Herr

Novelist and poet, playwright and philosopher Broch was born to a middle class Jewish family in Vienna in 1886. He worked in his father's textile business until 1928, when – at the age of forty-two – he sold the family business and returned to university to read philosophy and mathematics. A year later he left his studies to write. *The Sleepwalkers* was followed by *The Unknown Quantity* and his famous essay on James Joyce. After the Anschluss, Broch was imprisoned by the Gestapo. He was released – largely as a result of influence exerted by Joyce and others – and escaped from Austria to the USA. Whilst in prison, Broch developed an eighteen-page short story into the novel many regard as his masterpiece – *The Death of Virgil.* Broch was planning to visit Europe in 1951 when he died suddenly in his New York home. An incisive and important writer, Broch's reputation stands in the first rank of German writers of the first half of this century.

Photograph of Hermann Broch courtesy of the Austrian National Library

HERMANN BROCH

The Spell

PICADOR *Classics*

published by Pan Books

Originally published in German as *Die
Verzauberung*, 1976 by Suhrkamp Verlag,
Frankfurt
First published in Great Britain 1987 by André
Deutsch Ltd
This Picador Classics edition published 1988 by
Pan Books Ltd, Cavaye Place, London SW10 9PG
All rights reserved
9 8 7 6 5 4 3 2 1
English translation © Farrar, Straus and Giroux,
Inc. 1987
ISBN 0 330 30028 8
Printed and bound in Great Britain by
Richard Clay Ltd, Bungay, Suffolk

CONTENTS

THE SPELL

Snow lies on the branches of the spruces in the forest, it lies in my garden and clings to the crevices between the rocks of Mount Kuppron. I can see garden and woods when I look out the window, but I cannot see the rock wall of the Kuppron from the mountain slope on which my house sits, nor can I see it even from my rear windows, hidden as it is by the woods. Yet its presence is felt at all times. Those who live by the sea can hardly form a single thought of which the sea would not be part, and so it is for those who reside on the shores of great mountains: whatever reaches their senses, each sound and each color, each birdcall and each ray of the sun, all are but an echo of the great mute mass of the mountain, its folds bathed in light, brightened by colors and washed by sound, so that it is only natural that man, whose soul mirrors color and birdcall and ray of sun, himself turns into an everlasting resonance of that immense silent presence, a sounding board vibrating in unison with that silent melody.

I sit here, an aging man, an old country doctor, driven to write down something that happened to me, as if by doing so I could hold fast to what is known and what is forgotten; thus our life flows, rising and sinking and at times disappearing altogether, absorbed by time and lost in nothingness. Was that not what, years ago, had driven me from the city to the quiet of this modest country practice, what prompted me to forsake the scientific world in which I had been entrapped, to abandon it for the sake of a different kind of knowledge which was to be stronger even than all oblivion? I had spent year after year as one who had been granted the great good luck to labor along with others on science's inexhaustible edifice, a knowledge hardly my own alone but belonging to all of mankind, to labor as an insignificant link in a chain of workers and, with them, adding one small stone after another to the endless building, merely seeing the next step, and yet, like all the others, apprehending the infinity of the structure, blessed and illuminated by that infinite goal—yes, all that I forsook, as if it had been the Tower of Babel, I averted my eyes from that infinity that belongs not to me but to mankind, turned away from an infinity that cancels each yesterday and only acknowledges the morrow, so as to withdraw into an endeavor of the smallest dimension which no longer could lay claim to perception but is merely a living and a being in togetherness, at times perhaps a stretching out of a helping hand, as if thereby I had wanted to salvage my past even as I see my future growing shorter with each passing day. Did I want to throw myself into this chaos of immediacy? Or did I wish merely to escape the aridity of systematic intellection? Many years have passed since then, and today I hold only a faint memory of the city and of the loathing toward all urban life which suddenly seized me, a loathing of the punctuality which regulated the streetcars and so many other aspects of daily life, this world of rules which renders words superfluous, mutes the work in the laboratory and in the clinic, almost mutes all that preventive and therapeutic machinery of medicine, hardly deserving any longer to be called the healing art, mutes the language in which we communicated, mutes that infinity in which lay and still today lies the goal of all these strivings—though today I no longer aspire to them. Perhaps this loathing carried with it the fear of losing the diversity of life, for however various man's possibilities are, once he has chosen a path and has begun to follow it, that diversity increasingly diminishes; he stays on his track and nothing can deflect him any longer. Indeed, this may well be the way things happened, though now that it is as remote to me as a fugitive dream of long ago I would not dare assert that they did, but even if it were so, what did I get in exchange? Is the city which I fled not just as much part of the landscape as the village in which I now work? Is its order not as much part of an all-embracing humanity? Or did I merely seek solitude? Alone I walk through the woods, alone I climb the mountains, and yet the boundary markings of the fields, the life in the stables and the barnyards, the awareness of the old mining tunnels deep below in the mountain, all this human traffic among beasts and plants is of greater reassurance to me than nature itself, and even a single errant rifle shot in the forest reaffirms in me the feeling of being a link in the human order and existence. Why is it then that in the city I no longer perceived this order as a truly human order but saw it merely as mankind's weariness with itself, as a tiresome non-knowledge, while out here I am filled with a sense of belonging? I forsook intellectual understanding in favor of a knowledge that would be stronger than perception, strong enough to fill the time allotted to man to follow his steps hither and thither and to let his eyes rest here and there in the world, to fill his short term on earth with an almost blissful waiting, a knowledge redeemed from oblivion, full of yesterdays and tomorrows, replete with the meaning of yesterday and tomorrow: this had been my hope. Has it been fulfilled? To be sure, even in oblivion nothing is lost and whatever existed remains with me as it existed always and forever: our ship grows ever heavier as it nears the harbor, barely a ship anymore but only its freight, hardly moving and indeed motionless on the still mirror of eventide as it puts into port, weightless despite this overly heavy freight; no one can say whether this ship sinks or rises into the clouds above, nor can we name its freight or its harbor, unfathomable the waters we crossed and unfathomable the skies vaulting over us, unfathomable our own knowledge as, even as it continues to grow, it is lost to us. Years have gone by since my flight to this place, years filled with impatience to make use of this last span of time still remaining to me, year after year has gone by since I abandoned the step-by-step findings of painstaking scientific research, restored now to my own life, joyless yet happy in the awareness of my growing knowledge and of the fusion of past and future, even though it is an awareness so intangible as to be hardly more than a faint apprehension, gain and loss at once. And now that I wish to write it down, the unforgettable in the forgotten, as I try to record it I start out with all the hopefulness of the young and all the hopelessness of the old, wishing to gather in before it is too late the meaning of all that has happened and of all that is yet to happen.

And I am writing it down because outside it is snowing and because darkness is falling, even though it is still early afternoon.

And what I really wish to record—as if otherwise I might forget it—is merely that there has not always been snow outside, that much else has occurred during this past year, bloom and harvest and the fragrance of resin throughout the woods, water dripping and trickling down over the rocks of the face of the Kuppron, wind blowing from afar and dying away, light that flamed and faded, and skies that changed from day to night and back again to day. All this occurred while my heart was beating, while wind and sun and clouds were there, all of them flowing through my hands and my heart.

1   Perhaps it would be more appropriate to begin with my childhood, and indeed it might well be enough to take hold of and set down in all candor a small portion of that childhood, such as the fact of a large house in the city with a staircase, where I had stood at the topmost landing, looking down into the cool and echoing abyss below. For this, too, I wish never to forget. And perhaps it would even be enough to record a single minute of the day just past, to hold on to it, so that it may remain standing in the slow ebbing passage of skies and mountains amid the gradual succession of shadow and light which flow, both ever so lightly and ever so heavily, through our own selves. But what I wish to recall is that day in March, now many months past, indeed almost a full year past, as remote as yesterday and as close as childhood, for this is the only way our memory works: it raises one event or another and thereby encompasses both living and dying; it takes hold of a single instant which in itself may not be significant at all, but because it invests such a moment with the meaning of its past and of its permanence and transposes the human experience into that of nature, beyond death and life and into the irrevocable, because of this transmutation into the irremediable, I wish to recall that day in March, even though surely it was not much different from all the other days and yet was innately significant.

It was a day when the sun was shining and when winter had been relegated into the shadowed corners of the world: though the ruts and wheel tracks on the country roads in some places still were iced over, already the fields in the valley were spread out in brown hues in intimation of the greenness to come, and green were the patches of meadows among the stretches of snow, meadows of new grass in which even some dog daisies had already made their appearance. The whole world seemed like a single awakening flower, and the motion of the small ragged white clouds against the hushed blueness of the sun was hardly noticeable.

I had tended to the few patients who had come to see me at home and was on my way to my clinic in the Lower Village. Three times a week, including Sundays, between noon and two o'clock, I see patients in the clinic which I had set up at Sabest's inn. In winter, I use the road which leads from Lower to Upper Kuppron and then turns to the Kuppron Saddle, and when there is enough snow on the ground, I even use my skis; but in summer, I take the path through the forest. To be sure, the return trip is less pleasant, for the climb takes almost an hour, but this is the lot of a country doctor: he must be a good hiker, even if he is past fifty. Of course, sometimes a carriage is available, or even a motorcar, which will give me a ride; this is the custom of the region and it is but fitting.

It was noon, a great all-embracing blue song, when I got to Lower Kuppron; the church clock struck the hour and immediately thereafter the two boys ringing the church bells joined the peals of the noon bells to the song of the heavens. It was in the village street that I encountered the stranger.

A dark Gallic mustache hung over the corners of his mouth between a sharp beak of a nose and a stubbly chin that had not seen a razor for a long time, making him look older than he probably was; I judged him to be about thirty or a little above. He didn't pay any attention to me, but when he had gone by, I had the impression that, even so, I had caught his glance and that it had been a dreamily rigid and yet bold stare. Perhaps I deduced this only from his walk, for his way of walking, in spite of his obvious fatigue and notwithstanding his wretched footwear, was both sprightly and stern; in truth, it could only be described as a sprightly and stern shuffling, and it seemed that such a manner of progression could be led only by a sharp glance directed at a distant goal. It was not the walk of a peasant but rather that of a traveling journeyman, and this impression was reinforced by an effluvium of petty-bourgeois airlessness that trailed behind the man, a petty-bourgeois self-righteousness which quite possibly was suggested by his dark suit and the almost empty knapsack dangling shabbily at the small of his back. A lower-middle-class man of Gallic appearance.

When I arrived at the inn, I glanced once more along the road. The man was about to disappear into Church Street. In front of the inn stood a truck loaded with white-powdered bags of cement; obviously it had arrived only moments before, for a small wreath of hot air still trembled above its radiator cap, a soft wisp of the ether of this earth and a precursor of summer to come.

The driveway is flanked on either side by the door of the inn's taproom and that of the small general store which also is operated by Sabest, the innkeeper, though both establishments can be entered from the driveway as well. Some steps lead up to the taproom, while the store is level with the street. The driveway, in the shadow of which I now entered, is wide and high enough to accommodate a hay wagon; somewhat needlessly it is whitewashed like a room and is always filled with the smell of empty beer kegs which stand waiting to be picked up by the brewery. It is here that my doctor's shingle is hung. Since I needed some tobacco, I entered the store, but I found no one; nor was there a soul in the adjacent butcher shop, a small, newly added extension with a flat roof that projects into the yard. The gray and blue tiles were freshly washed and strewn with white sand, and the steel strips with their meat hooks were brightly polished; no meat was hanging there, only some dried sausages hung quietly along the walls. The rough, deeply scarred chopping block also was well scrubbed, though naturally this cleansing had failed to remove the black blood ingrained in its crevices, and though the air was clean and cool, it nevertheless smelled like a large open wound. I walked into the taproom.

The truck driver and his two helpers were sitting at the long corner table with their beers in front of them. There were no other customers in the room, either at the second long table or at the round table in front of the window which was reserved for the village notables and was the only one covered with a blue checkered tablecloth, in addition to having a container of rough toothpicks next to the white flint cone with matches.

"He's got quite a mouth, that one," the driver was saying. I assumed that he was the driver, for he sat there more self-importantly and looking better off than the two others. And since it is in the nature of incipient portliness to use words and thoughts as redundantly as all the other things of this world, he repeated it after a brief reflective pause: "Yes, he sure has a big mouth."

"Yes, that he has," I said as I entered, to the general merriment of those present. But though I had said it with only that purpose in mind, I had already been thinking of the stranger and I was quite positive that the driver had been speaking about him.

Peter Sabest, the eighteen-year-old son of the innkeeper, also laughed from behind the counter. He had put on his grown-up face and was rolling a cigarette. "What's your pleasure, Doctor?"

I asked for the tobacco that I had vainly sought in the store, and he gave me a package from the glass case standing on the counter.

"I see you're sole master of the mansion today, Peter."

"Not for long," he said regretfully. "They only went to the market."

The driver and his two helpers had noted that I had been addressed as Doctor, and thus I was established as trustworthy. So they decided to continue the fun, and the older of the two helpers said, "A have-not but with a wide-open mouth."

"An empty mouth will talk," observed the younger one, a short man with a snub nose who could have been taken for a Czech, a recently married Czech perhaps, for he already sported a wedding band on one of his fingers although he was certainly not much older than twenty-five.

"Well," I countered, "that's not quite true as far as women are concerned, for they like to gab even with their mouths full . . . You ought to know, even though you haven't been married very long, right?"

That made them laugh uproariously once more, but Peter, who had inherited the blondness and the fair skin of his mother, blushed exactly as his mother was wont to do. Though undoubtedly he would no longer do so in a few years when his skin would come to resemble a whitish leather stretched taut over a layer of fat that allows no blushing.

And Peter asked, "So, what did he talk about?"

Probably because the sun outside seemed so summery, the older of the two helpers had taken off his jacket and reached into his shirt to scratch his chest. "Yes, what did he really say?"

The driver gave a grumpy show of disinterest and declared, "When one drives, one only pays attention to the road."

So I said, "What in hell! If you don't even know what it was he was talking about, perhaps he didn't talk after all."

"I sat behind on the bags," the younger one said apologetically.

"He spouted a lot of nonsense," the driver said.

"I believe he was a gypsy," the older one ventured, continuing to scratch. The flea seemed to have found its way to his back.

"A Gaul," I said.

"Aha," snorted the driver dismissively, since he had no conception of what a Gaul might be.

"Nice of you anyway to give him a lift," I said. "The fellow was dog-tired."

They looked at me, surprised that I knew whom they were talking about. And it irked them somewhat: no more fun.

"Ordinarily I never give anyone a lift," grunted the driver. "For one thing, it's against the rules." He pushed back his leather cap. His sparse hair stuck to his forehead.

At that moment, the innkeeper's big St. Bernard slowly emerged from the back room, rubbing his flanks against chairs and tables. He appreciates me as a dog owner and so he laid his head with the perennially slavering muzzle on my knee, the bloodshot eyes eloquent with the melancholy benevolence of a faithful nature and measured speech: "Here you are again, you human being, smelling partly of doctor and partly of your own dog Trapp, and also of the other things in life, which, however, I choose not to speak about right now."

"Yes," I reply, "yes, Pluto, and Trapp sends you his best greetings."

"So be it," came the answer in Pluto's eyes.

"Out with you, Pluto," I say, "outside is a March day that smells of sun and summer."

"Yes," he replies. "I know. I've already been outside and found it good."

It was cool in the taproom, though somewhat stuffy because of the closed windows. The sour smell of kitchen, beer and wine, of sweat and underdone meat, the smell of knights and mercenaries, in the fumes of which the Occident conquered the world and which now tamely survives only in humble pubs yet is always ready to break forth to cover once again the slaughter fields of the earth, that smell also pervaded this room, and the driver and his companions tasted of it.

The older one had given up the search for the flea; he withdrew his hand from the shirt and regretfully examined his coarse empty fingers.

But suddenly the driver became loquacious. "Have you ever heard such nonsense, Doctor? We are to live a chaste life so that the world may get better . . .?"

"Oh? Is that what he went on about?"

"Yes," said the driver, finishing his beer, "that pig."

"But you agreed with him," declared the older helper.

"Me? I didn't give a damn, I watched the road . . . if anybody went along with him it was you."

"And why shouldn't I say yes? I don't give a hoot for women anyway, whether or not this improves the world."

Wanting to participate in the conversation in his schoolboyish way, Peter interjected, "He must have been a priest."

"Priest or not," the young husband ventured, "when one of his sort can get his hands on a girl, he doesn't say no either."

The brass spigots of the beer taps shone like the March noon outside, the windows on the brightly lit white housefront across the street glowed darkly as if emulating the waves in the sun-drenched sky, and it is the time of day when the light, like a swarm of glassy gnats, sinks down to earth to impregnate it with its fecundity.

"Nor do I want to hear about all that bullshit," the young man continued merrily. "It's all a lot of bunk."

"I bet your young wife doesn't want to hear anything about it either," I said.

"No, she sure doesn't." And he laughed with the happy mien of a man who has been granted a miracle and wants to keep it intact.

"Well," I teased, "maybe the fellow will convert you yet. Why don't you have him sit with you?"

"No," said the driver, and although he looked quite fierce with his leather cap and almost like a locomotive driver, his voice sounded rather shy. "No, my helper will have to stay alone on the bags, we're not taking this fellow any further, I've no use for him and his baloney. Besides, the road over the pass is lousy, one hairpin after another, and the truck is heavy . . . I'll be glad to be over it and on the other side before it gets completely dark."

The three said "Good day" and left the taproom. I watched them through the window. Undecided, they peered to the left and right along the road, then they climbed onto the truck, the driver pressed the starter twice, and with a sudden jerk and a turning of the steering wheel, they rattled away. The young helper on the bags noticed me as I stood at the window and he waved.

"Are any patients upstairs?" I asked Peter as I turned back to the room.

No one had come as yet, and Peter seemed intent on continuing the conversation with me, not only because he was bored all by himself but also because we understand each other rather well. And who was that vagrant of whom we had spoken?

But as to that, I had no information to give him. Maybe the driver had given the fellow another ride after all and was sitting next to him now, as he slowly steered the truck up the road to the Upper Village, constantly changing gears because of the steepness of the climb. Or maybe the three had already forgotten the vagrant, a bit of the memory being jarred out of their heads with each jolt of the clutch, dazed and dozing on their way. I, for one, had every wish to forget all about it. I walked through the back room and out into the yard, from where an outside staircase leads to the upper floor and the open-air corridor giving access to the guest rooms and Sabest's own lodgings, and also to my own two rooms: the waiting room and my clinic.

The sun burned down most pleasantly. The rugous iron banister on which I leaned let the heat flow into my hands, and the song of early spring in the air, astounded at its own strength, had become almost mute. In the middle of the yard stands a surprisingly large chestnut tree. Were it not so well protected by the walls of the house and the stables, it would never have been able to prosper so mightily at this harsh altitude. Its leafless branches cast convoluted shadows, their greenness still dormant within.

As I was taking in the sun at my ease, listening to the ever fainter murmuring of the light all around me, I heard the drumroll of a carriage in the driveway. The innkeeper and his wife drove in, but they were not alone: a calf, child of a bull, child of a cow, lay on the flat bed of the one-horse butcher's buggy, its legs fettered and the head looking up sideways at the chestnut, without comprehending the rare nature of the tree.

The carriage stopped. Sabest jumped from the box and helped his wife to alight. While she sorted out her shopping, Sabest, with the help of the yardman who had come from the carriage house, lifted down the calf and unfettered it, so that it now stood on unsteady legs, loosely tied to one wheel of the carriage. Then they unhitched the horse.

Theodore Sabest does not conform to one's image of an innkeeper or a butcher. He cannot put on any fat and he fits much better his general store. But that is only the first impression. For quite soon comes the realization that he belongs to the lean type of slaughterer, one is almost tempted to say the lean type of executioner, and it is not easy for him to produce the hail-fellow-well-met bonhomie without which an innkeeping business cannot be successful. One can readily imagine how this brutal and passionate man at one time must have courted the blond girl who became his wife. She, who despite all her blondness is not too soft either, has become the model of an innkeeper's wife, efficient and endowed with that frank and yet sly sensuality that has its fitting place between kitchen and pub. Looking at her, one regretted that she did not have more children, but an executioner does not wish for a mother in his home but rather for a mistress, he cherishes that jungle in which human beings are joined together in bliss and misery, he derides those who wish to clear this dank darkness and escape from it, for he knows well that men, though they may build houses with large driveways and may even use motorcars to get around in, can never transcend the edge of that jungle, he knows that the beginning and end of all that is human lies in the darkness of primeval sleep and oblivion, and that each action, each spoken word, and any doing or non-doing can lead back into the darkness of that primordial maze, and that its gloomy fires are forever ready to break out again to engulf us. To be sure, one may safely assume that the innkeeper Theodore Sabest hardly ever thought about such matters, and it may also be that I, the doctor who knows quite a few things about his marriage, may impute altogether too much to the workings of his soul, and were one to ask Sabest himself, he would reply in all probability that he had been content with a single heir purely because of financial considerations.

Meanwhile Pluto had also joined the group and, with the best of good-natured intentions, was now sniffing the calf and, with a heavy raised paw, was even challenging it to play with him. But the calf became restive; it pulled on the rope and, stiff-legged, reared up on its hindquarters. And this somehow seemed almost undignified for a creature which, after all, was soon to be led to its death And so I retreated to my office.

This was the first day I meant to describe.

2   All was forgotten. The snow had covered every-
     thing. At a single stroke the cowering winter had
broken free once more, jumping over the face of Mount Kuppron,
behind which it had been hiding: for two nights and two days the
snow had been swirling, and when the wind turned and blew from
the north, the sun shone on a landscape in which sleds gliding on
roads polished to a gleaming silver and the tinkling of bells almost
brought back the spirit of Christmas.

But even though walls of snow bordered the roadways and a
glittering powder swept icily across the fields and slopes, this was
not Christmas despite all the trappings, for the winds of March are
not those of December and man in March is not the same man he
was in December. Everything was sharper and, at the same time,
softer than it had been in December, sharpness and softness were
distributed in different patterns, somehow the cold had been de-
composed into its components, it piercingly penetrated my thick
fur coat while at the same time a melted layer spread over the hard-
frozen snow on the paths, corrosive and sticky, and adhered in
heavy black clumps to the soles of my shoes and wedged itself
under their heels; it also jammed the paws of Trapp, who, at times
whining softly, would limp painfully along. But soon he would
jump ahead again when he encountered some powder snow, rolling
in it and joyful in the whirling clouds he was thus able to produce.
For a full-fledged wolfhound his comportment was a little too youthful, but Trapp has no conception of dignity.

"Come," I said, "come, Trapp, we've got to get down to the
Lower Village; they phoned for me. The Lenard woman is having
her baby."

I packed my instruments, told Caroline, my housekeeper, that
we would be back for dinner, and set out into the bright afternoon.
The north wind still whistled, though no longer as sharply as

during the previous few days, it had become, so to speak, mono-chordal, its upper and lower registers had fallen silent, and it had now become a solitary stroller, softly whistling to itself as it loped along above the treetops. The forest beyond was utterly silent; at intervals, a clump of snow detached itself from a branch, crackled drippingly, and flopped softly to the ground. From Wetchy's house, which, like my own, is embedded in the pines—truly ensconced in the forest since the garden and hedges were hidden by the snow—a thin wisp of smoke rises into the silver-blue brightness emanating from the infinity above, it shrouds the tree trunks and almost reaches to the ground, a thin smell of smoke, the somewhat harsh smell of humanity and of its shelters amid the odorless freshness all around me.

Smoke also rises from my own house. It is a home in which I have been living for over ten years. I had come upon this place while on a hike through the mountains and had remained, following a sudden impulse to accept the position of community doctor that just then had been advertised together with the lodging, had ac-cepted it, in truth, only for the sake of this house on its wooded promontory. Withal, the house really is a fake, true child of inflation and of a stock-exchange swindle, an unfinished child and one that even had had a somewhat premature birth. For in those inflationary times some gypsters had promoted a scheme to reopen the mining works in the Kuppron, and because they could not merely issue shares, they had also built these two houses and a portion of a cableway which was to lead down to Plombent. Of course, that's where the matter rested, the mine drifts were never opened and the smelting works in Plombent were never built. A bit of cable stretches senselessly over the forest, with a lone mine cage dangling from it near the Cold Stone; the two houses remained unfinished and were taken over by the community for back taxes, and the former manager of the project, Wetchy, also remained in a way unfinished: he now lives in one of the two houses and ekes out a meager existence as an insurance agent and salesman of agricultural machinery. And because the community could not find any use for the other house, it was assigned to the doctor, for whom it was deemed good enough, since in the eyes of the peasants a doctor is a bit of a luxury anyway.

The equinoctial shadow, flowing down from the Kuppron, can already be felt in the forest although it has not reached it yet, but when one takes the path to the village, a path yellowed by treads among which I recognize this morning's imprints from my own hobnailed boots, and when one emerges into the open, then there stands to one's right, shadowed and shadowing, the mighty face of the mountain, its loins girded by the forest as by a cloth, while the topmost edge of the fields, their white expanse dotted with dark snow-capped hazel bushes, has already been touched by the glancing kiss of dusk. In front of me, a short distance farther on, lies the Upper Village, still under the sun, and behind it, in an immense semicircle, starting with the gap of the Kuppron Pass flanked by the Vent Alm and the Raw Venten, there stretches the high golden chain of peaks, their foothills falling away in infinite steps to the east and the north, their first dip to the left, the round trough of the Kuppron Valley—though from this spot it cannot be seen in all its length: the end of the valley is shielded by the slope, as well as the village of Lower Kuppron in the center of the basin, and one can only make out its ascending southern half and some isolated farmsteads scattered across the opposite slope. Through the sunny wintery stillness could be heard the striking of the church clock, and—embedded the valley, embedded the dwellings in the translucent azurine cold—the sound reverberates and floats skyward, reaching beyond to a sky above the skies, the icy breath of the sun.

To reach the road, one does not have to go all the way to the village; one can turn to the left—this path, too, I've trodden out myself in the snow, for Wetchy and Caroline do not count in my reckoning—and one feels proud to have saved some ten minutes of walking by taking this shortcut. With the sun at my back, the light northerly breeze in my face, and the happy dog in front of me, I am taking long strides and I am even a little worried because the Lenard woman has already gone through two births and neither was easy. I should have taken the skis.

Even without these, though, after another quarter of an hour the church tower with its simple gable roof came into sight, shortly thereafter the snowy roofs of the village, and after another quarter hour I was down at Lenard's, where everything was already in full swing. It all went like clockwork, the Hulles-Mary, who acts as midwife, could have handled it all by herself, and exactly at six o'clock, in the last rays of the sun, we brought this new human being into the world, this everyday miracle had been accomplished once more, and I, the old obstetrician who has worked long years in the women's clinic, was astounded once again that this creature which we had taken out of a human body now had become one itself, equipped with everything that is needed with which to manage and endure this world. It was a boy whose cord I had cut, the second Lenard boy, for the last one had been a girl, red as a shrimp, fluffy down on his head and with cute little fingers and half-moon nails, and he was furious at the outrage inflicted upon him. But a big smile seemed to hover over the entire house.

Happy as I was with my accomplishment, there was nevertheless little sense in remaining any longer in the house, so I washed up, packed my white smock and my instruments, and notified Trapp, who had been sleeping rolled up in the kitchen during the whole procedure, that we would be on our way. Trapp assented, and so we went out into the street, where dusk was already setting in.

Since I was down there, I went to the inn to learn whether any medical news had arrived for me. There was nothing. At the gate I met Peter, who was about to leave the house.

At first, we talked about this and that, of his aversion to butchering, of his preference for the less bloody storekeeping business, and together we started on our way. At the corner of Church Street he became restless, and I was indiscreet enough to tell him that I knew where he was going and that I would even go with him.

He blushed and we turned the corner, for if one wishes to visit the cottager Strum, or rather his sixteen-year-old daughter Agatha, this is where one must turn. But we had gone only a few steps along Church Street when I said, "There he is."

I had said this before I had fully perceived, let alone before I could truly identify the figure in the growing dusk, leaning there in front of the house of Lorenz Miland, because it seemed so perfectly natural that he was the person sought. The person sought? Yes, sought. For though I had forgotten him, forgotten him so thoroughly that I had not been impelled even to ask whether he was still to be seen in the village, I nevertheless knew that he was still around. Such things happen.

And thus it was quite proper that, as we approached the man, I said, "Good evening."

"Good evening," he replied. He stood in the light from the window, hatless—no peasant ever leaves his house without a hat—and without a jacket or jersey he stood there in the cold and kicked a bit with his heel against the uneven ice border that ran along the wall of the house. All this seemed to make little sense. Was he waiting for someone? Somewhat puzzled, I looked at him.

"Good evening, Peter," he finally said. "I guess you haven't yet learned to greet a person."

In some embarrassment, Peter then also said, "Good evening, Mr. Ratti."

Ratti; that sounded Italian, and it fitted in with the man's curly hair, which is quite rare in this region.

He seemed quite cheerful and said, "Nice evening."

"Well, yes, but a bit on the chilly side." And to say something concrete, I added, "You're staying at Miland's."

"Yes, he's taken me in."

Taken him in? As a wanderer who stays a few nights? Or as a hired hand? If it was as a hired hand, I was surprised that the man was still here, for Miland demands hard work, and with his one hundred acres of ground scattered all over the district he has to get the kind of labor for which this man hardly seemed suited. It was also surprising that Miland should take on a hired hand that early for the spring sowing. Well, it would all come out soon enough, I thought, and so I merely said, "We've already seen each other. You came in on the cement truck."

"You didn't see that," he corrected. "I had already gotten off."

Despite all the cordiality with which this was said, it was nevertheless proof of a petty disputatiousness, and it was more: a chal-

lenge to be hated, for in the sham-chummy tone and gesture there
was something that seemed to say, Hate me, hate me, so that you
may love me!

It is possible that I am wrong. But Trapp, who had been sniffing
the stranger and who is never wrong, had stopped the *perpetuum
mobile* of his friendly tail-wagging and held his tail aggressively
ramrod straight.

I didn't feel like hating the man, but since I was standing in front
of my friend Miland's house, I thought I might as well pay him a
visit. So I merely nodded to Ratti and entered the house.

There was light in the stables, and since Miland was obviously
still working there, I went inside. Nine head of cattle stood there,
mostly of the shorthorn type with the dark brown glossy hide that
is generally bred hereabouts, in addition to a pair of heavy draft
horses. At one end of the stables, in a larger stall, the community
bull, which is kept by Miland, rattled his two chains. Everything
looked efficient and properly attended to, the concrete floor was
clean, and there was a water tap, even though the water had to be
pumped over from the well. But that still is more efficient than
having to haul it in pails, and it is also pleasing to the eye.

"Well, if it isn't the doctor himself," said Miland, who had heard
me coming and had emerged from one of the stalls. "That's a mighty
rare pleasure." And because a peasant's thoughts always are practical and only admit of tangible causes for any event, he continued,
"Do you need anything, Doctor? Is Caroline out of eggs?"

No, Caroline hadn't sent me. I just happened by.

He had rinsed his hands under the tap and now stretched them
out toward me. "That's really good of you."

Suddenly I was aware of a strange resemblance between Miland
and his new lodger. The peasants in this region sometimes are of
a Mediterranean type, dark-haired, sinewy, and with sharp eagle
profiles—hunter types. Miland, too, had a dark mustache hanging
over the corners of his mouth. "Finished with work?" I asked.

"Finished, yes, but haven't had supper yet . . . Surely, you'll
share it, yes?" and he switched off the two ceiling lamps. In the
dark, one sensed the warm breathing of the cattle.

The house is at a right angle with the stables. We crossed the yard. By now, the sky was full of March stars and the air was milder than in the afternoon. The sleep of the creatures of this world always seems to warm up the sky.

His wife is a strong-boned, hard being, almost as tall as Miland and of an increasingly masculine cast, although she is not yet forty. She comes from the Upper Village and it is said that there were some strenuous battles before Miland finally won her.

But the marital relationship of the couple is not quite clear, despite the many children that they have had together. Some of these children died and it may be that this is what made her so hard. No one's death comes to pass without making some impression, and those close to the deceased inherit part of the liberated soul and become richer in their humaneness. But a mother cannot be heir to her own child and her countenance is marked by the hard lines of those who live in the hell of the disinherited.

"Good evening, everyone," I said as I entered the room. "I see everything is still in full swing."

With the exception of Karl, the twelve-year-old, who might have gone to bed already or might be prowling around somewhere, the whole family was there: Miland's wife with the infant boy in her arms, the ten-year-old Cecily dozing at the table, Andreas, the hired hand, sitting on the bench with his pipe, together with the maid, Hermine, who was already stretching herself and ready to slip into her wooden clogs to shuffle off to bed. The oldest daughter, Irmgard, stood at the stove and was boiling tea; in this region, it is the custom of many peasants to drink tea.

We sat down at the table, still greasy from the meal partaken by the others, and Miland started stroking the blond head of sleepy Cecily. Bread and a thick slab of bacon were in the middle of the table, together with a plate of dumplings that had been left over for the master, but first he spooned his milk soup without removing his left hand from the head of the child. Then it was the turn of the dumplings and the bacon, and I, too, cut off a bit of bacon from time to time and ate it with a piece of bread. There was silence while we ate, and Trapp watched us and pondered at length whether the bacon rind, inedible for us, would be reserved for him or for the yard dog.

When we had more or less finished, Miland asked whether Marius had had his supper yet.

"No," said his wife, on her way out to put the infant to bed. "No, he only eats once a day, he says; that's what he's used to."

"Yes, but he likes his tea," Irmgard said from the stove.

"So his name is Marius," I said.

"Yes, Marius Ratti . . . You already know him, Doctor?"

"He's standing in front of the house with Peter."

"He likes doing that," Andreas, the hired hand, said, and giggled.

"Well, maybe Peter has already gone to see Agatha . . . I'd prefer that."

"No," Andreas insisted. "They're still standing outside."

Had Peter been embarrassed because I had caught him meeting with a vagrant? And I asked: "How did this man happen to land in your place?"

Obviously this Marius Ratti was a favorite topic of conversation for the Miland woman, who, though she had just come back into the room, knew immediately what we were talking about and replied, "Irmgard found him."

Irmgard put down large mugs —much too big to be called cups— at each place and filled them with tea. "No, Karl brought him in . . . He had asked the children in the street if there was another inn close to the church."

"Why didn't he stay right there at Sabest's?"

"He thought it too fancy for him . . . He doesn't have much money. So I asked him whether he wanted to eat something . . . That's what one has to do . . . after all, he's a wanderer, isn't he?"

"Yes," I said, "he's a wanderer all right."

"That he may well be," said the wife, "and if he was hungry I'm glad he was fed, but I don't care for such people in the house; for all I know, the police may be after him."

"Then you'd be rid of him soon enough, missus," giggled the hired hand.

But Miland said, "I've never turned anyone out and I've not fared badly for it so far."

All of them now padded silently to the table in their heavy gray socks, and we all stirred the reddish-brown water that faintly tasted of tea, while our thoughts were with the wanderer. For even the sedentary man is a wanderer at heart, though he may not wish to admit it, and when he shelters a wayfarer he may well do it so as not to be reminded of his own inescapable leave-taking.

"I'll go get him," Irmgard said, and went to the door.

Miland took Cecily's tightly braided pigtail. "And you, do you like Marius?"

The child merely nodded into her tea mug and smiled dumbly. But then, following a sudden impulse, she slid from the chair, skipped to the bench, which she climbed, and in the dim light of the alcove—for the electric bulb under the tin shade hung low over the table—she groped for the switch of the radio which stood in all its brown-lacquered urban ornateness on the ledge among the meager household utensils. Thus, the entrance of Marius was accompanied by the lazy rhythms of jazz music which now crept from the brown box and danced around the smoke-blackened ceiling of the room.

But on the floor it was Cecily who was dancing. She jumped from one leg to the other, raised one little arm and then the other, and a grave and holy awakening could be seen on her face, soundless was her dance, a hushed skipping on heavy gray woolen socks, nor did she stop her angelic dancing as the jazz rhythms now switched to that of a tango.

Marius leaned against the doorjamb and watched this idyllic scene with an affable sideways bent of his head. He paid no heed at all to Irmgard, who, without turning her eyes from him, placed his mug of tea on the table, and the way he ignored her gesture inviting him to join us seemed almost deliberate. But suddenly he bounded over to the alcove—I almost thought he was about to join in the child's dance—and switched off the radio.

Cecily froze in the midst of her motion. She was so startled that her delight would not admit of the mortification that had already taken hold of her: one leg slightly bent, so that she almost stood on one leg, one arm raised with the palm of the hand turned toward the ceiling, as if trying to snatch back from there the vanished strains, and her face, not yet aware of its awakening, awakening forever, could not yet slip back into the restraint of the flesh, frozen in eternal awakening and yet already bearing the mask of sorrowful sleep.

But finally it crumpled, and a tearful "Booh!" was wrested from the distorted mouth as she fled into the arms of her father.

However, we, too, were transfixed, though we merely sat with our tea around a sober electric bulb in this warm and sober kitchen, sat in this semi-darkness through which the plates on the board glimmered in pale whiteness, in this warmth in which for generations the tenacious vapors of spluttering fat had been mixing with the exhalations of human bodies, behold, all of us were transfixed, including Irmgard, whose hand still was stretched out bidding Marius to join the table, as well as her father, who held Cecily pressed against himself, and even Andreas, the hired hand, was frozen as he held a match stiffly ready without rubbing it against his hind-quarters. It was Miland's wife who was the first to regain her speech. "Give the music back!"

"Mistress," said Marius politely, "give the box back."

"Foolishness and nonsense," exclaimed the woman. "Are you out of your mind? And all the good money the box cost us . . . You put the music back on right away."

"If the mistress so orders, I have to obey," agreed Marius in theatrical submissiveness, "but parents are weak and often they yield to their children with no thought of the harm they may be doing them . . ." And after an artful little pause he added with an ingratiating smile, "I just thought it might be bedtime for the children."

Cecily, to whom this was addressed directly, gave no sign of having heard. She sat quietly and contentedly let herself be caressed by her father.

Marius had his hand on the switch and waited.

And then Miland said, "That's city music."

This was true, but it was also a city-bred gadget, and even if country music had emanated from it, this would not have changed anything.

"City-like or not," said Marius, "it's costly music and the mistress wants it." But in so saying he looked at Irmgard as if the decision were up to her.

"Drink your tea and hold your peace," ordered the wife with a short hard laugh.

But Irmgard stood immobile under Marius's gaze, and I, too, looked at her. She stood with her arms folded under her bosom, exactly as her mother and her grandmother are wont to stand; she was in everything a true Gisson, the face with the wide bone structure under the reddish hair, the skin warmly transfused and the lips a bright pink. Was that the face of her mother when she was brought down to be wed in the Lower Village? Where is the human core and permanence to be found, as the past draws veil upon veil over our faces and yet unveils them at the same time?

No one knows what goes on in another being; and the hired hand, Andreas, heaved a sigh—"Ah, yes"—after finally deciding to light his match and now brought it to his pipe behind a shielding hand.

And Irmgard, turning away from Marius, said, "It's true, it's time to go to bed," and without looking again at Marius, she led Cecily by the hand and left the room. Whereupon Marius joined us at the table, stirred his mug, and began to drink in small gulps like someone who has done his day's work and has earned his refection. We spoke of unimportant matters, and after a while Miland got up and switched on the radio and we listened to the news.

Then I left for home, Trapp behind me, for he had become tired and no longer felt like running. The snow crunched under my boots and was full of small uneven mounds and black shadows as the moon stood at my back. It was both cold and mild. My walk is easy; I would not have walked differently as a child, and though my face may have become utterly unveiled, as seen from inside it is more puzzling to me than ever. Nothing is answered as yet; how then can it be time already for leave-taking? Thus I walked. Here and there, light showed in houses, in some of them people could be seen sitting together, much as we had been sitting in Miland's kitchen, but when I left the village the face of the Kuppron stood in front of me, white and huge in the light of the moon, the farther peaks traced in delicate silver, uplifted and slaked by the fogs of the nocturnal horizon. And as I moved higher behind my two-legged shadow which showed me the easy path, the night became ever more luminous, and everything became so mild and radiant that one hardly could discern the lighted windows in the houses of Upper Kuppron; steadily I strolled upward into the cool softness of the heavenly vault in which the stars swam as if they, too, had been warmed and made lighter by all the mildness around.

3 Irmgard Miland was a Gisson as much as her mother was, but the truest Gisson of them all was her grandmother, even though the name was hers only by marriage. With women of such strength one always feels it to be somewhat improper that they should lose their own name instead of passing it on to daughter and granddaughter and great-granddaughter. However, in the case of the Gissons, in some ways a truly exceptional one, the name Gisson has been so totally assimilated, so completely absorbed by Mother Gisson, as she is known by one and all, that one cannot even conceive that once there must have been a male bearer of that name, and if one thinks about it, it then seems as if that man could not have died at all, though he most certainly did, but as if he, too, had been absorbed in that woman, as if he had not returned to the earth which now shelters his remains but rather had become one with the woman, and not by any means because he might have been a weakling, far from it, but because, quite to the contrary, one could imagine him only as a strong, even an overpowering man who, in his might, would have wished for just such an end. And this even went so far that in the case of his own son, the red-bearded Mathias, who is said to greatly resemble his father in strength and appearance, one constantly forgets that he, too, bears this slightly foreign-sounding name—of which there are quite a few here in the Upper Village—this rather pleasing name, Gisson; if one speaks of him, he is merely called Mathias of the Mount.

By now it was April. Heavy rain poured down from low skies onto the blackened snow through which peeked spots of dark earth and bleached grass, though both sky and rain seemed ready to transform themselves soon again into snow. In the fog, all things seemed blurred when one came close, the fir trees dripped, and smoke lay on the roofs of the houses like thin broth.

It was around eleven when I left the Sack house, which lies a bit beyond the Upper Village, and turned homeward. It was an unpleasant case. The woman had furunculosis, was feverish, and had to feed her child; and I didn't like its looks either. And, as always in such circumstances, I felt anger at the dumb self-perpetuation of the human race under such handicaps. Why didn't they simply give up? Just because everybody is afraid to die alone and without help like those who remain childless? Of course, now I would have to switch the child to bottled milk, and since there was no question of pasteurization in these remote parts, it was an unrelieved misery. With these wretched thoughts in my head, I walked down the village high street, which, unlike the one in Lower Kuppron, is bordered by contiguous buildings only over a few stretches, interrupted repeatedly by undeveloped lots and small wooden huts; as I slogged along past the wet houses, planting my stick in the snowy morass, the hood of my loden cape deep over my eyes, I suddenly thought of visiting Mother Gisson at the Mountain Manse.

The Mountain Manse is a long, low structure, the Gothic origins of which are evident in its window casements and corbels; it undoubtedly had been the seat of the mine's management in the days when Upper Kuppron was a miners' settlement. Since those times the Mountain Manse represented a legally not altogether clearly defined communal property belonging to a few families, probably descendants of the former mine masters, chief pitmen, and other privileged officials, who have transformed the complex as best they could by adding separate entrances and partitioning the large yard to make a number of single-family dwellings. Though this naturally did not produce true farmsteads, there really was no need for that up here since there are no true individual field boundaries either and since none of the properties, which mostly developed from simple forest clearings, exceeds the size of a small cottage homestead. But it may well be that the continued existence of this communal building provides for the villagers of Upper Kuppron the glue that holds them together in the fading memory of the old unity which long ago the miners' guild had bestowed to the communality.

The farmers in the valley have no understanding of this, and although few of them can be called rich, they view the Upper Villagers with their minuscule holdings as proletarians rather than true peasants, and the Mountain Manse, despite all its venerable tradition, to them is a kind of barracks. And they resented for a long time that Miland should have taken a woman from up here.

The windows of Mother Gisson's house, as is customary in this region, are decorated with hanging carnations, at present still bare of flowers; their gray-green stalks hung from the window boxes like thickly tangled, weather-beaten beards, and the rain streamed from them. And as in the other lodgings of the Manse, one of the windows had been transformed into a door, the outer wooden leaf of which always remained open during the day and was fastened to the wall by a wire hook. To the left of the door, a wooden bench was rammed into the ground, providing a shelf for the wooden clogs which it is the local custom to slip off one's feet before entering. Through the inner glass door one enters directly into the kitchen.

As I stood and took off my rain-heavy cape, Mother Gisson scolded all menfolk for always dirtying her white-scrubbed boards with their hobnailed boots and their dripping clothes. There is a bright coziness to this room; it is as if the sun, which, for many centuries, entered here to stay all through the mornings, had stored up in this room a nest egg of brightness from which to draw on such gray days. In one corner stands the stove on which the noon broth already simmers, two glass-paned wardrobes, peasant workmanship of the eighteenth century, are filled with flower-decorated china; under one of the windows stands a large table and the corner bench, and that is where Mother Gisson now sits and scolds.

"Instead of scolding, Mother, you really should give me a drop of something in this beastly weather."

"So that's why you came, Doctor."

And she goes to fetch the bottle from the pantry. But this schnapps of hers is something very special, a hellishly potent brew of mysterious herbs. Each August, in the season of the shooting stars, Mother Gisson can be seen in front of her door peering attentively at the sky; for a long time I had no inkling of what that meant, but once I had gained her confidence, she began to give me some hints. "I'll go in eight days," she would say, or "Tomorrow I'll go," and when that time comes, she climbs the mountain in the first light of dawn, clambers around the slopes like a kid goat, and returns with a carefully wrapped-up bundle of herbs. Not a word does she ever let slip of its contents or of the secret places where she finds them. "Who's going to inherit all that knowledge, Mother Gisson?" "Irmgard, one day, but we're not there yet."

Along with the bottle, she brings a loaf of bread.

"Schnapps alone is no good," she says.

My friendship with Mother Gisson is already of long standing and grows stronger with each passing year. Soon after I had taken up my position, she sent for me; her son Mathias had collapsed suddenly and I diagnosed acute appendicitis, more than ripe for surgery. Yet despite my urgent pleas, she didn't send him to the hospital. For a long time she peered deeply into his eyes and then said to me, "No, we couldn't get him there alive, we've got to manage right here." And took his treatment into her own hands: she had the patient's cot set up in the stables between the two cows—later I found out that her therapies always involved animals—and there, amid the fumes and the raw exhalations of the cattle, she made him fast for eight days. Whether she also spread warm cow dung on his sick stomach, I never could find out for sure, for she wouldn't even allow me to touch the patient, on whose face peritonitis was writ already in bold capital letters. And when I asked her about it later, she merely smiled and said, "Perhaps." But somehow she pulled her son through, and since then I've seen other, similar cases of her powers. It isn't that she despises medical science, or at least no more than I do myself, but she is keenly aware of its limitations, and that I acknowledge this has brought me not only her friendship but also some valued help. And it seems almost natural that she, who at seventy is barely fifteen years older than I, should treat me as a youthful daredevil on whom one has to keep a tight rein, even if he has proven himself already.

"So," she said, "here's your schnapps and the bread is freshly baked." After exchanging two sentences with me, she switches to the familiar *Du*; here, in the Upper Village, this informal address is the custom, particularly among coevals.

I ask about Irmgard.

Mother Gisson laughs softly. She has strong yellow teeth. Once, when she had a toothache, she herself pulled the offending tooth; how she managed that, I still haven't figured out.

"Have you seen Marius yet?" she asks.

"Hell! Is he still at Miland's?"

"Irmgard sent him to see me today."

"Does she want to marry him, by any chance?"

Now she no longer laughs, merely barking a short "No," and it seemed like a prohibition addressed to the granddaughter.

She brooded silently for a while, and to judge by her gaze, it seemed as if she was pondering something very far away. And it sounded almost threatening when she said, "The time may have come."

"What time, Mother Gisson?"

"The time for change." And then she added, "That Marius is knowledgeable."

Knowledgeable in her vocabulary means eager for knowledge. I nodded.

"He went to the mine," and with her thumb she gestured toward the back of the room in the direction of the Kuppron.

Mother Gisson is one of the very few who could give precise information about the old drifts. Little by little she has identified for me and even shown me a number of the sealed adits, the Rich and the Poor, the Drift of the Dead Heathen, the Pit of the Dwarfs, the Silvery, and the Plombon. I suspect that she might even know quite a bit about the potential productivity of the old sites, even more than her son, Mathias of the Mount. Once he had shown me a fist-sized rock in which, weirdly and ominously glittering, a gold vein was encrusted. "Found?" I asked. "Yes," he replied, "by my grandfather, or even earlier." And he put the rock away. An old miner's pick hangs above his bed.

"What business does Marius have at the mine? And in this weather?"

"Looking for gold, I guess." Mother Gisson laughs again, and there is something sly and roguish in her merriment. "There's many have tried it."

Why is it that I, too, am still troubled by the mountain? What is it that at times still makes me shiver when I walk along the age-old mining paths which, in places, still show some traces of masonry underpinnings? Or when, in the underbrush, I come upon some collapsed and blocked-up tunnel entrance? All this should no longer be strange to me, familiar as it is after all these years.

I said, "The mountain won't yield anything anymore."

"It has to rest," corrected Mother Gisson.

I've heard that quite often from her, but once more I ask, "How much longer, Mother?"

"I won't live to see it and neither will you; the mountain's time is wide-spanned."

And then I said, as if there was a direct connection, and because I suddenly knew why I had come to see her, "Sack's child won't make it."

"Oh," she said, "the child, too."

"Why too?"

She said, "Because the mother won't make it for long either."

"Hm," I grunted somewhat incredulously, for usually one does not die of furunculosis.

The wood crackled in the stove, outside the rain splashed down monotonously and gushed from the eaves. Mother Gisson went to the stove, opened the stokehole, and put in another log. And while attending to these trivial chores, she remarked, "That's how it is, I know her after all, the Sack woman."

Probably no man, not even a doctor, would be capable of stating this with such implacable certainty, and I would rather not have heard it. But though I found it impossible to doubt her, nevertheless I felt I should try to mitigate her verdict. "Well, Mother Gisson, once in a while and exceptionally you too may be wrong."

She removed the lid from the cooking pot, stirred its contents with a wooden spoon, tasted it, and said, "Dying is a blessing . . . but you don't understand this, you're still too young, and in addition you're a doctor."

I thought of Sack and made no reply.

"You city people don't get older anyway, you're born old and you stay that way until it's over . . ." And she nodded to me from the stove.

Someone who has attended as many deathbeds as I is bound to have some inkling of the fact that there are different kinds of dying, that even in this great solitude in which so much becomes equal, there still can be a singling out, the true death which is so immense and so utterly beautiful, a true coming to an end and yet not an end in itself, that even the physician, the enemy of death, yields to it willingly and willingly gives up a fight that is directed not against death but against the ending of life.

Mother Gisson took out the plates and said, "And because you think that everything comes to an end, you cannot see and you don't want to see that for someone the time may be ripe . . . though there's already some improvement in you and one day you may even be allowed to die truly . . . but when you are supposed to see it, you refuse to accept it . . ."

"That's what I'm here for, Mother Gisson."

"That's what you think because you're dumb and young." She laid the plates on the table, folded her arms under her bosom, and planted herself directly in front of me. "One thing I tell you right now: when my time comes, you're not going to doctor around much with me but just let it happen as it happens, even if I should no longer be in a condition then to do much about your little shenanigans . . ."

"What in blazes are you talking about, Mother Gisson?"

"Of that which is to come that you don't wish to see."

This was ridiculous. There she stood, a picture of rude health despite her seventy years.

"Now I realize that in your conceited quackery you wouldn't allow me even to set you to rights . . . but that's something I mean to discuss with you at greater length and, thank God, we've still plenty of time to do so . . ."

"Just you wait," she said, laughing, and it sounded more cryptic than I cared to admit.

Just then I saw through the window the approaching figure of

Marius, a loden cape around his shoulders, coming up from the left along the street with that sprightly shuffle of his, the wet trousers clinging to his legs: he hardly cut a very prepossessing figure.

I pointed outside. "He doesn't look as if he's bringing a lot of gold."

She looked out. "No gold, but he has found something."

Nothing could surprise me anymore; we would see soon enough.

Then the glass door tinkled and Marius appeared. Only now did one realize fully the condition he was in: the soaking-wet boots encrusted with earth, the trousers full of dirt all the way to the knees—small wonder when one goes looking for gold in such weather.

"Take off your shoes and socks and hang them next to the stove," ordered Mother Gisson.

Childishly, I felt good about Mother Gisson not using the familiar *Du* in addressing the vagrant.

Marius did as he was told. Next to the stove, a double rail is specially provided along the wall for the drying of boots, and that's where Marius stored his things. He came to the table barefoot. He had well-formed and surprisingly clean feet.

"So show me now what you found."

From the pocket of his wet pants he drew a long greenish splinter. It was a thin flint knife.

Mother Gisson took the knife in her strong weathered hand. "You have good eyes," she praised.

I commented, "That has seen at least five thousand years."

"Did you find that near the Cold Stone?" asked Mother Gisson.

For once, this was not an astounding but a rather obvious assumption. For the stone slab which has given its name to the hillock on which it rests originally and without doubt was called Celt Stone; unmistakably it had been a Druidic sacrificial altar, and since it had most probably been erected on the site of an even older sanctuary, it is not surprising that such objects sometimes are found thereabouts. What was surprising, though, was that Marius should have located this spot and that he should have such an uncannily sharp eye to have found the knife in spite of all the snow and morass.

"Yes," he said. "Where I come from, such things are also found."

"Where's that?" I asked.

Marius replied willingly enough. "In the Dolomites. That's where my grandfather still has a farm."

"Want to eat something?" Mother Gisson asked, and pointed to the loaf of bread.

"Many thanks," said Marius, taking the loaf, and since he still held the flint knife, he attempted to apply its jagged edge to the bread.

Whereupon Mother Gisson angrily snatched the loaf from his hand, turned it upside down, and pointed to the three crosses notched in the crust. "This is holy," she said, "and that knife is also holy, but the two don't go together." And she cut a hunk for him with her kitchen knife.

What did she know of the holiness of a Stone Age sacrificial knife? Did time have no meaning for her? How far back did her memory reach?

Marius took his knife, and as if to show Mother Gisson that he had understood her, though in an almost unthinking gesture, he drew the knife across his throat. Then he smiled, pocketed the knife, and took a bite of his bread.

"Beware," Mother Gisson gravely warned him. "You have some knowledge, all right, but you don't know enough yet. That's a bad mixture."

"I know more than others," replied Marius with some smugness. It may be that this was also meant for me, for right from the start I had been under the impression that he hadn't been too pleased to run into me here, of all places.

"And that's precisely why you should watch out, for if you are looking for gold, you are just like all the others, only worse, for, as I said, you have some knowledge."

"And what if I find gold with the rod?" bragged Marius.

"Even then you better beware," said Mother Gisson. "There are antics and masquerades that may have an air of solemn holiness and may take hold of people, yet they remain what they are, a mockery of the real thing." Her voice was indignant. "Better eat and stay content with what you are." And despite her anger she cut another piece of bread for him, as if for a naughty child about whom one cares nonetheless.

But I was reminded of the legend told by the people of this region, according to which only the tunnel called the Pit of the Dwarfs, the entrance to which lies high up next to the Mountain Chapel, reaches all the way down to the depth of the gold lode, a tunnel which, though it begins in a huge hall, soon branches out into an immensely complex maze of tiny drifts which none of those who belong to the tall-grown species, who long ago expelled and exterminated the original pygmy-like mine builders, ever could penetrate, try as they might by crawling like snakes on their bellies; much less could they ever enlarge or raise the ceiling of these infinitely ramified, labyrinthine toy tunnels without being crushed by the collapse of the surrounding stone, perishing among the teeming monsters of the netherworld. Recalling this curse of the dying king of the dwarfs, I shuddered at the thought of the bottomless pit of time into which all those people who had worked this mountain have since vanished and I shuddered at the thought of the abyss of time over which human life rests suspended.

At that moment Mathias Gisson entered through the back door of the kitchen, the one facing the mountain. Obviously he had come into the house through the yard, for he had already cleaned up and stood there, big, broad-shouldered, and in shirt sleeves, an archangel with a red beard, guardian of the door which he filled all the way to its frame; he carefully examined the newly arrived stranger, for he is one who thinks thoroughly and slowly, and anything out of the ordinary he ponders at length.

"Yes," said his mother, "and this is Marius Ratti, who came up from Miland's."

Whereupon Mathias of the Mount, who not only loves his sister but also has a liking for his brother-in-law, sat down at the table, shook hands all around, and in keeping with peasant ritual, which is both more complicated and rigid and more subtle than any urban ceremonial, inquired about what had been said, so that our intercourse should not be interrupted because of him.

So I continued my thoughts. "In my opinion, the gold in the mountain lies so deep that it cannot be found with the rod."

In his plodding miner's speech, Mathias elaborated: "The divining rod is but part of the man who handles it. There are times when he has the feel for gold, and there are others when he can look for copper or for the dullish lead, and then again there are those times when the rod will show only water. He can only find what he truly needs, and if he forces himself nevertheless to look for something else, then the rod twitches toward evil and everything turns calamitous for him. That is why long ago they gave up the gold drifts, and later the copper as well. Everything has its own time and man has to bow to it, for it is man's own time."

He may not have finished and, in his deliberate way, may have meant only to pause for a moment before filling in the gaps in logic that would have been apparent to an attentive listener. But Marius, with his quick wits, had already pounced on these and impatiently retorted, "That may well be true if you assail the mountain with drilling machines and turn its insides upside down to wrest its treasures from its core. But when I hold the twitching rod and feel the gold through every fiber of my body, then this means only one thing, that the time for gold once more is upon us."

Mathias Gisson had propped his chin in his hands, so that the hairs of his beard flowed through his fingers; like many strong men, he likes to laugh, and Marius's fervor seemed a bit funny to him. Without mocking or rebuking him, he merely removed one hand from his chin and, laughing, slapped Marius on the knee. "There's always plenty to say for and against anything."

But Mother Gisson, busy taking off one pot from the fire hole and replacing it with another, said from the stove, "The rod can be misused as much as any machine, and it can also corrupt the one who uses it . . . I can merely warn you and whether you believe what I say is up to you."

"No, please," exclaimed Marius with all the engaging courtesy of which he is capable, "don't put me off like that . . . let me show you what I can do—don't laugh at me, Mathias, before giving me a chance to convince you."

Whereupon Mathias got up and forthwith returned with a copper wire loop, which he silently offered to Marius. I recognized the gadget: some dowsers prefer these metal loops when looking for ore.

But Marius was not to be beaten so easily. He had much to fight for, as one whose concerns were larger than I could imagine at that time, and he said, "No wonder you didn't find anything; this can hardly be called a rod anymore, it's almost a machine . . . You've got to try it with a living willow rod in which there still is the tender flow of life . . . Did you ever try that?"

"I've never tried it with anything . . . We know the will of the mountain without any rod." And Mathias held his hand knee-high, flat over the floor, as if listening through it to the depths of the earth.

It was brighter now in the cheerful kitchen, for gradually the rain outside seemed to have slackened. Marius was silent, and we, too, said nothing. Finally he spoke, and it was almost a plea. "You know the will of the mountain and you are so sure of yourself and so self-righteous that you cannot admit to anyone else's knowledge and instead reject it out of hand . . . Test me, take me in and let me serve you, and do not deny my powers before having tested them."

He had risen, and as he stood there, barefoot with his head slightly bowed, he resembled almost a waiting penitent.

Mother Gisson looked him full in the face and then, using the familiar *Du*, she said very calmly, "You're not capable of serving, even should you wish to . . . and though I do not doubt your knowledge, it cannot bring us any good."

"So you reject me," he said.

"Not in anger but in deep concern," she replied.

"Yes," he said, and went to the stove to collect his socks and boots.

"Mathias will give you some dry socks," she said with a look at the drenched, blackish and shriveled things. "You can bring them back whenever you like." She also took his loden cape from the hook next to the door, under which a small puddle had formed, and brushing off the drops still clinging to it, said in an almost motherly tone of voice, "You should have done that yourself earlier." Mathias brought the socks, which Marius accepted with polite thanks, and it was somehow as if a lost son, who partly still belongs to the household, were about to leave once more for far-off lands—and surely they were sorry that they could not keep him for the meal which now stood ready on the stove, but that no longer was possible after what had been said and what had come to pass.

"The rain has let up," I said. "It's time for me to go, too . . . There are patients to see, after all."

It was now better to leave mother and son alone.

So we both took our leave, Marius and I, and left through the glass door for the slushy and muddy street stretching between the whitish walls and the dark windows of the houses, whitish and black under the hazy bleached noonday sky, a black-and-white photograph. The gray air met us, dank and limp, and silently we walked down the street together.

At the end of the village I said, "Good day, Mr. Ratti."

"Aren't you coming down with me?"

"No, I'm going home." And I pointed to where the red tile roof of my house peered over the dark pines near the Cold Stone.

"There are two houses there," he said. "Is there someone living in the other?"

"Of course."

"Who?"

"Well, a sort of manager who has remained from the construction project . . . He makes ends meet more or less by representing some technical firms . . . engines and things like that."

"Ah yes, the radio salesman."

"Yes, that too."

He showed me that he was well informed. "His name is Wetchy." Ratti's face was contemptuous; the neighborhood was not to his liking.

"Well," I said in conclusion to avoid any further questions, "here is where I turn left."

"Good day, Doctor," he answered curtly, and walked off.

He will hold it against me that I had been a witness to his rebuff. But no matter. When I reached the edge of the woods, I saw the first crocus in flower.

4   It was Easter and white clouds drifted in broken rows westward to disappear beyond the Kuppron, succeeded by still others in the cool blue skies. The spring that was now upon us was the real thing, gentle and lasting, resembling in no way the frigthening vernal explosion of the first days of March, for now this heavenly blueness poured down softly on all beings, like a gentle rain to which one readily exposes one's skin.

I had gone down quite early to Lower Kuppron and was now strolling along the lane that borders the fields on the northern edge of the village. The orchards of the farmsteads are still transparent and the fruit trees at the point of burgeoning, but the wobbly gray fences running along the slightly raised path already show mossy streaks and the ditch by the lane is full of weeds and coltsfoot. The green fields and meadows drink of the sky in little gulps; it is as if a faint and playful breeze was about to blow just above the earth, an animated matinality otherwise experienced only at the seashore when at dawn the first gusts ripple the surface of the waters. Soon the meadows will be full of primroses.

As I turn toward the village next to Strum's cottage and the cemetery, I meet our man of God between church and parish house, the priest Rumbold. Sickly and pale, his shadowy existence takes place well-nigh invisibly between the four walls of his presbytery, and he never calls on me, perhaps because he feels that one should not oppose human decay, or perhaps because he fears the fee for my services, even though he well knows that I would not accept one from him. I once advised him to eat as much liver as he possibly could; Sabest always could put some aside for him and this would have helped his anemia. The vague gesture he offered in reply implied that he could not afford such costly victuals. "Well, then a lot of spinach, Father," I said, because I knew that he himself worked the few vegetable plots in his overgrown garden, in which he also cultivates his beloved rose bushes. He nodded happily. "Yes, yes, spinach is very healthy."

Nevertheless, we get on well together and he bears me no grudge on account of my calling him too late in most cases for the administration of last rites.

Quite recently it had been reported to me that once again he had been bedridden, and I remonstrated with him, as is my time-honored custom, that on such an occasion he should call for my help.

With the touchy humor of the neglected, he replied, "Well, you're not making much use of my services either, Doctor."

"True, Father, but you know of my agreement with our maker . . . I pay Him my respects at Easter, Pentecost, and Christmas, but at other times it's His turn to find His way to me . . ."

He smiled his lopsided grin, under which one always expects to see the heavy woolen scarf out of which his face peers in winter. "But that's not right, Doctor, it's not right."

"After all, it's not the church visits that matter . . . anybody can manage that . . . what counts is that the rest be in good order."

"Yes," he said with a sigh. The timidity he feels with his peasant congregation also inhibits his relations with me, and it always takes some time before I can draw him out from his shell. Because of my physical stature, he apparently lumps me with the peasants. He barely reaches to my chest.

Neither of us was much inclined to start a theological disputation.

And so I said, "Soon your garden will be in full bloom." And was struck by the thought that probably his faith did not exceed by much the olfactory confines of his roses. Gardeners are often like that.

He sighed again. "Whatever I can do with my own hands, I do willingly . . . but just have a look at the roof of my poor church . . . the eaves all broken down, and here the presbytery . . . oh, I can hardly bring myself to talk about it . . ."

"No one's got enough money, Father."

"There should be enough for that . . . but the peasants believe it suffices for them to come to church on Sundays and listen to my sermon . . ."

"You see, I'm right about those church visits . . ."

"I've already gone to see the mayor twice . . ."

"He doesn't do anything without Lax, and that one is a wild heathen . . ."

Lax is the chief municipal councillor.

The priest looked at me sideways to see whether I was serious, a glimmer of his feeble humor again skimming over the crooked mouth. "Heathen? I guess they are all heathens . . . even when they cross themselves, it's still heathenish."

"Man is an obstreperous beast, Father."

"Of course, of course . . ." An insect-like giggle escaped from his puny chest. "Obstreperous, yes . . . and no sermon does any good . . . for when I call them heathens, they take it all in and afterward, in the pub, they may even boast about it."

"It may not be quite that bad, Father."

He peered up at me. "We're all only human . . . obstreperous human beings . . ."

"I'm the last to deny it."

"And all of us know how little it takes for man to lapse . . . to lapse below the animal. It is no easy task to do justice to God's image."

So, after all, we almost landed in a theological dispute, for I, in my own banal understanding, was more than ready to grant priority to animals and certainly to flowers in their ability to equal God's image.

"Yes, the flowers," said the man of God, and he was transfigured by a weak inner light.

The bells above us had ceased their Easter ringing; the bell ringers, whose joyful labors could be observed through the open door of the church tower, released the ropes with a last "bam" and emerged like concert stars, surrounded by their jealous comrades. Duty called the priest to his sacristy. The most pious of the old church spinsters had arrived hours before and had been tripping back and forth among the crosses of the cemetery, looking for the old names, in the presence of which they became young once more and nodded their greetings to them. The church began to fill up.

Oh, for the sound of the organ, which gathers together the wind of the clouds, the wind of the hills, and the wind of the earth within its rippling waves, so that all this flowing multitudinousness of the world, guided in all simplicity by a humble organ-playing village schoolmaster, may find time and space in a small rural church, so that the widely scattered faith, here fortified and made corporeal, may be sheltered under this defective roof resting on Gothic walls. And as unbelieving as the wind that is forever seeking, ever drifting, faith itself unbelieving, the congregation has come down from the hills to join together in the captive organ sounds and in the Word made tangible, all have come here to pray, assuming manifold positions of devotion: there's stingy Krimuss with his yellow mastiff's face, from which at any moment one expects his tongue to loll out sideways as he gazes upward into the timberwork; there's rich Robert Lax, the real ruler of the village, who could easily afford two hunting districts and yet, until quite recently, was a well-known poacher, looking down with his strong black eyes to his hands folded over his belly; there's Mayor Wolters, his white hair cropped short, looking more like a baker than a farmer, reading attentively from his prayer book, following his pointing finger and mumbling the words; there's the whole Miland family, including the wife, a black taffeta reticule on her head, looking inward with closed eyes; there is Bartholomew Johanni with the heavy and empty look of his oxen, his heavy and empty glance now fixed on the sacrament; there is also the merry Thomas Sack with his seaman's beard, whose wife lies sick at home; and all the other Upper Villagers are here, including Mathias of the Mount, all of them seated more or less according to their standing and importance on the benches bearing their names on brass or porcelain labels, harbingers of those that will identify their tombstones. But up front, on the rug-covered altar, the gentle gardener bows before the picture of the Holy Mother, who, in the windblown folds of her starry-blue mantle, holds the baroquely playful and kicking Christ child, while the rest of the children of the community are assembled in the gallery, a quarreling and pugnaciously devout host of angels under the bespectacled glare of the organ-playing schoolmaster, who, in this capacity, is called the *regens chori*.

Not far from me, leaning nonchalantly against one of the pillars supporting the gallery, Marius stares with coarse ostentatiousness at an image of a mining accident shown on one of the wall paintings. There's a bit too much defiance in his posturing. That he should have conformed to the churchgoing custom of the Miland household is hardly such a taxing concession. After a while, he becomes aware of my glance and greets me with his eyes, affecting a somewhat ironical politeness, and then, quite suddenly, he has vanished. Even later, when I walk through the groups of peasants who have taken up positions in the main thoroughfare, standing there in strictly hierarchic order, the groups of old and of young farmers, the Upper Villagers, the elder sons, the cottagers, and the hired hands, all standing there separate as they have stood for centuries past, unconscious of this ritual and yet dimly aware that the spiritual happening in which consciously and yet uncomprehendingly they partook should not be followed without pause by everyday life and by the visit to the pub, as I then walk through the dissolving and constantly regrouping crowd, greeted by most and greeting them in turn, the womenfolk already hurrying away, their skirts blowing, to prepare the midday meal, I see no sign of Marius anywhere, and it doesn't surprise me: for to which group would this wandering stranger belong? To none. And none misses him. Here they all stand under the vernal sky, their black suits in sharp contrast to the sun-whitened walls, in each suit a naked man and in each man a naked soul, hardly aware of the fact that it has rested a while and yet awaits to be transformed once more into wind and cloud. Only the one who is not among them and whom none misses is always wind and his everlasting drifting is without goal and unappeasable.

On such holidays there are few customers for my office: they save their visit for the following day. Thus, I have time to visit the pub, and this, too, is part of the custom.

As I enter, Sack, as is his wont, is monopolizing the conversation. Here he plays the part of something akin to an Oriental storyteller, a part he has conceived for himself either because he gets his fun in leading the others or simply because he takes pleasure in the telling itself.

"And since you are talking about foreigners and the Italians . . . why, you don't know anything of the Eyeties . . ."

"Oho," protested one of the younger peasants.

"Yes, you think you know them because you've been there during the war . . . but what were you? An artilleryman; all you did was shoot at the Eyeties from afar . . . And anyway, what is a war without horses? It's a shitty war, that's all it is . . . But my father, he was a horse soldier, a cavalryman, and he fought a real war near Novara . . ."

He stroked his round seaman's beard and, out of long practice, interpolated an artful pause, then filled it by greeting me with a "Good day, Doctor," which I returned with "And a good day to you, Sack," while, in accordance with my standing, I took my accustomed seat at the round table at which were already seated the mayor, the black-haired Lax, the mastiff-faced Krimuss, and the goat-bearded Selbander. Sabest placed my beer next to the white flint cone, and Sack continued.

"Yes, my father was a horse soldier, and he wore his beard as I wear mine today, in his honor and in his memory, but in those days he was still young and his hair was dark. And so he rode with his comrades along the roads that lead into the big plain that is called Italy, all the time getting deeper and deeper into the Italian heat. And that is a heat of which you have no conception, for the whole world is like a golden baking oven and a red sky stretches over it . . ."

Another pause for effect.

"Perhaps you don't believe me? You all think you know what heat is like because you have tasted the bitter sweat running over your lips at harvest time? You think the sun is just as powerful around here? Like hell it is. For what is the sun without the help of the sea? Sometimes you can feel the sea even in our parts when you climb real high on a mountain, and that's why at times you're drawn to those peaks where the chamois are hopping around . . ."

"Shut up, Sack," said Lax.

". . . But down there in Italy where the sea is, you feel the ocean at all times, even if you don't see it, and its salt rises to the sun and follows it on its course and then comes back with its heat and turns it into the sweat of man and beast, but also into the whitish green of the olives and the black sweetness of the grapes. Did you ever see olives? No, you haven't, you haven't even seen any vineyards . . ."

"How's that?" could be heard from Krimuss. "You mean to say that these days you even have vineyards in the Upper Village?"

"No," replied Sack, "but we've got a lot of other things, and you, Krimuss, don't you interrupt when I'm telling you something about my father and the Eyeties. Because my father, he knew all about it since he and his comrades rode between olive groves and vineyards, tasting the salt of the sea on their lips and looking forward to the Eyetie girls."

"At last, it's getting interesting," Lax said to me.

"Of course," said Sack. "Just you pay attention, Lax, and you'll see how interesting it'll get. You, too, would have been glad to ride in all that heat without meeting anybody far and wide. Not a soul. From time to time they asked, 'Where's the enemy?' But no enemy was to be seen. The villages down there aren't like ours, they're like small towns; sometimes they even went into real towns, and these, too, were all empty, the people had fled at the approach of my father and the other horsemen or had hidden in their houses, and when the soldiers needed water for their horses or for themselves, they had to break into the closed yards by forcing the doors open with their long lances. But in one house they did find a man who showed them to a well and even helped them to water the horses. But when they had finished, he tore open his jacket and his shirt and shouted, *'Evviva Garibaldi!'* That shout was punishable by death, and thus the man meant for the soldiers to pierce his chest. But my father—who was not my father yet at the time—that made him laugh, and he merely tickled the bared chest of the man with the point of his lance. And then they all rode away. Which shows you the way of the Eyeties. And that's what I wanted to tell you about those people."

Did not the tale circle around Ratti? At first, everyone was silent. Only the innkeeper, with the coarse humor of his trade, laughed, and when all eyes were on him, he commented, "I'm sure he also found other chests to tickle, your father . . . and with a much shorter lance? Heh? A short stubby one . . ." and with his fingers he measured the length of a penis.´

Naturally, this brought general laughter. Nothing is so idiotic or so obscene that men will not accept it gladly when inscrutable and complex issues have somehow been brought to the surface of their souls and when they feel the need to cover up their uneasiness and dread. Lax, who happened to be close to the serving girl, could not resist making things even plainer by pointing at her breasts.

Only Mathias, who sat at the second table, objected, grunting, "You're all a pack of pigs."

But Sack, who always likes to be among the funmakers and who may also have welcomed the chance to forget about his sick wife for a while, smiled, and when all the noise had abated he said, "I'm the last to deny that I may have a brother or sister down there; there's plenty of our children in enemy country . . ."

And someone sitting with him at the first table exclaimed, "Oh no, a second Sack, that really would be too much!"

"Don't worry," called Sack in reply. "He wouldn't have my gift of gab since he would be speaking in Eyetie . . . but it's quite possible that he'll show up here one day. And why not? All war children are restless, they wander to seek their brothers. Indeed, he may arrive at any moment, another oldster like me, with a beard like mine . . ."

They all looked at the door, and then general laughter broke out once more.

"You don't mean that seriously?" asked Miland, and he seemed to ponder the theory of the war children.

"Wouldn't that be real nice if every vagrant could claim to be a war child," said the mayor. "There's enough trouble with those people as it is."

"They're arsonists," said Selbander, the goatee next to me.

"As long as they don't steal, I don't mind the arson," Lax said, and laughed explosively.

Sack understood him perfectly. "Yes, a barn fire can be a damn pretty sight . . . and as for what was inside, only the farmer knows . . ."

"One doesn't talk of such things," the mayor reprimanded him.

"Wetchy's not here anyway," said Lax, finishing his beer. "Sabest, another one."

Wetchy happens to be their insurance agent.

But the goatee insisted. "Who comes from fire has to set fire."

And Bartholomew Johanni, who has few thoughts in his head, added, "All gypsies put a hex on the cattle."

It may be that with the rise in temperature during the morning, the drinks had gone faster to the heads of some of them, certainly to that of Krimuss, who now stood up and announced with his yellow mastiff's mouth, "Who roams runs away from death."

And the hired hand Andreas, who sat at the second table with the other help, nodded, adding, "And draws death right after him." After which he went back to his pipe.

Miland said calmly, "Death squats everywhere, wherever you look, on the roof, in the garden . . . He needs no stranger to be brought into our midst."

But Krimuss, who had remained standing and was now slanted drunkenly over the table, so that his watch chain with its amulets, silver coins, and half-moons swung over his beer, blared in a croaking voice, "He may be in our midst, but he is our own death and our friend . . . We have no need for a death brought by a stranger."

I thought it was time to interject something myself. "In my humble opinion, if anyone of you sees death squatting anywhere, it's time to call the doctor."

"So as to speed it up . . . right, Doctor?" called Sack into the general merriment, which now was at my expense.

The small, chubby cottager Strum, who sat next to Sack, now mused, "In heaven's name! I've never seen death squatting anywhere."

"Right you are, Strum," I said. "What we see is life, and I much prefer being called for a birth than for a death."

But Mathias laughed and said, "And yet both are the same."

"Shut up!" said Krimuss with the hoarse insistence of the drunk. "Death up there on the mountain is also an alien death . . . That one, we'll cut down to size . . . and if he should come down here, I'll strangle him myself and throw out his bones."

There was a short pause, and once again everybody looked toward the door. I felt that something was about to happen. Even Pluto, who had resigned himself to the fact that his master ran a noisy pub and who drew from it his own rewards, arose on his four soft, gigantic paws and looked in sad anticipation toward the entrance. And, indeed, the door opened, and who came in but Marius.

"Good day," he said simply, and since all the seats were taken, he posted himself at the counter. Calmly he stood and observed the assembly with some derision.

"A beer?" asked Sabest suspiciously, for he knew that Marius had no money.

But Miland said, his gesture including his hired hand Andreas, "The beer for my people is on me."

"Thanks, farmer," Marius said, and drank a little of the beer that Sabest placed in front of him.

Krimuss, still standing, asked with aggressive suspicion, "And why did you come?"

Marius Ratti nodded to him. "Because you spoke of me."

"What in hell!" exclaimed Lax. "You think we have nothing better to talk about than you?"

"No," said Marius.

Such was his arrogance. But to Sack, who had not yet had a taste of it, this was cause for merriment. A few others joined in.

"Throw him out, Sabest," screamed Krimuss drunkenly, "or I'll strangle him."

"Stop." Lax caught Krimuss by the arm and pulled him back on his seat. "Sit down, Krimuss . . . let's have some fun."

"Are you an Eyetie or aren't you?" the goatee next to me asked aggressively.

"If you mean me, no, I'm no Italian." That was said sharply, fearlessly, and with firmness, emphasized by the formal *Sie*, which in these surroundings was hardly customary and even quite inappropriate.

"But Ratti is a somewhat Italian-sounding name," interpolated the mayor in a conciliatory tone.

"Yes. So what?"

"They say you can find gold," said Lax, changing the subject.

"Yes, that I can," said Marius, strangely calm and accommodating.

"Make gold?" The stolid Johanni was still following his own train of thought. "If you can make gold, then I guess you also put the hex on the cattle."

Sack called to him, "Why don't you let him put the hex on your cattle, Johanni? . . . A calf with three heads will make you rich . . . Sabest doesn't pay you much anyway for a normal calf . . ."

"I can find gold but I can't make it."

And then could be heard the firm voice of Mathias of the Mount: "Nothing will come of that, I can assure you."

Shaking his head, Johanni insisted, "Make gold, find gold, it's all the same."

It had become oppressively hot in the room. The tobacco smoke hung in a broad layer in midair, and there was a sour stench of beer and sweating bodies. Acting on impulse, I took off my jacket.

"The doctor is all ready for the brawl," a voice from the crowd shouted.

Again, there was a howl of laughter. But no one imitated me; they all kept their jackets on.

"And why should nothing come of the search for gold?" inquired Lax. "If he can find gold, let him try his hand at it."

"No," said Ventlin from the Upper Village, "the mountain no longer yields any gold."

Some of the younger men, whose interest had been piqued, had gathered around Marius and were now asking questions.

"You want to do what? Find gold . . . up in the mountain?"

"He's a nut . . . just a crazy nut."

They look at each other and laugh foolishly.

"He wants to bring death down from the mountain, the golden

death," Krimuss said, baring his dog's teeth. "Sabest, throw him out."

"Why don't you try?" says Marius, and it is as if he were baring his chest for the lance.

The young lads seem quite willing to follow Krimuss's suggestion, if for no other reason than for the sheer fun of it. It is then that Mathias Gisson intervenes. He pushes the lads to one side and plants himself in all his breadth next to Marius. "What is it you really want?" he asks him with great affability.

No less strange is the comportment of the goateed Selbander next to me. He has risen, and as if thunderstruck by Mathias Gisson's question, he gasps out an answer. "Gold."

Krimuss's attitude also changes. "The one who holds the gold also holds death . . . Let him bring us the gold, and then we'll strangle him . . ." Then, turning to me, he adds, "Let him bring death, so that we can strangle death."

"Hand over the gold," someone shouts from the first table. Now Miland also has stood up. "Marius is my hired hand, and I haven't hired him to look for gold . . . so let him be."

Lax, to whom the whole thing is hellish good fun, shouts, "You're as much a fool, Miland, as your hired hand . . . Why don't you let him look for gold? . . . He doesn't do any real work anyway."

"That's my business."

Marius says calmly, "I do my master's bidding . . . In any case, I wouldn't be looking for gold for myself."

Selbander gesticulates wildly. "The gold belongs to the community . . . It is the community who decides . . . Miland has nothing to say in the matter at all . . ."

That arouses Ventlin. "The mountain belongs to the Upper Village . . . and it's not to be touched . . . We won't stand for it."

Krimuss has followed the discussion with the mean look of a vicious dog, and now he pulls on my sleeve. "The Upper Villagers won't let death go . . . The Upper Villagers are smart . . . but it won't do them any good."

The goateed Selbander now intervenes like a shyster lawyer. "The prospecting licenses belong to the community as a whole . . ."

It is Miland who replies. "The community can wipe itself with those licenses . . . There's already one useless cableway up there . . ."

But Lax, perhaps merely so as to heat up the discussion or perhaps because he really has been enticed by the lure of the gold, says, "No, no . . . that's got nothing to do with it . . . We want our gold."

The mayor again tries placating the opponents. "Who knows whether there really is any gold?"

"He promised it," declares Selbander furiously. And someone calls out, "Miland is on the side of the Upper Village."

Marius is at the center of the row, but he belongs to neither faction and he merely smiles. Yet he is the target of menacing looks from both sides.

Johanni repeats once more, "Gypsies who put the hex on cattle should be thrown out."

"Bravo, Johanni," shouts Lax delightedly.

It was pretty clear what was about to happen. And Sabest had already begun to clear away the beer mugs. Strum, who was a peaceable sort, made ready to leave. But the young lads around Marius were showing signs of militant expectations.

The goatee could be heard. "The richest community . . . that's what we once were . . . the richest community in the whole country."

If I didn't want to have to fetch my bandaging kit from upstairs, I had to intervene now. I put on my jacket. "Well, men . . . I'm going . . . it's already noon . . ." And so as to get the chief rabble-rouser out of harm's way, I continued, "Well, Lax, how about going with me . . . ?"

"Now? Just when the fun is starting?" But he had already grown a bit thoughtful, his hard, capable head had begun to work, and he got up and said, "It would be a pity not to have a try at it, though . . . One has to think it over."

Krimuss growled like an old mastiff, and there was disappointment among the young lads. It was possible that one of them would still leap on Marius at the last moment. And Marius was not someone who would retreat of his own accord. One had to offer him an honorable retreat to save face.

"Come with me, Ratti," I said loudly.

"Not all that glitters is gold," proclaimed Sack. "How much do I owe, Sabest?"

Marius was in no position to refuse me. He took his leave with an airy wave of his hand and followed me out.

"Well?" I said once we were outside.

"Thank you, Doctor," he replied, "but I could have managed those lads by myself." And he walked away with his sprightly shuffle.

There was still a lot of noise inside, but the mayor was able to drown it out. "Folks, it's time to settle up."

Lax appeared outside and, looking after the receding figure of Marius, he observed, "He'll look for the gold anyway."

"Is that why you tried to have him beaten up?"

"You would have made him whole again, Doctor."

"Why, many thanks, Mr. Lax."

He laughed with his strong white teeth under the black mustache. "No hard feelings, Doctor."

The noonday heat was upon us. The drifting of the clouds had slowed, and when one of them stood still in front of the sun, its edges silvery, the milky stillness filling the world was that which is felt only at noontime in spring. Caroline was waiting with the Easter meal, and I started on my way home.

At the end of the village, Sack caught up with me.

"Such a clever chap," he said.

"You mean Marius? Yes, but what does he really want?"

Sack gave me a knowing look. "Snare them"—and with his thumb he pointed back at the village—"and snare them all he will."

I turned around. We had reached the first of the three chapels along the road to the Upper Village. From here one already has a full view of Lower Kuppron. It lay in the midst of its orchards, over which a first veil of greenery was spreading, and the noon smoke of its chimneys rose thin and straight into the air. Singly and in pairs, the Upper Villagers in their dark suits came up the road after us, and all of them were thinking of the noon meal that was waiting for them and that they would soon thrust into their naked bodies.

5　　On an afternoon in the middle of May there seemed to be no end to my clinic. I had a whole string of patients, among them some decrepit little women endlessly emptying the excess of their sufferings into my hands, who, when finally finished, were all too ready to start all over again; some dental treatments of the type that any country doctor must be able to cope with; and, finally, I had to prepare my prescriptions. It is not only that commercial medicines would be much too expensive—a doctor not able to concoct his own preparations would not amount to much in the eyes of the peasants. So I brew my potions on the alcohol burner, crush my powders and mix my ointments on the glass plate, while my dental instruments boil in the electric kettle. My hands are used to the work and no longer make any errors. I could almost watch them work by themselves or, if I wanted to, I could think of something else, for instance of Marius, but today I find myself unable to do so because, for the past hour, the pig that Sabest has stuck has been squealing for the loss of its emptying blood and fills my ears with the bottomless sorrow of all suffering creatures. As I label my bottles, boxes, and jars, I hear its last death rattle, heralding its transformation into pork roast. Such things, too, the country doctor needs to be able to take in his stride, and not only the doctor but whosoever later enjoys his roast, and not only the glutton but all those who tolerate war, murder, and bloodletting, of which every single one of us is guilty. Still, I was glad when the air was no longer filled with the screams of death. I took my preparations down to Sabest's wife in the kitchen, so that—as is our custom—she would take them into her safekeeping and later hand them out to the patients coming to fetch them.

Minna Sabest takes the medicines and heaves a big sigh.

"The poor pig," I say.

"Not the pig," she says, and once more sighs heartbreakingly.

The sighs are a bit too ostentatious. I can't quite believe in them; perhaps they are to be taken only as a formal opening.

"So, what's wrong, Mrs. Sabest?"

She casts a glance at the kitchen maid, busy peeling potatoes near the window, and we move into the taproom.

"Doctor," she says, "it's about Peter . . ."

"Why, I haven't seen Peter in a blue moon."

Nervously she looks around the empty room and then whispers, "That's just it, Doctor, not even we, his own parents, get to see him . . . All the time he's hanging around with that man . . . with that Marius whom Miland took in . . . You know him, don't you?"

"Of course I know him."

"And believe it or not, Doctor, that man has bewitched our Peter."

"And what next, Mrs. Sabest?"

"Oh, don't laugh, Doctor, it hurts me . . . I won't even talk about the fact that Peter, when we do see him once in a great while, brings home a lot of wild ideas, like"—and she points to the radio—"like he's going to get rid of the radio . . ."

"I already know all about that foolishness, Mrs. Sabest, and I wouldn't take it too seriously if I were you . . . though there are times when I wish that damn gadget to hell and gone myself . . ."

"Well, fine," she went on, "and it's not the radio I want to speak of, though I can't believe that you'd go along with him in this matter either . . ."

"No, I don't agree with him, for you need the radio for your customers." But secretly I was impressed by the intransigence with which Marius pursued his objectives.

"Oh, not just for the guests," she says. "In the old days he would sit with us and we would listen to it together . . ."

"Children grow up, Mrs. Sabest, and as far as I know Peter flew the coop quite a few times even before there was any Marius . . ."

She dried a tear. "Yes, Doctor, I know you're talking about Strum's Agatha, and you well know that I did have quite a few objections against a common cottager's daughter . . . but now that he's forbidden it to him . . ."

"Come, come now, if it comes to that, there's no forbidding that'll hold, let that be the business of Agatha . . . and who ever heard of such prohibitions anyway . . ."

"The whole village, Doctor. Don't forget that I stand in the store all day long and that I hear a lot, last but not least the humiliation to myself . . . They all talk, the Selbander woman and Mrs. Lax, who . . . Well, I don't want to name names . . . but all of them come to me with tales about Peter being bewitched by this vagrant, this good-for-nothing tramp, or perhaps having been perverted to even worse things, disgusting things . . . Oh, Doctor, don't laugh, the whole village is laughing already, and to whom shall I turn with my worries if not to you?"

"Hm." I thought of the truckers and of their indignation at Marius, whom they had called a pig because he had been preaching chastity to them.

"You're not laughing, Doctor?"

No, I didn't laugh. Behind this hearty and knowing woman who always seemed in sound accord with life and all of its pleasures, there now stood a little girl, innocent of worldly knowledge and probably surprised that she should ever have given birth to another, a different kind of being. Indeed, man will do anything to keep the true powers of life at arm's length and to remain blind to them as long as he possibly can. I know this only too well.

"What's your husband saying about all this, Mrs. Sabest?"

"He's one of those who laugh . . . I even think he may like this tramp . . . He says every animal knows best with which to mate . . . but he would still cut the bum's throat if I asked him to . . ."

If she requests it in bed, he may indeed do so; I wouldn't put it past Sabest. But I'm not giving her that advice. Nor does she need it, probably.

"I shall follow up on the matter, provided that meanwhile you don't take it to heart, pretty Minna . . . I really see no reason to do so for the time being . . ."

That made her smile. I fondle her full cheek and accompany her across the driveway into the store to buy my usual allotment of tobacco. The small store smells of sundry things, but mainly of indigo and other calico fabrics, the bales of which are stored on the shelves on a slant, so that their patterns can readily be seen. Whatever the peasants need can be found here; the store is a true gold mine, although Sabest treats it as a minor adjunct to his business. But that's mainly for show.

"Yes," she continues, "and he even runs down the store, he calls it a cheap panhandling shop and we ourselves are usurers in his eyes."

"Stop it now," I say. "You promised not to take it to heart anymore."

She looks at me trustingly, and I leave the store accompanied by the tinkling of the doorbell.

The street, in the spring afternoon, was white and dusty, but the dust did not as yet have the biting sharpness of summer; there still was a great deal of moistness in the fragrant air, and in the midst of this mountain village street I suddenly was reminded of the seashore and of spring-green dunes. For a moment I was overcome with longing, the longing to travel once more, to be young again and to be allowed to wander from place to place, if need be to drift as a harebrained and utopian fool like this Marius, still a wanderer through this world. Yes, such was my sudden longing, and while it lasted I felt it to be of greater import than the complaints of the blond wife of the innkeeper, and I understood Peter despite my better knowledge of the aberrations of Marius and of all maverick drifters like him who, in their confusion and lunatic restlessness, are nothing but nature's trial-and-error experiments, the innumerable failures that must precede the creation of one true genius. Yet I had no use at all for that knowledge in the pangs of my longing which made me feel as if the world itself had been set into vernal motion. As the clock on the church tower struck half past three, I felt joyful that the Kuppron wall, bare of snow at last, greeted the village in kindly friendship, kind to me, kind to Marius and to all wayfarers. The pasture hut on the Kuppron ridge above the large meadow was clearly visible, the skies above had withdrawn into a higher silence, hardly perceptible anymore; the time of upward striving had begun for all of nature, but I, I once more realized that my wandering years were over for good and that nothing remained but the staid path of aging. And so I went across the street to the barber to have my graying hair and beard trimmed.

Master Steppan, in accordance with his twin professions, stood at his cutting table in front of the window, ironing a jacket. Both the tailoring and the barbering scissors hung in harmony next to the mirror which served both kinds of customer alike.

"Right away, Doctor," he said as I entered, for he was just in the process of ironing a sleeve.

On the back wall and above the door which leads to his living quarters hangs a picture of the Madonna with an eternal light in front of it, indication that, in addition to his twin main professions, Steppan also serves as sacristan. The eternal light glimmers behind a purple glass on which is painted in fading gold a cross entwined with a flaming heart.

He is more or less my own age, and since he may well brood over the same things that had been in my own thoughts, I said, "It's spring again, Steppan."

Looking up from his ironing and blinking over his steel-framed glasses that sit low on his red-veined nose, he philosophized: "The older one gets, the longer spring lasts."

He said this with his usual, strangely confident cheerfulness, a cheerfulness all the more surprising as his life takes place between a cantakerous wife and a greenish sickly daughter, and as he spoke he calmly continued to iron.

I had sat down in the barber chair. "Yes, we're getting old, Steppan, two old barber-surgeons."

He laughed. "Since there has been a doctor in the village, I'm no longer a barber-surgeon . . . Though my father, yes, he was a true barber-surgeon."

He won't admit that he still practices the art of pulling teeth, which he learned from his father, or that he still applies leeches— to which, incidentally, I have no objection at all. And then he adds, "But soon there won't be any need for a doctor either . . . there'll be medicine machines; tailoring machines we already have . . . I even suspect you of wearing machine-made clothes yourself, Doctor . . ."

Guiltily I stroked my pants. It was true, I had bought them ready-made in the city.

"Machine shirts, machine socks, machine jackets, and pretty soon man will have a machine skin, and so it'll continue all the way ever closer to the core until finally he'll have a machine heart. And then the whole human being will stink of machine oil."

"Is that why you smear your hair oil on people's heads?"

"I won't let anything be said against it; it smells powerfully sweet."

He placed the flatiron on its stand and straightened up. His tailor-like slightness is compensated by a jolly little belly. "Though it's true that for the Almighty even the hair oil stinks," he added as an afterthought, "for He is surrounded by the fragrances of paradise."

"Who knows, maybe paradise smells of hair oil."

He smiled. "A little of it is bound to be mixed in."

To be sure, right here the smells were not those of paradise: a mixture of barber and tailor odors, the steam of the ironed jacket, and some kitchen fumes from his living quarters.

"Yes," he said, "the devil stinks, the plague stinks, death stinks, the machine stinks, and all evil stinks to high heaven, and that's why a good man yearns for the sweet fragrance."

"Open the door," I said. "Outside the air blows straight from paradise."

"Yes, yes indeed," he said as he ironed the other sleeve of the jacket. "In spring the world is God's mouth. He breathes the air of paradise and His breath is His word."

"Tell me, barber, why don't you have a garden the way your priest does? Then you could have your own roses and their fragrances . . ."

"Bah," he exclaimed, like someone who doesn't want to bother with trifles, "not much longer and we shall all be in the Great Garden where spring is everlasting and where forever we shall dwell in His breath and in His word."

And as he finished ironing the sleeve, he added, "The world beneath heaven is a mean mouth which rarely smiles and much conceals."

Then he was finished and he trimmed my hair and beard. "So," he said, and went for the dread bottle with the threatening amber liquid, "and now for the oil."

"Skip it," I told him. "I'm handsome enough without your smells . . . I don't need it even though I'm about to visit a pretty young girl." For during the trimming procedure the decision had ripened in me that, for the sake of the unhappy blond Sabest woman, I would go check with Agatha on how things really stood with Peter and Marius.

"Give my best regards to Irmgard," he said in answer, "but you still would have been prettier with a drop of oil."

"Wrong," I said, "I'm not visiting Irmgard . . ." But at the same instant I reflected that I might as well stop by at Miland's and talk to Marius personally. It was too early for that, though, for everyone would still be in the fields. My work for the day was finished and so I had time to visit at my leisure. And I added, "You're right, maybe I'll go see Irmgard as well."

And so I walked slowly past Miland's house on Church Street, glancing briefly inside, past parish house and church, and then entered the dead-end alley closed off by Strum's gate. The gate is open, the yard tidily swept, but, except for some chickens, there's no one around. It is then that I catch sight of Agatha in the garden, in back of the yard.

There she sits under the apple trees at the rough table rammed into the grass between two similar rough wooden benches, her nose close to her work, and she sews with those slow rounded motions that are part of woman's earliest dignity, as characteristic of the youngest girl as of the aged crone, weaving both of them into the fabric of time, irrespective of the fact that one, like Agatha, may be barely sixteen, while the other, like Mother Gisson, is past seventy.

I was about to open the slightly jammed gate in the fence between yard and garden when, alerted by the noise, Agatha came running toward me with a somewhat startled and confused expression on her face, as if she had to forestall my entering the garden; and, indeed, she falters before reaching the gate and merely says, "The Doctor."

"Yes, Agatha," I say, and remain in the yard. As she stands there before me in her blue apron, hands clasped behind her back, still half pigtail girl, half future mother of pigtail girls, it is difficult for me to imagine what has been or still is happening between her and Peter. Although fully aware that such things are quite usual between young people and that I myself had been subjected to them, and indeed, if luck or misfortune should so decree, might once again be subjected to them, it is but an abstract knowledge, and as far as I am concerned, it is more like knowing some past or future gossip about myself which I don't have to take too seriously.

"How are things with you, Agatha?" I ask, because that is what one is supposed to say.

She is much too shy to answer, quite probably she wishes I were at the North Pole or, because that is too far for her imagination, quite simply in my grave.

"Father still in the fields?"

She nods. Her thoughts are elsewhere or nowhere, they are within a happiness that is inconceivable to her because her thoughts cannot say much more than "Now I have to sew," or "Now I have to cook," or "Father is in the fields"; she cannot form that happiness into thoughts because no thought can express it, it does not consist in the pronounceable but rather in the rounding turn of the needle which leads the thread, in the crackle of the fire in the stove, in the sleeping and waking and in the constant stream of time turning into time, in the being of time which flows thick as an arm through her young body, the heart in its center, beating ceaselessly, a ceaseless, formless and unformable prayer to the overarching powers of which it is a part.

I was just about to leave when the formless dreaming found an access to reality; it smiled and said, "Here's Trapp."

Yes, Trapp was there, he, too, caught in his dream, surely a friendly one, for his tail wagged back and forth, a wagging prayer to the powers of which he, too, was a part.

"Wait, Agatha," I said. "We'll join you."

But the gate proved stubborn, so I finally vaulted it. Trapp followed with an easy jump and Agatha laughed.

"Splendid," I said. "Now watch, Agatha." I found a stone, to which Trapp barked an enthusiastic "hurrah," and threw it in a big curve back into the yard. Trapp returned it with great verve, dripping with saliva. Then it was Agatha's turn to repeat the game, and this sealed once more our friendship for the day.

We continued to stand like that for some time, she with her naked legs, solid pink-marbled girl's legs with mosquito bites, so that she frequently felt the urge to rub them together, and as we stood and watched Trapp, tirelessly challenging us to continue the game, over and over prodding the stone temptingly before us with his paws, she gradually fell silent and became thoughtful.

"Come, Agatha, I'll sit with you for a while."

We sat on the benches, I facing the girl, who had taken up the linen fabric from the table and once more started to sew. The farmers hereabouts are not fruit cultivators, they don't tend or crop their trees, so that the adjacent gardens and their trees, their crowns entangled with those of their neighbors, form a single dense canopy of foliage and a single dense carpet of grass, capturing between them the shadows and the cool of the summer, hardly leaving any patches of sun on the ground, only small playful curls of light which tremble in unison with the blades of grass. Through the trunks one could discern the wheat field on the opposite slope, a horizontal band of sunny green, framed by the edge of the fence and the lowest branches of the foliage, some of which protruded as dark silhouettes into all that brightness, a brightness that from our shadowy bower shone like a faraway land, barely green anymore in all the sunlit brilliance and becoming increasingly brighter and colorless until finally it was but a bluish shimmer of the firmament that traveled and yet rested over it. It is this restless and yet restful sheen which is the summer. All around us the chickens pick in the grass, cackling sporadically, and from the water ditch at the edge of the garden a mosquito may come over, carried by its thin shrill whine. Trapp lies with us, his stone between his paws. Agatha sat with her back to the brightness of the field, her eyes on her work, and over her naked arm, going to and fro with the needle's motion, there flitted always the same squiggle of sunlight.

And then she started to speak:

"There are two cows and a young calf in our stable."

"Yes," I said. "I know."

"When the calf wants to drink, it bends its neck
and lifts its head. Its lips become long and soft.
And it kneels."

"Yes," I said. "That's how calves drink."

"Its whole coat smells of milk. On its forehead
the coat is dense and black. It has no horns as yet.
Its forehead is hard and flat and heavy.
And it stretches its head for drinking."

"Yes," I said.

"The mother licks its forehead and its flanks.
She licks its thighs.
Were it to stay with the mother, the mother
would let the little calf drink and drink until she is empty.
It has to sleep alone.
And the mother also has to sleep alone. But
she always has her head turned toward the child.
The night is dark and very large. The moon
has a white belly and he lets it flow
toward my bed,
and there is nothing for me to look at."

Then she fell silent and sewed. I cleaned my pipe by folding blades of grass and threading them through the stem. The gift of speech, which, for a moment, had floated on Agatha's soul, seemed to have blown away once more.

But then she said, "The storm."

"No," I said, "there'll be no storm today."

She smiled as if she had caught herself at something secret and let the needle do her work. From time to time she gave the spool of thread, standing on the table and bearing on its top a white trademark, a little turn, so as to release another length of thread.

"What are you sewing, Agatha?"

"For later," she answered.

Ever more sun squiggles seeped into the garden as the sun sank lower.

Agatha let her work sink into her lap.

"But when we were sitting here nights, the night
was like a cow that breathes and I
lifted my face, my mouth was that soft.
And it became bright.
Between the horns of the night
came the storm and it sang
like the sun.
I drank the storm and its milk,
drank the milk of the storm and
I was white as the belly of the moon and most fair.
But now I am a witch."
She fell silent and stared into the void.
"What are you?" I let slip from my lips, startled.

She did not hear me. But she placed her hands under her small round breasts, as if offering them to someone, and it may be that she saw her lover sitting next to her on the shaky wooden bench, for she turned a bit to her right and the cloud-like breath on which her soul curled into speech took on a different rhythm and was borne by another tide.

"Why, oh, why did you leave me?
Was he stronger than the night?
Was he stronger than the storm
and stronger than twenty bolts of lightning?
Twenty cows and twenty bulls
dance around my breasts
and the beat of their hoofs
follows my song.
And yet you left
because the weak one called you,
the one who cares for no one.
And so he called me a witch."
The last words were a childlike lament.
After a while I said, "That's how much you loved him?"
She looked me full in the face and said, "Yes."
"That's how much you loved Peter?"
"Maybe Peter, yes," she said.

Then we were both silent and I looked out to the sun swaying in the wheat field. Through the field strolls the wayfarer, the weightless one, blown by the wind, the foe of mothers, coming from infinity and receding into infinity; he cares not for the fields and not for the mothers, his strength is not of their making, it is in the borrowed strength of chance encounters, it is not that of growth but that of gathering.

"And now you are a witch," I said.

"Yes, that's what he called me."

"Marius did?"

The witch bent down to scratch the mosquito bites on her shins, and since Trapp had noticed that the witch was sad, he sought to lick her face but only managed to reach her hands and legs.

She indulged the dog's wet caress and then she said, "Yes, that's what Marius called me because he forbade it to him."

"I know," I said.

"Oh, Doctor, sir, you knew," she lamented. "Why did you let it happen?"

It was not a reproach directed against me; it was a lament addressed to life as a whole because it had left her alone in the storms of the moon. And she stretched herself in pain and let her hands glide downward from her breasts over her womb and all the way to her knees.

She had come to know the "it once was" which enters the world and fills all of it, penetrates and fills all its pores and that of all its creatures whenever anyone dies. When she had reached her knees, she twitched slightly, like a dog in its sleep. "That's where the lightning sits," she said, "it sits in the legs and waits."

"Don't be sad, Agatha," I said. "Life is long and beautiful."

"Yes," she said. "I know. But they're sitting at the blacksmith's and they make him sharpen their scythes."

"The blacksmith is a good man."

"He makes the plows and the scythes," she said, and let the thread glide through her fingers as far as her arm could reach, "and time runs short for them as they sit and watch him work with fire and anvil."

"Yes," I said. "I'll go there and see what they're up to." And I got up.

She nodded and looked a little happier. "Would you like some milk, Doctor?"

"With pleasure."

So we crossed the garden and the yard to reach the house, where Agatha disappeared through the low wide door that leads directly from the yard down into the cellar. That's where the big brown earthenware jug stands in which the milk is stored and forms a thick skein on its surface. There are also a few smaller vessels down there for the decanting of the milk, and that is how Agatha will fill a glass for me, taking care that the skein not glide into it, though she may well fish the milk skein out for herself on the sly with two greedy fingers and let it disappear into her own soft mouth, and all this was as fitting as that she is now coming back, climbing the stairs step by step, the glass in her hand and her eyes on the sloshing surface of the liquid, all of it profoundly good and fitting, for the smile that drops to the ground from a human face together with the drop of spilled milk for which it is meant, that smile is the essence of a simple and true humaneness. Thus Agatha returned with a glass filled to the brim and said, as is proper, "May you enjoy it, Doctor, sir." And with like good manners I replied, "Thank you, Agatha."

I drank standing in the yard. The blue of the skies all around us was vernally tender like soft porcelain and wherever it reached all the way down to the earth it grazed the new green of the hills and the blossoming whiteness of the trees, and this produced a soft gentle sound replete with a satisfying human fulfillment. In between one heard the noises of the village and the hammering from the blacksmith's shop. I returned the glass and said once more, "Thank you, Agatha."

And although I had lost all desire to meet Marius, I was nevertheless so deeply moved by Agatha's behavior that I decided to look into the matter. Followed by Trapp, I entered the Miland farm.

And immediately was met by a surprise: I came upon Marius already in the yard, but with him was another man, who unmistakably was also a drifter, a puny little fellow with a mouse face who had planted himself in a mock-respectful at-attention position in front of Marius and awaited his orders or his lecture with an amused twinkle in his eyes.

As soon as Marius saw me, he said loudly for my benefit, "Go to the kitchen and tell Irmgard to give you something."

The little rogue—one could not define him any other way—tripped off to the kitchen, and I said, "Well, another visitor."

"A good day to you, Doctor," said Marius, to remind me of my manners.

"And a good day to you, too, Mr. Marius Ratti," I replied, and sat down on the bench next to the entrance, under which all the wooden clogs of the family are stored, starting with the huge ones of the farmer, all the way down to the dainty clogs of Cecily.

Marius had remained standing nonchalantly in the sun, his arms folded. "What brings you to us, Doctor?"

That was a bit too thick for my taste and so I snapped quite gruffly, "I'm waiting for the farmer."

That he remained polite and calm and didn't turn tail either was rather to my liking. He replied, "I believe I may say 'to us,' for I live here, after all . . . That makes me part of the homestead."

All right with me.

After a while he said, "All the others are in the fields."

"Yes, the spring sowing . . . And you, you're under house arrest?"

"Oh," he said, "there's plenty of hands out there . . . My time will come soon enough."

"And when's that?"

"At threshing time, for instance."

"Well, that's a long time off . . . You mean to say the farmer has taken you on only for the threshing? After all, there's always plenty of harvest hands around and we already have a local mechanic."

"I'm hoping that this year the threshing will not be done by machine."

"What?"

"Yes," he said simply.

"I don't for the life of me understand what you mean, Marius."

"Doctor, machine threshing is a sin."

Quite obviously he was mad.

"Hm . . . a sin?"

"One could think that bread is bread . . . and yet our bread no longer is true bread." And he repeated, "Bread."

"Yes . . . and so what?"

He became impatient. "Bread comes from there"—and he pointed to the sky and then to the ground—"and it comes from here . . . and in between is man with his hands but no harvesting machine . . . That's the way it has always been."

I was rather stunned. Any discussion was probably futile. Nevertheless, I said, "Mills are also machines, after all."

"Yes," he said, "the big ones, the steam-driven mills . . . and they've made the people sick, too."

Was he one of those apostles of nature healing who draw their half-baked knowledge from popular weeklies? One of those who have read of the pollution of the world through the proliferation of electric waves? And was that why he wanted to do away with the radio? And had he ensnared Miland with such naïve back-to-nature talk? To get him to say some more, I observed, "So you find whole-wheat bread healthier?"

"I don't know what that is," he answered gravely.

"Well, bread made of rough-ground grain."

This seemed to irritate him, either my thickheadedness or the existence of whole-wheat bread; he shrugged impatiently and turned away. "What is prepared in sin can never be healthy." And he went into the house.

Left alone on my bench, I contemplated the yard and the manifold useful things that it held—enough to bring it back, very nearly, into the realm of nature. And I imagined that Marius Ratti might have come from one of those Italian stone villages, ensconced in the surrounding mountains, with their almost windowless unplastered walls of rough-hewn stones and steep outside stairs. From such houses, too, fields are cultivated, vineyards are tended, and there is joy at harvest time in the fall. What is his business here, where there is the same order though perhaps less joyfulness, and what is he up to? The stable walls along the yard are well plastered, though in places the humidity may creep up darkly from the ground, the ladders are hung in neat rows below the eaves of the roof, a large swallow's nest has found shelter in the angle between stable and barn, flies swarm through the stable windows and over the dung heap, the stench of which drifts over to where I sit, green weeds already grow from the compost pile and the grass pushes through the joints of the flagstones at my feet, and all of it stands for the permanence of mankind between the growing and the petrified, a semblance of permanence and yet one that is real, for man comes out of the flight of grasses and wind and returns to flight when all that surrounds him once more petrifies, man who himself is but wind and grass in the stony abysses of the cities. A fly disappeared into the blue and it could have been an eagle, and I forgot the here and now as the vineyards of Italy extended all the way to the chestnut tree in the yard and the store of the blond wife of the innkeeper. But then I heard agitated voices from the kitchen, remembered why I had come, and went in to see what it was about.

The situation I found was rather strange. The little man, who had been sitting on the corner bench or had fled there, was being held just above his seat by Marius, who had taken hold of his jacket and was bouncing him up and down mercilessly, so that the toes of his feet hardly touched the floor. While not fighting back in earnest, he shouted, "Let me go! Let me go!" as Irmgard, perhaps somewhat frightened but with obvious satisfaction, stood next to the two and looked on. It was an odd scene, a featherweight bit of violence, a fluff of a drama, and I couldn't help laughing out loud. The little one, who had been the first to see me enter and laugh, also was overcome with merriment and began to smirk.

Marius dropped him abruptly. "Remember this for the next time." And without paying further attention to the midget or to me, he started to leave by the door through which I had entered.

"Listen to me, Marius," I called. "You could have broken his tailbone." The wretch was white as a sheet and could not catch his breath.

Oddly enough—but everything had become strange in this bizarre situation—it was Irmgard who replied. "Serves him right."

"Irmgard!" The commanding voice of Marius could be heard from outside, and Irmgard obediently followed his call.

I approached the little one. "So, how do you feel? . . . Take a deep breath." He now had the hiccups, which made him grin again, though his whole body was still shaking violently. I took the green-and-white earthenware jug which always stands here full of water, filled a glass, and made him drink.

He drank, thanked me, and seemed once more his jolly self.

"What have you been up to?"

"Oh," he said, "nothing really but a bit of courtesy . . . I paid some compliments." He extended a hand and rubbed his fingers together as if testing cloth, and I understood that the compliments had been of a tactile kind.

"And Marius didn't like that?"

He made a gesture as if I had asked him something so obvious as not to deserve an answer. So he was evidently well acquainted with the particular traits of Marius, and I asked, "I guess he's jealous?"

"Terribly," the midget replies, and comically throws out his puny chest. But somehow I feel that he is mainly intent on pulling my leg.

"So why then do you make him jealous?"

Under his breath he declares, "Passion."

"But it would seem to me that your esteemed tailbone is a rather high price for that."

"Another time I'll get it cheaper . . . It all comes out even."

"So you have a kind of running account with him."

"With him? No, I meant it generally . . ." He gets up, rubs his behind, and tries a few steps. "It's all right . . . after a time, one can stand a lot."

He must be about forty, quite ragged, not a real farm worker either, even though one finds such types at times in the stables and among machines. For an instant the idea got hold of me that Marius had only injected himself in this household to have his crony join him here and perpetrate some devious swindle. The much-wrinkled and multifaceted mouse face of the midget observed me with amused irony.

"You're a farm worker?"

"If need be . . . why not? I'm a jack-of-all-trades . . ."

"Well, yes, but it's hard work."

He straightens up, and with the pride of those whom nature has made too short, he makes me feel the huge muscles in his arms; all the more strange are the fine-boned hands at the end of these arms.

And that gives me an opening. "With muscles like these you let yourself be manhandled like that?"

"Ah," he says with a supercilious expression, "one must know when to defend oneself . . . With someone else it would have ended differently."

What was it that linked these two? There was the one with huge arms on a puny body and with delicate hands, a wide thin gap of a mouth under a pointed nose, a mouth with which he spoke and breathed. And there was the other one, he, too, a breathing human being, whom in comparison one could describe as well-proportioned and handsome—though why, in fact?—whose power was not in his arms but in his eyes, in his strangely rigid bird-like glance. What linked these two? What is it that joins people together? Why are they stuck with each other for good and bad and forevermore? Their paths through the landscape of this world can no longer be separated, for it is the landscape that follows them, no longer confined to the here and now but interweaving vineyard and glacier, and it is so powerful that it binds and directs the steps of the wanderers. And I said to myself, "It is in the glance."

"Yes," acknowledged the sly face from below me, as if he had guessed my thoughts, "yes, indeed."

For the man whom we meet does not come from this or that region, he doesn't come from a space that has width and depth and height, yea, not even animals originate in such space, but man comes from much farther away than he himself knows, and the glance that emerges from his body betrays its origin in that inconceivable infinity of space in which both body and space are constantly being reborn and in which being is joined to being, so that man never again can live without infinity and fancies himself a traitor to ineffable eternity, fancies himself as animal, grieving in its blindness, when he is called upon to abandon and turn his back on the wanderer who, with his glance, has granted him a shimmer of his own innermost being. And this probably is the answer to the question I had raised and which this incongruous vagrant had affirmed with such a resounding yes.

And because this is how it is and because any slipping away of infinity, once apprehended, will throw us into despair, a despair of which the most trifling and most clearly physical expression is jealousy, I pointed to the door behind which Marius and Irmgard had disappeared and asked, "And as for you, you're not jealous?"

"Jealous?" And once again he snickered his mousy laugh with the many wrinkles. "Jealous? . . . He's right, after all." And he once more rubbed his behind in his torn and much too wide, long knickerbockers.

"Well," I said, "although I don't understand this since I don't know your private arrangements with Marius regarding women, I guess that's probably true."

This at last brings out something deeper. "No, you won't understand that . . . To understand it you would have to be with him for a few years."

So I said quickly, "You've been wandering together . . ."

But now he doesn't reply. He takes the green-and-white jug and, to make things simple, drinks a great deal of water directly from its spout and then says, "Everything's all right," and sits down on the corner bench.

So—at least a few years.

I said, "Fine," and leave the kitchen. As I enter the small passageway I hear Marius holding forth. He speaks so clearly that I can hear every word without even eavesdropping, and now he says in conclusion, "This is so by rights, and for the sake of justice this is how it has to be."

It is no coincidence that he, too, speaks of rights. Irmgard had already said that it served the midget right, the midget had admitted that the other was in the right and had resigned himself in renunciation, for people always speak of rights and of being in the right when, drifting between trees and mountains and impelled hither and thither by infinity, they are driven to each other, driven apart and again driven elsewhere, oh, no other word can they find to express it, at least not a loftier and holier word, and every wrong that they inflict can only be done if they truly believe that in inflicting it they are in the right. Everywhere they sense justice at work, in all that happens and in all of nature, for the rightfulness is the consolation in the grief of leave-taking, because it is only in rightfulness, whether it be called law or given some other name, that the infinity beyond infinity wherefrom all of us derive can be apprehended, often apprehended only in distorted form and broken in its corporeal embodiment, often emptied of content so that it no longer appears animated by a higher principle, yet holy and eternal in the word and permeating the ineffable. And such a shimmer of the eternal trembled even in that rather odd system of rights between Marius and the little wretch.

But now the voice of Irmgard answered, "It is your justice and that is why I believe in it."

The voice rose upright and shapely, as shapely and upright as the whole girl. And that is precisely why I am outraged. There is no justice that belongs to Marius alone, and even if lovers deem each other as representing infinity, indeed, even if to each other they truly are infinite, there must be no words in the merciful gift of immediacy that is bestowed upon them, least of all words of right and justice, notwithstanding the fact that all true justice must mirror love. Only a fool or a charlatan reverses the relationship and supplants the immediacy with that which is derived. Did Marius seek to enthrall this strong, upright girl with such balderdash? Could she really fall for that? Had they kissed, I would have had no objection, for in my aged brain the image of a good-looking couple evokes grandfatherly fantasies of matchmaking, but Marius and his queer behavior made me see him as a kind of itinerant preacher of some abstinent cult with communistic colorings, and I was filled with deep suspicion of all such unctuous fussing in which the sly mouse in the kitchen perhaps would be assigned the second fiddle, so as to bring off some scoundrelly scam. I joined them outside.

The itinerant preacher stood there in his typically bold attitude, half turned toward her, and she, with a slight smile, had her eyes directed into the distance. Nothing remained of the pompous dialogue. But I was still enraged and said, "What is to be done with that man inside?"

Marius made a disparaging gesture, as much to show that this was none of my business as to underline the irrelevancy of the topic. "Ah, Wenzel . . ."

"Wenzel? Is that his name?"

"No, I called him that because he looks like a Wenzel, a wenching runt . . . and now it's his name."

Irmgard laughed.

Marius's jokes are not funny to me. He was a shapely, handsome man and yet much closer to the animal than many whose features are more bestial. But animals do not joke. Eagles have little sense of humor. At most, pigs and mice may have some sense of the comical.

"So it's Wenzel . . . and he's to stay here, too?"

They both ignored my question, as if I had spoken of things that had become totally insignificant. Finally Marius deigned to reply casually, "The farmer may be quite happy with him."

Without another word, Irmgard went into the house.

What was the order according to which the world was to be organized around here? Or was the anarchic about to overtake all order, the enticing lure that makes itself manifest when order is overcome by revulsion against itself? The voluptuousness of decay. Yet it seems unthinkable to me that a peasant such as Miland could be so nauseated by the time-honored order of his ancestors and forebears as to succumb to such temptation.

Marius struts back and forth in the yard. My presence seems to bother him, and this is probably why I ask, "And how are things going with the gold?"

He evades the question diplomatically. "The farmer doesn't favor it."

But because I want to arrive at some clarification for Peter's sake, I become blunt. "I understand that finding gold requires chasteness."

"Certainly," he politely acknowledges.

"But you also preach your morals to people who have no intention of ever looking for gold."

"Are you perhaps in favor of whoring, Doctor?" came the somewhat surprising reply.

All of a sudden I realize that, despite all his diplomatic skill, he doesn't mean this ironically, but in all seriousness, as deadly serious as anything said by a madman.

And he instructs me: "All diseases are the result of wantonness."

"Why, I thought it resulted only in children."

He throws a contemptuous glance in my direction and continues to strut back and forth. I wouldn't be surprised if the man had already been confined once. But be that as it may, he certainly was a borderline case.

As if he had guessed my thoughts, he stops in front of me. "You think I'm mad . . . But does your medical science know the origin of diseases?"

I could reply that, yes, in the case of infectious diseases one does know their origin. But since there is a question to any answer, I content myself with simply saying, "It would seem, Mr. Ratti, that you've had some personal experience with medical practice."

He smiles, stretches his arm toward me, and with fingers spread but without touching me passes his hand along my body. "Your trouble sits right there," he says, and points to my left shoulder.

That is true; I suffer from chronic rheumatism in my left shoulder and left upper arm, to which I pay little attention but which bothers me recurrently when the weather changes. It was, of course, possible that he got his knowledge from Miland, to whom, often enough, I had complained of my rheumatic pains, but it was also possible that he really had the gift of magnetic diagnosis. A dangerous gift in a madman. And so I say in some annoyance, "Do you know any other magnetic tricks?"

"Oh, so you take it simply for sleight of hand . . . ?"

"No, but it does not prove anything against medicine."

I was rather pleased when I heard the creaking of a carriage along Church Street and when a moment later the wagon turned into the yard. Wife and son sat on the box next to Miland, the maid was in the back with Cecily, and Andreas, who had gotten off earlier, closed the gate of the yard behind the wagon.

Marius helped with the unhitching of the horses. The way he lent a hand showed that he was familiar with animals and knew how to handle horses. He stroked their coats almost tenderly, and his touch was delicate in stripping their bellies and the inside of their thighs of the blowflies that clung there.

Meanwhile I had greeted the family. They weren't surprised to see me. The doctor himself is seen as something of a wanderer: he goes from house to house to visit a life here and there, this so evanescent life, sinking into earth molecule by molecule, and his task is to halt for a short while the decay which with one begins in the shoulder and with some other in the kidney or elsewhere, to halt it on the strength of the principles which he derives from infinity.

And in accordance with this function of mine I asked, "Everybody in good health, thank God?"

"Healthy, thank God," replied Miland, who had been silent up to then, pressing Cecily against him.

Thus we all stood for a while, all of us on our lower extremities, which, oddly bifurcated, protrude from our bodies, and I wondered whether wantonness was not in truth the cause of our decay, of our body's slow decomposition, whether it was not an expression of our revulsion against order, of the voluptuous pleasures we find in decay, and I waited for the happening that had not yet happened because Wenzel had not yet shown himself. In her quiet slyness, Cecily had attracted one of the young kittens and had grasped the animal, which had approached her with arched back and stiffly raised tail, in one surprisingly quick motion and now held it in her hands. The sun disappeared behind the Kuppron, the world was edged in red, and the sudden soft evening breeze brought the fragrance from the daffodil slopes down to the valley like an invisible herd of flowers.

Andreas had climbed to the barn loft and, from inside, pushed open the wide gray double doors to throw down the hay bales for the horses; the two long iron wing hooks clanked for a while before their dangling came to rest. And now Irmgard came out from the kitchen, but the guest was not to be seen as yet.

Then Irmgard turned and called, "Come out here for a moment."

The man called Wenzel appeared immediately and grinned, one cannot say in embarrassment, but nevertheless in some trepidation.

Marius joined him and said with great simplicity, "This is Wenzel and he seeks a place to work."

I looked on in some suspense. Miland's wife did not let on anything of what she may have been thinking. She examined the newly arrived man with a straightforward glance and no amenities could be expected from her, but she respected the form and would not anticipate the reaction of her husband. The latter took the hand of the obsequiously smiling rapscallion, who reciprocated with a highly unpeasant-like bow and scrape, and said to him, "We have enough help, but if you wish to look for some work elsewhere in the village, you're welcome to stay here meanwhile; it's all right with me."

"As the master may see fit," said Marius with his suspect pliancy.

The cat, which had sat quietly on Cecily's shoulder, suddenly jumped away, its tail gliding through the vainly grasping fingers of the girl.

And to my surprise, Miland's wife, in whom the Gisson character usually found its harshest incarnation, said to the midget, "Maybe my brother in the Upper Village has some use for you."

And that was all. What was strange was the general atmosphere of amiable pliability that seemed to have taken hold here and that could only have been generated by Marius. I remembered the old Miland who was still alive when I arrived in the village some fourteen years ago. Of his grandchildren he had known only Irmgard. But this has little to do with pliability. And yet it does: Miland's father had passed on the farm to the son only with great reluctance; he was full of distrust against him for fetching a wife from the Upper Village. Nevertheless, an amicable relationship developed in the last year before his death, not with the daughter-in-law but with his son, whom he may have suspected perhaps of suffering under the wife's harshness. In those days Miland frequently sat with his father in the garden, for though the old man's diminishing life also became ever smaller in space, it would not let go of the growing, burgeoning, and ripening soil with which it had been entwined. More than ever he sought to identify himself with the ground and the growth that had been the driving force of his life, even though it had now become confined to the enclosure of his garden. And that is where he had fallen asleep, back there in the garden, his hands in the low branches of a tree, and had passed away long before anyone noticed. When he was found and carried back to the house, he still grasped a young twig in his hands, and this we twisted around the crucifix which he held in his coffin.

Yes, this has nothing to do with Marius's pliability, it is another kind of compliance, but it is significant for my own relationship with Miland, and that is why I remembered these events as we stood there and everything around us grew ever more still and golden.

6 An hour's walk above the Upper Village, not far from the adit called the Pit of the Dwarfs, stands the old miners' chapel, a small Late Gothic structure which in the eighteenth century, as with so many other such buildings, had been plastered over, whitewashed, and adorned with the customary decorations of the period, but which now is slowly falling into ruin. There are two chipped stone steps, grass growing from their cracks, that lead up to the entrance door, which is always locked, to be opened only once a year to admit the priest for the saying of a mass, the so-called Blessing of the Stones, always celebrated on the first Thursday between the new moon and the summer solstice.

I go there at times and it is almost my favorite walk; I visit it again and again, driven by the strange and yet so human desire to commit to memory with special intensity and forever a place one likes, despite the better knowledge that this is a desire and a challenge exceeding the powers of the human mind, even the superhuman ones of those in love. Nor is it any different in this case. Much as I try on each visit to memorize in all their details the gray shingle roof of the chapel, the pines rising above, the two windows with their pointed arches and their delicate center columns, at the foot of which a thick layer of rubble has already accumulated, memory nevertheless fails me each time, for each time much comes to me as an unexpected surprise, such as the fragrance of the woods which hangs like a cool cloud around the decaying walls, the fissured rock faces above, which from here appear so close as to lead one to believe that one is standing at their very feet, though in reality they are still a goodly distance away, and last but certainly not least, I am always astounded anew by the view which opens from up here: the chapel lies at the topmost edge of a small stony mountain meadow, quite obviously an old clearing which once had been laid out for the Pit of the Dwarfs—through it the old miners' path zigzags steeply upward, and below, after a broad belt of bushes and shrubs overgrown with yard-high, sharp-leafed grass, there again are the pine woods, over the top of which one has a clear view of the entire expanse of the valley.

I have often sat here in the past and still like to sit on the chapel's steps, my hand resting on the head of my dog. And often this contemplation of the vesperal valley and of its trembling golden and shimmering smile is filled with a great wonderment at the constant transformation, as I realize that my glance does not rest whereon it is directed but rather watches my own self in astonishment, as I contemplate the steadings of this world: for the one who observes is not the one who sits here, not the aging man who once was a child and who has endured all these many years, climbing up from the mist-laden gorges of time, and neither is he the one in whom memory has accumulated layer upon layer, interspersed with trifling pieces of medical knowledge, indeed, he is not even the one who once slept in the breath of a woman and who, in a not too distant future, will stretch out in utter solitude, extinguished the never-resting memory, the memory still growing toward the sudden oblivion of time, no, none of these is the one who now looks down into the valley, no, I am none of these, I was never any of these, for I myself am nestled in an innermost and supremely safeguarded shell as in a diving bell, a bell lowered into my deepest depths, sunk so deeply into my own hereafter that this whole life's course, together with the end set at its culmination, is no real concern of mine, and if I don't begrudge my brother who dwells in me and who, in truth, is but a lodger of mine, either his pleasures or even his pains, if, like the simpleton content with merely watching and clapping his hands, I waste my time because I simply have none or because time no longer counts there where my last gaze shall rest, in that sphere—oh, where may it be?—in which blindness and knowledge have become so much one that another and more discerning vision would be required to once again separate these two, a separation from which surely blindness no longer would emerge as blindness, nor knowledge as knowledge, if thus my diving bell still floats in the darkness of my oceans and in the shadows of my unfathomable sunken landscapes, yet and despite all the darkness of my solitude, it grows lighter around me, and as I look out of such deep and almost final darkness, piercing with my glance through all the shells of my own self, as I sit here sealed up in my flesh and in my life, listening to the music of the light departing the mountain peaks, I, enraptured and looking outward from the inconceivable of my own being into the even less conceivable of ever more extending realms, seeing and yet seen by myself, I apprehend the interwoven texture of all knowledge, I apprehend the apprehension of myself being both mountain and hill, myself being both light and landscape, unreachable because it is my own self and yet forever striven for, goal which I shall reach in spite of everything when in the deepest depths of the oceans, of the mountains, and of the sunken islands, when on the golden bottom of darkest darkness the great oblivion will overtake me one day.

Thus do I often sit on the steps of the chapel, the mountain and the Pit of the Dwarfs at my back, grieving for the unreachable and yet enraptured at being allowed to perceive it. The dog, whose hairy head, soft and warm, perfectly fits my cupped hand, so that always I clasp it fondly time and again as if to encompass the infinity inherent therein, the dog whom we envy because he is exempt from the cursed blessing of discernment and because to him his greedily eating and so frequently pissing existence seems one with his powers of seeing, bound up in a single happy state of being, a being of which one may assume that in all its aspects it constitutes the dog Trapp, yet not truly happy, or only very rarely, even when he rolls in the snow or spurts madly across the fields, for unswervingly and wherever he is, he searches for himself, searching for that shimmer of infinity in his own head that man has awakened in the animal, seeking that infinity of which only the grief but not the ecstasy has become his share. But in this grief, of which we, I and Trapp, jointly share a part, we look into each other's eyes, lovingly and searchingly, into the loving remoteness of our infinity from which both our glances derive and which we share in our mutuality, we look at each other until finally I turn his muzzle away, telling him that it is not proper for a well-behaved dog to stink from the mouth. But he can't help it. His teeth are already going bad.

Often as I come up here and much as I like this place, by no means do I participate every year in the Blessing of the Stones. Not only because it has become—like many such invocations of nature—a rather paltry celebration but also because a poor church-goer such as I has no business bothering with such incidental religious functions. This year, too—when it fell in Whitsuntide—my participation came to pass only by the purest of coincidences. I had come to the Upper Village on my morning rounds, had found the houses decorated with leafy twigs and the street covered with grass, and so, after having concluded my work, including a visit to Sack's wife, instead of going home I went to the Mountain Manse, where a simple open-air altar had been erected in the street—a wooden scaffolding covered with red cloth edged in gold and the whole topped by a picture of the Virgin surrounded by foliage. The participants in the procession were already waiting there, the village girls in their Sunday best, who act as the bridesmaids of the Mountain Bride, the spectators, even some from the Lower Village, and, of course, all the children of the village, for it is here that the parish priest was expected. Nor had the Mountain Bride arrived as yet. I greeted some of those waiting and was about to enter at Mother Gisson's to pay her a casual visit, when she emerged in her beautiful silk Sunday costume, followed by the Mountain Bride, who, to my surprise, was none other than Irmgard. Yes, it was Irmgard, the bridal crown in her hair, carrying a floral spray and all decked out to beat the band.

"Ah!" breathed the crowd, as was her due, and "Ah! Look at Irmgard!" shouted the children, who relished all that pomp. The sky was covered but bright, it didn't rain, nor was there any threat of rain, for the wind flowed from the north, soft and in broad cool waves, filling the skies and the valley. And in that opalescent light which flowed so uniformly and in identically smooth invisible waves throughout all of space, Irmgard appeared even more resplendent than if the sun had burned down with a more ostentatious glitter.

"What a surprise, Mother Gisson," I said after having duly admired Irmgard myself.

Now the mother of the Bride, Miland's wife, also came out of the house and joined us. I had already noticed Cecily among the children. The Bride's mother was in her everyday clothes and she looked neither at us nor at her daughter but into the milky sky and into the wind which so tenderly had brought the light and left it here while continuing on its own way.

"Yes," was all she said when I greeted her, "today it's Irmgard's turn to be the Mountain Bride."

"I, too, was once the Bride," Mother Gisson said, "but that's so long ago it's hardly true anymore."

And that made me understand that Irmgard was still considered a Gisson and that she owed her exalted position on this day to this inherited quality, a position otherwise never bestowed on a "Lower One"; for there had been a time, it is said, when the Lower Villagers were not admitted even as spectators. Obviously, many of them had been lured up here today because a "Lower One" was for once acting the role of the Mountain Bride.

The Miland woman, who may have been thinking of the time when she herself had stood here in full fig before she had become a "Lower One," said, "She's come home."

"That may well be," assented the grandmother.

I asked, "Is Irmgard to stay up here for good?"

"Yes," said the Miland woman.

Mother Gisson explained. "Yes, after the harvest, I'll take her in."

"I'll pay for her board," said her daughter.

"If you wish," said the grandmother, "but Irmgard will earn her own keep."

At that moment the carriage with the priest turned into the village street below us. The farmer's horse trotted with heavy tread, constantly reverting to a stumbling walk, prodded on by Sack with many clicks of the tongue, "tsk, tsk," "hees," and slight strokes of the whip. On the box with him sat the ministrant with the large black wooden cross used in deathbed visits and processions; and behind them sat the priest in full robes on one of the small benches, while on the other sat the sacristan in red vestments and the prayer leader Gronne, who lives in the Mountain Manse and who, as custom dictates, always went with Sack to fetch the priest. And that's how they had brought him up here also today. I looked at my watch: half past seven.

They climbed down from the carriage, taking with them all the utensils required in the Blessing of the Stones, among them the still-rolled-up red damask church banner, whereupon Irmgard, in the midst of her companions, approached the priest and recited the verses with which the Mountain Bride is to greet the man of God:

> Blessed be Jesus our Lord
> Whatever's in the mountain hoard
> Will be set free by His grace
> Satan and monsters He will chase
> All evil return from whence it came
> In Jesus' and in Mary's name.

And while she recited this in the tone of a village schoolgirl, she proffered the bouquet of flowers to the priest for his blessing. The shy little divine hesitated for a moment since, as the friend of flowers that he was, he felt in duty bound first to appraise the offering, but then with a weak, friendly, and so to say expert smile gliding over his one-sided face and with a light nod of approval, he made the sign of the cross over the bunch of flowers.

Trapp, who has no manners and merely saw that some of my close acquaintances were all assembled here, approached the ceremony, so as to have a clearer view of what was going on, and I called him back, not wishing him to interfere with ritual proceedings. He obeyed, patently disgusted with the incomprehensible stupidity of man. But meanwhile the sacristan had swung the censer and the priest had planted himself before the open-air altar to intone the first prayer, in which, however, the congregation did not attend him as yet in full devotion since they had already been standing here for quite a while, nothing really had changed in their eyes, and their attention was still mainly centered on the altar, which impressed them as mighty pretty as it stood there, a patch of scarlet amidst the green foliage. This has nothing to do with piety or worship but merely with the human desire that the world should be somewhat pleasant to look at before anything momentous is to happen and as one is sailing along on it, either with or against the wind, which, in any case, is hard to differentiate, for the wind of this world is but a small and diluted echo of the larger breathing impelled by that sweet power of which only the sea is able to speak when it deems itself unobserved and holds its ceaseless dialogue with the moon through the gentle and yet mighty swaying of its tides. The trembling of the leaf, quivering still after the wind has died down, when all is stilled and only the heart beats, is it not like an echo of an echo? Like a last mirroring of the sea on the heights of mountains? The foliage of the branches adorning the altar rustled softly and almost cozily, as its leaves had already begun to stiffen and to roll up their edges. Again the sacristan swung the censer, slowly it swayed to and fro as the line of procession began to form and to move, led by the ministrant with the towering cross, on which the silver-glittering Saviour bowed and swayed, sur-rounded by all the children, followed by the priest and the sacristan, then by the Mountain Bride with all her bridesmaids, and finally the prayer leader Gronne and all the lay participants, the few men that took part followed by the fairly large crowd of womenfolk. Thus it is prescribed by the traditional ritual of processions and funerals, an age-old ritual of mankind, as anyone observing it can readily believe.

And now the prayer leader started the litany for the procession:

> The Lord's voice on the mountain shone
> Stars and moon all have flown
> His great mercy He has shown
> Early before dew and dawn
> Risen on the world's tower
> On the mountain of His power
> Praised be Mary on the Mount.

And this he continued monotonously, though somewhat out of breath, since the way led upward. I kept behind the men, so as to be able to converse with Mother Gisson, who was at the head of the women. I had sent the dog home. For a long time he looked after us before finally turning back, but even then he stopped several times as if he couldn't quite believe in his dismissal.

"Wouldn't have mattered if he had been running after us," said Mother Gisson.

"Well, better that way for the sake of sanctity."

Not only Trapp disappears down the road, but also the Miland woman, who, with Cecily holding her hand, hurries with long steps back down into the valley.

> . . . On the mountain of His power
> Praised be St. Peter on the Mount.

Obediently Mother Gisson joined in the "Praised be," so obediently, in fact, that one could suspect that she was making a bit of fun of it and was only striving so valiantly in order to set a good example.

But much of the doings of man are both serious and in fun, infinite and finite at the same time, particularly when his knowledge has already outstripped the first level of reality and when he has been blessed with the gift of humor. Sack, too, son of a horse soldier, lowered and yet risen to the rank of coachman, allowed to drive the frail priest, the lover of flowers, Sack, a few steps in front of me, obediently joined in the singing.

"Fifty years ago things were different," said Mother Gisson in the manner of old people who see only the difference, although they know well enough that even fifty and a hundred years ago the woods stood as they stand today, the grass grew, smoke rose from the chimneys, and the path snaked upward, sometimes in easy serpentines and sometimes steeply.

But the little priest was a poor climber and we advanced very slowly. It was hazy in the woods, the wind ran over the tops of the trees but did not penetrate to our level, the air was still, impregnated by the forest, by the fragrances of wood, both living and felled, impregnated by the smell of the grass and of the sweetish rotting of humus. To the left and the right of the path everything was covered by huckleberry bushes, a hard green carpet.

> . . . His great mercy He has shown
> Early before dew and dawn . . .

And one could hear the call of the yellowhammer.

"In those days we had a priest who knew his business," Mother Gisson continued her reminiscences. "We got up there in a bare half hour."

"Now, Mother, isn't that laying it on a little thick?"

But she still has the long sweeping step of the mountaineer and, in reply, permits herself a small superior smile. "Why, that's no great feat, in a half hour. I could do that even today . . . and the Arlett priest, he knew how, he also understood the Blessing."

"And what's there so special to understand?"

Mother Gisson laughed. "Praised be St. Michael on the Mount."

I thought I knew what she meant: she had a strong aversion to the puny and shadowy kind of men to which our flower-cultivating cleric belonged.

After a while she said, "For a Blessing of the Stones to be worth anything it needs the night."

"But marriage is celebrated during the day, Mother Gisson, not during the night."

"But the blessing comes at night."

> . . . Stars and moon all have flown
> His great mercy He has shown . . .

"Of course, Mother Gisson, but there's no wedding night without a bridegroom."

"To be sure, the one up there in front is no bridegroom."

"And the Arlett priest, he was a bridegroom?"

"My, yes, that he was . . . He was a terrible man, one could not send a girl to confession to him . . ."

"Wild stories, Mother Gisson . . . And that's when you were the Mountain Bride?"

She made a sly and almost regretful face. "At that time, the mountain had already been dead and sealed up for some time . . . but when it still stood open, wide open, if you know what I mean . . ."

I understood: "The mountain labored . . ."

"Yes, if you wish . . . When it was still open, then there was a night blessing on the wedding night, with dancing and all that belongs to a wedding night, and worse . . ."

"At the pub?"

"No, up there, of course."

"Is this what is said?"

"Yes, that's how it's told."

I recalled that a harmless folksy celebration with a bit of masquerading and hopping around is still held each fall near the Cold Stone at the time of the shooting stars. There's no denying that the garland of festivals and invocations which the people have wound around the mountain has by now become quite faded and shabby, badly disheveled in the storms of the centuries.

". . . His great mercy He has shown," and as if it belonged still to the text, or rather to a truer one, Mother Gisson continued: "Miner in the mount, child in the womb, safe and born . . . Praised be St. Pancras on the Mount."

"What was that you were just singing?"

She laughed a bit and then she said seriously, "When the time is right, the Blessing works with both the Bride and the mountain . . . that's one and the same."

I was suspicious and merely said, "Oh." What I really wanted to ask her was whether she had thought of herself as the bridal womb of the Kuppron when she herself had been the Mountain Bride these many years ago, or whether Irmgard, walking ahead of us with her bridal crown, had such feelings and was ready to receive the fecund blessing, ready to be delivered by the holy knight. Once upon a time, when language was born, perhaps even before the earth rose and folded itself into mountain ranges, there indeed may have been something like a womb of mountains, but today this is but an empty term that has strayed into the vocabulary of geology. But Mother Gisson is not receptive to such notions.

"The Lord's voice on the mountain shone . . ."

But then I said nevertheless, "Mother Gisson, in all seriousness, there are any number of living mountains which are being subdued by digging machines and cableways . . . even without any priests or mountain brides . . ."

"Why not," she said, indifferent.

"Quite apart from the fact that a priest like this Arlett who knows, as you say, how to handle all that would be not so easy to find . . . that's pretty strenuous business . . ."

And that made her laugh again. "If it's the will of the mountain, the priest has to perform."

"Yes, but it would seem that the mountains can do without."

"Not all mountains are the same . . . risen on the world's tower, on the mountain of His power"—she interrupted her singing once more—"what's more, they're patient and some of them will stand for a lot."

"God in heaven, Mother Gisson, if only I knew whether you really believe in all of that."

She looked at me pityingly. "Just wait . . . wait and see for yourself when they lose their patience and take their revenge . . . Then you'll know."

"No," I said. "I won't see anything at all, for the evil in this world is not revenge and punishment, but, a senseless, idiotic game . . . Poor Sack would be punished for nought and nothing if his wife, God forbid, were to die and leave him alone with the children."

Sack, who may have heard his name spoken, turned around.

"Life does not punish," she said simply. "It is everywhere, also in evil."

"Agreed, Mother, and there is no objection to that . . . but what life is there in the evil of the mountain and its alleged revenge? Perhaps the lindworm?"

She did not answer. Such remarks make her cross. Whether she believed in giants and dragons could not be fathomed and was not to be queried. She was full of tales of these beings and of their doings and workings in herbs and rocks, she was in constant fruitful consort with them when she looked for plants and in her unremitting listening and hearkening, the fabulous constantly reaches her from a past which lies beyond remembrance and which to her is almost as valid as the present, despite her standing firmly with both feet in everyday reality. No doubt, this is how things are: who truly loves is never bereft of the loved one, not even in death, the one who loved truly knows of the deceased with absolute clarity, he knows of his constant return which has become his enrichment, and although he cannot say in what form this occurs, even though he shrinks from saying "It is a ghost" or "It was a spook," he nevertheless is filled with a great certainty but refrains from putting it into so many words and is vexed when questioned about such matters. This is also how things stand with Mother Gisson, whose love reaches back deep into time and who is capable of calling back a great many things from that nameless beyond, and it is only natural that she gets cross when one asks her about it because she cannot say "It was a fabled creature," "It was a fairy," or "It was a dragon," for she simply knows that all of this is alive in and around her. No, one must not ask her and it had been wrong of me to do so.

The path was getting steep. Interrupted by many gullies, the wheel tracks cut deeply into the rock, traveled by foot and wagon for thousands of years, ground down by primitive sleighs even before the wheel had been invented, path of miners, path of giants, path of dwarfs. The fields of huckleberry bushes became thinner and now we had to stop often because our little cleric could not go on. I would have liked to help him, but I had neither caffeine nor any other suitable medication with me in my satchel, and, in any case, he would have refused to take anything before saying mass. It was outright idiocy to exact such a climb from someone with a patently weak heart, particularly on an empty stomach. And so I called to him against all custom, "Sit down for a while, Father!"

He turned around stiffly in his cumbersome vestments and gave me a grateful irresolute smile.

"But of course, Father, a bit of rest will do us all some good and our dear Lord won't object."

He gave it some more thought and then, with the gesture of peasant women who wish to spare their skirts, he lifted his robes up behind him and sat down on the rocky edge of the path, revealing a pair of masculine striped and patched trousers. The others copied his example. The ministrant leaned the Christ against a fork in a tree and disappeared with the children in the bushes, his white surplice shining out from between the tree trunks. The prayer leader Gronne got rid of the damask church banner and took out a bottle—which explained the strange bulge at the back of his coat—holding it somewhat undecidedly in his hands while he settled down among the womenfolk, who, gabbing among themselves, now lined the entire slope side of the path. "It's only coffee," he said apologetically, "for the moistening of the throat," but although all of them longed for such moisture after all the singing and even though they looked quite covetously at the bottle, none dared to take a sip before mass and neither could I bring myself to ask Gronne to offer some of his balm to the priest, even though the sacral had now dissolved more or less into the secular and, one might even be tempted to say, the touristic.

"Well, Mother Gisson," I said, "don't you wish to rest a bit, too?"

She had already forgotten her earlier vexation and looked at me and all the others with the tolerant indignation of a master of ceremonies. "Not before the Blessing," she said, and then she called to Irmgard, probably so as to enjoin at least on the Mountain Bride the confines of dignity.

But Irmgard, in spite of the pearls of sweat showing on her brow and even under her bridal crown, presented a solemn face.

Sack joined us. Now that the singing had stopped, the air was full of the buzzing of insects. An army of ants crossed the path, a busily teeming mass. Sack's usually so merry face was worried. "Did you visit her today, Doctor?" "Yes, Sack, and it's not too bad." But as I say this, I look at Mother Gisson, who knows better, probably because I don't want to look into Sack's eyes and perhaps also in the hope that she may now rescind the verdict she had pronounced on the sick woman. Nothing like that happened, even though she must have heard Sack's anxious question and could have felt my own concern; unperturbed, she rearranged the ribbons that hung from Irmgard's bridal crown and had become disarrayed.

Sack asked once more, "Will she get well?"

"Yes," I said in a kind of bitter rebellion.

"Your boys are getting big and handsome, Sack," said Mother Gisson, pointing to one of them who was running around nearby.

Sack smiled into his round seaman's beard. The boys look like him as much as he himself still resembles his father, sturdy and stocky little fellows and cheerful like all the Sacks. They had been given to him in the fitting dictate of life that compels men to seek women, and their sight evokes all the astonishment one feels at the fact that a woman had said yes to such a lad with a seaman's beard and had grown to love him, she, too, subjected to the same fitting dictate of life. I don't know whether Sack had these thoughts, but were I in his place and had I children, this is how I would feel.

And then the boy had approached us, had admired the bride and wanted to have her floral spray.

"No," said Mother Gisson, "that's not for you; it already belongs to the Almighty, but you may look at it."

I, too, examined the bouquet in Irmgard's arms. It consisted in the main of mountain pinks, mixed with delicate aspen grass, but there were also a lot of other plants, many of which were quite unknown to me and presumably came from Mother Gisson's mysterious collecting trips. But I did recognize the lanceolate leaves of the snakeweed, so called in these parts because its extract is supposed to be an antidote against viper bites.

"Yes, the flowers belong to the Almighty," Mother Gisson repeated in a louder voice, for the first time addressing the priest. "Isn't that so, Father?"

"Yes," he replied softly, in his exhausted voice, "they do." And he dried his pale face with a discolored kerchief.

I joined him and asked him to let me feel his pulse. Oh, he protested, everything was all right and he only had been climbing a little too fast. And it was only because he wasn't really accustomed to climbing.

"Well, Father, I'm not exactly in favor of your training to become a mountaineer but some short little walks would do you a heap of good."

The dalmatic hung between his spread legs. I would have liked to suggest that he divest himself of all these appurtenances and negotiate the last part of the way in shirt sleeves. The Arlett priest certainly would have had no qualms about doing so.

"And next year, I won't let you climb up here. You may count on my medical veto."

"Next year," and he smiled again his weak, one-sided smile, "that's a long time off and I don't count in such extended periods . . . As it may please our Lord."

And with that he rose, smoothed his cassock and vestments, and readied himself to continue the climb. But once a work is interrupted, its resumption is always in doubt, and rests at the wrong time are not propitious when climbing mountains. The women, once they got their tongues wagging, enjoyed sitting in the shade, no one was particularly eager for the mountain blessing which now seemed like nothing so much as an uncomfortable duty saddled on them by their forebears and preserved by their own inadvertence. Nevertheless, Gronne, the prayer leader, conscious of his duty, pulled himself together, and when he once more intoned whiningly, "The Lord's voice on the mountain shone," a semblance of order was restored to the procession with the help of the sacristan.

Nor was the climb as difficult as before. After a while, light shone through the tree trunks, and when our litany had reached St. Genevieve on the Mount, we emerged into the clearing. The sweating human mass was buzzed by swarms of blowflies and gnats, ahead of us stood the chapel, to be reached after one more loop in the path, and the rock face rose up huge behind the last wooded strip, gray and divided by rust-brown stripes. The sky was still coated in light-grayish white but where the sun stood it had become of blinding opalescence. It smelled of grass, of low bushes and live copsewood. One of the black lizards common in this region sat on a tree stump and observed us with its snake head raised and its tail looped in an S.

Our advance had now become dead slow. I had given my stick to the priest, but because he nevertheless slid and faltered time and again, Sack had taken his hand to pull him along. And as we crawled upward, following the swaying cross which the ministrant now held at a sharp slant because of the steepness of the path, and as I, as is my wont, examined the cliff wall in front of me, I discovered to my astonishment—because this had never struck me before—that a horizontal bulge of perhaps some six to nine feet in thickness extended about midway in height along the entire wall, resembling nothing so much as the relief of a gigantic snake. With the slight annoyance that I always feel when I realize my incapacity to fully grasp and recall even those features in nature for which I care the most, I persisted in my scrutiny and found that this bulge turned downward in one place and ended in a triangular formation, weirdly like the head of a snake and pointing directly at the sealed entrance of the Pit of the Dwarfs. So what, I told myself, but I was brought up short the next instant and again became uncertain. I had already heard too much today about dragons and lindworms from whose claws the Mountain Bride Irmgard was to be delivered, and so I wondered: Was what I saw in fact as I saw it? Had I—or one of the observing parts of that I—become so captivated by a ceremony in which I thought I had not really been involved that I saw things that were not there? It is possible, after all, to fantasize all kinds of things into rock formations, they lend themselves to this kind of imaginative interpretation as readily as stalactites, so why not a snake encircling the mountain? There stood the rock wall, itself milky gray under the milky white light of the skies, it stood there like eternally congealed light, an age-old smiling of the earth, nay, rather her laughter as she opened herself to light for the first time, and we approached it with our invocations, these, too, age-old themselves but worn threadbare by time. Why, then, should the rock not have its fun with us by girding itself with a snake? The litany could no longer be managed; Gronne had lost his voice, and Sack could be heard shouting in the lead, "Hup, hup, Father, we're almost there, only a few steps to go." And then the children had arrived, and the ministrant, who had climbed the last stretch on all fours, triumphantly planted his cross in the ground. "Hup, hup," Sack shouted, and dragged the priest to the small flat piece of ground in front of the chapel.

So there we were. And most were of the opinion that today the walk had been especially steep. Smiling and fighting for breath, the little priest leaned on the open chapel door, which had been garlanded with brushwood, and he was mighty proud of his athletic achievement. He still held my stick.

"Who walks slow tires fast," Mother Gisson said, and smoothed her skirts. "This is going to be a tired Blessing."

"Certainly," I replied, turning halfway to the priest, "and that's why our Reverend Father shall have a breather first."

But the priest smiled and shook his head before disappearing into the chapel, followed by the sacristan, so that the congregation also had to enter. There developed a slight bottleneck.

We were here at the center of the bright luminous mist that had filled this morning, so utterly did it permeate the whole of the valley and the rock and the sky. And one could imagine that all of us were standing on the shore of the very morning itself, the shore of a sea which in its matutinal stillness extended beyond the farthest infinities. Sack, next to me, said, "The rock is mild today."

"Yes," I said, and we both looked up at the Kuppron.

"Tell me, Sack," I said. "That thing up there looks like a snake to me."

"Yes," he confirmed, "that's the Snake 'round the Mount . . . and, indeed, it goes all the way around."

"Strange," I said.

"Why? Maybe it became petrified . . . That happened, after all."

"Come on, man," I said. "A snake around a whole mountain? What nonsense."

"Prehistoric," he replied. "There were strange things going on then."

Meanwhile quiet had been restored, and I had to push my way into the chapel since I wanted to see Irmgard in her role as Mountain Bride and, besides, Mother Gisson would never have forgiven me if I had not attended.

The small whitewashed space was bright in the flowing morning light that entered through the door and through the two windows with their pointed arches, and the light of the candles duly burning on the altar table was paled by all that brightness. But what strange kind of divine worship was being performed here! The candles seemed like waning stars at dawn, and below them, sweetly and kitschily smiled upon by a cheap plaster-cast Madonna, an artifact undoubtedly installed on the orders of the Arlett priest, there lay the stones, those stones responsible for the whole ceremony being called the Blessing of the Stones, and these in reality were rather pieces of ore which probably had served in cultic rites long before the chapel had been built and before they had been consigned to storage in this Christian chamber, for the surface of these mineral lumps, the size of an infant's head and streaked with metallic veins, was ground down and rubbed smooth as if they had rolled for thousands of years in the stream of human contact. An old miner's pick hung under the cross on the wall behind the altar. The priest celebrated the mass in front of these objects, and what he did must have seemed to him, the servant of the church, as bordering on the very edge of blasphemous superstition. What then were the feelings of his congregation? Here, in the first of the few rows of prayer stools, knelt Mother Gisson, and, by virtue of a knowledge derived from other sources, she was at best a smiling though respectful guest at this ecclesiastical ritual and, besides, she was thinking of the Arlett priest; there knelt Irmgard, the Mountain Bride, in the solemn piety and dignity of a prettily decked-out peasant girl, and it was hard to say whether her piety had to do with Marius's justice, in which she believed, or with the joy she felt at being able to show herself to him in all her beauty and finery; and there were all the children, rejoicing in having entered the customarily locked chapel; and then there were the women, each of whom had the day's victuals in a knotted scarf in front of her on the floor. And yet this rather paltry ceremony was invested with the quiet dignity of the summer morning in which it was performed. Being there that morning was like gazing out over the twilit sea, and the gestures of the priest and the faces of the crowd seemed like flitting mists or like nebulous sails drifting over a shadowy infinity, for, however earthbound the gesture of prayer may be, what matters most is the ability to perform it, this simple capability of man which, even though it may be disparaged as theatrical, nevertheless is, as it were, man's guaranty—no, not as it were, it is man's actual guaranty that his roots are in infinity, that he cannot live without it, and that he has been granted the power to turn back toward it. It is his guaranty of the infinite. Though the little priest may be greatly exhausted, though his vestments may be covered with dust and his feet burning painfully in his coarse country boots, and though Irmgard may parade her bridal finery accompanied by all kinds of worldly thoughts, Mother Gisson may already be at home in a remoteness whose simplicity no longer requires any ritual effort, nevertheless the dedication to this otherworldliness and to the incomprehensible found expression in the priest's performance and the gesture of the prayers, for man who folds his hands in prayer is uplifted so irrevocably by the humbleness of his inward-directed glance that the white sails of his devout attitude carry him through many layers of his being, many and manifold layers, and all the way to the barely apprehended shores of infinity, to the shores of an invisible heaven, yet apprehended by the blind glance of the worshipper. Beyond the chapel door the crickets chirped their white song.

But the Blessing of the Stones itself does not take place in the chapel. During the three Our Fathers recited at the end of the mass, the sacristan and Gronne had cleared the altar of the ore stones and had placed them in a stretcher carrier, an implement widely used in the mining methods of yore, when there were neither tubs nor rails. Two young lads took hold of the carrier, and before the rest of us could reestablish some order in our procession, the Mountain Bride and her bridesmaids together with the children and all the youths had crowded around them and the whole group with their burden had vanished into the woods behind the chapel. There they were to wait for us at the entrance of the old adit of the Pit of the Dwarfs.

The sacristan had taken the miner's pick from the wall of the chapel and carried it together with his censer, the ministrant was in charge of the cross, while Gronne had taken the church banner, which had been set up next to the altar, and had inserted it once more in his belt, intoning again his litany, though this time without invoking all the saints of the liturgy but ending each verse with "Praised be St. George on the Mount." Thus we marched into the woods, and at our slow speed it took us well over twenty minutes to reach our vanguard at the Pit of the Dwarfs. The Mountain Bride stood there, her back to the sealed-up adit, at her feet lay the carrier with the minerals, and her bridesmaids, holding hands, had formed a semicircle around her, as if they were to protect both bride and mineral stones. As soon as they caught sight of us singing, they started to sing antiphonally, a bit childishly and comically, for they bawled out the militant verses as if in school:

> Not a soul shall ever dare
> Enter the giant's dreaded lair
> Unless he's offered a maiden fair
> Then all good men he shall spare.

In spite of this warning we advanced valiantly. In days gone by, this singing must have come out of the tunnel and probably sounded quite gruesome, particularly in medieval times, when all this occurred in the darkness of a new moon night. I looked up at the rock wall; the great snake relief could not be made out from here, but from the overhanging rock that I had identified as the head of the snake two rust-brown runnels darted downward like a forked tongue.

We steadfastly persevered in our litany:

> The Lord's voice on the mountain shone
> Stars and moon all have flown
> His great mercy He has shown
> Early before dew and dawn
> Risen on the world's tower
> On the mountain of His power
> Praised be St. George on the Mount.

And finally it led us to victory. For when we arrived in front of the chain of girls, they had already swallowed their pride and merely sang:

> When Christ comes the world to free
> From the devil's gaping snout
> All that's evil has to flee
> Dragons, monsters hereabout.

At these words the sacristan touched the interlocked hands of two girls with the miner's pick, the chain opened, and the priest was thus able to enter the semicircle. The Mountain Bride sank to her knees with graceful decorum, though not before having spread her kerchief on the bare earth, and the priest made the sign of the cross over her head, as well as over the sealed-up entrance to the tunnel, and blessed her virginal body and the mountain with the aspergillum, while the congregation recited the Lord's Prayer and the Ave Maria. After this was done, the Mountain Bride, from her kneeling position, raised her hands with the flower spray toward the priest and declaimed: "Thou hast delivered me, now take my flowers." The priest then had to answer: "I take thy flowers, now receive this blessed one"—pointing to the minerals in the carrier— "carry him and thou shalt be delivered." At these words we could no longer restrain ourselves and, our throats rested, we began once more for the last time:

> The Lord's voice on the mountain shone
> Stars and moon all have flown
> His great mercy He has shown
> Early before dew and dawn
> Risen on the world's tower
> On the mountain of His power
> Praised be St. George on the Mount.

Meanwhile Irmgard had risen, she had taken up the gold-veined piece of ore designated by the priest and had swaddled it in a strip of linen that had been given her to cradle it in her arms. Thus she mingled with us, and the women touched her and the ribbons floating from her bridal crown with loving hands, touched also the stone in its linen covering, saying over and over again with feeling, "Yes, Irmgard, yes." But Gronne would not allow such emotional tomfoolery to go on for long, he set his parade in order and rushed us on, for everybody was eager to have a bite to eat. And since this was a most convincing argument for all, we soon were on our way back, in front the ministrant and the children, then the girls with the Mountain Bride, who was followed by the stone carriers, the priest with the sacristan, the prayer leader and the congregation. Gronne was now silent and only the girls and the children sang:

> When Christ comes the world to free
> From the devil's gaping snout
> All that's evil has to flee
> Dragons, monsters hereabout
> Blessed St. George, blessed St. George

> On the mountain our prize
> From the mighty dragon's blood
> Fairest maiden shall arise.

"So there . . ." said Mother Gisson, and this didn't sound very solemn. A lot had happened, after all, the mountain or at least her own granddaughter had been delivered from the clutches of the dragon, Irmgard carried a piece of ore, we had done our part and were tired, and to dismiss all this with a "So there" seemed to me a bit shabby.

> Victory bestowed your lance
> All the pagans on the ground
> With her child the maid will prance
> Reigns the Christ the world around
> Blessed St. George, blessed St. George
> On the mountain shall arise
> Hosts of angels for the dance
> Surrounding Christ in paradise.

Yes, and nevertheless Mother Gisson had been right with her "So there." The ceremony had been celebrated, the mountain had been exorcised, the shrine had been opened. Once a year. Once a year and every year, throughout the stream of millennia. And yet it seemed that precisely the infinite which had stood at its beginning and which was to be called forth each time, somehow had been diminished, almost as if the part that man had once been able to raise by his invocation had fallen back into its original and inaccessible condition, leaving only a petrified shimmer of itself, a piece of gold ore, an earthly shimmer, and maybe not even that. It had become a harmless and prettified infinity, all too easily was the dragon vanquished, its many heads had become a chain of girls' heads, the champion of the faith that the church had delegated was our little gardener-priest, who all too clearly betrayed how glad he was to be rid of this chore, and even the paean on the suppression of pagan forces had become a childish singsong. It was as if the infinite had lost the connection with itself, as if the soul were suspended between the times, condemned to let that which had been raised degenerate time and again into the playfully infantile;

it was as if there were, between the living infinite of yore and the infinite that is to come, both apprehended, both known when man closes his eyes in devotion, a dead interval that stretches before him when he reopens his eyes, so that he, in his knowingness, is no longer capable of grasping the chthonian forces which once he was empowered to invoke. Mother Gisson was right to have concluded, "So there."

I said, "One should at least reopen the tunnel for the ceremony."

"And what good would that do?"

I had to reflect for a moment. "It might give us the shivers . . . we might then become more conscious of the subterranean powers."

> . . . Blessed St. George, blessed St. George
> On the mountain shall arise . . .

"That's what the Arlett priest wanted to do . . . and he went in, in fact . . . In those days the entrance was not yet sealed but only barred by a few boards . . ."

"And?"

"He thought of trying it by sheer force . . . everything he did, he did by force . . . in the pulpit and in bed . . . but here it was of no avail, the underground powers cannot be forced . . ."

"No," I said.

"The girl got with child, all right, but the mountain remained mute . . . so then we sealed all of it up."

"What, including the priest?"

She laughed. "No, he lived to a ripe old age and we all cried when he died."

"But, Mother Gisson, he was a fiend, after all."

"No, that he wasn't . . . he was violent and confused but he was a good man and great, also, in his faith, and he had the Word . . ."

"You call that the Word?"

"Yes, he had the Word as only a few have, and faced by him, men were like women . . . and that's why he also wanted to force the underground woman into his power, for the sake of his faith . . ."

> Victory bestowed your lance
> All the pagans on the ground . . .

sang the children.

"And what if the mountain were not a female, Mother Gisson?" I had wanted to say that for a long time. "It might just as well be the dragon instead of the bride."

"Ah-hm."

I looked at her questioningly.

At that instant the sun tore the bright veil that had covered the world. The white-haired trunks of the pines turned brown-golden, golden-black was the needle-strewn earth and dappled with shadows and patches of sun that reached up into the foliage.

But I insisted, "Rather than the mountain, it is the valley who is a woman . . . or the sea . . ."

"The sea"—she said it devoutly, like someone who has longed for the sea all his life, although she surely had never felt such longing—"the sea . . . the snake encircles the sea and yet it rests at its bottom."

For a moment I felt a weird silly shiver in the region of my belly as if the stone snake of the Kuppron had wound itself around me.

"Have you any idea where man and woman truly are located? Whether the mountain sinks into the sea or whether the sea pours into the mountain?"

I dared not raise any further objections.

She continued: "The one who is strong impregnates and is being impregnated, in everything and by everything . . . and all we can do is listen and hearken when the time is ripe for the one and when it is ripe for the other, for both these times are and live in every single thing. And you should know that, Doctor."

"Yes, Mother," I said, "maybe one day I shall know it."

"Hasten it," she said, "and let it grow."

> . . . From the mighty dragon's blood
> Fairest maiden shall arise . . .

sang the children.

The short walk through the woods had ended, the weathered

rear side of the chapel came into view, we entered the clearing and the sunlit valley stretched wide before us. We climbed down the last slope; the priest supported himself on my stick, and when he slipped nevertheless in the gravel, Sack lent him his arm. As the children sang their last "Surrounding Christ in paradise," we had arrived in front of the chapel, in the open door of which the sun now slanted its rays, so that in contrast to this yellow prism of light the rest of the room seemed almost dark.

This is where Irmgard then laid the stone she had carried, laid it on the barren earth in front of the chapel steps after having removed it from its covering, and then the same was done with the rest of the stones from the carrier. This was the last act of the ceremony. The priest remained standing on the threshold, the Mountain Bride knelt down in front of him and was blessed once more together with her stones. Then the priest went to the altar, on which he deposited the flower spray, and called out "Aurum," and Irmgard brought him the piece of gold-veined ore; he then called "Argentum," and she brought him the silver ore; and then finally he called "Cuprum" and "Plumbum," and she brought him the pieces of copper and lead ore, and that was like a baptism and at the same time an orderly taking of stock, for therewith the stones were once more returned to be stored for another year. While the final prayer was recited, the sacristan returned the miner's pick to the wall where it had hung, and this restored everything to its former condition. Then the candles were extinguished, everyone left the chapel, the door was locked, the priest made the sign of the cross over it, and the key was removed. The ritual had ended; only the flowers remained on the altar, their dusty remains to be swept out the following year.

But even before all this had occurred, the provisions had been removed from the scarves and the bottles uncorked. A general hastiness had set in, not only because of the onset of appetite but probably also because everybody felt that, despite all the harmless and childish masquerading, something had happened that left an uneasiness which everyone tried to put behind him as fast as possible. It was a general feeling of relief, and quite a few gave it bodily expression by stepping behind the chapel and befouling the sacred wall. Nor was it surprising that the priest, too, felt relieved, since he had labored mightily, all too mightily for his poor heart, and now he rested beside me on the sunny steps, for to reach the shade of the woods had been beyond his strength. He rejected the solid victuals offered him from all sides, for he still felt too weak for any food, but he accepted some sips of cold coffee from Gronne's bottle.

"Next year we'll have a substitute climbing up here, Father, on that I insist."

"Yes." He smiled apologetically. "Yes, Doctor, maybe . . . but a substitute will cost money and this way I can do something at least for my flowers."

No doubt he was in such straitened circumstances that even the few pennies for the reading of a mass made all the difference to him. But I felt sure that he also said it because he suspected in me a pagan who would only comprehend material considerations. But when Mother Gisson now appeared before him and said with all the dignity peculiar to her, "Many thanks for the edifying mass, Father," he slanted his head even more, spread his hands as if to imply that he had merely fulfilled his duty toward God and to this small Christian congregation, and replied with great pureness of heart and touching candor, "It was a great pleasure for me, Mrs. Gisson." And though this occurred on those levels of polite ritual which are so frequent in rustic customs, such courtesy, both with Mother Gisson and with the priest, emanated directly from their innermost beings, a being that in her was great and rounded, while with him it was somewhat meager and puny but nevertheless of such convincing simplicity that Mother Gisson let go of his hand and ordered him with all the authority of which she was capable and which no one could easily deny: "But now you take off those vestments immediately, Father, or I'll take them off myself . . . We no longer need them." And the priest obeyed with such alacrity that he could hardly acknowledge the curtsy with which Irmgard, who had followed her grandmother, also thanked him for the blessing she had received. But with Irmgard, this was merely a formality in which she herself had no part.

Ten o'clock sounded from the church tower down in the valley. The morning sea had ebbed from the valley, green lay the cultivated land below, darker green where it is crossed by numerous mountain brooks, darker still the green of the orchards of the Lower Village and of the wooded hills on the opposite shore of the valley, and cowbells could be heard from the scattered farmsteads. Over it the sky stretched in unbounded and impeccable blueness, higher over the valley, even higher over the stony peaks which, as yet beyond the grasp of spring, were still carrying a late sun-blown winter. Thus is man framed by his existence from his remotest origins to his remotest future, and his primeval forebears and his most distant descendants in an unimaginable future are for him no longer members of the same species as his own, hardly do they seem to him human beings, neither gods nor stones and yet stone and god, standing at the infinite first beginning and at the ultimate end, a oneness so great as to recapture after aeons the unity of its origin, while in us, who are standing in the middle, only memory and prescience are alive, yet both so strong that they have become knowledge of the eternally changing and the eternally flowing together, knowledge of the indistinguishable into which all that is divided longs to flow together and in which all shall once more become one. Man and woman, streaming down from the sun, heaving in mountains, flowing in the sea, man and woman bent over the fields, sheltered in huts and speaking manifold tongues, speaking the still much-broken and unwieldy language that is filled with rites and empty flourishes, man and woman one day shall once again be as one among their flowering fields when their language, inventing itself and singing of the earth, returns into its innermost depth, so as to express the ultimate oneness.

"Yes," said Mother Gisson, who had observed me, "so what do you think, Doctor? Is the valley woman or man?"

"The devil with you, Mother! What I think is that you should now start the descent and rest in the woods . . . It's getting too hot up here."

"And you?"

"Since I'm already up here, I'll walk over to the pass and look in on the two Mittis oldsters."

I should have visited this old couple a long time ago. And so I took my leave and left it to Sack to help the priest, who at long last was happily in shirt sleeves, and pilot him all the way down to the valley.

7   It had rained for several days in succession, a rain that slackened until one night it had blown away. I had been awakened quite early by the smell of summer which had been carried into my room by the south wind through the wide-open window in great intermittent bursts. I got up and leaned out the window. The small garden was still moist and shadowed by the surrounding pine woods. A merle busied itself on the gravel. But now it flew away, for Trapp had noticed me and had hastened to crawl out from the doghouse, where, a moment ago, nothing could be seen of him but the black tip of his nose lying over his crossed forepaws. Now he stretched twice with open mouth, arched his back, and began to dance in front of the window, barking and wagging his tail.

Is it these mornings, both in summer and in winter, that have kept me, an aging man, all these many years in this mountain village? Is it they which no longer will let me go?

Caroline also has awoken, and I hear her busy in the kitchen as she prepares breakfast for both of us. I go to the bathroom, which, like so many other things in this house, is a fakery from inflation times: the nickel-plated faucets are dry, for the catchment at the source that was to feed the pipes to the two houses was never built and, as a result, I have to make do with a few buckets of water in this elegantly tiled bathroom. Strangely enough, in some remote corner of my soul, this is rather to my liking—even though, were the municipality finally to put in a pipeline at my insistence, I could quite easily install two or three sickrooms, which would be a real boon for this remote community—and I rather relish this primitive state of affairs, as I relish anything that will distance me from the city and the urban amenities which I fled so long ago. Of course, this is nonsense in itself, but man requires at times some outside milestones when he is engaged in an inner progress. And since I have dissociated myself from the city even in surface matters, I did make some progress, or I at least believe that I am making some.

Later I sit with Caroline in the kitchen and have my breakfast. The window was open, the shadow of the garden sent its cool breath into the kitchen and absorbed the smell of freshly ground coffee. But one also felt that outside the tops of the firs were already gilded by the first slanting rays of the sun, for, swaying in the southerly wind that releases in their wood a creaking sigh of a smile, they shower the sparks that have caught in their branches like seeds of light, sinking down into their shadows and impregnating their breath. And mixed in with the smiling sighs of the trunks and branches, there rose the singing of all the birds.

But man is not placed in this world only to rejoice in its beauty, an opinion emphatically held by Caroline, and so she once more lamented that she would not have such a lonely old age if the scoundrel who had left her with child had not decamped to America. For some time now I've been wondering whether that lad in America may not have answered to the name of Arlett. But the child is in service in the city and she concluded the tale, as always, with the bitter adage: "A servant's child's lot is to serve."

I had business in the Lower Village but—since it was a Wednesday—no clinic, and so I decided to stroll down right away, maybe also because the glory of the morning tempted me to take the path through the woods. As soon as Trapp had finished his milk, I took my stick and my satchel and we started out, first past Wetchy's house, then walking over to the clearing where the unfinished cableway originates and points its route northward down into the Plombent Valley—though without ever reaching it, of course.

We paused for a moment in the clearing. The rock walls of the Kuppron can be seen from here in all their expanse, all the way to where they sink down to the Kuppron Saddle. They stood out clear against the azure sky, and no less clear stood the Raw Venten on the other side, which still carried snow on its heights. Bordered by the long black shadows of the trees, the alpine meadows up there lay green in the golden morning sun, and the cool freshness of its light by now had filled to the brim both the Kuppron and the Plombent Valley, the confluence of which can be seen from this point. On the lower hills to the north and the east, each farmstead could be distinguished clearly with its meadows and clumps of trees, the homely doings between house and stables lay openly revealed, all that wide-spanned human life and labor, the water wells and their troughs; occasionally a rooster crowed and at times even a human call crossed over to where I stood. All this I saw and heard in the rain-washed clarity of the air. The morning breeze had died down.

A waiting for knowledge.

We followed the narrow clearing which had been laid out for the cableway and which each year gets more dense and overgrown with underbrush and fat grasses, teeming on this moist and shadowy slope; we passed the gray concrete pedestals of the cableway masts, huge cubes with coarse-grained surfaces, abhorred by every plant and avoided by every blade, showing only the horizontal imprints of their forming boards, until we arrived at the small brook which comes down on the left from the Cold Stone and crosses the cableway in a deep gully. Together with the brook we turned to the right and entered the woods.

Innumerable such runnels come down from the Kuppron's face after these days of rain; turbid with sand, they rush through the ordinarily dry bed of the brook and over the moss-covered stones, while at the edges ferns and grasses snake in the rapid flow; sometimes one of these tears loose with its clump of roots and earth, swirls around a few times, and disappears in the surge. Since the path leads over smooth and moist needle-strewn ground, I have to plant my stick firmly so as not to slip, and when it gets too bad I make small detours to find footholds on moss or fallen twigs. The blue sky is visible through the blackish branches, the variousness of the trunk-filled woods has begun to play with the sun, a game of sun dapplings and of rustlings, there was laughter in the resin drops of the trunks and glittering pearls adhered to the cyclamen leaves which here and there and particularly around the tree trunks had turned their dark-speckled reptile leather toward the sun. I, too, had turned my face toward the sun, I walked straight toward it, and I, too, may have been laughing. But then the stand of trees changes and almost from one moment to the next one finds oneself in the golden-green light of a beech forest; after a few paces one steps on the softly rustling lawn of sharp-edged forest grasses, underbrush presses in from all sides with delicately emerald leaves, and to get through these obstructions one has to bend away twigs which spray one's face with dewdrops, playful last stragglers of the rain; it is cooler and leisurely flows the brook. I light up my pipe, it feels solid and pleasant as I clamp it between my teeth and my mouth fills with the warm sweetish smoke; I hear the cuckoo and the wren and all those calls carried from throat to throat throughout the reaches of the forest, far and farther away and into the inaudible and once more echoing back to me, as again I am filled with wonderment, arising from the inaudible limits of my own being, wonderment at being human, a man in the woods who walks through dew and dawn, a man who forgets yesterday's rain and today's sun, himself an evaporating drop of dew, himself call of the cuckoo and warble of the thrush, passed on from remoteness to farther remoteness and only recaptured in the inaudible. It gets darker now, the trunks rise higher and their foliage is more dense, while their bark becomes more splintered and gnarled. Presently the brook cuts deeper into the soft ground, so deeply indeed that soon it turns into a small ravine, in which much debris has been deposited and on the dark slopes of which bushes and bracken grow, as well as the huge leaves of the butterbur.

Suddenly Trapp slows down and walks stiff-legged, he points his ears and attentively straightens his tail, and then he stops altogether. A hardly discernible growl rises from his throat. Without his permission, another human being has invaded the forest.

The being becomes visible and is of great shabbiness. In one hand he carries a knotted red kerchief and in the other some fine mushrooms. Skinny, gray-haired, and of undefinable age and growth of beard, it is Waldemar the cobbler, who has taken advantage of his great knowledge of mushrooms shooting up after the rains.

We greet each other and I admire his mushrooms, for he is a simpleton.

"This one is for Marius," he says, and holds the largest one, a flat cepe which he carries in his hand, under my nose. The mushroom smells cool and earthy, one could almost say rubbery.

"So, for Marius, and what for?"

Waldemar is generous. He need not be as poor as he is, but he is defenseless and the people have great fun exploiting his simple mind. Lax has never paid him a penny.

"He will redeem us all," he says.

That something like that was coming, I had always expected; nevertheless, I was surprised.

"Did he have his shoes fixed by you?"

"Yes, and the other one, too."

The other one? Yes, that must have been the one called Wenzel. The path we now followed together runs at times along the edge of the ravine and at times at some distance before again approaching it and finally meeting the road, which leads from the left over the heavy log bridge and then down to the right to the end of the woods and into the village.

I stopped.

"Did they pay you for the shoes?"

"Yes," he said with a blissful smile.

"Aha, that's why he's going to redeem us."

"If you laugh, I'll go back into the woods," he threatens, and is about to do so.

"Come," I said.

The wheel tracks on the road are sharply delineated, their rain-softened edges break under our steps, and in the ruts the gravel has been crushed flat by wagon wheels. There are times when we walk behind each other, for in some places the road is hollowed out between loam walls over which there are still constant runnels of water. But the closer we get to the end of the forest, the flatter the road becomes, and finally it gently skirts the woods, separated only by a few trees and some bushes from the slopes of the meadows on which the mown grass already lies in long windrows and fades into hay. Now we walk again next to each other.

"He is poor and he will give to the poor," says the cobbler.

"And take from the rich," I said, "so that they, too, finally may pay you for their shoes."

"No," he says, "he won't do that; he doesn't take anything away from anyone . . . I'll give him one more," he says finally, and is about to loosen his kerchief to select another mushroom.

"Fine," I say.

Behind the next fold in the ground the village appears, and so I shake hands with Waldemar and break through the bordering bushes to walk more speedily down across the mown meadows. Trapp, happy for the open space, rushes ahead.

The village lies in front of me down there in the dark well of its orchard greens. The walk down the meadow is easy, the grass is interspersed almost everywhere with moss, a moist long-leafed moss into which my stick penetrates deeply as into a great yielding pillow. All over the meadow there are stems of primroses which long ago lost their flowers, poisonous-pale, snapped, and malignant stem cadavers. I climb over the simple fences that cross the meadows to restrain the cattle, and for a while I rest on one of them, my hands holding on to the gray, longitudinally fissured wood, one leg swinging lazily and the other levered against the center plank, taking in the morning view. Up near the woods stands Waldemar the cobbler, who—obviously to see what I was up to—had also come out on the meadow, and when he notices that I am looking in his direction, he makes several of those deep bows for which he is mocked by people and lifts the hand with the mushroom bundle in greeting. All around are the mountains, the forest, which farther off turns into a large flat bluish eiderdown, the mown meadows, the light green wheat fields and the almost blackish clover, the stands of oats in a stiffer shade, but right in front of my eyes lies the village, the church and cemetery straight ahead and the school, almost surrounded by fields. It is the village that shelters Marius. So I leave my perch and walk down the short remaining distance.

I arrive just behind Strum's farm. The gardens, already stripped of the sweet sorrow of their white and pink spring, have matured, the foliage hangs in sated plenitude from their shoulders and arms, the grass is lush at their feet, and their head is a many-voiced birdsong. From the open windows of the school can be heard the chorus of a poetry recital.

Of course, I recall Agatha and her sewing in the garden. But she is not there. However, I catch sight of her father, who is carting a wheelbarrow of earth to the vegetable patches that border his yard. I call to him from the field and he comes over to me.

"All's well, Strum?"

"Yes," he says, and he gathers up his blue apron in front of his rounded belly to make himself more presentable. "Yes, we are both fine, Agatha and myself."

"Of course, Strum is always fine."

He laughed. "Especially when he's becoming a grandfather."

This was news. "What a surprise, Strum . . . and I hear about this only now?"

He beamed. "I hope it's a girl."

"Well then, I must get over to your side to shake hands . . ."

I climbed the garden fence and we shook hands.

"When is it due?"

"She's in her third month."

"By Peter?"

"Of course."

"But those two are a little too young to get married."

"Agatha doesn't even want him anymore."

"Really? . . . Well, maybe later . . . Just think, the girl would be well taken care of and she would make a fine innkeeper's wife . . ."

"They don't want the daughter of a crofter, they aspire to something better."

"That may change."

"No," Strum said, and stuck his hands in womanly fashion under his apron. "Now it's us who no longer want to."

The garden is not as bright as six weeks ago; its leafy canopy has become dense, the carpet of grass is thick, and the coolness of summer is captured in its midst.

"What's more," he continues, "Peter's gone crazy . . ."

"Never mind, Strum . . . This Marius business will blow over soon enough and then Peter will be all right and back to his senses."

"We don't need any Peter."

"Ridiculous. Every girl needs a man . . . and then it's always better if it's the father of the child."

Strum reflected, and I looked out at the fields. The ears of wheat, which had still been heavy and bent by rain in the morning, had straightened up and now swayed lightly in the shimmering heat.

And then he said, "No, we don't need a man."

"You don't, Strum . . . That I can well believe."

And with that we walked over to the house.

We found Agatha at the kitchen stove.

"That's some news, Agatha . . . You couldn't have started much earlier."

She didn't seem to understand what I meant, for she merely smiled and said, "Yes."

But Strum said happily, "Yes, she's been real quick."

It was strange; he neither needed nor wanted a man for the girl. But what had happened before, that he fully acknowledged and approved. That this round puerile womb had received Peter in sweet compulsion, that a great and sad and gentle need had held both in its sway and had borne them in a hand that closed their eyes and swept them beyond the edges of their own selves, this Strum accepted like a woman who thinks only of the future child. And now a new child was forming in this child that stood before us, a new body in this body facing us, and a new skeleton was hardening in this not yet fully formed bony basin, and it is the joy of life ongoing.

"What are you going to do with this tiny being, Agatha, once it has arrived?"

Agatha's round child's face still seemed as if it were coated with a thick and almost immovable layer of youth, one could not tell as yet if her face would later show one or another of the innumerable layers of the human condition—few faces gain such maturity, and the face of her father, whom Agatha resembled, also showed, as it were, only a single layer—but now her face became animated as if by an inner light, as she said, "I'll sit with it in the garden under the trees . . ."

"Yes," I said, "I'm sure you'll do that. Why, you do that even now."

And the thought came to me that maybe the unborn was already hearing the rustling of the trees and the blowing of the wind and that it may well carry with it all through its future life this preternatural, prenatal hearkening as an eternal longing.

"But it will be November before I take to bed."

"True," I said, "and then the trees will be bare and I guess you'll have to change the diapers of the little one inside."

And Strum joyously concurred. "Yes, that'll be great fun."

But the girl in whose womb the human seed was germinating said, "Our room will be kept warm and I'll keep the light burning through much of the night. And the cradle will stand next to my bed in the shadows . . ." And then she added, "Maybe I'll cry at times."

"A cradle of almond wood," I suggest. Why I thought of almond wood, God only knows.

"We have a cradle," said Strum. "Agatha herself lay in it as a baby."

Suddenly I felt a hurt at having no child myself and I felt my age. And so I merely asked, "What are you cooking today, Agatha?"

"Noodles," Strum answered, and licked his lips.

But the pregnant girl would not yet let go of that cradle. "When I'll bend over it, it'll grasp for my breast and I'll open my shirt . . . and after it has fed, it'll make little fists and go to sleep again." And as she spoke, her whole body became a gentle swaying.

Strum listened delightedly. The sounds of summer entered through the open kitchen door, there was no smell from the stables, and somewhere someone played on a mouth organ as if it were Sunday.

"Yes," she said, "that's how it will be."

"Of course," I confirmed, "that's how it will be . . . feed and sleep, that's what babies do . . . Wouldn't it be nice, Strum, if we could do that, too?"

Agatha's light eyes gazed past me, perhaps to the garden and its trees, under which next year the basket with the infant was to stand, the trees into which it would be looking up when it was not sleeping, but it may be also that she gazed farther away and to her grandchildren and their great-grandchildren who will carry along the stream of life coming from infinity and conceived by infinity, carried along between trees and fields into all eternity, for the human eye is better able than man's reason to grasp an allegory of a higher and lower reality because the eye forever thirsts for security in the empty space of nothingness—an allegory that also can be found in the trees of a simple farmer's garden.

And this was confirmed as Agatha cupped her hands as if to collect the not yet forthcoming milk of her breasts or as if she were carrying in front of her something valuable and irreplaceable, and said, "When I was small, I knew my great-grandmother and now I shall one day know my own great-grandchildren."

Seven generations! That is quite something and it can occur when one becomes a mother at sixteen.

The Sunday sound of the mouth organ could still be heard, and I recalled that during my clinic hours I had often cursed Peter for producing this thin, tinny music, but in Agatha these sounds did not seem to trigger any memories.

I raised her chin. "I'm sure we'll manage fine, Agatha."

When I was standing once more with Strum in the yard, the morning freshness of the air had evaporated. With the rising sun, the sky had become whiter and thicker, the heavenly pathways were like a milky cupola clapped over the dark pastures of this world.

"You should really tell the Sabests what's happening," I said, "even if there isn't going to be a marriage. The child should know where it came from and the world should know it, too . . ."

He scratched his round head. "Yes, I guess one should . . ."

"And last but not least, you're not exactly swimming in money either, after all . . . The child support will be most welcome . . . and you have to demand it, if only for the sake of Agatha and the child . . ."

"I wouldn't want to do that, Doctor . . ."

"But why not?"

Strum hesitated a bit. "Peter knows about it anyway."

"And so?"

"And then, the other day I ran into Wenzel . . ."

"What has he got to do with it?"

"It could be that it was just one of his jests, but he said that henceforth girls who ask for child support will get their windows smashed . . ."

"You're not going to take this seriously, I hope . . . because if anything like that were ever to happen, I would really drag this Mr. Wenzel over the coals . . ."

"We've got plenty of time." He laughed. "A full six months . . ."

"I have no liking at all for those jokes of Wenzel's," I said in parting.

I had some letters to mail and went first to the post office, which is located at the corner of Church Street.

In the small chamber-like room with a single window, in which the walls are plastered with official announcements, so that next to the infrequently changed weather forecasts one can also read about the opening of the telephone connection with Pernambuco, Miss Baldan sat bored as usual and welcomed the unexpected customer.

"Quiet days, Miss Baldan . . ."

She smiled with her long uneven teeth, which I know well from my practice. "Soon there'll be a lot to do . . . I may even need an assistant . . ."

"Really?"

"Yes. Mr. Lax thinks that when gold is found here, there'll be a great deal of business and plenty of visitors . . ." She said it proudly, and it was hard to tell whether this pride was based on the expected increase in the importance of her functions or on her relations with Lax, which it is gossiped are of a more delicate nature and to which she likes to allude. She is bent over my letters; the meager black bun is held in place with steel pins and the skinny neck is yellowish.

After leaving, I see Johanni standing with a horse under the canopy of the smithy, and since in any case I had wanted to look up the blacksmith, I cross the dust-white street, squeeze through the farmers' wagons standing in front of his shop waiting for new axle pins or wheel rims, and greet both men.

The smith was in the process of examining the neck of the animal, letting the two soft sinews glide through his hand as Johanni looked on with a worried face.

"Nothing wrong," said the smith.

"No," insisted Johanni. "The horse has the heaves. You have to give him the powder."

I know about horses; there was nothing wrong with the animal. But Johanni, wiping the sweat from his brow, seemed to have acquired, in addition to his ox-like obduracy, an obstinate ox-like fearfulness; neither the bright morning light, nor our soothing words or the fire flickering in the darkness of the shop, nor the merry hammering of Ludwig, the apprentice, who was working a scythe blade on the anvil, could assuage his dark and confused fears, and he simply repeated: "Give him the powder."

"All right," the smith finally said, and went to get the powder. I helped him as he grabbed the horse by the nostrils and blew the powder into its mouth, its teeth bared in a painful grin.

When Johanni had gone with his horse, I sat with the smith on one of the wagons and we both lit our pipes.

"Well," I opened the conversation, "and what do you make of that?"

We looked after Johanni, who walked next to his horse with the heavy tread of an ox. The horse chased the flies from its thighs with some swipes of its tail.

The smith looked quite grave as he said, "If it catches on with a few more like that, we'll have a disaster. Then the cattle really will come down sick."

"That's Marius," I said.

"I'm only the smith," he said, "I only know about animals; you're the doctor, it's for you to cure human beings."

Under the canopy stood the plows, their blades flashed in the sun, some of them in bluish shades, and along the wall the scythes were lined up in rows. I looked the smith in the eye. He had brown eyes with golden sparks, like warm polished wood.

I said, "When someone comes to redeem the world, the doctor is helpless."

"Yes," he said, "but those like Johanni don't believe that he'll redeem the world, they just believe that he can work magic."

"Well, he does. As you can see, he casts a spell on people."

Ludwig, the apprentice, had joined us, the finished scythe blade in his hand, and, laughing, he said, "He doesn't cast a spell on anyone . . . They're only afraid of the gold which we'll dig out of the mountain."

"Shut up, you," his master rebuked him, "and get back to your work."

Ludwig continued to laugh. He was a big lad, wearing a scanty undervest instead of a shirt which revealed his powerful shoulders; dark blond hairs sprouted on his broad chest.

"Marius is not going to go after the gold, at least not as long as he works at Miland's."

"Yes, but Wenzel works for Krimuss," the apprentice replied gleefully, "and that's something else again."

The smith said, "That Wenzel is nothing but a clown."

"Marius, too, perhaps," I said.

"No," said the smith. "That one is for real."

"And Wenzel will carry it out for real, too," said the apprentice, beaming.

At that, the smith laughed, too, a hard laugh, yet good and worldly, like warm wood. "No one who jokes can be for real; iron is for real."

"Marius is no iron," I said.

"We have the iron," said the apprentice.

A huge scale was suspended under the canopy on a heavy chain; the big iron trays each hung on three smaller chains and they were large enough so that a whole sack of grain could be placed on them. This is where the peasants weigh their grain.

"What is it you want?" I asked the smith. "And you, what is it you want?" I asked the apprentice.

The apprentice was the first to answer. "There's laughter in gold. This is where we'll weigh it."

"There's laughter also in death," added his master. "Death laughs like a horse, but he also can be grave and good."

What was it they had wearied of? They had their anvil and their bellows that transform air into fire. They had their own knowledge. Were they seeking another knowledge? "You both want the same thing," I said in parting, and left to do my own work.

The chestnut tree in the yard of the pub was wrapped in the glory of its belated spring. It blossoms here later than all the other trees of the region, and the pink candles stood in close ranks all around its large soft body. But its spring is the spring of the city, of which I had wearied, of which I am still weary, even though I have fled and forgotten it so long ago.

Around six o'clock in the evening Wetchy came running over to my place from his house.

"Maxi is feverish."

"Children are easily feverish, Mr. Wetchy . . . Any other symptoms? Red throat? Digestion?"

But he was in no condition to give any reliable information, he was much too upset and chattered away without making any sense while we crossed the short distance to his house. There was nothing but woe and trouble wherever one turned. It was hard enough to make ends meet. No business. Not any business worth mentioning. How was one to feed one's children? And now there is some crackpot in the village who is agitating against radios. Though he sells nothing but the best brands.

"Hm."

Some chap they call Wenzel. Who the other day had followed him in the street and shouted over and over again, "Wireless Wretchy." And the children and the young lads had stood by and slapped their thighs.

And he concluded with great indignation: "And that fellow is even smaller than I."

Yes, it had been Wenzel. And it's true that there isn't much height or girth to Wetchy. I had to laugh. "So the little clown doesn't like your chatterboxes either . . ."

He was hurt. "A business like that is hard to build up, Doctor, and all too easily ruined . . . yes, indeed."

By then we had arrived at his place. His house is identical to mine, but here not only the plumbing is missing but other appurtenances as well, which in my own house I have installed myself.

The sickroom was darkened. Wetchy's little wife, who had been sitting at the bed, rose, and at first I only saw a touchingly small gesture of imploringly raised arms. At times I see something like that with kneeling women in dark churches.

"Good evening, Mrs. Wetchy . . . How about letting a little light in?"

"Yes?" It sounded full of hesitation and anxiety.

Lacking blinds, she had hung a large blanket over the window. I removed it.

"But his eyes are hurting him."

The small boy looked up at me with suspicion and fear.

Everything in this family has an undertone of anxiety, both the love that holds them together in a thin and tenuous warmth and no less so the authoritarian posture of protection with which the little paterfamilias Wetchy exercises command over his family.

He danced around me, blocking my way. "Is it something serious, Doctor?"

"How about if you let me examine the boy first, Wetchy? . . . Bring me a spoon."

"A spoon," he ordered his wife.

The boy patiently let me place the cold spoon on his tongue, and he was hot with fever. Measles? Not one case of measles near or far. But fear attracts disease and it draws microbes even up here in this pure air.

"Is it something serious, Doctor?"

"Well, maybe measles."

"Mea . . . dear God in heaven!"

"But, my dear woman, which of us hasn't had his measles and put them behind him? The sooner, the better."

She looked at me dubiously but did not dare contradict me, and she even smiled a little as she took the hand of the child, who had sunk back into the pillows like a small old man.

Afterward, I washed my hands in the kitchen. Of course, I could have done it at home, but for pedagogical reasons I've made it my habit to do it at the patient's house. Wetchy, with a fresh towel over his arm, watched me devoutly, as if the health and life of his child depended on my ablutions.

Near the kitchen window sat the older of the two Wetchy children, a five-year-old girl, at a child's desk, quietly cutting colored paper into strips.

"You know, Wetchy, for the duration of the sickness you really should send the girl to some relatives . . . because of the danger of contagion."

He looked at me aghast; he simply was not equal to such a contingency.

But meanwhile I had reconsidered the whole matter. It might well be that by now the contagion was already in the girl and this would only lead to further complications. So I offered: "Better still, send her over to my house to be quarantined . . . old Caroline has nothing to do anyway . . . and if any symptoms should appear in the girl, I'll return her to your house . . ."

Wetchy made a movement as if to run back to his wife. But then he thought better of it or his legs simply may have failed him. He dried his upper lip, on which grew a small reddish salesman's mustache, and then he wiped his bald head, which held a few sparse red hairs; the profuse perspiration left him weak and mute.

I looked at this resigned sufferer, this city dweller cast up here much against his own will. It may be even that the anxiety with which such a person safeguards and withholds the small meaning of his life contains more insight into the vital concerns of existence than the comportment of the peasants and of the rough rural lads who have nothing but derision and a scornful shrug for such a creature. Nevertheless, I found his pitiful behavior annoying and I turned to Rosa, the little girl. "Well, Rosie, would you like to stay with me? With Trapp?"

But the child only shook her head gravely and continued to cut her colored strips. And Wetchy made a gesture as if this decided the matter.

So it's no; fine.

I approached Rosa to look at her work. When I stepped on the wooden planks which Wetchy had installed under the desk—a similar arrangement was in front of the stove—so as to protect woman and child from the cold rising up from the stone kitchen floor, the planks seesawed noisily under my great weight.

"Once more," called the child with surprising animation. Wetchy also laughed fatuously. "Do it once more," he, too, said. He seemed to have forgotten both the measles and my offer.

So I repeated what suddenly had become an effective joke and stepped with all my might on the planks, so that they reverberated thunderously under my feet. Which once more scored a success with both father and daughter.

But since I didn't want to continue this idiotic game indefinitely, whatever both of them might have wished, I said, "Wetchy, you better go now and consult with your wife."

Wetchy, who was still rubbing his hands in foolish pleasure, made a regretful face and left, not without turning back at the door, because I had stepped once more on the planks, eliciting a loud cheer from Rosa, who threw up her arms in delight.

When he had left, the child suddenly said, "Will you play this game with me if I come to stay with you?"

"Yes," I said rashly, without realizing that now I would also have to get a plank. As if fate were meant to warn and deter me, she once more shouted, "Do it again!" But at this point Wetchy and his wife returned; he was calm, he no longer perspired, he held his hands quietly.

"So what have you decided?" I said, with what I believe was little encouragement.

Faced by the child, they once more became uncertain, an uncertainty which Mrs. Wetchy tried to mask with polite phrases: they could not put me to such trouble, and since they had been struck with this disaster, they knew only too well that they had to bear it alone and were not permitted, oh, by no means, to be so importunate.

Impatient with all this balderdash, I cut her short brusquely. "So it's all right with you if Rosa catches the measles?"

Tears sprang to her eyes. "No . . . no," and she raised her hands beseechingly to ward off such a fate.

"My dear woman, I didn't mean to be harsh with you . . . but if it is to be, then let's get it over with . . . and smile a little . . . it suits you much better."

Obediently, she immediately forced a smile. "Yes . . . but in this frock . . ." and she was about to approach the child, obviously with the intention of making her more presentable for the visit.

"Nothing doing," I ordered. "Anyone who was in the sickroom is not to touch the girl . . . Caroline can come over and get anything we might need."

"Don't go near her," Wetchy seconded, and looked sternly at his wife. "But I may accompany her, yes? . . . I'll wash my hands."

And so we left. Wetchy had a few of the child's belongings and extra underwear stowed in his briefcase, Rosa carried her doll and a carton with her cutout work, and I was curious about what Caroline would say to all this. A few moments before, the sun had disappeared behind the Kuppron, the breeze from the cliff faces had freshened, and Wetchy held the briefcase pressed against his chest so as not to catch cold. I turned around. Mrs. Wetchy stood at the door and waved a superfluous farewell. Her belly bulged under the faded light blue apron; she was to have another child in September. And it would be another small reddish Wetchy with a rachitic disposition.

Through the tree trunks to our right the vesperal rocks shone gray in rigid stillness, they let the evening wind glide down over their faces and into the forest, which received them with a crepuscular sigh. And at that moment I fancied that I would take in the little girl forever, and as my own child, instead of her staying with me only for the duration of the sickness, and although I well knew that this was nonsense, probably brought on only by the fatuous farewell wave of the woman, the thought, strangely enough, was not unpleasant to me. True, I would have greatly preferred a real peasant child or the child of a lumberjack and one that would not answer to the silly name of Rosa, and so I turned around once more as if to ventilate the possibility of a return. Mrs. Wetchy still stood there, waving her hand; I waved in return and tried to induce the child to do the same. But the little girl was not interested; she was firmly holding her doll and spoke to it, and she would not turn around.

8 There are days when the whole world is like a cozily furbished room, the sky is a restfully painted blue ceiling, the mountains are like green-and-white wallpaper, and on the many-colored carpet of life all kinds of toys lie strewn about and make sweet childlike music. With such days spring reaches deep into summer and even all the way to fall, and then they become the childhood days of old age, as heartrending as those and a memory of that which lies behind each childhood game and also is contained in ultimate peace.

It was July and I thought that just such a day had dawned, for a peculiar gentleness had infused the world, a cloud of transparent softness, yielding and muffling and yet as inelastic as the surface of clear water, invested with a wooden softness, as it were; one could not yet tell whether the day would be merry or sad. The clinking of the breakfast china was different from the usual sounds, the crickets outside made an ungodly racket, but Rosa and Caroline sat having their coffee, the fifty-year-old and the five-year-old both equally old and equally young, both stirring their conversational tidbits in their mugs, and they may well have been talking about their illegitimate children.

But when I got out into the open, the day was no longer to my liking. True, all was bright and quiet, a fittingly animated quietness in which the furnished tameness of human existence was settled on the slopes of the mountains with toy-like peacefulness. But the sounds of the valley, which ordinarily rise so freely and with such liquidity, as if they were being drawn upward into the thinner air of the immeasurable beyond, these sounds today had a different shading and a different velocity; they rose almost hesitantly as if merely out of habit, and a strangely fusty seclusion was contained in this gradual deceleration, for the blueness of the morning was not open to infinity, but rather appeared as an occlusion stretching like a dense cellophane bubble over the mountain peaks, and every

sound reaching it from below seemed to stretch its rigid imperme-
ability ever more tautly. I listened: all sounds came from below,
nothing from above, not a single birdcall.

Nor did this blue cellophane bubble burst open during the later
morning. On the contrary. Around noon it had become a solid
dome of blue-painted lead.

I walked toward the village along the Venten brook which snakes
through the valley floor in a wide curve pointing east. The fields
ripened and the grass stood ready for the rowen. This is the time
of year when every man who is subject to the growing earth walks
with the gait of the reaper, his arms always ready for the swing of
the scythe, even when, as I, he merely carries a doctor's satchel,
and his life begins to flow from the head into his arms and downward
into his legs, drawn by an earth which no longer sprouts upward
into infinity but once more pulls down that infinity toward itself,
imbibing it for the coming stillness of winter. When harvest time
draws near, man no longer speaks his thoughts, for he no longer
has any, he has become one more harvester among the untold
multitude, all subject to the same mind-numbing force and what
they think is nothing but the blind sucking power of the earth. As
I walked along over the brittle ground of the lane, I looked up at
the sky, waiting for the leaden dome to sink down, drawn downward by the power of the waiting earth. The stillness of the morning
had become even heavier. Where the brook passes over some small
sills, its rippling babble could be heard, and once in a while someone
up there where the meadows reach into the woods sharpened his
scythe. Small and black were the figures of the harvesters on the
slopes, sometimes a scythe blinked and at times the white of a shirt
caught the light.

Between the bushes edging the banks of the brook and the path
there is a narrow strip of marshy meadow grown over with hemlock
and marigolds, and in a few places there are islands of reed grass.
The reed stalks stood stiff and high, and this is where I suddenly
heard the crunching saber cuts of a scythe and the rushing fall of
the layers of harvested reeds. On the edge of the path lay a patched
blue shirt next to a covered basket.

It was Wenzel and he was cutting reeds for stable litter.

"Good morning, Doctor, sir," he called out.

"Good morning."

His naked torso was perfectly formed, the skin brown and hairless, but the huge long arms, ape-like, were densely covered with hairs. He hung with one arm on the upper handle of the scythe, which he had planted next to him, and it was a good deal taller than he. From his waist dangled the leather scabbard with the sharpening stone.

"Hot work," he said.

"For sure."

"You should take off your shirt, too, Doctor, sir."

His whole face was beaming, as if he were delighted at my arrival, and he was full of a cordial jolliness which one felt could turn suddenly into hostility. He was simultaneously a rogue and a hangman's henchman, both a wag and a strangler from no-man's-land, who well may be thought capable of quite a lot, maybe even of the reopening of an old sealed-up mine, but certainly of the merciless persecution of a poor and defenseless radio salesman. He laughed and licked the sweat from his upper lip. Since I had thus come upon him by happenstance, I thought it right not to beat around the bush. "Good that we meet, Wenzel . . . What is it, actually, that you have against Wetchy?"

With his heel he probed a molehill, parched by dryness into a heap of pale loose sand, and he sighed deeply.

"Well?"

"Doctor, what is one to do with such a wretch?" he replied with a desperation that was at once guileless and feigned.

What he intended happened: I had to laugh.

"And now he is even related to you."

"How's that?"

"Well, you got his daughter."

"True."

"And the other one has the measles."

"Yes."

"Sad," he sympathized.

"And that's why you should leave him alone."

"And something like that even dares to propagate itself . . ."

"That's a fairly widespread habit, I believe."

"Would be a lot better if something like that had never been born."

"Your harassment of him is not going to stop that."

He pouted. "He, too, is harassing everybody with his insurance policies and his wireless claptrap . . ."

"What's it to you, Wenzel?"

"Me? . . . Nothing . . ."

"But you're meddling in a lot of things which are none of your business . . ."

He made a disparaging gesture. "But, Doctor, I'm a nobody . . . It's just that the people can't stand Wetchy . . ."

"Yes, but up to now he lived in peace . . . It's only when you came on the scene . . ."

"I? . . . But, Doctor, sir!"

"Who else? Marius?"

He scratched his head. "Marius, that's another kettle of fish . . ."

"Yes," I said, "it's another kettle of fish, indeed, if on his orders you stir up the peasant lads . . ."

"Marius doesn't order anything," he said almost scornfully.

"So what else does he do?"

He thought that over quite seriously and then said, "Marius only speaks out loud what the others are thinking."

"Really? You mean to say that they, too, had always been thinking about the nonsense with the gold?"

"Always, Doctor, always." Again there was in his face his usual merriment, but he meant it seriously nevertheless.

I looked across at the Kuppron, which stood there silently, gold in its stony belly, holding up the weight of the leaden dome, the mountain a part of the earth, thrown up by the earth perhaps against its own will, thrown up against the heavens, so that they might not tumble downward into its down-drawing power—whether giant or giantess, it could not be said. But in front of me stood the dwarf-like scamp bearing his scythe, he, too, thrown up by the earth and cutting its reeds.

"Yes," he said, "the people only do what's in their own thoughts."

"More likely in the thoughts of Marius . . ."

"That's the same . . ."

Trapp, his tongue lolling out, had lain down on the hot earth and growled under his breath. It was as if he growled into the earth.

"If you really do what you're thinking of doing, you will all get into trouble with the police . . . As far as I know, that's happened to quite a few who simply went ahead and acted out their thoughts."

"The police also think that way," he said, and winked at me slyly, "just like you yourself, Doctor, sir."

"Kindly leave me out of your jokes, Wenzel," I said. "What you are thinking of doing to Wetchy is a barefaced infamy and I can only warn you also about your gold-mining schemes."

I had to say that, of course. But I would much rather have taken his scythe from him, so as to do some reed cutting myself. The strangely leaden air felt hot in my lungs, and even though I know about human anatomy, my own breath seemed to me dark and inscrutable.

He again twisted his heel in the sand of the molehill, smiled, and then said, "People always want something new and one must let them have their bit of fun."

"And that's what you call redeeming the world?"

"I don't."

"Well, Marius, then."

He again made his cynically sneering gesture. "Maybe."

"So all you want is to have your fun . . . but these are pretty mean jokes, Wenzel."

"The world has to go on, Doctor, sir."

Age-old and overpowering, the Kuppron stood and threatened, there threatened the mountains of rock towering in the blueness, covered by the immense and immeasurable life of the woods and their millions and millions of trunks, of bushes and leaves, and suddenly it became the sneering threat of a decrepit old man who soundlessly strips off the thin clothing of life and raises his arms to stand all at once in the terrifying armature of his nakedness.

"The world has to go on," repeated the dwarf with his scythe.

Yes, it has to go on, it has to rise time and again against the superior might of the naked oldster, against him who over and over again reveals the terror of naked death in the midst of shining fair beauty, it has to rise against him, seeking to undermine his power, so as to wrest the secret of the gold from his core, so that he may tumble down and the heavens be recaptured once more by the sucking and absorbing breath of the earth.

"Yes," I said, "the world has to go on, but probably not the way you have in mind."

"No matter, as long as it goes on at all." He laughed. "I'll show you something, Doctor."

He went to the basket at the edge of the path and lifted the lid. Among the grass and leaves with which he had packed the basket, there teemed a dozen or so greenish-black crayfish, moving their claws.

"I fished them from the brook," he explains. "They are for Krimuss, he loves to eat them. He's something of a crab himself."

Trapp sniffed at the basket.

Wenzel held one of the creatures under the dog's muzzle. "These are the moonfish," he said.

"Well," I said, "better to look for crayfish than to look for gold, Wenzel. That makes more sense."

He grinned again. "The crayfish, too, are under the stones."

"Yes," I said, "but catching crayfish does no harm to anyone and doesn't stir up trouble . . . I'll be seeing you, Wenzel, and leave Wetchy alone."

And so I left.

"At your orders," he called after me, and when I turned around he stood there like a sentry and held the scythe at present arms, its curved blade glittering in the blue sky like a white and overly elongated crescent moon.

Not far from the village I caught sight of Marius on the slope of one of Miland's meadows. In a staggered row, he, the farmer, and the hired hand Andreas marched across the meadow, swinging their scythes in uniform rhythm, and behind them followed the wife and Irmgard, who, with smaller and more irregular motions of their long rakes, spread out the mown grass. From where I stood one could almost mistake the farmer and Marius for each other. Irmgard waved to me and I waved back. It may be that she also shouted something, but the day had become so motionless that the air seemed too stagnant to carry the sound; it, too, sank into the earth and was absorbed by it.

The village was dead; one might have believed it was a nocturnal noon, so dark was the cloudless light that sank down in wave after wave of soundlessly resounding drumbeats. Pluto lay in the narrow shade of the wall of the pub, his head deep between his forepaws, and it seemed as if he, too, were growling into the earth. He sent a mournful glance in my direction, but he did not rise, not even to greet Trapp; they had nothing to say to each other on this day or what they wanted to say may still have been buried too deeply in the earth at which they both growled. Nor did Mrs. Sabest have much to say; she sat in the public room and stared into space.

"I guess no one's coming to my clinic today," I finally ventured.

"No," she said.

"I'll just wait for the beer truck to take me back up."

"Yes," she said listlessly.

But after a while she said, "Peter's now working in the butcher shop."

"Why, that's news," I commented. "All of a sudden he doesn't mind blood anymore?"

"Wenzel ordered him."

"Does that mean that he no longer wants to go into the business?"

"Marius says that all the junk shops should be closed . . . They're only good for the womenfolk."

"So, and what do you say to that?"

"My husband likes it."

"Including what he says about the junk shops?"

She smiled. "For the time being the pub is crowded every night . . . The farmers come because Wenzel makes them laugh. But there are some real bad brawls sometimes."

"So I noticed last Sunday."

After a while, Sabest joined us. He wore his bloodstained butcher's apron, and the long, straight-bladed splitting knife hung at his side like a sword. He sat down next to his wife and grabbed her soft armpit with his red hands so as to make her laugh. Her giggle sounded strange on this motionless day.

"So business is good, Sabest?"

"Yes," he said. "That Marius is quite a guy. There's a fresh wind blowing in the village."

"But he himself never comes to the pub?"

"That little scoundrel, Wenzel, is enough by himself . . . He even won Krimuss over."

"So Krimuss is happy with him . . . ?"

"I should say; the lad works like a horse . . . and what's more, he's going to get the gold."

"This may bring some real trouble."

"The others will give in, the ones from the Upper Village . . . They're like women . . . They're only afraid."

"Well, that's not exactly my own impression."

He tested the blade of the knife with a finger. "If they don't give in, some blood will flow . . . It would be about time, anyway . . ."

"Have you forgotten the war, Sabest?"

His fleshy lower lip protruded in a far-off, pensive smile as he fingered the full arm of his wife. "The war? No, I haven't forgotten it . . ."

"And so?"

He continued: "That is, I've forgotten almost everything, Doctor, everything . . . but there's one thing that stayed, one thing stayed with me: it always smelled of woman . . ."

He fell silent and snorted through his nose.

"And the world has to smell of woman once more . . . It needs some blood for that . . . and not just the blood of calves and pigs . . . When I stand in the slaughterhouse, Doctor, I can feel it. I feel it under my feet what it is that the earth wants . . . and if it doesn't get what it wants, then it no longer gives us any force . . . then we're no good for the women anymore, we become useless and everything on us droops . . ."

He didn't laugh, even though he made an effort to do so, but in his face was a great panic and the hand that had grabbed the woman no longer had a hold on her but rather clutched her as if seeking help.

"It sucks from down there," he said hoarsely, and pointed to the floor.

The smile on the face of the woman also had faded. She took the hand of the man from her arm and placed it over her bosom, covering it there with both her hands.

"And Marius is supposed to preserve that force?" I finally asked.

He didn't answer for a long time. And then he said, "What is to be, is to be . . . Someone has to do it."

Later, after I had gone up to my clinic, the beer truck arrived. Its honking could be heard from afar, and when I glanced out the window it had just turned into the village street, a puffing and rattling machine, somewhat awry because the road down there is strongly cambered, a machine equipped with eyes and indicators, with all kinds of signs and even with a flag, an earthly monster filled with beverages for human bellies. I heard the moistly hoarse voice of Sabest and barrels being rolled in the entranceway. So I prepared myself to leave, and soon after we drove away and left the village, three human beings on this noisy monster, three humans whose bodily recesses were clammy with sweat, while the machine on which we sat sweated oil and stank of grease and gasoline, thus we drove, three humans on a man-made contraption, drove through the motionless rigidity of the afternoon amidst fields that called for the reaping and slowly sucked up the hot still air all around; what had not yet been sucked up trembled like a glassy glare on the surface and waited. Behind us on the truck bed the empty barrels danced and the chains that had been wound around them clanked.

I got down at the third chapel and Trapp followed with a slow, almost clumsy jump. We took the shortcut through the woods. I looked up at the face of the Kuppron. It seemed as if the trembling glare, hardly perceptible, originated up there, for the Kuppron also seemed to tremble, a tremor as of someone under an overly heavy load who does not wish anyone to notice his great labor. The air trembled also between the pine trees, and the swarms of gnats stood almost motionless in the air.

I had dinner with Caroline and Rosa.

The child said, "Tell me the story."

And Caroline told the story. "Long, long ago, many hundred years ago, the heavens were lying on the earth . . ."

"Why?" asked the child.

"Just because," said Caroline, "because that's how it was . . ."

"Yes, but why?" asked the child.

"Because it was paradise," I said. "Whenever the heavens lie on the earth, it is paradise and the people walk about in heaven."

"No," said Caroline. "In those days there were no people yet . . . First, the giants crawled from out of the earth."

"Because the heavens were lying on the earth?" asked the child.

"Yes, maybe," Caroline said, and paused, probably wondering whether the giants who had thus been created were the first domestics in the world.

"Go on," said the child.

"Yes, and the giants could not stand for the heavens to lie on the earth. They were angry and jealous and wanted the earth for themselves, for themselves alone . . ."

"And then?"

"Then they took many stones and built them high up, one on top of the other, until the heavens were lifted away from the earth."

"Yes? And so they weren't lying on the earth anymore?"

"They weren't lying on the earth anymore."

"So the heavens were sad?"

Caroline was affected unpleasantly by that question. "Yes, maybe the heavens were sad . . . and that's how the giants built the Kuppron with their stones."

"As well as all the other mountains," I added.

"And now heaven can't come down anymore?"

"No, it can't."

The child wondered: "Maybe it still comes down during the night when nobody is looking."

"No," said Caroline quickly, for she knew that no one comes back from America.

"It can happen at times," I said.

Caroline glanced at me with disapproval.

"At times," said the child, as if remembering.

After dinner I went out into the garden. Dusk was falling, but the usual evening breeze was missing; the dry sultriness of the air was deadly still. All of a sudden Marius appeared at the fence and greeted me.

"Marius? You here?"

He nodded.

"Is someone sick?"

"No, Doctor."

"And you came to see me?"

"Yes, also to see you . . . You spoke to Wenzel today."

"Aha, so that's why."

"No, not only because of that . . . I have to go up to the mountain . . . The mountain has called."

"It did what?"

"It hasn't done anything yet . . . but it's drawing me up there."

"Well, fine, so then sit down at least."

"Thank you, Doctor."

He took a seat on one of the benches and I sat on the other. I offered him a cigarette, but no, he didn't smoke.

"You told Wenzel that I'm up to no good," he said with faint reproach.

"What you yourself are up to, I don't know, but if Wenzel is your executive arm, I don't particularly like what he does."

"Wenzel," he pondered, "Wenzel is a clown but he knows what he wants."

"And what does he want?"

"He wants what the people want."

"Yes, he also tried to have me believe that . . . but in fact he does what you want, Marius."

"The farmer doesn't want to have anything to do with the gold, so I gave it up."

"And so what is it, then, that you want? . . . For you're not going to convince me that you're a mere spectator here . . ."

"I want justice, Doctor."

"And in this you include the campaign against Wetchy?"

"I have nothing at all to do with that . . . That is simply the people's voice, but the people are always right."

"Well, Marius, my own concepts of justice are rather different."

"It is better that one suffers than all."

"Marius," I said, "justice comes from infinity."

"No," he said, and pointed toward the ground. "Justice comes from down there, and it can be divined with the rod just like gold or water . . . That is all one and the same . . . Though, in the last analysis, it is also infinity . . . The mountains are infinitely large, the earth is infinitely large, and if one hearkens to them, one hears infinity . . ."

"One should listen in here," I said, and pointed to my heart.

"The heart, too, comes from the earth," he stated simply, "and because it beats in the earth, one can also hear everything else in the earth . . . All of them, all that are here," he continued, "they all listen into the depths of the earth . . . Wetchy is the only one who doesn't . . . and this, you see, Doctor, this is justice."

He had risen to his full height, a man, upright on two legs, the sex sheltered between them, a man composed of a thorax on which two arms are appended for the purpose of grasping, for the clasping of earth and the holding of the divining rod, composed of a vertebraed neck on which sits the head: from the opening of that head speech came forth, a speech about justice, and the man believed in it.

Marius walked to and fro with his long rolling gait that still held the swing of the scythe. The gravel crunched lightly under his feet and the crickets stridulated; nothing else could be heard.

Then he took up where he left off. "We all have to hearken to the earth together, then justice will be established . . . and if they are not ready for such togetherness, they must be made to accept it."

"You want power, Marius."

"Yes, for justice."

If there had been a breath of air, I probably would not have let him continue; there was a malevolent and crazy mysticism in all that ranting, I felt this as clearly as I had felt it in our first meeting, but I was strangely paralyzed, as lethargic as this evening and the whole day had been, and even the man's speech came as if from a paralyzed mouth; indeed, it seemed as if this speech had risen through his whole body all the way from the soles of his feet and as if it were merely gushing over on top without his intending it.

Nevertheless, I said, "And what is this togetherness to be? Is it to be a communal gold-seeking expedition?"

But he did not hear me and said, "The truth . . ."

"Yes?"

"The truth sinks into the earth for evermore; it is the women who always and forever swallow the truth . . ."

"And the women are in the earth, Marius?"

"Yes . . . but they do not release the knowledge they have swallowed, they only release children from their wombs . . . they swallow and swallow and they forever suck . . . but the end of their time has come, they cannot listen to the earth because they are themselves in the earth . . . their time has ended, their power is over, the earth won't stand for it any longer."

I only heard words which I registered without comprehension. And yet it seemed as if the ground were sinking, sinking ever deeper into its immobility, deeper beyond measure and below the sea of an infinity whose nocturnal waves slowly and silently reared up to the heights of the highest mountains. But up above, the first pale stars appeared on the stony dome of the skies, and they, too, were motionless.

"The mountain calls," said Marius.

And then he had disappeared as suddenly as he had come.

I remained where I sat. The darkness flowed down from the rocks, but it was not a flowing but rather a motionless expansion and spreading, a dark silver-black beard growing from the mountain, filling all space and so dense that the stars, even though their number had increased, could hardly be perceived in their glimmerless dimness. I listened so as to hear the voice of the mountain that had called Marius, the voice of the father who calls for the redemption of all, but I only heard the motionless and mute murmuring of darkness, the soft creeping of that dark beard. Black moonfish crawled over the branches of the firs and pines and ensnared them as in cobwebs, so that they, in spellbound immutability, might escape no longer, and the crescent of the moon rose thin, long, and dim above the tops of the trees, a motionless scythe, ready for mowing. Motionless myself, I looked up, looked into the shaft of infinity—whether upward or downward I could not tell; indeed, no longer seeing it at all, I could not tell, for the ultimate depth is in both directions equally motionless, aimless, and immovable, neither man nor woman but merely knowledge, an ultimate common denominator innate in all human knowledge and yet no longer within its ascertaining power.

Thus I sat in the immobility of the night which grew deep and late. The crescent moon again disappeared behind the rigid trees and it was quite some time later that I heard thunder. It was a far-off, strangely muted thunder coming from the direction of the Kuppron, a dream-like thundering which nevertheless had torn me from my own dream. I stood up to look for gathering clouds and, as stiff as someone who has mowed all day, I took the path that leads out from the garden and into the open. Not a cloud could be seen; the storm had to be located behind the Kuppron, I thought, but I did not think so for long. For now the drumroll was repeated and I realized that it did not come from behind the Kuppron but from inside the mountain itself; it was an oppressive, weirdly dull sound which began softly, swelled up harshly, and then abruptly ceased. The next moment tiles splattered down from my roof, a creaking sigh swept through all of the woods, as if its end had come, and it was only then that I felt the jolting sway of the ground under my feet and felt at the same time a total helplessness, a helplessness that is greater in the face of an earthquake than when one is confronted by any other power of nature.

I rushed into the house and to Caroline's room, in which the child also slept; I switched on the light and shouted to the woman,

"Earthquake, Caroline, out into the garden!" The lamp still swayed violently from one side to the other, pieces of plaster fell from the ceiling, and I grabbed the child to carry her outside. But before I reached the entrance door, there was another jolt; the whole house creaked on its beams, a door sprung open, there was a dribbling of sand in the chimneys, and outside I could hear again the falling of roof tiles. The entrance door was jammed shut, I had to use all my strength to force it open, and I was glad to be outside with the child. But then it was over and nothing else happened.

Rosa, frightened by the sudden awakening, whimpered in my arms, and I deliberated on what should be done now. Caroline seemed to be dressing in her Sunday best in honor of the earthquake, for she still had not appeared. I did not want to go back into the house with the child, nor could I leave the crying girl outside alone, and so I called several times, "Caroline!" but without getting any reply. All remained silent, though there was still creaking in the woods, it was as if the forest were stretching and bending its numb limbs, and, indeed, it seemed as if the immobility of the world had been broken, as if it had awoken from a nightmare, and there was the intimation of a far-off breeze.

While I was still wondering rather helplessly what to do, Wetchy came running.

"What was that, Doctor?" He was trembling all over.

"I guess it was an earthquake . . . Did anything happen at your place?"

No, nothing had happened. But hadn't I heard the terrifying noise coming from the cableway?

Only then did I recall the sharp whistling and crunching intermingled with the creaking of the woods. Why I had dismissed it from my consciousness, I could not imagine; but it was a fact.

"Tell me, Wetchy, did you bring the boy outside?"

"Yes, my wife is sitting with him in front of the house."

"And is he well covered?"

"Very well covered . . . Can we now go back into the house?"

"I think so . . . but watch Rosa for a moment . . . No, don't touch her, otherwise our whole quarantine will be wasted . . . Just sit next to her."

I laid the child on a bench and went back into the house. Maybe old Caroline in her fright had had a stroke.

But no, she had had no stroke. She was sleeping quietly in her bed, not without having taken the precaution of turning off the light once more. She may not even have realized what had happened. And this was probably the wisest comportment one could adopt under such circumstances. Nevertheless, I did not dare bring Rosa back into the house so soon.

"Stay a while longer," I said to Wetchy as I joined him again in the garden. "I'll go see your wife to calm her down and then I'll run over to the village to find out the reaction over there . . . People have had some experience with such occurrences, after all."

And that's what I did. I first visited the Wetchy woman who was sitting with the boy in her arms. The child was well covered and nothing was to be feared on so mild a night. Then I continued on to the village.

There was light in many of the houses. Some people stood in the street, more or less scantily clothed. They were not particularly disturbed. Yes, things like that happened from time to time; today it had been a little worse than usual, but it was always odder during the night than by day, when one hardly pays any attention. If I would only recall four years ago, in autumn. Yes, I remembered; at that time I had been in the Lower Village, though, where hardly anything was noticed. Were more jolts to be expected? Probably not, not likely, though the mountain, of course, does as it pleases, but one generally had a feeling for it.

I shared that feeling. The air blew up now from the valley, light and warm. The whole sky was full of twinkling summer stars. A beautiful night, and peaceful.

There were also some windows lit in the Mountain Manse. I wanted to look in for a moment at Mother Gisson and was astonished to catch sight of Marius in front of her door. He stood there with Mathias and seemed to be engaged in an argument with him which, on Marius's part, was considerably more emotional than on the part of the always calm and deliberate Mathias.

"Mathias," I heard him say, "the mountain has spoken, the time is ripe."

"Yes," replied Mathias, "the mountain has spoken all right, but what it has let you know is that you are to leave it alone."

There was no doubt that Marius was in a highly agitated state; he tore at his curly hair, as Italians are wont to do when they get desperate. "The cableway has broken," he shouted. "Isn't that enough of a sign?"

Approaching them, I said, "Really? The cableway snapped? Were you there when it happened, Marius?"

"It snapped right in front of my eyes; in front of my eyes the mine cage was flung to the ground." His eyes had a mad gleam.

Yes, it was true, he had disappeared in the direction of the cableway. Was that why I had dismissed from my mind the noise of the snapping of the cable?

"The mountain never did like the cableway," said Mathias calmly. "It didn't need you to bring it down."

Marius snarled: "The mountain has warned you . . ."

"Yes," replied Mathias, "it's warned all of you down there . . . It wants to be left in peace . . . You better tell that to all of the Lower Ones . . ."

Mother Gisson appeared at her window, bent over the blossoming beard of the hanging carnations, and smiled benignly.

"So you're here, Doctor," she said, "just because the mountain has spoken a bit?"

Marius jumped at her furiously. "The mountain spoke to me, it spoke its warning, all mountains are threatening, the earth threatens, for it's been far too long that it hasn't been placated . . . The women's time is over."

"Yes," said Mother Gisson genially, "you may be quite right . . . and it's not a pretty time that's about to begin."

Marius laughed, showing his white teeth. "Close your window, Mother . . . A new time is coming, the time for our knowledge."

"Yes," said the old woman in the window, "and more's the pity."

"Go to sleep, Marius," said Mathias in a conciliatory manner.

"No!" shouted Marius. "No! Come and sing, Mathias, sing with me . . ."

And he sang: "The cableway has broken. Now comes a brand-new time . . ."

"Well?" he asked when Mathias showed no sign of joining him in his song.

"You're drunk," said Mathias.

Suddenly Marius turned serious. "Why, maybe I am," he said, and turned to leave without a farewell.

But after only a few steps, he began to sing again: "The cableway has broken. Now comes a brand-new time . . ."

The few people still in the street turned to look after him in wonder.

Mathias Gisson laughed. "What a crazy fool."

"Yes," said Mother Gisson in the window, "a fool he is, but his time is about to come."

"And what next, Mother!" I said. "Just because a few down there were taken in by him?"

Mathias said, "The mountain isn't taken in by him."

"The mountain isn't, but the people are," said his mother.

"And Wetchy will be the only one who'll have to foot the bill," I commented.

"There's not that much difference between him and Wetchy," she said, "and that's also why he hates him."

I didn't understand her.

"Wetchy also is afraid of me," she said.

"It doesn't take much to frighten that one . . . He's sitting now at my place with the child . . . Can I send him home, Mother?"

"Yes, you can send your people to bed; nothing more will happen today."

"Thank you, Mother, that's all I wanted to know."

And so I went home, sent Wetchy back to his house, put Rosa to bed, and went to sleep myself.

But Caroline was greatly surprised when I told her the next day what had occurred during the night and she refused to believe a single word of it. Even the roof tiles on the ground couldn't quite convince her. It is true that the morning was so gorgeous that all the terrifying happenings couldn't even be imagined. The wind from the north had stiffened, one could count on a spell of fine weather, and there was every reason to expect a good harvest.

9   August walked the earth with the swinging gait of a reaping angel, and Anna Sack could no longer withstand the sucking power of the earth. She died as the first heads of wheat were gleaned, and we buried her in that hole dug six feet deep in the earth that reaches all the way to infinity. There weren't many who freed themselves from the harvest to pay their last respects to Anna Sack and to watch her swallowed up by the grave while the hot glare of the ever more majestic sun trembled over it, and, indeed, they hardly watched but instead looked out into the land and to the fields where their work was waiting for them in the sweet dryness of the grain. Anna Sack was more quickly forgotten than at any other season of the year.

For the work's rhythm is a good master of men, it relieves them from choice and from the freedom they know not how to use. Oh, they no longer have time left to make decisions as their life runs out ever more quickly, and they are as if benumbed by the swift passage of time. Am I not numbed myself at times by that swiftness? Yes, I am numb myself, I in particular, I who have been called to patch up as best I can the earthly existence of others, so that it may last a bit longer and so that they may return once more for a while to their assigned work and fall into its rhythm, full of hope that the power of its ever repeated course, the eternal tides of tilling, sowing, and harvesting, shall carry them over the human woes and the terror of death that rises so swiftly and mightily that no span of human time is sufficiently long to overcome it. Like the obediently toiling laborers they are, commanded to plow the next or, at most, the next after the next row of field, they long for the voice calling to them: Be true, do your work, endure, carry on for this one harvest even though it be meager, carry your grain to the threshing, till the fields once more, be a faithful servant, follow the example of Andreas, Andreas who toils diligently even though but a few scant years separate him from his end, do it for the sake of your own eternity, for I, the voice of your conscience, I have taken upon me the burden of your decision making and of your consciousness, I am the voice of your conscience and I lead you, for I am the fated meaning of your life. This is the voice for which man longs, for which he yearns, so that it may redeem him, and it is for the sake of that voice that the plow is received from the hands of the father, for its sake it is being given over to the son, so as to overcome infinity in eternal succession, the meaning of life that resides both in the past and in the future, inconceivable in the ungraspable present, carried on arduously from harvest to harvest, from father to son and to grandson, from furrow to furrow, a fragile and yet heavy burden, but when the plowman at the end of the furrow turns about, almost despairing that, notwithstanding the many furrows he has already plowed and all the many more he still is to plow, he shall ever reach the end of the field, then it can well happen that in his despair he may apprehend high over his head the breath of his very own meaning, gliding along in the highest realm of the empyrean with the calm wingbeat of the invisible and the inaudible, as wide and light and heavy as the skies themselves, though also as equally inconceivable and of such ephemeral power that, were he to raise his eyes upward to apprehend the unapprehendable, he could hear only the expiring breath that once may have risen from his own mouth, a word once spoken or a single birdcall from the past, echo of an echo, yet reaching him as the all-encompassing command: Begin once more, begin all over again, for once again you stand at the beginning of infinity.

It was in the midst of the harvest that, coming one afternoon from my clinic, I saw to my surprise that Lax, whose house stands on the main street, was setting out from his gate in his light buggy. His son sat at his side. Lax waved to me and stopped.

"Want to ride to the Upper Village with us, Doctor?"

Of course I did. I asked him what his business was in the Upper Village, now in the midst of the harvest.

"I'm driving up to the mill."

Lax owns a small sawmill not far from the pass, an old broken-down shack, fed from a tiny outlet from a lake in the forest, which at one time in the past was connected with the mining works. He had bought the patently worthless mill in one of those acquisitive urges peculiar to some peasants and now operates the saw from time to time when he or someone else happens to need a few boards.

"Oh, to the mill? Why, Lax, in that case I could go visit the old Mittis couple . . . If you'll just wait a moment, I'll go fetch some medicines for them . . ."

"Sure, Doctor, we're in no hurry."

Old Mittis and his wife live in the so-called Notch in the Mount, a small hill farmers' settlement which lies in the meadow in the midst of the woods below the head of the pass. Old Mittis has liver trouble and his wife suffers from dropsy, and so I take with me not only some medication but also—and more important—some tobacco and sugar from the general store.

Then we started out. Young Lax, a wiry lad who resembles his father with his sharp poacher's eyes, had climbed into the back and I sat on the box with Lax. We progressed slowly in a cloud of creaking, squeaking, and jingling, for farm horses are not made for trotting, even when they are such fine animals as those of Lax. They wore their large brass-studded harnesses, on the sides of which the round brass plates and brass crescents dangled on thin chains and glittered in the sun. Their silky dun-colored rumps moved in slow unison before us, and from time to time one or the other of the horses raised its tail, extruded its anus, and let fall a few apples or released some wind.

"Any other animal stands still or squats down to do that," commented Lax. "Only the horse has to go on running . . . Wonder what would happen if we had to do that . . . Gee up!"

But once the climb had begun, no gee-ups made much difference; the two horses walked at their own gait, a long powerful stride which clearly let it be seen that the weight of the light carriage hardly mattered to them. At the chapels Lax crossed himself dutifully, sometimes he merrily greeted the people in the fields with a wave of his whip and they waved back and looked after us in surprise, for it was as if we were driving to a wedding on the hardest workday.

"They're wondering," said Lax.

But that's all he said, and I didn't ask why he was driving to the mill with a light buggy on which he could not even load boards. The son sat behind us with Trapp and was silent.

In some fields there were already sheaves standing, in others the mowing was still in full swing, but those who had started earliest were already loading the crops to bring them down to the threshing floor. The thresher still stands in its shed next to the coach house of the fire brigade behind the blacksmith's shop, but when I happened to pass by recently, the doors were wide open and the machine had been cleaned and readied for use.

"What about the threshing by hand, Lax?"

"Huh?"

"Well, Marius wants to do away with machine threshing . . ."

He laughed. "Oh yes, a few are in favor of it . . . Let them do it if they want to . . . Gee up!"

The few trees and bushes bordering the road are all coated with the dust of harvesting, their leaves and even their branches seemed faded and were hanging in trembling lassitude as after a hard day's work. A drove of wild pigeons, startled by our creaking and jingling, rose at the edge of the woods and their wings blinked in the shimmering air.

"And why are they in favor of it?"

Lax shrugged. "God knows . . . Marius has convinced them that because of the machines too many people have lost their jobs and that wheat prices have fallen as a result."

"Hm, these are utopian do-gooder ideas he's picked up somewhere . . . And what do you think of all that, Lax?"

He laughed again. "Let the others try it. I'm all for it if the prices go up . . . A small farmer who does everything by himself can easily also thresh by hand anyway, but if I had to hire threshers, it would be too expensive."

"But you're in favor of Marius's search for gold?"

"That's something else again," he replied curtly.

We passed through the Upper Village. It smelled of peacefulness and empty stables. A few children came out, lured by our noisy passage. No one could be seen at the Mountain Manse, nor did Mother Gisson show herself at her window.

When we had passed the village and come in sight of Sack's house, I suggested we stop and look in on the widower.

"Why not," Lax said, and gave the reins to his son as he himself jumped down over the wheel of the buggy. "Why not, we've plenty of time."

We climbed the little hillock on which Sack's wooden house stands. He had seen us and was coming out from the small stable building to greet us.

The round face with the seaman's beard had lost some of its usual color, the cheeks were a bit hollow, and one could see that he grieved for the being who had deserted him.

"Well, Sack, more or less all right?"

"So-so . . . a widower with a bunch of children."

"You better marry again, Sack," said Lax.

"I guess I'll have to," said the widower.

Lax grasped with both hands a pair of imaginary breasts. "Get someone who has some of that . . . That's worth something, too." He laughed. "At least in the beginning."

Sack sighed. He had every reason to sigh. There had been someone who could say, "Remember when we first danced together?" and when you went to bed, you remembered together. And that someone had rotted away and stank of death toward the end. While now there was going to be another one, for whom there was no "Do you remember," someone who will be there because the sex urge in man never dies out and because men and women will always get together, even if this is done only on the pretext of children or housekeeping, and he even will beget some more children with that other one, but it will be done without remembrance of the past and without thought of the eternal, it will be only for the sake of the moment. And the moment doesn't exist.

"Yes," said Lax, "and you should take someone who has something of her own, too . . . You could use that quite nicely."

Sack nodded. Then he asked, "Where are you going?"

"To the mill."

Sack was less discreet than I. "But you've taken the buggy."

"Yes," said Lax somewhat uncertainly. "We only have to fix something up there."

"Aha," said Sack, and something of his humor of old flitted over his face.

"Aha is uncalled for," said Lax, irritated.

"Well, I only meant that you won't need any lumber yourself just now and that you'll keep it up there."

"I'm not going to cut any lumber. I'm only going to fix the saw."

"Yes, but just in case you should be cutting one of these days, maybe posts, for instance, like those used in mines, you shouldn't rely too much on Wenzel . . . He's not an expert on everything, you know."

Sack said it with his customary sly grin and I had to laugh.

Lax escaped into the role of the offended. "I've come to pay you a visit because you've become a widower but you're still full of the same old silly jokes."

And he turned his massive belly to leave.

"Are you driving up with them?" asked Sack.

"Yes. I'm going to call on the Mittis couple."

And then he whispered, "Are you going home by way of the chapel?"

I nodded in silence. By way of the chapel and the miners' path it is almost shorter than by way of the road and certainly prettier.

"Could be that you'll chance on me there," whispered Sack.

Lax turned around. "I'll be seeing you, Sack," he said, and patted his shoulder. "Get married soon."

But when we resumed the drive, he was somber and taciturn and it was some time before he opened his mouth again. "One shouldn't give too much credence to all that secret-mongering about the mountain . . . Am I not right, Doctor?"

"Well," I said, "when it comes to secret-mongering, no one can outdo Marius."

His face showed his displeasure. "I have no use for any of that mystic claptrap . . . Wenzel tells it as it is, and he isn't mysterious about anything."

We were driving at a walk along the winding road through the pine woods. At the edge of the road there were some deciduous trees, grass, and bluebells. From deep in the woods could be heard the soft crashing sounds of trees being felled. A few birds chirped and fell silent at our approach. Above, the harvest sky shone bright, but down where we drove the air we breathed was cool. Nevertheless, the horses now showed dark shiny bands of sweat on their flanks.

At a bend in the road, in the middle of a small clearing, stood a crucifix. Lax crossed himself again. "Who knows, maybe that's more the right thing after all," he mumbled under his breath.

"More right than what?"

He didn't reply.

When we came to the junction that leads to the right and up to the Green Lake and the mill, I alighted and said, "Many thanks."

"You're welcome, Doctor, it was a pleasure. And if you want to drive down with us, we can meet here later."

"Thanks, Lax, but I'll go home by way of the path. Dinner stroll."

He gave a salutation with the whip and veered the buggy off onto the forest road.

I continued on the edge of the road, where it was less dusty, thought of Sack and the mysterious meeting he had arranged with me at the chapel, and after some twenty minutes I arrived at the settlement of the Notch in the Mount under the head of the pass.

The people up here live a lonely life. They have little in common with either the old miners' settlement or the Lower Village, and if it weren't for the automobiles which now cross the pass quite frequently and for which even a shack selling draft beer has been set up, life would be going on as it did five hundred years ago.

The house of the Mittis couple surely has seen a couple of hundred years. It stands dark brown and covered with moss in the midst of this alpine meadow, not far from the white wooden beer shack, and next to it and not much more recent are the pigsty, the goat shed, and the woodpile.

As I enter, old Mittis sits in the kitchen. At my appearance, his much-wrinkled leathery face, out of which the china-like eyes hardly look at the world anymore, shows a few more wrinkles, which may pass for a pleased smile.

"Well, Father Mittis, still going strong? . . . All's well?"

He immediately adopts a querulous tone of voice. "No tobacco . . ."

That was customary; I unpack the tobacco and the sugar.

"You shouldn't smoke so much, Father Mittis. It's not good for you . . ."

He quickly filled his cold pipe and played deaf.

"Don't smoke so much . . ."

"She doesn't give me anything to eat either . . ."

This was aimed at the wife, who had just entered, and it was not news either but an often repeated litany, even though the two aren't as badly off as all that. Marie, the unmarried daughter, tends the few acres they own, and occasionally the son, who is employed somewhere by the state forestries, sends a little money.

"He lies," said the old woman. And now came the countercharge from her. "He beats me."

There may have been a time when the old poacher and lumberjack had indeed beaten her. For her it was yesterday and today. The closer man draws near death, the closer he draws in his past life; the threads of memory get ever shorter and entwine ever more to form an inextricable present. And so these two still continue to fight out the squabbles of half a century ago with a vitality all the more astounding in view of their decrepitude.

"What are you having for dinner tonight?"

"Dumplings, milk soup."

The usual menu. "Well, then, Father Mittis," I said, "so you'll enjoy a fine meal."

He didn't want to hear it. No quantities of food and no dishes could satisfy his fantasies. What was it this fantasy sought? What exotic delicacies did he crave?

Suddenly he said, "Poaching is now going to be legal, I heard."

"What's that? Are you thinking of getting out your rifle once more in your old days?"

"My man never did that," interrupted the old woman, in whose memory there was still a glimmer of recollection that this was something that had to be hidden.

Angered by her contradiction, he insisted, "I shot a lot."

"Not true."

Which explained the puzzle of his gastronomic fantasies: the remembrance of the venison and chamois steaks of his heroic poaching days made him despise all other food as not worth mentioning.

"Father Mittis, milk soup is much better for someone who no longer has any teeth."

Yes, I had found what his mind had vaguely been searching for; the wrinkles in his face multiplied and, clicking his tongue slyly, he said scornfully, "Milk soup, ah no . . ."

"Let me examine you now, Father Mittis. Take off your jacket."

"Venison leg, that yes . . . but the young people today don't know how to shoot . . ."

"The shirt, too . . . That's right." I tried to auscultate the swelling of his liver. "Does it hurt?"

"No . . . but if they now allow shooting . . ."

"Who told you that?"

"Marie . . ."

"Not a word of truth," could be heard from the old woman at the stove.

But Mittis calmly persisted. "It's true."

"And where did Marie hear this?"

"She was down in the village."

There must have been something to it. As I saw it, any rumor seemed to have some foundation in this village, at least for as long as Wenzel and his jokes were holding sway.

Old Mittis continued the thread of his confused thoughts. "Then all the game wardens will be shot . . ."

"I wouldn't put it past you, you're getting healthier all the time." My examination was finished; surprisingly, his condition was unchanged.

Of course, I still had to examine the woman; I took out my stethoscope.

"The Murner warden shot at me . . . Now he's gonna get it."
He laughed.

That would have been some sixty years ago. But hatred knows
no time.

"Can't you forgive, Father Mittis?"

He looked at me uncomprehendingly. "Someone will have to
come who'll shoot all the game wardens . . . but, of course, the
young lads of today are no good for that . . . but someone will
come, that's for sure . . ."

I had begun examining the old woman. It had probably been
years since these bodies had been in contact with any water; but a
country doctor is used to such things and he learns from them not
only scorn for much of today's poppycock about hygiene but also
an increased respect for the human spirit: how little it often matters
whether that miraculous creation called a body is washed or not
when compared to the spirit for which it merely serves as an im-
perfect vessel, compared to the spirit in all its perfection, perfect
even in so raw and unfinished a form as in this old couple, neither
of whom could either read or write.

"This is where he beat me," the wizened old crone said, and
pointed to her shoulder.

"Does it still hurt?"

"Yes, a lot."

A tenacious pain, as tenacious as the hatred that alone still glimmered in the ashes of this overlong life. And what was the harvest
that remained from an overlong togetherness which, at one time,
had even been one of mutual lust? Nothing but a wedding photograph that hung on the wall in the other room as the only decoration above the two narrow unaired beds which still stand there
as in those far-off days of bliss; nothing has remained but hatred,
and yet that hatred, too, was a marvel of creation, earliest and
malevolent heat lightning of the human spirit, yearning even in
that earliest coarseness for a redeemer, though he merely be one
who will shoot all game wardens.

"Here's the medicine, Mother Mittis, and also some sugar . . ."

Of course, she had noticed the sugar on the table long before.

But now she quickly dried a few tears because this was the proper thing to do and was meant to express gratitude.

"Now make sure that you take the medicine and also the tea . . ."

"Yes."

"And where's Marie?"

She pointed to the door.

"Well, maybe I'll meet her . . . and may God be with you, folks."

I wouldn't have minded seeing Marie, so as to impress on her the need for the medicine. But it didn't matter that much. The sugar was more important than the medicine in any case.

The path to the Mountain Chapel joins the road at the head of the pass. But I don't have to go all the way there; instead I climb straight up the stony grass slope to the right of the road, then a short distance through a fir wood where I have to camber my feet sideways so as not to slide on the ground slithery with needles, and then I'm already on the path which from here runs almost level along the rock faces of the Kuppron and on to the Pit of the Dwarfs and the Mountain Chapel as a continuation of the miners' path, which, much older than the road, formed the only connection with the pass in prehistoric times.

It was about six o'clock and the woods had become mild. When I came out on the alpine meadow, the Kuppron walls stretched in their full length to my left; they, too, were already mild and gray and only their uppermost ridge was still bathed in sunshine. A few haystacks are scattered on the meadow, which smells vesperally of the stilled woods and of herbage, and very gently slopes upward into a sparse stand of pines. One could hear the cowbells from the pastures near the peaks, and in the lowering skies, from which the diurnal cover had already been stripped, a solitary bird of prey floated soundlessly.

Now the noises of the mill in the woods below were all the more audible, the slow ticking of its wheel and the muffled and rhythmically discontinuous screeching of the saw. Lax was sawing and presumably he was sawing mine lumber, he, a circumspect and profit-seeking man, was sawing lumber for stock, without knowing the dimensions and without even knowing whether it would ever be needed, he did so out of deeply veiled motives in his soul and it may well be that he crossed himself over his broad and fleshy chest each time he put another piece of timber in the saw. The closer I came to the junction that leads down to the Green Lake, the louder the noise became. And then it stopped.

The turnoff leading to the Green Lake is really the bed of a brook. The lake, which opens down there like a calm eye between the fir-grown lids of its shores, is fed by a number of such mountain runnels, and this particular one originates right here. Between rocks and salmonberry bushes, the little thread of water snakes down almost motionless before reaching the slope, and its source seeps out from a small marshy mead. Mullein and hemlock, marsh marigolds and bluebells are growing there in the sweetish-tart smell of moldering plants, in that cool and invigorating smell which hovers over mountain sources even under the blazing sun but nevertheless retains that sun-drenched warmth well into the evening and even into the night like the silvery echo of a reverberating and imperishable trumpet call. The water in the grassy hollows was of an extraordinary clarity, each root fiber could be made out distinctly at its bottom, there were plenty of cow pats around from the cattle grazing on the pastures and the numerous scree rocks scattered around were coated with fresh, light green moss. This is the watering place of stag and doe, and Trapp also drank at length and with relishing strokes of his tongue. The rock faces darkened, their shining slowed, and the sunlit band at their upper edge had vanished.

Yet remnants of the sun were still alive in the underbrush through which the path now leads downward in a slight incline, alive in the pale bushes full of cobwebs and the evening humming of insects, until the woods closed in again and bordered the path in brownish nocturnal shadowing; though when I stepped out again into the open, the evening was bright, stretching over the Mountain Chapel in front of me and over the entire valley, which, on the opposite side, was still filled with sun, filled also with its own sunshine from the yellow sheen of its wheat fields in which the sheaves stood in

long luminous rows. But to the left and over the Pit of the Dwarfs
hung the stony head of the snake.

On the steps of the chapel sat not only Sack but also Mathias of
the Mount.

And between their legs they held their hunting rifles.

"Well, I'll be . . ." I exclaimed at the sight of them.

They both laughed.

"So what's going on?"

"Just wait and see," said Mathias.

"Later," said Sack.

They rose. "Let's go, Doctor, high time."

We went up to the Pit of the Dwarfs, both stayed mum and
acted secretive, but they couldn't keep the laughter from showing
on their faces.

"Are you two about to go poaching, by any chance, and taking
the doctor along as an alibi?"

"Could well be."

When we arrived in front of the sealed entrance to the tunnel,
they both seemed a bit undecided and Sack scratched his head.

To the right and not far from the adit there is an outcropping
of fractured rocks that guards the walls of the Kuppron.

"Up there," said Mathias.

At its rear, the scree is quite easy to ascend and the top is like
a great pulpit. Sack was about to chin himself up on a small rock
platform when Mathias said, "Stop!" and first tapped the stone
with the crutch of his stick.

A small black snake which had been lying on the stone, still hot
from the sun, fell down. Trapp snapped at it, but the snake escaped
in a quick flitting motion.

Mathias went on cleaning the whole slab and then we pulled
ourselves up. Trapp remained lying below.

We sat here as if on a pulpit or on a treetop shooting perch from
which we had a fine view of the adit and of the woods. Sack and
Mathias placed their rifles at their feet.

"Nice and comfortable here," Sack said, and leaned back against
the overhang behind him.

"Are you finally going to tell me what the meaning of all this is?"

"We're waiting for the game," said Mathias.

I looked at Sack. Over his calm and peaceable face, which a moment before had been full of laughter, this face in which sorrow had dug two soft hollows because his love had rotted away in stinking decay, there flitted the malevolent glimmer of hatred, and the mouth that just earlier had smiled said, "And the game is Wenzel."

"Wenzel? He's coming up here?"

"Yes, to the pit."

"And you want to kill him?"

Silence.

Sack laughed but it was a mean laugh. "Would be best."

"No," said Mathias. "But he shall not touch the tunnel."

"Is he coming alone?"

"Hardly. He has his lads."

"His honor guard," I said.

They laughed again because they liked the expression.

"The worst are the two Laxes," said Sack, "the father and son both."

"I thought it was Krimuss."

"Krimuss isn't so bad, he's just an old skinflint, he's only after money and doesn't want to die, so that no one can inherit it after him . . ."

"And Lax?"

"He's the real driving force behind it . . . and he's the one pushing the municipality to take up the mining rights."

"But for that you have to apply to the Bureau of Mines and God knows what else . . . And most of all, you need money . . . Lax wasn't born yesterday and knows all that, and that's why I simply can't believe in this whole business."

"Lax doesn't give a damn about all that."

"So what does he want?"

"More, more, more . . . gobble, gobble, gobble . . . maybe he wants to gobble up Krimuss and this may be his opportunity to do so . . . The one who really deserves to be shot is Lax."

Again there was a mean gleam in Sack's face.

"Well, Sack, but this afternoon you two had quite a pleasant conversation."

"He only came because he wants to get me to come around. He's been making the rounds to worm himself into everyone's favor."

It was getting dark.

I asked, "Have you heard anything about poaching being no longer prohibited?"

"I guess that also came from Lax, the younger one," said Mathias, who up to now had sat silent.

"Well, Sack," I said, "wouldn't that be something if suddenly the game laws were to be changed? Then even Lax might be good for something."

But Sack exclaimed wildly, "Even if Lax, for once in his life, were to do some good, I would say no to it." But then he had to laugh at his own impetuosity. "Never say yes to a scoundrel."

"Oh my, Sack, you almost frightened me, too, this time."

"And what's more, Marius is behind everything," he added.

"So he, too, is one of the bad ones . . . ?"

"Worse," said Mathias. "He may not be bad yet but he's about to turn bad."

The evening breeze drifted over us and we fell silent. Mathias and Sack probed the slowly darkening woods with their sharp hunter's eyes.

"Now they're coming," said Mathias.

I heard nothing, but a low growl came from Trapp.

"Quiet, Trapp!"

It took a few more minutes before I, too, heard singing and the cadenced marching of many feet in the woods.

And then they appeared in the clearing.

In front, the midget Wenzel as general, and behind him, his troop in file, by twos; I counted fourteen lads.

They sang a strange marching song which I was to hear often later:

We are men and no mere boys
Our soil no one destroys
Agents and tradesmen we despise
Our earth they bastardize
We hold the future in our hands
Bravely defend our fathers' lands
Chaste, loyal, proud and pure
Day and night we shall endure!

"Halt!" ordered General Wenzel.

"Rear rank, front!"

Every other rank stepped forward, so that they now stood in three rows of four; the two last men in the rear, somewhat in the position of subalterns, were Peter Sabest and the smith's apprentice, Ludwig.

"First and third row, fall out in square!"

The first row wheeled to the left, the third row to the right. They now formed a square horseshoe, on the open side of which stood Wenzel as the commanding general.

"Men in the rear, step front!"

Peter and Ludwig took three steps forward.

I'm an old soldier; the drill had been clockwork perfect. Sack nudged me with his elbow to share his amusement.

"Close ranks . . . 'Ten-shun!"

They followed orders and rigidly stood at attention.

"At ease!"

The right feet moved forward; all stood at ease as instructed. It was obvious that this wasn't the first time they had gone through these motions. They had been drilled often.

Wenzel paused artfully. A whiff of the harvested fields wafted toward us over the darkening tops of the trees and the last twitter of a bird could be heard in the woods.

Then Wenzel began:

"Comrades, I know you can keep discipline even if one or the other among you may have a girl lying now somewhere in the hay who without her lover is somewhat at a loss what to do with herself . . ."

Laughter. He knew how to grab his men.

"Quiet."

The laughter died down.

". . . And I am convinced that you will continue to keep discipline. Never forget that you have sworn an oath, a holy, voluntary oath, and that whoever breaks an oath is a dirty swine, a swine that deserves to be stuck dead. Unfortunately, one can't make sausages out of such a swine . . ."

More laughter. I was curious to hear what would follow. Caesar exhorting his soldiers.

"The time for deeds is drawing near. The day of retribution. The day of revenge. And then woe to our enemies. Of course, if you are cowardly swine it would be better if you run home to Mama right now. All those types are released from their oath forthwith. It is easier to whore around than to do one's duty. If one of you prefers to go whoring, he better say so right away. We'll let him go without any regret whatever."

Dramatic pause.

"Good. No one has come forward. I regret that Marius isn't here. He would have been pleased with you."

Then Wenzel ordered: "'Ten-shun!"

And it was done.

"Left and right wing, fan out and post guards!"

The two wings of the horseshoe ran in opposite directions and distributed themselves as watchers around the clearing.

"Center wing, tools out!"

It was only then that I noticed that the center wing, which had remained in place, carried backpacks to which were strapped shovels, picks, and other tools. These were now taken out, and Wenzel, who had removed his jacket, grabbed one of the pickaxes.

He ordered: "Jackets off. Start work."

With resolute steps the dwarf marched toward the Pit of the Dwarfs. In front of the sealed entrance he took a big swing and sunk the pickax with all his might into a crack in the wall. There was a crunching crash and one could hear the dribbling of mortar and sand, and then the crash reverberated in a faint echo.

He hit the wall once more.

But then Mathias of the Mount roared, "Leave the mountain alone!"

Wenzel froze in his movement; the guards who had secured the edges of the clearing came scurrying down and peered in our direction but were unable to see us. There was a moment of silence. Then Wenzel gave a laugh and shouted, "Shut up, up there!"

And he struck the wall a third time.

No sooner had that happened than a shot detonated deafeningly at my side, reverberating in a long drumroll. It had been Sack and from the direction of the rifle I could see that he had shot into the air.

"Treachery!" one of them called down below. "We've been betrayed."

"Treachery," the others repeated. A terrible racket broke out. And already there was the gleam of knives. Sack and Mathias next to me snorted with pleasure.

"Quiet, damnit, quiet!" screamed Wenzel. "Discipline!"

But discipline was now in a bad way and it was some time before a semblance of quiet was restored.

"Who are you up there?"

I thought it appropriate to answer myself. "The doctor."

Wenzel immediately became obsequious. "Good evening, Doctor. Is it you who are shooting?"

"Not I but the others."

"There could be an accident," said Wenzel reproachfully.

"Wenzel," I said, "this time your jokes won't be of much help, this time it's serious."

He reflected a moment and then asked, "How many are you up there, Doctor?"

"Enough to pick you all off one after the other," Sack replied in my stead.

"That's Sack," was heard from some of the lads.

"Yes, it's Sack," Sack confirmed, and pointed to himself, although no one down there could see him.

"Doctor, sir," said Wenzel, "couldn't you come down for a moment?"

"I don't think we have much to say to each other . . ."

"But, Doctor, it really would be important . . ."

"Better get the hell out of here, you and your whole herd of piglets," shouts Mathias of the Mount.

"Pig yourself, you shitty bastard," one of the lads shouts back. "Come on down if you dare."

Mathias laughs thunderously. "If I dare? Why, I'll put you all in my pocket, along with your pocketknives, you little snotnoses . . . And I tell you, off with you from the mountain or I'll chase you all the way back down to your village."

Wenzel intervenes. "Mathias, you talk as if you own the mountain . . . The mountain belongs to the municipality, the whole municipality, and we work for the municipality."

Mathias gets up, leans the rifle against the rock, and makes ready to climb down.

So I say, "Let me talk to them."

"But I don't want to talk, Doctor. They'll get something else to hear from me." He laughs, but his red beard bristles and his hand is around the haft of his hunting knife, which sits in a scabbard along the seam of his leather shorts.

"No, Mathias, that's not necessary. Trapp can handle this by himself . . . What are you thinking of?"

He groans but stays put.

I call out, "Wenzel, what is it you want to tell me?"

"Please, sir, Doctor, may I request a more confidential interview? . . . It's important."

I glide down from our rocky pulpit and almost immediately I hear the uncertain steps of Wenzel looking for a way up the scree. I give him some light with my flashlight.

"So what is it you want?"

He looks up at me guilelessly. "Doctor, such a great big fuss over a little military exercise . . . What have we done to the mountain, after all?"

"Don't try to play dumb, Wenzel . . . You know exactly what this is all about."

He immediately shifted his tactics and said respectfully, "Yes, Doctor."

"So then . . . ?"

"Doctor, sir, I request an honorable withdrawal."

"And what kind of a joke is that supposed to be?"

"No joke, Doctor, but we cannot simply decamp after what has happened, the lads wouldn't stand for that . . ."

"It'll only be a good lesson for them."

"If you, Doctor, were to leave with us, for instance, that would greatly alleviate the whole situation."

"Certainly not. I leave with Sack and Gisson."

He looked up at me with a despairing smile. "One shouldn't humble men needlessly and embitter them, Doctor. One should not sow hatred . . ."

"Oh yes? And how does this fit in with what you're doing to Wetchy? A little humiliation for your war games is very much in order."

"Yes, but the lads will hate you for it, you and Sack and Gisson," and he added with great warmth and sincerity, "And that I really would like to avoid."

"We'll manage to bear their hatred."

The dwarf made himself even smaller. "Today you won but . . ."

"Yes? Come, out with it, Wenzel! When and how is Marius thinking of winning?"

"But, Doctor, Marius? . . . Whatever are you thinking of?"

"Don't try to tell me that all this military theater isn't of his making."

With his peculiar mixture of candor and slyness he said, "With Marius it's a funny thing . . . Somehow one is in his grasp, yes . . . but he never does anything himself, he's only full of ideas and then nothing happens . . . so one has to take matters into one's own hands."

"You're a wily scoundrel, Wenzel, that you are."

"Yes, Doctor, that I may be . . . but Marius is a good man and you mustn't harm him . . ."

"And you will now kindly march off with your gang . . ."

"If you so order, Doctor, but as to Marius, I mean it in all seriousness . . ." He saluted again with military precision and departed.

But after a few steps he turned around once more. "And what do you think of my drill practice, Doctor? Isn't it snappy? I bet you liked that yourself." And then he disappeared for good in the darkness.

I returned to our post.

From below Wenzel's voice could be heard: "Form ranks . . . 'Ten-shun! . . . On special request of the doctor, today's exercise is being called off . . . File in twos."

"Wenzel," called down Sack, "are you really marching off?"

"Yes."

"I better tell you something . . . We're not going to stay up here either, but if any of you should try to ambush us on the way home, there'll be some shooting . . ."

"I vouch for my men," said Wenzel grandly. "We're soldiers."

"All right," I said, "fine with us."

" 'Ten-shun! . . . March! One, two, hup, hup . . ." sounded from below. And then they all marched off.

Sack and Mathias were disappointed. It had all been too simple and peaceful for their taste. "They should have gotten a few behind the ears, so they'd have to crawl home on all fours," said Mathias in his slow miner's speech.

"I'm afraid there'll be plenty of opportunity for that in days to come," I said.

When we reached the miners' path, we heard the troop below singing their marching song, and Mathias, who was still intent on the same thought, repeated, "A few good ones behind the ears, then there would have been peace once and for all."

"Not so long as Marius is in the village," said Sack.

The woods were pitch-dark. Here and there a firefly glowed. Eight o'clock rang from the village church. The days were becoming shorter. The stars of the August sky blinked through the tree canopy, and the deeper we penetrated into the woods, the darker the smell of the air became, the denser were the woods filled with the crops of the fields. And in that dark communality which rises from the harvested earth and extinguishes the individuality of man, so that he is capable only of either love or hatred, barely aware whether he clasps his fellow creature in love or hate, we three, walking through the dark woods, hated Marius and Lax, but also Wenzel and his whole gang. And we lit our pipes as if to dull all that hatred with our smoke.

At the first fields of the Upper Village, Sack took his leave to take the shortcut to his house, while I went on with Mathias to Mother Gisson.

We found Irmgard and Agatha at her place, and the two girls were just about to leave when we arrived.

"You're taking pleasure strolls in the midst of the harvest?"

"I asked for the girls to come up and see me," replied Mother Gisson in Irgmard's stead.

"After the harvest I move up here for good," said Irmgard.

And Agatha added with a glance at Mother Gisson, "Irmgard's lucky."

"You're luckier still," said Mother Gisson. "You're having your child."

The kitchen windows were open. Outside, evening and night exchanged their last tremulous farewell and in the street some voices could be heard—voices of those who have ended another day of their lives and now were soon to bed down, voices of women and children, and sometimes the bass of a man.

But Agatha sits down once more and laughs. "I'll wait for it right here, Mother Gisson . . . Why don't you keep me, too?"

"Throw them out, Mathias," said Mother Gisson.

And Irmgard, leaning against the doorjamb, said, "Let him try . . ."

"You two puppies I'll take by the scruff of the neck and throw you all the way down to the Lower Ones," comes the good-humored reply out of Mathias's beard, and so he grabs the two girls by the neck and they let themselves be pushed as far as the door, but there they resist being thrown out into the night, which is like a basket lined with black velvet. But their struggle is to no avail, they are expelled, and as if this had brought all the folds of the night into disarray, a swarm of gnats and moths streams through the open door into the room and dances around the light bulb.

"Good night," comes out of the soft warmth of the darkness, and then farther away and softer yet: "Good night, Mother."

Then Mathias is back with us and says, "Yes, Irmgard belongs up here . . ." And after a while he adds, "All the children should be taken from Miland as long as he keeps Marius."

Bare of secrets and hard is the kitchen in the electric light of the bulb, and Mother Gisson says, "Only Irmgard is at risk."

And then she goes on: "The danger is in her, not in Marius . . . If she were like Agatha, there would be no danger . . ."

"And Peter?" I venture.

"That was love," she said, and after a short pause she continues: "Hatred played no part in it . . ."

"Yes," said Mathias, "hatred . . ."

And then we told her what had happened at the Pit of the Dwarfs.

Mathias concluded his tale: "And now that hate has broken out betwen us and those down there, it might have been better if we had shot Wenzel on the spot . . ."

"No," said Mother Gisson, "hatred goes against knowledge."

"It might have been better if you had taken in Marius yourself when he begged you," I said.

She shook her head. "He would have left of his own accord soon enough . . ."

"But he did ask you for the knowledge."

"He didn't want it really, he couldn't want it, for he is one who came from knowledge but who has lost it, and such a one never can find his way back to knowledge, even were he to want to . . . but he cannot really want it."

And then she said, "He is a wanderer."

"Aren't we all, Mother?"

"That's what you think, Doctor, because you're a man . . . Only men wander . . . Women stay put and they are in knowledge . . ."

"That's bitter wisdom, Mother, for we, too, want that knowledge."

"Be content with what you have."

"No, that's just what we're not content with."

"Doctor," she said almost solemnly, "do you think there's a man who can do more than want to know? It is that wanting that is his knowledge! And that is why it can grow . . . It's different with us womenfolk. We have our knowledge; it can be small, it can be large, it even can become more beautiful, but it cannot grow . . . We cannot multiply that knowledge, we can only hold on to it, we have to hold on to it. That is our love . . . but your love, and that's what we love you for, we stupid women, is your need for ever greater knowledge."

"And Marius?"

"He believes he knows . . . he believes it because he has the gift of the rod and because he can feel it if someone else's shoulder aches . . . He sits on his knowledge like a woman . . . and that's why he can't ever want to know, that's why he is without love . . . A spellbinder he is, and nothing else."

"Yes."

"A woman who wants to go beyond her own knowledge, she is without love and she is in hatred, and a man who rests on his knowledge, he, too, is in hatred."

"But, Mother Gisson, one who wanders does not rest."

"Wandering," she said, "wandering, yes . . . they like to wander, the spellbinders, the gypsies . . . They think that by wandering they can exorcise their hatred with their feet . . . for if they don't move, if they don't wander, they would become aware of their lack of knowledge . . . The one who hates is a poor devil and he always needs a devil whom he can hate . . ."

"But he calls it justice."

She looked at me. "But that is . . ." And she opened her empty hands and spread her fingers, their nails already somewhat bluish and discolored by old age, and it was as if she let naked nothingness run through those fingers and away into nothingness. "That's what it is," she concluded, and let her hands sink into her lap.

Where is that knowledge which we seek and which Marius no longer sought? Where is that unreachable mystery? And dimly I apprehended that it was contained in the simple and sober knowledge of the human heart and that such knowledge encompasses all that is and all that ever will be: for all that happens, all that has happened, and all that ever will happen is mirror of the human heart, and the one who knows about the heart also knows about the primeval old and the primordially new, he is no mere spellbinder but sage and seer whose simple everyday utterance is of such power that at every moment it can enfold all of reality. This is what I apprehended as I looked at the face of that old woman who sat across from me smiling.

"And yet you say, Mother, that his time has come."

"Yes," she said, "because there is no longer any outlet for the hatred, so they have to follow the one who hates and promises them that knowledge which he lacks."

"The gold," I said.

"Only the Lower Ones," said Mathias.

"He who casts a spell bewitches," said Mother Gisson, "he who bewitches casts a spell."

"Miland, too, is from the Lower Village," I said, "and he, too, has fallen under that spell although he wants the knowledge and wants no part of the gold."

"Miland," said Mother Gisson, "Miland didn't get the love he needed and now he seeks a brother and is blind to the hatred."

"And Irmgard?"

Mother Gisson sighed. "She loves him truly and she would have been the right one for him, but he is her father . . ."

I said, "Maybe she loves Marius also. The finest woman can fall in love with a scoundrel if he is a spellbinder . . ."

That made Mother Gisson laugh again. "But not if he's not a man . . . And I already told you that he's no man . . ."

"Really? Does it go that far? He's nothing, there's nothing there?"

"Of course it goes that far with his pride, with his woman's pride . . . Any girl could get into bed with that one without fear . . ."

"Or none at all," I said.

"Sure, or none at all . . . That's why he is so cruel in his hatred, more cruel than any woman."

Man's prerogative is the search for the ultimate immersion of his own self, and for him love means the assumption of the fate of the loved one, love for him means the apperception of what is ultimately hidden, it means the assumption in their totality of an ungraspable future and of a past sunk in oblivion, both carried deep in himself as his forgotten past and his darkly unknown future, a hiddenness unreachable for himself and yet one which every human being yearns to reveal so as to partake of love, laying open the innermost core of his own self, that which is sunk in his deepest shaft, laying it open lovingly and ready to be loved; but while love thus attempts to descry and offer its innermost core, hatred, on the other hand, cares not for anything hidden, it cares not for the essential core, nor for any past or any future, it cares not for any concealments of fate, but hates that which is, the apparent surface and the visibly real, and while love ceaselessly strives toward that which lies at the hiddenmost center, hatred only perceives the topmost surface and perceives it so exclusively that the devil of hatred, despite all his terror-inspiring cruelty, never is entirely free of ridicule and of a somewhat dilettantish aspect. The one who hates is a man holding a magnifying glass, and when he hates someone, he knows precisely that person's surface, from the soles of his feet all the way up to each hair on the hated head. Were one merely to seek information, one should inquire of the one who hates, but if one wishes to know what truly is, one better ask the one who loves.

And Mathias said, "He hates the mountain even though he climbs all over it with his rod trying to divine its workings."

And Mother Gisson said, "Were he a man, I would fear less for Irmgard . . . any girl can handle a true man . . . but his strength is in nothingness . . ."

"But, Mother," I said, "you are stronger than nothingness."

She said, "My fear is greater than his."

"Yes, Mother, but your fear is for Irmgard and not for yourself."

"Fear is fear," she said.

And I said, "One who merely acts as the world's redeemer but in truth is nothing cannot touch you."

But she said, "The true redeemer always sends the false prophets ahead of his coming, so that they may make room for his advent . . . First hatred must come with its fear before love can make itself manifest."

"Dear God in heaven, Mother, now even you start talking of redeemers . . . Let the people behave decently, then they wouldn't need any redeemers and they would find their love already in themselves . . . And all they'd need for that is to listen to you for a change."

She smiled in calm confidence. "To redeem the world . . . yes, that's what it all comes down to . . . When the men seek the knowledge and when the women have their knowledge and safeguard it, either one or the other, both boil down to the knowledge of the good dying, Doctor . . . And when there comes a man who goes toward knowledge and wants it so much that he can show it and can die for it . . . then it is both knowledge and love at the same time . . . The women are merely in the here and now, Marius is only in the here and now, and where the men are exactly they themselves usually don't know . . . Isn't that right, Doctor?"

"True, we don't know it ourselves."

"But if one should come who is here and in the beyond at the same time, both in his life and in his death, a human being who is both"—she nodded to me—"well then, Doctor, then there could well be something like redemption . . . Isn't it so?"

"Yes, that's all well and good, Mother, but that's still no reason why you should yield to Marius."

She still smiled. "We yield when the time has come, and when the time is ripe, then what happens is also good . . . It merely has to ripen." And through her benign smile she asked, "Don't you want a little schnapps, Doctor?" And it may be that she no longer wanted to speak of Marius and of her fear.

"Yes," I said, "of course I'd like a schnapps, but irrespective of that you must not yield to Marius . . . And I must get home, for Caroline is waiting for me with dinner."

So I had my schnapps and went home, with something of a bad conscience but also with a hearty appetite, for it was past nine. The valley was to my right, resting from its labors, resting in the fruit of its soil, resting in a world that already was turning itself in before folding up in sleep, and when one took a deep breath one almost could imagine smelling the ripening of the apples down there in the orchards. Did I myself walk toward knowledge? When after dinner I went to my study to look through the issues of medical journals I had not yet read, I felt for a moment that instead I had fled from that knowledge which had been allotted to me. Had it not also been scorn for medical research, scorn for the small, quiet successes of laboratory work, scorn for what is called scientific progress that had contributed to my fleeing the city? Had I not merely been presumptuous and impatient? Presumptuous because I deemed myself entitled to abandon all that, trusting that what counted more was the confidence and the inner determination of the physician at the bed of the patient, regardless of whether he prescribed this or that medicine or, perhaps best, none at all? Impatient because I did not truly strive to reach love through knowledge but instead had been hoping that in the immediate exercise of love, a kind of dutiful love that moves from sickbed to sickbed and is not a hatred merely because hatred is excluded from the medical profession, hoping that in such professional love ultimate knowledge would come to me somehow by itself? Was it not so in truth? Wasn't I, too, merely a small would-be redeemer, content with his little store of magic? Had I not failed, I, too, to make good use of the freedom granted me to decide about my own life? Toward what knowledge could I still strive? But as I thus sat under the lamp surrounded by swarms of insects, reading and yet hardly reading anymore, deliberating instead whether I should look in at Wetchy's and see about his child who refused to get well, I all at once heard the voice of the here and now: Endure, carry on for this one harvest, meager though it be, tend the fields once more, be a faithful servant, start again and carry on, for you stand ever anew at the beginning of infinity, of knowledge, and of love.

10 August drew to its close. The harvest had been brought in and Irmgard was with her grandmother up at the Mountain Manse. She was not needed below for the fruit harvest still to come. The weather had held throughout, hot days and great clear nights full of shooting stars. Some rain wouldn't hurt now but the weather remained fine.

I sat with Sack in my garden as evening was coming on. His boys had been visiting with Rosa and he had come to fetch them after returning from his work in the woods.

Rosa sat on the lawn with Albert, the oldest of the Sack boys, and wound grass braids, not paying much attention to the two younger ones, much to the sorrow of the youngest, who followed her everywhere.

Sack was once more on his favorite subject. "You should have let us shoot, Doctor."

"But, Sack, this whole comedy will peter out into nothing at all . . ."

He put on his most knowing face. "Doctor, if one lifts an ax against you, you won't hold still either . . ." And to illustrate his point, he raised his lumberjack ax, which had been leaning next to him.

"Yes, Sack, but the ax of Wenzel won't shoot any more than the one you hold in your hand . . ."

"You never can tell . . . and the one who hits first wins . . . and a rotten apple like that has to be got out of the way for good."

He had stood up, not only to emphasize his words but in a fit of wild rage, even though it made him laugh at himself the next instant.

"Those two scoundrels have already stirred up the whole Lower Village."

"So you think Marius is rotten, too?"

"He's gone bad and he's getting worse."

I recalled that Mother Gisson had said something like that as well. But I merely shrugged and said, "Well, a crackpot has no trouble finding other fools like him . . ."

"Mother Gisson," he said, and it was strange that he, too, should think of her just then, "Mother Gisson did the right thing in taking in Irmgard."

"Of course."

Sack is in one of his dramatic moods and walks back and forth swinging his ax. "Mother Gisson knows what she's doing. Irmgard belongs up here with us."

And then he ordered, "Home, boys!"

Frightened by the man swinging an ax and by his loud bellowing, Rosa began to bawl. Immediately Sack put down his ax, picked up the crying child, and kissed the tip of her nose, and when this failed to have any effect, he crouched on all fours and took her on his back. Thus they made the round of the lawn, after which he carefully reared up and let his rider sprawl on the grass. As I had fully expected, Rosa immediately requested, "Again, please," and climbed up on his back. Heroically, Sack had to begin all over again. In the end, I liberated him from his charge and brought Rosa back to her grass braids.

"She's not a pretty child," he said as he joined me, "but a child is a child nevertheless."

At that moment Wetchy appeared. Catching sight of Rosa, his eyes filled with alarm. "Girlie, come here right away, the grass is moist, you're going to catch cold . . ." But then he fell silent, appalled at having interfered with my medical authority, and he stuttered, "Don't you think so too, Doctor? . . . It's getting cool . . . quite cool, in fact."

"No, Wetchy, I don't think so at all."

"Oh . . ." And he was both disappointed and guilt-ridden.

"Well, don't feel bad, Wetchy . . . How is the little one?"

"If you could please come and see for yourself, Doctor . . ."

"Something wrong?" I was a bit worried, for the little boy simply wouldn't get well; now he had trouble with his kidneys. And that was another reason why I still kept the girl. The poor little woman over there hardly knew whether she was coming or going, and with the ready adaptability of those used to bad luck, she and her husband hardly noticed the absence of their daughter anymore.

"The fever is up again . . ."

"Well, in the evening . . . but I'll be glad to come have a look."

Sack sympathized, "Yes, the children."

So I said, "Don't you complain, Sack. No doctor is going to get rich on your little scamps . . . They take after you . . ."

"There isn't much in me worth taking after." Sack laughed.

"Splendid sons, splendid sons," Wetchy complimented.

"Shut up, Wetchy," Sack said, and acknowledged that bit of pomposity by giving Wetchy a resounding whack on the shoulder— somewhat to my own satisfaction, I confess.

"Bad man," was heard from Rosa, to everybody's surprise. The presence of her father had emboldened her and, taking his part, she pointed an accusing dirty finger at Sack.

"Will you be quiet, girlie," Wetchy fearfully rebuked the child. "That's a nice man, a velly nicey man."

"Yes," said Sack soothingly, "I velly nicey man."

"Don't be too sure, Sack. I bet poor Wetchy's shoulder is still burning."

"Yes," agreed Wetchy, encouraged by my words to speak out also, and rubbing his shoulder but nevertheless sporting a forgiving smile, he said, "Everybody mistreats me . . . even you, Mr. Sack."

Sack became serious. "Don't let them get away with it . . . Show them your teeth and then you'll have peace once and for all."

"What good will that do?" lamented Wetchy. "What good will that do if they throw me out of my house?"

"We won't let that happen," declared Sack. "After all, we're also part of the municipality . . ."

"But Mr. Wenzel . . ."

"Wenzel shit . . . I've heard enough of Wenzel," said Sack roughly.

"What about Wenzel?" I asked.

The little agent swallows before speaking with some difficulty. "He says . . . he says there will be another earthquake and that the whole village will be destroyed if I'm not evicted."

"That's too stupid," I declared. "Let's go, Wetchy, we'd better look after your patient."

I let him walk ahead, for Sack held me back by my sleeve.

It had become dark and a lamp is lit behind the window of the kitchen; a yellow rectangle is cast on the gravel and a shadow appears at the window. It is Caroline leaning out and calling, "Rosa!"

"There you are," says Sack. "That's not Wenzel's brainchild . . . It's Marius's idea . . . but he'd better watch out or he'll be the first on whom the mountain will take revenge."

He said it so seriously that I could not help feeling a weird sense of apprehension, even though the mixture of municipal politicking and mountain magic seemed laughable enough to me.

"Well," I said, "let's keep the mountain out of it."

Sack laughed again. "All right, Doctor."

Darkness was now total. The grasses and leaves moved in a dark cool breeze, became still, and then swayed again. We both listened. And then Sack left with his boys and I went over to Wetchy.

He was waiting for me at the entrance.

It was a real mess. The kidney inflammation apparently had subsided, but now the child put his hand to his ear and his head and, indeed, there was an unmistakable irritation in one of the eardrums. Wasn't Wenzel right, that something like this would be better off not born? I was almost angry with worry, angry in my eagerness to get the child well at all costs. At least, everything that could be done so far had been done, but with someone pursued by bad luck like Wetchy, one had to expect the worst. For the time being, though, nothing could be decided and this could still go on for hours and even days; all one could do was to keep the child warm and try somehow to lower the fever. The little boy was apathetic, only whimpering from time to time. I would have to have a look at him later on that night. "I'll bring you some more medicine," I said, and returned home.

I took my time. Sitting in the garden, I wondered whether I shouldn't order the ambulance first thing in the morning. A three-hour drive to get the patient to the county hospital; a tympanoscopy I could perform myself if need be, although the need for a trepanation could not be ruled out. The woods were quiet; some fireflies glowed here and there on bushes, water was being poured into a pail in Wetchy's house, then one of its windows was opened, the thin trembling of glass could be heard and then the hinging of the window hooks. A shooting star fell and disappeared behind the firs. Then I got up, emptied my pipe, and went over. It must have been about ten o'clock.

The light in the sickroom was shaded, the air smelled sour. I drew up a chair next to the bed and waited. Mrs. Wetchy sat near the window in obvious exhaustion and watched me with fearfully imploring eyes. Wetchy had gone to sleep; he had kept watch the night before and they spelled each other.

"Don't you want to rest while I'm here?"

"Oh no," came the sorrowful reply.

Thus we sat and I felt old beyond my years. It would have made better sense to leave instead of giving the impression by my continued presence that things might be in worse shape than they already were, but I was restrained by a strange feeling that by merely staying at my post I would be able to compel a turn for the better; somehow it seemed to me that I, an aging and already stoutish man, could help this child onward to recovery by my sheer will, that I could help this patient reach a crisis from which he would emerge victorious, and it was not kindness, nor was it love, which kept me there and made me perform these nursing duties, nor was it medical ambition, but rather a kind of fighting spirit, albeit a slightly sleepy one, that was persevering, for the automatism of weariness and somnolence to which I ultimately succumbed not only dissolved some of my consciousness but also unleashed new energies and invested them with their own trance-like powers, powers beyond our reach during our normal everyday functioning.

It was about four o'clock in the morning when I heard Trapp bark over at my house. And in my diminished state of consciousness it seemed to me that this was merely a friendly reminder to go to bed at long last. He was right, after all. How much longer I would have to wait for the decisive crisis to set in with the boy could not be foreseen; what I was able to do I had done, and I couldn't very well go on sitting here forever. I got up.

Mrs. Wetchy, who had observed me incessantly, asked, "Is he better?"

"I hope so, dear lady. As you can see, he's sleeping. Don't wake him."

And I left.

It was still dark and the woods stood in nocturnal rigidity. But as I stepped out of the house, two female figures came toward me. That was what had alerted Trapp. I switched on my flashlight. It was Mother Gisson and Irmgard. And I immediately realized that they were going herb gathering.

"Good morning, Mother. On your way for my next year's schnapps, I see . . . Why, that's real nice of you."

"Yes," she said merrily. "Now Irmgard has to learn to make it . . . for when I'm no longer around."

"Nonsense, Mother."

"Don't argue with me in the middle of the night . . . And what are you doing here at this hour? Is the boy in bad shape?"

"He's not in the best of shape . . . and you really should have a look at him yourself . . ."

She made a rather comically repelled face, one I had not seen on her before. "I'm not too fond of those people really . . ." But then she added, "However, a child is still a child."

In view of the stark stupidity graven and frozen on most adult faces, children indeed are infinitely more bearable, even when they are ugly.

"Yes," I said, "have a look at him, Mother . . . And what are you carrying there to the mountain?" I pointed to a rather heavy bundle that Irmgard was holding in her hand.

Mother Gisson grabbed a handful from the bundle and held it out for me to see.

I directed the beam of the flashlight on it. It was grain, grain glistening golden brown and almost as if moist in the electric light.

"New grain," I said, without comprehending what meaning it could have.

"When the mountain gives us its herbs, it also should get something in return . . . This time Irmgard is going to make the offering."

"I see."

"She was the Mountain Bride, after all."

"Is that what the Mountain Bride always does?"

"If she goes looking for herbs, of course."

"And the mountain accepts the grain?"

"Wherever you find an herb, you have to put down a few grains, that's the way it has to be done . . . and you've got to give some also to the water . . . Man must show his thankfulness." And she laughed gently.

"And that's where my schnapps comes from?"

"Yes, your schnapps, too."

"Then, good luck, Mother Gisson. Good luck, Irmgard."

They continued on their way and I went to bed.

Around eight o'clock, just after I had gotten up, the telephone rang. Would I let Wetchy know that he was to come down to the village? Something had gone wrong with the engine of the thresher. Wetchy is also the representative of the manufacturer of the thresher.

I sent Caroline over and asked her to inquire about the condition of the boy.

Wetchy appeared after a few minutes.

"How's the boy?"

"He's sleeping, Doctor . . . Is that good?"

"I think so, yes."

"So I can go without worrying . . . or should I merely telephone?"

"No, you can go without worrying."

"Now they're calling me from down there," he declared in an offended tone. "Now I'll again be 'Mr. Wetchy' to them, but at other times they shout after me quite openly, 'Wireless Wretchy' . . . and right out on the street, too . . ."

"Pay no attention to it, Wetchy . . ."

"Maybe I should merely . . ."

"No, get going . . ."

He disappeared.

It was strange that I, too, couldn't quite stomach this worthy and diligent little man. It may have had something to do with the variousness of his businesses: equipment representative, insurance agent, salesman of wireless sets; God knows what else he did to make ends meet, a multiplicity of professions and of bustling deal-ering which didn't add up to any real whole, to any true profession which would be under the dictate of a divinely ordered rhythm. To be sure, my own work, too, is circumstantial and leads me to this or that sickbed, it consists at times of dental work, at times of obstetrics, and occasionally of surgery, as is the norm with any country doctor, and it lacks the tidal constancy regulating the life of the earth and of the peasants, and yet it is endowed with the background of that larger rhythm which is that of birth and death, it is to that rhythm to which I am subjected, even if I merely fill a tooth, and it is from that rhythm that I derive the dignity of my life, so that it may not be wasted senselessly on this earth.

Besides, it was a day filled with joyous confidence—either be-cause Mother Gisson was scattering her grains on the mountain or because my night watch seemed to have had some success. Like someone who expects something pleasant to happen, I took my time, and the morning was half gone before I went to look at the child. And, indeed, his aspect had greatly improved. The child lay in bed, his eyes clear, he had no fever and was without pain. And because man is made that way, I now noticed the breeze coming in through the open window, a fresh friendly breeze in which there was already a hint of autumn.

"Great," I said, "great, my dear woman."

She started to cry. After a sleepless night crying comes easy; both pleasant and unpleasant occurrences go straight to the eyes and one has to blow one's nose.

As I left the house, Wetchy was just coming back from the village.

I called to him, "The boy is much better."

He stopped and piously folded his hands. "Dear, dear God in heaven and all His saints, dear God, I thank Thee."

I was touched. "Well, Wetchy—I'm glad."

But he was suddenly alarmed at having given precedence to God and all His saints over me in expressing his thanks. "No offense meant, Doctor . . . I'm so grateful to you, so grateful . . ." And we shook hands.

"So what happened down there?"

He was still too dazed to give me a coherent account of the matter. Yes, during the night someone had broken into the shed that housed the thresher and some rascal had placed a metal strip between the contacts of the engine. And when they had started the engine in the morning, there had been the mess that was to be expected: a short circuit and all the coils burned through.

"That's big trouble . . . I guess now they'll have to thresh by hand?"

"No, no . . . That's why they called me . . . I'm the agent for Clayton . . ."

"What? You can repair engines? . . . I wouldn't have credited you with that."

"No, that I can't . . . I'm only the agent . . . But I wired them, a detailed telegram, the whole motor has to get new coils . . . a replacement engine has to be sent by car, it'll be here tomorrow."

"So then it wouldn't be worthwhile to thresh by hand?"

"Of course not, not at all."

"I hope you make some money out of all that."

"Oh no, I wouldn't want to make any money out of an accident."

"Is anyone under suspicion?"

Wetchy's gesture implied that any search for the perpetrator would be hopeless.

And then he explained. "No one is interested in that . . . The threshing cooperative is insured against breakdowns and the repair costs are covered by the insurance . . . and although the insurance company is supposed to bring charges, no one around here is going to help find the culprit . . . and the county police are well aware of that, too."

"Of course, that changes the matter."

"I wrote the insurance policies myself," he concluded with some pride.

"Well, then you can hardly complain."

"No," he said humbly.

"But you yourself, do you suspect anyone?"

"I don't want to have anything to do with it," he answered

fearfully. But then he rolled his watery blue eyes. "Peter Sabest stuck his tongue out at me and shouted, 'Wireless Wretchy,' right out on the street . . ."

Well, well, Peter himself!

"What do you think, Wetchy, could it have been Peter . . . ?"

"No, no, I don't think anything at all. I'd rather not know."

"And Wenzel, how did he behave?"

"Wenzel? . . . He looked on and laughed . . ."

"Well, that's to be expected," I said. "So now you better go, Wetchy, and look after your boy . . ."

He was aghast. "Dear God, how could I have forgotten!" And he ran into the house.

When I was struck by sorrow over the loss of Anna Sack and was then granted joy at the rescue of the Wetchy boy, I did not know that both that sorrow and that joy were rooted in an experience which had happened some fifteen years earlier in my life. The image of that woman, so deeply engraved in my memory as to give it an entirely new backdrop, an ineffaceable and indelible image, however much I tried to erase it, this image has become actual presence once more, not only as a mere dim background but as hard and concrete evidence within the space of memory.

It had happened in the first years after the war; I was forty-two and had returned to my post with the State Hospital, where I had been promoted to the position of deputy chief medical director and was about to receive a chair at the university on the strength of my work in biochemistry. A winter of hard work lay behind me, a winter, moreover, which had been long and gray and without sun before bursting now suddenly, almost violently, into spring. Thus it was on one of those leaf-green, clear, and luminously blue afternoons that I saw her for the first time. Carrying a light suitcase that showed signs of frequent use, she was walking from the administration building to the main pavilion of the pediatrics department, striding out with long, elastic steps, an almost unfeminine gait, purposeful and severe like the remote gaze of her eyes; I took her for one of those mothers who at that time of day usually came to visit their hospitalized children, but when, hampered by the suitcase, she had managed with some difficulty to open the pavilion's heavy door, which, in addition, was checked by an automatic closing device, I could not help but follow her with my eyes—am I not doing so still? indeed, I can still hear the soft pneumatic sigh with which that door snapped shut after her—as if she had been carrying with her, despite her inconspicuousness and her ordinary clothing, an aura of remoteness that subtly lingered in her wake and raised her above the commonplace. And I felt somehow disappointed that in that hospital garden nothing had remained but the young greenery of the burgeoning chestnuts and lilac bushes.

Naturally, this first impression soon dimmed, especially since it very soon turned out that she was a newly appointed doctor, so that our relationship promptly shifted to a professional level. When I took over the management of the hospital while the medical director went on vacation, my contact with her became closer. Her professional abilities were remarkable; knowledgeable, capable of making decisions and of an almost angry self-assurance, she, although the youngest of the assistant doctors, soon and unobtrusively had assumed authority over her whole department, and while it is true that she may have found little opposition to her rise—her two colleagues did not amount to much and the head of the department, Professor M., was too old not to have been more than glad to get home as quickly as possible after his rounds—such a success nevertheless was possible only because behind it stood a whole human being and, even more important, that rarest of persons, not merely a medical practitioner with high professional skills but a born healer of clairvoyant sureness in her diagnoses; such extraordinary intuition for all forms of afflictions predestined her to become the friend of the patient, his ally in the struggle against illness and death, superior qualifications of an order bound to impress everyone, colleagues and nurses alike, who together with the rest of the staff were at her every beck and call; but it was the children who most patently had fallen under her spell, and there one could almost speak of hypnotic magnetism, since it was enough for her to sit down on one of the cots for the little patients to become so happy and serene that one simply could not doubt their ultimate recovery. And when she walked through a ward, a long row of eyes followed her with eagerly hopeful devotion. Yet this dominion was not in any way gained by some sort of ingratiation, for she courted no one and, quite the contrary, was always quick at brusque hectoring, an angry champion of healing, particularly so with the children: the jocular playfulness with which so many pediatricians approach their young patients was quite alien to her; she examined them rather with a soberly concentrated attention, and the children instinctively approved.

She let the children call her Dr. Barbara and, by way of the nurses, that was the name by which she became known throughout the institution.

Apart from minor controversies arising out of her unbridled urge to assert herself, I got along with her very well during my tenure as chief of the hospital; she felt that I respected her knowledge and ability, and we established a healthy masculine, or rather an asexual, work relation, particularly so since this unaffected, thoughtful, and energetic colleague awoke in me no reminiscences of the woman who, a few weeks earlier, had crossed the hospital garden. Thus things stood until my last round of inspection; the chief's vacation had ended and I was about to take my own and, therefore, felt little inclination to make any decisions which I would not be able to implement or which I could not personally answer for. Nevertheless, a last-minute discussion arose between us regarding the advisability of an operation in a specific case—I myself am opposed to overly prompt interventions, such as are advocated all too often by surgeons—and finally she let my arguments convince her, even though with sullen reluctance. When this was settled, I said, "Well, Dr. Barbara, we don't have to say farewell; I hope you will have frequent occasion to call on me at the lab." "It's bound to happen, I'm sure," she replied, still sullen and smoothing out her soberly parted hair with both hands. I shall never know why at this very instant I see before me these hands in all their vividness, why I experience their femininity in so profound a way, such as I had not felt since my childhood so long ago when my mother stroked my hair for the last time, and why the sight of these hands suddenly filled me with a yearning that upset my entire life and invested it with a totally new background. Of all this I became conscious only much later, for at the time I merely said, "You are an excellent physician, Dr. Barbara, but you would be an even better mother." A deep shadow darkened her face for a moment, but then she said with a laugh, "The former falls under your competence and pleases me." And before I could answer, she was gone; but she turned once more at the door and called out, "Have a nice vacation!"

On that day in early summer the chestnuts in the hospital garden were still in full bloom, although their glory had tired somewhat and awaited the next rainstorm that would sweep it away. And when, that evening, after having packed my suitcases, I leaned out the window of my apartment above the laboratory and looked down at the trees, their pinks and whites slowly dissolving into grayish shades while the sea of the city's roofs gently sank into the spent, smoky haze of the darkening night, the diaphanous veil of the evening appeared to me like a translucently gossamer flower, an eye crowned by the brows of angrily tempestuous clouds that edged the far-off horizon, and duskily disclosed an ivory face framed by tea-black auburn hair, gray-eyed and illuminated by an ineffably tender smile, truly seen for the first time although I already knew it so well. I gazed into this face, I could not draw away from it, and I remained leaning at the window until night set in, and the night was like an infinitely gentle and feminine hand, softly resting on the brow of the world.

This was no vision, it was a second reality, a reality that all of a sudden had entered the visible world, and it was not limited to that single evening but accompanied me when I left for the south on the following morning. I fought against it, certainly, for I felt painfully alienated from the reality which I had built and at which I had been working for so long, I felt that something was striving to tear me loose from everything that existed before without my being able to find any connection with that overwhelmingly new

experience which already had taken an iron grip on me, I felt the
terror of being unable either to advance or to turn back, and often
enough I was seized by the thought of escaping into the mountains,
where, in a hardier atmosphere and in the brisk air of the glaciers,
I might go climbing and even might succeed in climbing out of my
own soul and shed, at the same time, that new, unbidden reality
of my life. Yet I could not bring myself to do so, not because I could
have reflected perhaps that fated encounters occur in a space without
landscape, in a space removed from the impact of any environment,
and that, therefore, any geographical changes could be of no avail
whatever, no, that was not the reason, rather it was because I found
myself incapable of leaving those southerly shores where the sea
so mirrors the human face, animated by the same smile, frozen at
times into the same graven immobility, pulsing to the same rhythm,
the landscape of humaneness embedded in the tartness of its olive
groves, in the gray of its vineyards, in the darkness of its laurel
bosks, and in the dappled gloom of its oak copses, that land, gray-
eyed, moody, and cloud-shrouded, that radiant and thought-laden
landscape, ivory-colored like its porcelain clouds under which roll
the waves of the starry-eyed, star-glittering sea, dream-heavy and
dark like a field at night, the sea in its tempestuous mantle and then
once more stilled and green-blue, changing to bluest blueness and
to indigo, the sea sparkling under the sun when, far out, a fishing
boat with tilted sail slowly crosses the shimmering path of the sun,
the southerly sea, the Mediterranean. Image of that unity toward
which all mankind strives, image of man's ultimate humanity, thus
nature became for me the image of that woman's second reality,
and though that landscape could not truly be called feminine, though
its wave-blown diversity was altogether beyond the here and now,
its tides beyond life and death and beyond all sexuality, the longing
to enter it and penetrate its image had fused so incontrovertibly
with my longing for that woman in whom I had found a second
reality, the homesick yearning for the beloved being had merged
so insolubly with my deepest memories that the sea in all its manifold appearances, in its noonday blaze as well as in its ominous
roarings, in its stillness under the morning's white-flitting wisps of

fog, as well as in the mild chant of its eventides, wave cresting after wave, together with its laurel-leaved, its oak-shaded, its pine-studded, and its olive-veiled coastlines stretching all the way to the boundlessness of heavenly shores, that sea became for me the single image of an all-embracing You in which, springing forth from the wealth of the visible and the invisible, that second reality is bestowed upon us, chosen as the image of the great "You are" whose deeply vouchsafed certitude twines with the original "I am," enclosing both of them in that selfsame infinity and therein fusing to a oneness that is the goal of all longing.

We had not exchanged any letters, not even a greeting on a postcard, and despite the deep certainty that we are granted by all that is truly fated, I also knew that fate is merely the subordination of the mind to a specific conceptual world and that the fate of the physician that led him into his profession, more than any other, is determined by the all-encompassing rhythm of the eternal reiteration of death, by the ever-present evocation of that hour in which man divests himself of all sexuality as if it never had existed; he who fails to imagine himself constantly at that hour knows neither the reverence for death nor the reverence for life, and such a one was never destined to become a physician: thus aware that the return into my profession might also mean a return to this possibly more limited conceptual reality, I not only feared—even while hoping for it at the same time—that I might then lose that newly gained second reality but that, worse, if this were not to happen, I might find myself alone in my yearning because the woman for whom I longed was tied to her profession with such irrevocable fatefulness that she would never be able to detach herself from its grip. And as I reminded myself, moreover, of the age gap of fifteen years that separated us, my thoughts lingered intentionally on those fears as if to shield myself from any possible disappointment.

But things were to turn out otherwise.

The return to everyday life did not change anything but rather yielded an ever-growing astonishment, the astonishment at a closeness which in no way had I been able to anticipate in my remembering, the astonishment in the face of a homesick yearning that came alive truly only by virtue of that closeness; it became the astonishment at a femininity of which I had had no inkling and that permeated this closeness, oh, such closeness that when I faced her there was no need for me to gaze at her hands or to examine her face—although I would have found it well-nigh impossible not to—in order to realize on the strength of her mere presence, her mere existence that that which I had experienced through the imagery of the landscape resides in infinitely greater profusion in our own soul, that the non-landscape in which ceaselessly weaves the soul's own deeply veiled infinity is greater than any individual and any landscape because it includes every single one of these, and that the otherly You of our sexuality that for me had exalted and animated and transmogrified the landscape is in no way diminished by reality but instead is resurrected anew in a more vital and a more manifold form: being allowed to experience the You in the other being, utterly and with every fiber, as our sexually apposite complementation, that is our ultimate attainable love, strength-conceiving, strength-endowing in the unimaginable and ineffable equilibrium of existence, and in an almost agonizing straining of my perception I was given to apprehend this the moment we met upon my return.

I hardly dared assume that she might have experienced something similar and that she might feel something akin to my own emotions, and perhaps I shrank from that unfathomable abyss which lay behind such a possibility, yet I could not doubt for an instant that during the past weeks she had been aware of my thoughts and of my yearning, that she knew how things stood between us, and even though her welcoming words, "It's nice to have you back," could be interpreted partly as an empty courtesy and partly as an expression of her always underlying, slightly ironical, slightly dour readiness to lock horns, I clearly perceived in these words a first signal of reassurance and of intimacy. And I replied in the same vein, "Why? Did something happen where you needed my assistance?" — "No, not really." — "Or did you merely lack the right opponent for your contentiousness?" — "That's more likely . . . I'm always ready for a good fight." — "Well, then why don't you invite me up to your place; let's not leave it to chance, and it's too long a wait until it's my turn again to take over the chief's duties." — She squinted at me through slightly narrowed eyes, not in surprise but somewhat quizzically. "All right . . . tomorrow evening, if that suits you." Thus went our first meeting when I came back.

I went to see her for tea after supper and I told her outright and without any preamble that I was profoundly affected by her, affected to an extent exceeding by far any appreciation of her womanly and human attributes, certainly exceeding by far my respect for her qualifications as a doctor, an extent inexplicable and incomprehensible as is the case in every truly fated encounter. "Yes," she said, knitting her brows wearily, "I know." — "Of course, you know," I confirmed, "for not only does every woman have a clear intuition of such happenings but, moreover, bonds of such intensity can never be one-sided—in such occurrences certain impersonal or suprapersonal factors are involved, and this is a conviction that has nothing to do with male vanity." — She looked at me steadily for quite a while, and then she said soberly, "Yes, I guess this is true." Strangely enough, this clear and unambiguous admission did not make me happy at all; in its straightforward soberness it implied rather the opposite. And, indeed, she went on: "But whether legitimately or illegitimately—and it wouldn't make any difference to me now one way or the other—I cannot be your wife."

Much as it was on the tip of my tongue, I dispensed with the silly question "Why?" and we remained silent for several moments. Outside the night faded away, heavy and sweet, sodden with July and with the dying noises of the metropolis. And then she went on: "If it were only a matter of love, things would be quite simple and everything would be all right. But I don't want merely love, I want a child. I am twenty-eight. The time is ripe for me to have a child. I could not love without a child. But precisely that is unthinkable for me. It's out of the question." She had clamped her hands around her knees, those tenderly feminine and yet strong hands, the gray eyes, wide open, gazed calmly under the womanly delicate line of the somber brows, feminine was the gloss of the tea-dark hair, and her lips in that ivory-colored face were stubbornly pressed together. "No," she repeated, "it's not possible . . . it's not compatible with my profession." Somewhat tritely I objected that many married women doctors are also mothers and that, after all, one can relinquish one's profession when more important things are at stake. And I concluded hopefully: "It is enough if one of the parents practices." Presently she smiled, and the smile in her solemn face was as lovely as a spring day in winter, like a streak of sunlight shimmering on the sea, but then she shook her head. "If need be, children may be compatible with a single profession—but not with two professions . . . Yes, you are surprised, but I owe you an explanation, for obviously you don't know that I am a militant communist, with everything that this implies."

At the time I hardly worried about this state of affairs, for there were other things much closer to my heart, and I said, "One can give up even two professions." — "You don't understand," she replied. "I am not and never would be able to do such a thing . . . No, I could not, even though I am aware that there is something unnatural in this, and although there is nothing I yearn for more than to have half a dozen children by a beloved man with whom I could live somewhere quietly in the country, yes, although, although, although . . . yes, and although sometimes I almost hate those children in the hospital because they stand in the way of my own, and although I hate all this political activity because it robs me of the last vestige of human freedom, I feel that I have no right to lay claim to anything for my own life, and I guess that this must be truly so, for otherwise it could not be so strong, stronger than whatever else I wish for."

"Barbara," I said, "each of us is given only a single life and this life is short . . . and yet we are always ready to squander it; beware, beware of throwing your life away . . . ."

"This, too, is my life, and what I do is not done because of cheap altruism; I have no such illusions . . . but I cannot do otherwise, I am obsessed . . . I am obsessed with something one may call justice, if one strips that word of all its implied loftiness, this is my obsession because I myself have already seen and endured much too much misery . . . ."

Mechanically she lit a cigarette and continued: "Why this had to have this particular effect on me is difficult to fathom, nor do I want to probe into it . . . It may have something to do with the fact that I am the child of a marriage of convenience in which, from the very first, there was nothing but hatred and revulsion . . . Later, my mother remarried out of love and, true to her rebellious nature and in contrast to her first marriage, into the most wretched circumstances—to a man, moreover, who was rather dull of mind and jealous of his predecessor, so that he was never able to overcome his rage at the child my mother had conceived with her former husband, and in the passionate frenzy in which these two lived it is little wonder that he managed to infect my mother with his own angry aversion . . . I was the typical stepchild among my half sisters and half brothers, and I had to endure all the injustices that only a child can feel so keenly . . . And then, when I was fifteen, I simply ran away, ran away into the starkest wretchedness, sinking to the very depths of body and mind, and also into the worst moral depravity; I consorted with men whom I did not love but who gave me a meal from time to time. I told myself, what's right for my mother is fitting for me, and out of a sense of revenge I gave free rein to any passing urge, without restraint and without a thought; it was no longer a life, it was sheer chaos . . . But precisely because I had sunk so low, I slowly realized that I had gone so far astray mainly in the hope of being able ultimately to study, for this, too, I had been denied at home . . . and later, yes, later the wish awoke in me to become a doctor, at first merely as a kind of hygienic instinct, yet strong enough so that, while I slowly, ever so slowly cleansed myself of all the filth in and around me, I managed in the end to realize and achieve my goal . . . Yes, I achieved it and all the while the pediatric field as the ultimate objective gained in strength and clarity, the idea of making amends, of compensating all those other children for everything that had been done to me, for never must such a thing happen again, and I was driven by the thought that such injustice had to be wiped out throughout the world . . . Of course, I always knew and I know today better than ever that the justice for which I strove is sheer utopia, an infinitely remote goal of mankind of which I myself shall never see even one iota, yet we cannot exist without infinity and we live for the vague hope of a future in which mankind one day may find such ideal justice . . ."

She fell silent, and then abruptly going off on a tangent, she pointed to a photograph which hung as single decoration on the soberly white-painted wall of her room, a doctor's room similar to my own and yet filled for me with an all-pervasive femininity. "This is my mother," she said. "I have hung that picture there as an admonition . . . perhaps also as an admonition to mankind, which no longer has the right to beget children so long as justice is not established throughout the world."

Since she could not help smiling again in the face of this somewhat absurd conclusion, I joined in her amusement by assenting. "Obviously a rather awkward contradiction." — "Yes, quite obviously this may entail some difficulties . . . but you will understand that all this brought me into the mainstream of communist thinking, both because of its inherent idea of social justice and because of the admittedly harsh postulate to subordinate the individual to the collective so as to extricate mankind from its chaos and misery; it is within the collective that man is able to forget these iniquities most readily . . . Justice is the earthly paradise . . ."

"And on that account you wish to put a stop to the bearing of children, Barbara?"

Her smile faded and she was serious again. "No, of course this cannot be stopped, since this would mean putting a stop to infinity . . . Nevertheless, one has no right to satisfy one's own personal claims to happiness as long as there are still tasks to be solved for the sake of higher goals, as is still presently the case . . . That also applies to myself . . . and it applies as well to my desire for a child . . ."

With narrowed lips she drew on her cigarette. "I felt duty bound to tell you the whole story and I had to be totally candid . . . Please don't take it as one of those autobiographical confessions which lovers are prone to use to make each other happy or jealous . . . I also know that the appeal for a child is likely to touch a tender spot in a man, particularly when its potential paternity is being offered him at the same time; yet I hope that the whole constellation of facts will have the contrary effect on you and that your marital intentions will decrease accordingly—for all I care, for reasons of jealousy, for which admittedly my past life would offer you more than sufficient grounds."

Her voice had become progressively colder, and now she concluded harshly: "Shall I pour you more tea?"

"I love you," I said, or rather, it was spoken thus by my innermost self. At first she stared at me, her angry gaze probing my own, and then her eyes dimmed and she started to weep. "Yes, I love you," it spoke out of me once more, for I knew that I would never again be able to leave her. "I love you very much and I love you forever."

"Please go!" she shouted angrily while the tears welled out of her eyes and ran down her cheeks. I had taken her hand. She let me hold it for a few seconds before withdrawing it, and then she gently stroked my hair, so lightly and tenderly as I had not felt for over thirty years. "Leave," she begged softly, "leave now."

I left as in a dream, yet I was led by the clear, sober feeling of absolute certainty. A younger man probably would have stayed to overcome the resistance of her unyielding soul or, had he left, he would have been motivated by jealousy or, at least, by some romantic notion. I was not jealous; nor did I feel particularly romantic. For once the ultimate perceptions of the soul and its fate are at stake, the desiccated past that continues to survive in jealousy with puppet-like spookiness evaporates in the heart's humaneness. The tortuous paths that this woman had followed and which had led her astray, those paths that she had revealed so ruthlessly, also had led her into a profession that had become her vocation, they not only had allowed her to fit harmoniously into the wholeness of ordered being and had brought her self-realization in a patiently persevering and sterling creativity, but more than that—a fact of which perhaps she was hardly aware—those paths constituted the worldly mirror image of her search for her own self, the paths she had had to follow so as to reach her own self in its all-encompassing unity through the symbol of her worldly doings, so that this self, apprehending its own immeasurability by testing and penetrating the measurable, could emerge from its measureless darkness into the light of consciousness.

To be sure, it had been a man's path which had been thrust upon her by her harsh childhood, a path which in its preordained radicality only the great world redeemers are able and destined to follow all the way to the exemplary goal of the ultimate secular symbol: inimitable for the ordinary mortal, even more inimitable for a woman whose womanhood, as in this instance and despite all that consciousness already acquired, is bound to assert itself all too soon and all too painfully. But it was precisely that consciousness that had become her irrevocable gain which conveyed to me this certainty and the conviction that she would emerge from her present difficult inner struggle with her personality enhanced, for even if this were to be at the price of a partial loss of that already achieved self-awareness, at the price of a return of part of her being into the anonymity of the instinctual for the sake of the desired child, this nevertheless could no longer constitute an abrogation of her bitterly acquired self-deliverance, an abrogation she obviously feared, but on the contrary would become the inception of a second and even more urgent act of redemption, namely the full acceptance of the child in whose existence the second reality of every woman is vested once and for all, the assurance of the otherly "You" and the luminous dream of togetherness, irrespective of whether realized in the love of me or of some other man.

Thus could have gone my reflections if I had indulged in them; but in retrospect I realize now that all my deeply felt certitude had emanated simply from her hand in that one single instant when I had felt it resting on the crown of my head, the hand that had drawn me into the dream of togetherness, dreaming and dreamt, dream within dream. It was that one instant which had been the source of the reassuring "You are" and of that premonition which perceives the realization of the self and of its oneness, no longer in inaccessible remoteness but in the immediacy of present experience because the other You has suddenly been revealed: listening to the echo of the other You, hearing one's own echo, man becomes his own metaphor and, able to surrender himself, he becomes ready for the great homecoming into the metaphor of his nature, sinking back into his being, into the all-surrounding All, into the living dying, he himself become nature in his beingness as procreating creature whose origin, bare of any landscape and beyond the three-dimensionality of space, pregnant with all the worlds, pregnant with perfectibility, encompasses any and all landscapes.

Borne by such certitude of the future which, at the same time, was certitude of the present and even of the past since her memory had become no less my own, so that all was in the present and everlasting, I left her without leaving her, and with the same certitude I knew that the waiting which I had enjoined upon myself was no longer a waiting in time but rather a timeless ripening in that timeless primordial sphere of the soul which houses the self, the maturation of the shared, time-freed redemption which is the staple of our ultimate reality. The celestial bodies swam in the mildness of the summerly heavens, mirroring our being in the counter-image of the immeasurable, all that is human and temporal was dissolved in the ineffable, and walking home through the hospital garden, I perceived the innate clarity and rightness of all that is.

My trust in the future proved unfounded, my speculations had been wrong, and my hopes were to turn into despair, and yet it would have been to no avail if, at that time, I had behaved differently: events would have turned out the same whatever I could have done. In the eyes of the woman I loved, I had acted as she had expected, and certainly the weeks of growing intimacy that followed were the fruit of my renunciation. It was intimacy and it was tension. And one morning she came to see me with a large sealed parcel. "I'm going to be unfair to you, unfair because you will not refuse my request . . . You shall have to muster enough courage to take some prohibited literature into your safekeeping, not a great deal of courage, for no one will ever look for it in your rooms."

For an instant, sharp and venomous, the suspicion flashed through my mind that her show of affection had only been a tactical maneuver to enlist my aid in her political machinations, but then I looked into her eyes and saw her somberly calm determination and her truthfulness. "You are not unfair," I said, "or do you think that now you are duty bound to give yourself to me out of fairness and so as to pay off a political debt? The way high-minded lady spies do in the movies?"

She didn't laugh. "No joking about politics or love . . . for it so happens that I take both damn seriously . . . oh God . . ." And she fell silent.

"So—and why 'oh God'?"

"Because all this is more than serious, cruelly serious and truly wicked, and because I have to be inconsiderate toward you . . . but revolutions are not made with fairness, and these happen to be our methods."

"You are inconsiderate and unfair primarily toward yourself, Barbara, and I'm very afraid that one of these days you will be made to pay for it." — "Yes," she replied, "I'm paying for it already, but otherwise than you think . . . I'm on the point of becoming a poor communist and probably also a poor doctor." — "That I haven't noticed yet." — "And yet it is so." I put the parcel away. She looked out of the window into the shimmering glare where, as if sucked up by the thirsting earth, the air burned in sweet lassitude and dryness; then she turned to me. "August is a cruel time, one senses the harvest . . . even here in the city."

"Barbara," I said, "give me your hand."

She smiled, and her smile was somewhat pained and tired. "The hand of the spy, Doctor?"

"No, your hand."

"Better not," she said, and left.

No man is free of vanity and, therefore, the professional success that came my way at just that time not only represented for me the fulfillment of my ambitions as a doctor but also served as proud homage to the beloved woman, and motivated by such somewhat puerile but comprehensible reasons, I welcomed the invitation of the medical association to give a lecture about the latest results of my work.

I had taken my leave of her on the eve of my departure and was surprised, therefore, to find her at the railway platform. "Are you meeting someone?" — "No, I'm seeing someone off"; and she laughed because I was so slow in understanding that this someone was I, she laughed because I looked so happy when this fact finally dawned on me, but she did not laugh when the train left the station: she stood there on the white concrete ribbon between the sun-glittering rails, her hand slightly raised and motionless, and her face was very solemn.

That was the image of her I took away with me, the image that imprinted itself on my mind for all time, immutable and complete in all its details. And its permanence saturated all the other images of this trip: the images of the summer clouds speeding toward the ivory-colored summits in the west; the image, lasting only a fleeting second, torn out of darkness by the blinding glare of torches, of some repair on the walls of a tunnel through which the train rushed with a hollow roar; the images of harvest-tired trees lining the country roads between windrowed fields; the images of meadows darkening into night and of a belated peasant's cart bumping along dusk-stilled lanes, inaudible its creaking progression up and down hillocks, at times disappearing in a hollow, wending its slow way between farmsteads becalmed in vesperal eventide; the image of a girl strolling over there among the orchards—image upon image, never to be seen again and yet lasting forever, anchored forever in my memory, borne by the image of the railway station and of our parting, merged into an indelible and unforgettable wholeness, alive in the harmony of the ordered universe, a permanent reality that increasingly gains in truth as it vanishes: a ripening toward truth. For at the core of this truth-ripening there lay a yet greater knowledge, and it was that which foremost I carried away with me; it was the knowledge of the ripeness of our togetherness. It was then, after my lecture, that I wrote her for the first time, that I had to write her, impelled by my total acceptance of her being and overwhelmed by the strength of my own yearning miraculously surging forth from the autumnally shifting light of those days.

The moment I returned, I went to the pediatrics department. I found her in the main ward of the upper floor at the bed of a small girl, and her perturbed state was in strange contrast to her usual calm, all the stranger since the case did not manifest any particularly remarkable features; the child had been admitted to the hospital the day before after an automobile accident and showed all the symptoms of a concussion: the feeble irregular pulse, the lowered temperature, and a somnolence which, though it had lasted for more than twenty-four hours, was by no means alarming either; on the contrary, her condition had shown relative improvement after some bloodletting and, all in all, everything seemed perfectly normal and straightforward. And yet Barbara was haunted by the idea that the child had suffered a brain lesion, a damage, in short, which for its possible cure would have called for so risky an intervention as a trepanation or a spinal puncture.

As I proceeded with the examination, she said with somber despair, "I cannot come to a decision." — "What is the opinion of our colleagues?" — She shrugged her shoulders. "Concussion, unanimously . . . That's why I counted on you . . ."

I was quite alarmed by her apprehension. "Look here," I said, "I know how reliable you are in your diagnostic intuition, and if you can give me the slightest reason for your suspicion, I would not hesitate to follow your lead, but failing that, I, too, can diagnose this case only as a concussion." — Her tone of voice became still more desperate. "My reliability is gone . . . I no longer have any insight, only premonitions and fears . . . fearful premonitions." — "That's not enough, of course, to justify such a difficult intervention." — "No, it's not enough . . . and that's precisely the crux of the matter . . . I can no longer practice my profession." — She was exceedingly overwrought and overworked, and obviously had not slept all night.

"Barbara," I said, "you are exhausted . . . you are seeing things. This is a simple case, you and I have treated innumerable similar ones . . . Everything that had to be done has been done. With a little morphine we'll manage perfectly well . . . Neither you nor I can assume the responsibility for such an operation . . . Calm down . . ."

She pressed her hands to her heart, those lovely hands, feminine yet strong, and said, "You may be right." — "Certainly I am right insofar as can be predicted by human foresight, and when I now order you to get some sleep and rest a few hours, I am right in doing so without any reservations at all . . . I'll be glad to take over your duties in the interim and the nurse can call me if anything should happen . . . but nothing is going to happen . . ." She nodded her assent.

This was around five in the afternoon. I had found a great deal of accumulated work upon my return, the nurse did not call, and so it was quite late before I could get back to the ward: of course, she had not slept but still—or once again—sat next to the child, who lay still under her ice bags as I had left her, unconscious as before. Nevertheless, I had the impression of some improvement, the heartbeat was stronger and more regular, the pallor was less waxy, and the breathing seemed deeper. "That's it," I said, "the case is taking its normal course." — "If we are to do a spinal puncture, it would have to be now," she countered with strange stubbornness, "or it will be too late." — "But, dear God, why, Barbara? Do you see any symptoms of paralysis?" — "No."

The manner in which she scrutinized the child by now was no longer that of a doctor; an almost hate-filled, uncharitable anxiety could be read in her eyes. And then she said listlessly, "I no longer can tell." — "Well then . . . let's get a little air, there's nothing you can do here except fall deeper into your panicky state of nerves . . . You have lost your sense of proportion . . . that can happen at times . . . Assign the case to a colleague tomorrow and come now . . ." Wearily she acceded and got up. "All right, let's go."

It was muggy and sultry under the chestnut trees, the air felt dead and numb, and so as to breathe more freely, I took the path to the belvedere which crowns the highest point of the hospital garden. We did not speak; the tension was too great, the oppression too heavy. To the left and right the walls of the hospital pavilions shone whitish in the moonless darkness, the light of the lamps along the pathways in some places picked out the boxes of geraniums adorning the windows as a kind of impersonal institutional embellishment, the flowers looked as if painted an eerie red, the night lights could be discerned dimly through the panes of the wards in which lay eerily impersonal and disembodied bipeds, neutral disease carriers waiting to be freed of their variegated afflictions, and I found it doubly ghostly that a single being in the whole world, the being at my side, should have been singled out from all that impersonality, and that it was a woman and, for me, the one and only woman. The noises of the city could be heard weirdly dampened, as if the air were unable to carry any sounds, and when we reached the lookout with its somewhat monumental and temple-like hemicycle enclosing the ring of a stone bench, the autumnal sky around us revealed itself as a dome of red-smoldering waiting, eerily lit up by the lights of the city, starless in its reddish haze, shrouding the human habitations below.

We sat down on the stony monumental structure, and the sight before us almost led one to fancy that this structure had in truth been erected as a lookout into a petrified hell: the luminous signs on the roofs of the buildings changed regularly in immovably mechanical monotony, the roar of the traffic rose in limp rigidity, intermingled with the hoarse sharpness of automobile horns and the clanging of streetcar bells, motionless all movement, motionless the air itself; but we two, surrounded by the non-nature of the city, ourselves part of this non-nature, subjugated by man's workings and subject to human thought, we two sat there in our white hospital coats like two health mechanics, subjugated by the lunatic power of human agencies and by their innate logic which is stronger than man's heart and soul and nervous sytem, stronger even than the elemental powers of nature, and nonetheless we were filled with the breath of creation surging from unfathomable depths, the creative breath, self-creating and re-creating in never-ending reiteration, the breath that alone was alive in the rigid immobility of the night, in the immobility of time elasping, an aging time that grew deep and late, detached of all spatial dimensions in the inaudible and invisible well of infinity, the red-smoldering and death-bearing well of non-nature.

"The child will die," said Barbara's voice at my side, and that voice, too, was unnatural, monotonous and failing. At first I did not know whether I had not merely thought this sentence myself, but when I looked at her and she once more said dully, "It will die," this brought me sufficiently to my senses so as to get hold of myself and set things straight. "Is this what I brought you here for, Barbara?"

She knitted her brows like someone trying to see something in a new light, and it was quite some time before she understood and was able to answer. "It is not easy to tear oneself out of such a state when it has lasted a full two days . . . but in any case I want to check on the child once more tonight."

The mention of the two days set me thinking of a contingency which, to be sure, I should have considered earlier. "Tell me, Barbara, have you had at least a bite to eat since yesterday?" — She thought quite seriously before replying. "Perhaps . . . I really don't know." — "Well, then let's go back . . . You're going to have tea, either at my place or yours . . . Fortunately there exists a prime moving force called hunger, and hopefully we shall also find the right remedy for it in the form of something edible."

I was happy to rediscover in her face the habitual features of her contentiousness. "Can't you stop ordering me around? . . . First I'll check on the child, and then . . . well, then we shall see . . ."

"If you'll let me, I'll do the examination in your stead . . . and I'm not abrogating my authority to issue orders to you; after all, I'm still your superior and I have relieved you officially of your duties . . ."

A hint of amusement crossed her face. "Superfluous, Professor, I'm already relieved according to schedule and at this moment officially off duty, so you may now go home with a clear conscience . . . but I shall call you and let you know how things are."

"In that case, I shall at least prepare tea for you." — "You're a dear," she said, and was gone.

It took quite a long while for her to call. I had set the tea to boiling, had assembled whatever there was to eat in my bachelor's household, and had done my best to set the table as well and as neatly as possible. At last the telephone rang. "How is the child?" — "Unchanged, rather better even . . . I'm coming over." — "Wonderful. Tea is ready," I added, but she did not hear it and, in the expectation that she would appear at any moment, I hurried to put the last touches on an orderly festiveness, hung my clothes in the closet, put the shaving equipment away, and soon could find nothing perturbing in the room except my own impatience. For, incomprehensibly, she still let me wait and I, infected by her fears, grew restless and began to imagine that some complication might have arisen with the child which required my presence. I had already put on my coat once more and was about to leave when I heard her swift steps in the passageway, and even before I could open the door, she had knocked and had entered. Taking in at a glance my preparations as a dutiful host, she stopped and smiled, but when I stepped forward to meet her, she switched off the light. As I felt her arms around my neck, I was enfolded in an ineffably maternal peacefulness, in a shroud of profound peace, harvest-ripe and memory-laden. I was home.

I don't know whether I may dare speak of happiness, but what I experienced was sheer and absolute bliss: beyond the visible, beyond the transparently luminous within the darkness, it was the soul's very landscape that I apprehended, I perceived it with closed eyes, the crepuscular landscape which softly divested itself of its veiling and of its formless depth, animating her countenance, nocturnally invisible yet visible, the tangible soul-filled beyond all tangibility, soul-filled each breath and each fiber of her body, soul-filled even the bones of her skeleton, radius and ulna and phalange and even her teeth, soul-filled with femininity, impregnating me throughout with the boundless dream of her womanhood; memory and oblivion became one, transfigured into the true memory of Being and of the world's beginning, while on the golden-shimmering bottom of all darknesses, in the deepest depths of the oceans, of the mountains, and of the sunken islands, weightless yet heavy with sorrow, unattainable to language, unattainable even to the eye, in the unperceivable where no call is heard, in that primeval sphere which lies deeper than all the mirrors of all the worlds, mirrors upon mirrors of worlds upon worlds, in that one aeon's instant which encloses all the continents of our forgotten memories, bare of images by virtue of the very profusion of images and yet creating all the images of our being, there shone her face, immune to time and space, invulnerable to life's inexorable course, shining in the star-studded dark floods, and it was the face of my own oblivion, it was both my own self and hers, resting and restful, dreaming and dreamt, responsive to all the senses and yet desensualized in the illumination of our deepest and most poignant, our knowingly prescient resting. Could that still be called happiness? Surely another and more profoundly penetrating eye would have been required in this sphere of silence and astonishment, in this sphere of resting, in order to gauge to what an extent I had been transmuted already into that other self to whom, admitted into its mystery-shrouded infinity, I so wholly belonged. For only he who still remains within the confines of his own self is given the ability to be happy or unhappy, only he whose seeing is still determined by the animal and the angelic nature of his dual origin knows in the aching nakedness of his soul of its joy and sorrow, but I, released from all confinement and thus granted the homecoming into the metaphor of the great all-encompassing unity, I had found in its unfathomable, its crepuscularly yielding and mystery-pregnant rebirth, in the echo of life's abyss and origin, which dream-like and shadowy surpassed any and all metaphor, I had found therein the other You, the You that I am, the oneness of all realities, its music, powerful and comforting in its mildness, yet terrifying in the sanctity of its coursing and passing in the knowledge of being. This was beyond happiness. Though later, of course—once she had left—I no longer heard in me the sweet song of joy: it was the world that sang as I stood at the window; the red haze under the firmament's dome had dissolved, the night had become weightless and was ablaze with stars, and through the matutinal world, magically released from rigidity, inexpressible its singing, blissful and lovely and sweet, the first breath of the morning breeze blew with silvery lightness over the crowns of the chestnut trees; timidly, a single bird began to twitter and greeted the redeemed stillness.

And the morning that followed was equally joyful and serene, the light smiling and almost spring-like, the air as soft as if it were afloat, as if it had turned altogether into floating clarity, eerily quietened and quietening, flowing like the glassily transparent lapping of waves, a playful manifold waving of diaphanous veils. It was still early when I got to the children's pavilion and I only had come to satisfy myself that here, too, the turn for the better that I fully expected had indeed taken place. And sure enough: the child had awoken from her unconsciousness, she smiled and I fancied that her eyes shone happily. "Where is Dr. Barbara?" I asked the nurse. — "Off duty, Doctor." — "Call her anyway—that is, unless she's asleep . . . but she'll be glad."

She came after a while. Solemn and sober in her white coat, wearing her usual severe frown, she walked through the rows of beds followed by the eager eyes of the children, and greeted me merely with a dry question: "When did she wake up?" — "During the night, Doctor," the nurse answered in my stead. She proceeded with a thorough examination, checked the heart and the breathing, but even then her features still reflected some puzzled worry. "It could be," she finally said. "Let's hope that it's over." — "Of course it's over," I emphasized, and then added needlessly, "I am very happy." She ignored this, and only mused softly and anxiously, as if speaking to herself. "If only it's not merely a free interval!"

Her solemnity impressed me so much that I saw not only the fate of the child but also my own fate endangered once more; I felt something threatening rising like a fog, as if the fossilizing and petrifying forces had once again drawn close, the rigid nocturnal world rising menacingly, shrouded by and sinking back into the darkness of the soul. "No," I almost shouted, "no . . . Everything will turn out all right now!" — "Continue to apply ice bags, Nurse, just to be sure," she directed, "and if you notice the slightest change, please call me." And thereupon she left. When I myself returned to the lab, the skies were still cloudless: nonetheless, I had the impression of the beginning of an overcast sky that could presage the setting in of oppressive weather brought in by a foehn wind from the south. The day became heavy.

Finally, in the afternoon, she called me; I had just about given up hope that she would. Yes, I was to come to see her. I dropped everything and rushed over within a few minutes like an infatuated schoolboy. "Forgive me," she said. I was mystified. "Dear God, what am I to forgive?" — "You won't have it easy with me, dear . . . It's not easy for myself either." — Embracing her, I placed her hands on my head.

This was on a Thursday. And, indeed, a steady foehn wind set in on that day. On Saturday the child manifested paralytic symptoms and, during the night from Sunday to Monday, she expired. The diagnosis of a brain lesion followed by a free interval had been correct.

She took it in silence. My own dismay was more audible, for it was of a different and a more exteriorized nature: although it is true that I had no reason to reproach myself for any diagnostic error—one can hardly be expected to treat each and every case of concussion by trepanation or puncture!—objective considerations play only a minor role in human relations, and by rights she could have accused me of overriding her hunch with irresponsible flippancy or even by the presumptuous use of my authority, and if, as a result, she had turned against me, a part of myself would have deemed it justified. That she did not do so was reason for me to be touched and profoundly grateful to her. She declined to mention what had happened in any way whatever, she remained enclosed in her silence and pursued her professional duties with even greater zeal than before, but since she also seemed to be as fond of me as ever, I, concerned almost solely with plans for our future, soon began to hope that not only her work but to an even greater extent my love for her would help her get over what she had been through. And especially when, after another three weeks had elapsed, she took my hand and told me with smiling matter-of-factness that she might well be expecting a child, this appeared to me the ultimate fulfillment and a totally fitting consolation. And though I thought nothing at all when I held her in my arms at that moment, nevertheless I was conscious of a great deal: I knew that the whole reality of this world rests in the depths of the human heart, the world itself submerged therein, I knew of the everlasting eternity intrinsic to all earthly happenings, I knew of time that flows through us, of our premonition reaching all the way from the elemental beginning to the last descendant at the final end, singing its own language freed of all words, and I knew deeply the feeling of existential security embodied in the We in whose center stood the beloved woman and her child.

I still held her pressed against me and already I spoke of our plans for the future and of their realization; gray-eyed and frowning, she looked at me, a glance full of affection and kindness, and smiled. That this was the smile of a being who plays with castles in the air in which one cannot truly believe, this I did not grasp, either then or later, although her behavior did not change; when I spoke of marriage, of giving up our practice at the hospital and moving to the country, her solemn thoughtful face lit up with that sweet wistful smile of hers and she was wont to say, "We have time, dear one . . . later," but apart from that nothing really happened. What did happen was merely a redoubling of the energy with which she threw herself into her work. In addition to her normal duties, she worked on serological investigations in my laboratory, threw herself with renewed passion into her political activities, and was always busy somewhere else on her free evenings, and still I did not recognize the urge for self-obliteration which drove her to all this frenzy: quite the contrary, I shared in it intimately myself, not only in the laboratory work, which I happily assumed she undertook to be close to my own interests, but even in her political concerns—though these, in truth, were totally alien to me—gratified by her successes, even glad of the progress in the formation of communist cells which she organized in the hospital and elsewhere, and despite the unwomanly nature of such propagandistic doings, there simply was nothing related to her that did not strike me as thoroughly feminine: I was captivated by the power of her conviction. And I failed to perceive that despite all the interest I took in her life, essentially I lacked any true access to her being, that the child for which she had yearned faded increasingly into the background, and that, at the same time, our whole relationship had shifted to an entirely different level. Only once did I become suspicious, when, bent over the lab table, a test tube in her hand, she casually and with indifference dropped the remark: "For the sake of our child, the other one had to die." But I did not wish to hear it, and it was soon forgotten.

In October, she took a three-day leave of absence, supposedly to settle a long-overdue matter of inheritance in the interest of our marriage. The haste of her departure did not strike me as particularly unusual and did not disturb my feeling of absolute security; on the very same railway platform on which three months earlier I had become conscious of her love for me, we bid each other a casual goodbye. In the following days the newspapers contained veiled hints of an unsuccessful communist putsch and of the thwarted attempt on the life of a minister. Since I am a poor reader of news items, I did not even pay much attention to it; moreover, there was just then a great deal of work at the hospital, work which I welcomed, for I missed her sorely and was looking forward joyfully to her return. Instead, the news came that she had poisoned herself in a hotel room. The cyanide she had used came from my lab.

What happened immediately afterward and in the months that followed, I no longer know. Much later and quite by chance, I came across the sealed parcel she had entrusted to me. At first, I hesitated to open it. When I finally did so, I found a letter on top; it contained a single line: "I loved you very much." The rest of the parcel consisted of detailed plans for the putsch and directives to the various cells and units in the eventuality of its success. I burned everything.

It turned out to be true that Marius was now working in the Upper Village. Coming from my house, I met him as he was headed there.

"What brings you up here, Marius?"

"Up here they thresh by hand," he answered with a meaningful look, as if this were his doing.

"Is that anything special? The small farmers up here have always done that and undoubtedly will continue to do so, since for them it is more practical."

But he was set on refuting me. "They still have to get the grain down to the mill."

"Sure, but it's easier to transport sacks instead of sheaves and they need the straw."

"Well, yes," he said. But he was angered by my contradicting him and, without further ado, made as if to continue on his way.

"Tell me, Marius, what actually happened with the thresher engine?"

"The cableway broke, too," was all he said, and he left abruptly, although we were going the same way.

It didn't bother me; on the contrary, it amused me to see him loping swiftly ahead of me with his sprightly shuffle while I followed more slowly. I was in too good a mood to let him spoil it for me, and I was in such a good mood because I had won out in the case of the Wetchy boy, because Marius up there in front of me was no real man and could do no harm to Irmgard, and also because the wind blew so invigoratingly.

Yes, the northeaster sent by autumn, which for some days had been dispatching cautious and timid harbingers, had now stiffened into a full-blown storm. The sky was clear, there wasn't a single cloud which the storm could have played with or propelled ahead of itself, it was a luminously transparent storm, and the entire valley and the line of mountains across from it seemed to have been caught up in its cool and light swaying. Behind me and to my right along the face of the Kuppron, the tops of the pines were bending in the storm, their crunching bowing could be heard, and the wind blew into my thin summer jacket and into my shirt and inflated both into a cold bubble around me. But I did not shiver; my stick and my instrument satchel in one hand, my other hand in my pocket, I leisurely strolled toward the village, Trapp was racing with the wind ahead of me, and Marius was walking still farther ahead. The wind shaves the landscape like a broad-bladed straight razor, as if it meant to mow and scrape away the scratchy stubble beard remaining after the harvest, and that is also the way it sounds, steely and recalcitrant, as the soft summery velvet that had been left spread over the fields, hiding among the bristles, is being wiped off the earth and carried away. But it is not only the summer's softness that is being erased but also its dry sharpness that had been embedded underneath the velvet, the sharp and edgy harvest dust of the fields, the sharply corroding dust of the road which slantingly rises from its serpentines in layer after layer to settle down on the slopes, coating the dry grass: it is this biting dryness which has dulled and jagged the wind's razor, so that much has been caught up in it; manifold invisible threads flutter within this invisible mass of the storm, manifold smells, smells of the harvested fields and the smells of the leaves and stems of cornflowers, fluttering in the storm are the smells of mint from the marshes of brooks, odorous threads of sunlit flowery fragrances picked up in some garden corner, smells of stables and pigsties through the cracks of which the storm had been whistling, smells of cow stalls and compost heaps, and all those smells, blowing and flowing, streaming and thinned out, become almost abstract in their increasing dilution, all these fluttering and elongating odorous threads are being carried upward to the rocky walls of the Kuppron, in which at last, fragrant still for a while, they are caught for good, for that is where finally the storm is broken up, by then barely able to detach a few pebbles from the inclines before it dies out. Only what is alive is subject to the storm. A hare, running for his life in a contest with the wind, crossed the road in front of me, doubled back as he caught sight of Trapp, doubled back once more as I came toward him, and in an absurd hunter's gesture I pointed my stick at him, as if I could have thus brought him down. Not only I but the hare, too, was full of jollity, and so was Trapp, who raced after him with a yapping highly improper for a hunting dog, for this whole summer day, suddenly cooled off and set in motion, all at once was filled with a so to speak implacable exhilaration, an almost cruel exhilaration compelling one's own merriment, a joyfulness that entered with the storm, penetrating the self from without and throughout its layers of fat, flesh, and muscle, and deeper still into one's very bones, so that even the skeleton man who, packed into fat, flesh, and muscle, was hidden within, even he rejoiced because the storm could harm him no more than as if he were a rock, and he didn't even feel cold.

Though had the Wetchy boy not gotten well, it wouldn't have been so.

Marius had disappeared among the first houses of the village. I was not interested in following him.

I looked out into the windy afternoon and over the valley, and I took my time, and if there had been a coffeehouse nearby, I might well have sat down in it. For the happy man has time to waste, the life stretching in front of him appears to him immeasurably long, so long that he can fill it with castles in the air, dimensions expand and time slows down for him, and he is like the child who is wont to say, "When I grow up . . ." Yes, so what did I want to be when I grew up? In all probability, once more a country doctor.

Thus I slowly strolled along the village street. As I approached the Mountain Manse, the threshing flails were just beginning their merry, yet muted cadence, the afternoon music of these days, for all those who do not thresh at their own farmsteads do so, in accordance with venerable custom, on the threshing floor of the Manse.

And because I had time, I let myself be lured by the jolly rhythm to have a look at the work in progress, maybe also because there had been so much talk these past weeks about threshing by hand. I entered through the pointed Gothic arch of the main gate into the large yard, which, of course, has not been a real yard for a long time but is now divided by many fences into small yards and plots of vegetable gardens; the whole space opens toward the mountain, for on that side there stands only the long, low building of the threshing barn, a two-story structure, the wooden upper floor of which can be reached directly from the slope behind while a ramp leads up to it from the yard, so that the wagons with sheaves and hay can cross the building from one side to the other without having to turn. In the yard the ramp continues in a driveway cutting straight through the fenced-in lots and leading to the Gothic stone gate, and this was the path I myself followed to the barn, pushed by the wind which had vaulted over the roofs of the Manse in one easy leap and now had grabbed me with all its strength from behind. But since the barn door at the top of the ramp was closed on account of the storm, I had to use the small door at ground level. Next to the entrance a gin was being turned by a small donkey; the wheel sighed and creaked, and the village children stood around and watched the laboring of the animal.

The stone-walled ground floor, half built into the slope, is a low-ceilinged room, the gloominess of which is barely relieved by a few tiny windows giving out on the yard. The threshing flails boomed above, and this room is where the seed dresser, driven by the gin outside, slowly revolved. Several girls were busy directing the flow of grain coming from above through a wooden chute into the dresser and shoveling the sifted grain into hoppers divided by boards which stood in a row along the rear of the room. The noise was deafening, and it was some time before I could recognize the girls in that hollow booming gloom; Irmgard was among them.

The sweetish smell of the fresh grain floated thick in the dust-laden air.

"Hello," I said quite superfluously, for one could not make out a single word. "Hello, Irmgard."

Some of the girls had noticed me and nodded to me in recognition. I approached Irmgard, who still hadn't seen me. "Hello, Irmgard!" I bellowed.

She looked up briefly from her work and seemed pleased to see me.

"Found many herbs?" I continued to shout.

She made a sign suggesting that we go outside to continue the conversation more comfortably. When we pushed the door open against the wind, it sent a quick whirling eddy inside which churned up the grain and made the girls cough before escaping to the upper floor.

Here the children stood, the wind whistled, and the little donkey made its rounds. This was no place to stay. There was a small strip in the lee of the wind close to the side of the building, and that is where we sat down on the grassy slope along the rubble wall. The noise from the threshing behind the wall was still quite loud but one could make oneself understood.

I repeated my question. "How was the herb gathering?"

"Oh, it was great," she said.

"And it wasn't too much for your granny?"

"Oh no, she's fine."

I had the unmistakable feeling that she wanted to ask me something, something which stuck in her throat and which she couldn't get out. And so I asked her straight out, "What's the matter, Irmgard?"

She looked at me with her amber-flecked eyes, and after a moment of silence she said, "Marius should leave."

That was indeed a surprise; she was the last person I would have expected to harbor that wish.

"Oh?"

"Yes, he should leave."

"Because of your grandmother?"

Her face showed utter astonishment. She obviously had no idea at all of Mother Gisson's dire premonitions.

"I had thought you were in love with Marius."

"Yes, I am," she said after a while.

"And yet he should leave?"

"I want a child."

"Now that makes sense for once, but there you picked the wrong one, of course . . ."

She was somberly silent.

"So what is there to do, Irmgard? . . . He, all he can do is talk big, and me you don't want . . ."

She laughed at last.

"What does that crackpot want of you anyway? Why is he after you? . . . He doesn't love you."

Angrily she burst out with "Oh yes, he loves me."

"Oh? . . . So what does he want of you?"

"He wants to kill me."

"Yes," I said in a rage, "he'll kill you all right with all his empty talk, many a girl has been killed that way."

A smile passed over her face; she obviously was amused by my rage. She had drawn up her knees to her chest and had clamped her arms around her legs so that the wind wouldn't raise her skirts, and with that serene assurance she seemed to have inherited from Mother Gisson she said, "No, he really does want to kill me."

"Hell's blazes, girl, don't make fun of your old doctor." But then I asked, "Are you afraid of him, by any chance, Irmgard?"

She looked at me a bit mockingly. "Afraid? No."

"Then why don't you send this bigmouth itinerant preacher to hell and gone? . . . Send him packing!"

"I can't," she said simply.

"That's how much you love him?"

"It's Father . . ." she said falteringly.

"What about your father?"

"Marius, he comes from far away . . ."

"Yes," I said, "and hopefully he'll leave for far away, too, and real soon."

"Yes," she said.

"Well then, if you do your part, I'm sure he'll leave . . ."

"I can't."

"Now look here, Irmgard, first you talk so sensibly about wanting a child and then you keep saying, 'I can't, I can't' . . . If you were one of those silly city ninnies who don't want any children, I could somehow understand it . . . But what does your father have to do with all that?"

She thought it over.

"Is he also to be killed, by any chance? . . . If this is allowed to go on, this Marius is going to wipe out the whole family . . ."

At last she was able to collect her thoughts. "Mother is hard . . ."

"Yes, rather."

"And that's why I have to stand by Father. Otherwise . . ."

"Otherwise what?"

"Father is already there where Marius came from or wherever he will go . . . He draws him hither and thither . . ." And now she was able to express what she had wanted to say. "Yes, I'm afraid for Father . . . yes."

"Hm . . . and that's why I'm to help in getting Marius to leave . . . ?"

She nodded in happy assent. "Yes . . . Father listens to you, Doctor."

"It's not an easy matter, Irmgard . . . It involves not just your father but the whole village."

Disappointed, she said, "I know . . ."

"Where is he now, this strange lover of yours?"

She pointed to the barn wall next to us, behind which the thresh-ing boomed.

"Well," I said, "I still have work to do, but when I'm through I'll pass by again . . . Then we'll talk some more . . . You won't be finished working that soon anyway . . ."

Sometimes they go on threshing well into the night; it is work that doesn't depend on daylight.

"Yes, Doctor," she said obediently, and got up to return to her work.

I climbed the grassy slope, for I could reach the upper houses of the village just as well from behind, by way of its upper edge. When I was up there I saw that the rear door of the barn was wide open and so I couldn't resist glancing in. The threshers stood in a circle around the heap of ears in their typical, sweepingly animated position, one leg slightly bent and placed behind the other and then straightened in cadence with each blow of the flail, while the grains jumped and spurted from the heap like so many golden drops. Marius stood with his back to the door, fanatically intent on his work, and at times I could see his bold profile, so reminiscent of Miland.

I whistled for Trapp, who was busy somewhere in the yard near the fences, and left. After reaching the narrow path that meets the main road at the end of the village, I had to step briskly so as not to shiver in the cold; the wind had stiffened further and was now so chilly that all the smells it had carried earlier had frozen and no longer could be perceived. I couldn't make much sense out of all of Irmgard's talking, and if one came right down to it, it only meant that she was unhappily in love with that fellow and that she hoped for some vague help from me that I was unable to give. Mother Gisson would be better equipped for that and I decided to turn to her in some form or other; one couldn't leave the poor girl in such confusion, after all. Though, of course, no one can do much about the fate of another, and a man in particular is incapable of such help, as he is only bound to make a mess of it, I trusted Mother Gisson, if anyone, to find some solution.

The afternoon ran out and it was getting dark when I was finished with my visits and was walking down the road toward the Mountain Manse. The storm, becoming nocturnal, continued unabated, but it was no longer as dry as during the day, it already carried some mild moisture in its strength, while black clouds massed at the northern edge of the skies. Some windows were lit and the kitchen windows of Mother Gisson also cast yellow rectangles of light on the street. I looked inside. Mother Gisson and Mathias sat at their evening soup, but Irmgard was missing; she must still be at the barn, even though the noises of the threshing had stopped. Of course, I could have waited for her in the house, but something told me that I'd better fetch her.

In the corner of the wall behind the arched gateway a bulb swung in the storm. The yard lay dark and silent; all around it were the entrances to the dwellings and across it was the black outline of the barn. One of the doors opened, releasing a swift beam of light, and a pail of dishwater was emptied into the yard. I crossed the orchards, where the storm shook the small fruit trees, sharply rustling their leaves, and arrived at the square in front of the barn. It was now empty, the little donkey had finished his labors, and a dim light came from the small windows of the ground floor.

There was no one down there. The light came from two heavily dirt-encrusted bulbs around which the dust trembled like a loose swarm of insects. But the air was still and now could be breathed. Tools lay about, two wooden shovels leaned against the seed dresser, the peacefulness of the coming winter sat in the corners of the bins and in the invisible depths of the room, but from the floor above voices could be heard. "Is that you, Irmgard?" I called, and receiving no answer, I climbed the stairs, which creaked mightily under my steps.

When I had reached the last steps and had a clear view of the whole room, I saw Irmgard and Marius standing in the middle of the bare, neatly swept threshing floor; they looked into each other's eyes and stood stock-still.

"Good evening," I said, though without getting any response, for they didn't so much as turn their heads, even after I had repeated my greeting. They were standing about a yard from each other, Marius bent slightly forward, his right arm raised as if arrested in the middle of a motion, Irmgard straight and lissome. Had they hypnotized each other? I, too, stopped and waited.

The man now said, "Your sacrifice will be great."

The room was in wide-spanned darkness. A single bulb hung from the ceiling, exactly over the two figures. The rear door had been closed, but the wind whistled through the planks of the walls and in the draft the tips of the stalks in the stapled sheaves moved incessantly with a scratchy rustle. Nothing else could be heard.

Marius repeated: "Your sacrifice is great and I love you."

Finally she, too, spoke, and I was relieved that it was in her normal tone of voice, though perhaps somewhat more stiffly. "Yes, it is a great sacrifice, for you are barren and your lips know no kiss and I shall bear no child."

He, on the other hand, spoke in his usual preacher's tone. "You shall do much more than bear, much more than conceive . . . Offerings shall be made to you for your sacrifice."

It was terrifying and at the same time absurd. The psychopathic state of this man was unquestionable, but Irmgard was no lunatic, even though she came from highly inbred peasant stock, no, she was no madwoman, and so I called to her, "Irmgard!"

"Yes, I love you," she responded, as if her name had been called by him.

Marius remained rigidly bent toward her. "Virginally the light bears heaven and earth . . . bearing the entwined siblings, newly born each day in the sun . . ."

Irmgard's hair moved slightly in the draft whistling through the gloom, a strand hung over her forehead but she did not remove it, the moist lips of her mouth were open as in a dream or as if to drink, breathing the motionless expectancy of a woman over-powered by love, breathing her own openness and her being.

"In the virginal blood of their embrace," he declared in his high-flown speech and with priestly unction, "heaven and earth once more shall be joined together and their longing will be stilled."

"Yes," said the girl.

I have always wondered and it has made me skeptical why persons in a trance are usually wont to spout forth such high-flown gibberish, and from what I knew of Marius it was not to be ruled out that he belonged to that species of madmen who, in addition to their derangement, are also putting on a show, that it was an act he now put on for the benefit of both Irmgard and myself—though to what purpose? to cover up his impotence as a man?—and yet a cold shiver runs down my spine each time I encounter the incredible verbal wealth of such lunatics. For is it not the original source of all human being that erupts in the deranged speech of such madmen? Is it not that which lies on the deepest bottom of the shaft of knowledge, that which lives in all of us and joins us in deepest kinship, the oddly irrational sources of thought and speech, the no longer comprehensible chthonic powers sucking and drawing us down to the dark roots of all harvests?

They had fallen silent once more. The bulb above them swung to and fro, its light was shed on the large heap of grain piled up behind them, already prepared for the next day and ready to be poured down to the seed dresser through the wide mouth of the wooden funnel, the soft wavy mounts of grain glistened moistly while the troughs of the waves were in deep shadow, but I, standing in full light and yet invisible to them, I, too, was spellbound and petrified, caught up in the surrounding gloom.

But now the man once more raised his voice. "The mountains have spoken, they tremble under the weight of heaven, the heavens eager to sink down once more into the embrace of the earth, the earth trembling in readiness to open itself and to receive heaven . . ."

"Who are you?" asked the girl.

But he continued unperturbed. "Harvest over harvest is borne by the earth and yet she remains virginal under the shadow of heaven . . ."

"Are you the heaven?" asked the girl.

"I am the lion," he introduced himself to my astonishment. And although I was still spellbound and rooted to the same spot, I found my voice and called out, "Irmgard!"

"You have been called," he said without shifting his glance.

"I do not wish to hear."

"You may go."

"You have called for me, no one else."

"I have called you up for the sacrifice."

"Yes, for you are the father."

"Not yet."

"When shall you be him?"

"When your blood has flowed back to the earth, when in your sacrifice the mother once more will mate with the father, the earth mate with heaven, the siblings of day after day . . ."

"But you are heaven."

"Putting to death you as father, I shall return as heaven to you, to you who have become earth, I shall return as your spouse . . ."

"Yes," breathed the girl, and it was as if night flowers blossomed out of the darkness.

And then she said, "Oh, do it."

"Not yet," he replied.

Now finally he moved, released her from his gaze, straightened up to his full height, and as if speaking to the large wooden funnel gaping at his side, he began the strange singsong which I had heard from him once before. "The cableway has broken, the time shall come, the earth is awaiting, the mountains already are trembling, already war roars throughout the land and the earth sucks up all the blood, yet she is not sated, nor is she redeemed, for she is drinking up guilty blood, guilty blood is being shed on her, not the blood she thirsts for, for such blood is naught but manure, dung serving nothing but new abominations, new lusts, and new profanations . . ."

No doubt of it, he suffered from logorrhea.

". . . until the one shall arise who is sent by the father, the one free of sins, he himself father performing the sacrifice, the voluntary sacrifice free of guilt, pure in the blood of the virgin, accepted by the thirsting earth, yea, oh yea, then the virgin once more shall become the womb of the earth, the mother turn into the daughter, bitterness and evil shall be extinguished in the strict strength of the mountains, purity will run down richly from the peaks' pastures and the sea shall carry the golden harvests all the way up to the sun, golden the trace of the lion in the bread of all men, in the sun's blessing of the mother, seeds of the sun, fruit of the father on the breasts of the earth . . ."

His singsong became ever more breathless, a plaintive jubilation through which the storm whistled. But then he suddenly gathered all his breath once more and shouted, "For in this grain heaven and earth are united again!"

"Yes," said Irmgard.

"Oh, Mother!" he screamed.

And with this he fell stiff as a ramrod into the heap of grain next to the funnel, his face and hands buried deep in the kernels as if he meant to mate with them his body and his entire being.

Thus he remained and moved no more.

Irmgard stood still as before, her gaze was directed into a far-off distance, and she seemed hardly aware of Marius's shenanigans.

The scene remained as if frozen.

And it may be that I myself would not have been able to rid myself so quickly of the numbness which had beset me as well if, all of a sudden, the rain had not come down, pelting the wooden walls of the barn and beating down on its roof. The wind still sweeping through the room was now full of loosening moisture, its whistling had become rounder and deeper in sound, so that I was able finally to approach the girl, though only slowly and haltingly as if I were walking on swaying ground. Cautiously I took her under the arms.

"When?" she asked in her dream.

"Come," I said, and led her down the stairs.

As I opened the door leading out, the rain met us in all its force. Trapp stood there, soaked through and wagging his tail, with a happy smile because his patience had been rewarded. He stood up on his rear legs and placed his forepaws on Irmgard's shoulders, and before I could prevent it, he had licked the sleeping girl's face with his long wet tongue.

"The beastie," she said.

"Yes," I said, "it's only Trapp."

It was good that it rained; the branches of the trees in the orchards now swished heavily in the downpour, the fences shone moistly, the gravel crunched wetly under our steps, but Irmgard began to wake up, and although she let me lead her meekly and with eyes closed, she nevertheless raised her hand to wipe away the raindrops from her forehead.

"Irmgard," I said.

And she said, "Yes."

"Are you still afraid, girl?"

Eyes closed, she shook her head.

"We'll have to get rid of all that sacrifice nonsense once and for all . . ." On her face appeared the tortured look of someone trying to remember a dream.

Then she said, "It's raining."

"Yes, Irmgard, it's raining . . . Do you know who I am?"

She still had her eyes closed. "The Doctor, sir."

"All right, then," I said.

But she was still searching for her dream. "It is the rain of the father and the earth drinks it."

"Just at the right time, too," I said. "If it had rained eight days earlier the harvest would have been ruined."

"Yes," she said, "the harvest."

But now she opened her eyes.

We entered the dwelling of Mother Gisson through the yard, crossed the small rear room, and entered the bright kitchen. Mathias still sat at his place under the window, but Mother Gisson had taken a seat on one of the two old chests along the wall. Trapp shook himself and made a beeline for the kitchen range, where he curled up.

Mother Gisson smiled. "Why, I almost worried about you two."

"Yes," I said, "the devil take all prophets and preachers."

"I guess you two have been baptized," said Mathias from the window.

Irmgard stood in the middle of the kitchen in her wet clothes and rubbed her eyes.

"Come here, girl," Mother Gisson said, and when the big girl stood in front of her, she drew her on her lap and stroked her gently like her dearly beloved child.

11 A small portly man leaned against the counter of the pub. On a chair next to him stood a sample case from which the necks of several bottles peered out.

"Sabest," he said, "you get your name printed on the labels."

Sabest, a cigarette between his lips, did not reply.

The liquor salesman continued: "The labels will say: 'Theodore Sabest, Hotel and General Store, Kuppron.'"

Sabest still did not react.

The salesman now took out a sample bottle and a liqueur glass from his case and said, "I drink to your health, Sabest . . ."

"Well," said the innkeeper, "I still have bottles left from last year . . . The farmers, they make their own liquor."

But the salesman was not to be put off. "Then you can stick new labels on them . . . Lower Kuppron is even more impressive than just plain Kuppron."

"That's not going to make the farmers buy any."

"You also have high-class clients," said the salesman with a sidelong glance at me, "and you can get delivery later, just before Christmas. As Christmas gifts, you tie silver twigs on the bottles, that's very elegant."

"Until Christmas," said Sabest, deep in his own thoughts, "until Christmas . . ."

"The terms are four weeks," said the salesman, "for you six weeks. Then you don't have to pay until February . . ."

Sabest barked a short laugh. "By then, who knows who's going to be alive . . ."

"Those that are alive will need schnapps," said the salesman.

"Put me down for ten bottles," said the innkeeper.

I got up and left with a word of farewell. It was a perfectly ordinary scene that I had witnessed. But that other scene between Marius and Irmgard was still so fresh in my memory that ever since, everything, even this commonplace exchange, for me had some trance-like quality. This may even have been a true impression and there are some indices for that, but it could also have been due merely to my own condition, for a solitary man such as I, one who has freed himself from many bonds in life, such a one can easily be pushed into the remotest realm by even the most insignificant contingency, into an alien world more remote than any foreign region, more remote than the most distant homeland, a space in which nothing subsists but the cold breath of death. Yes, that was entirely possible, even though I conceived of myself as perfectly sober and reasonable both in my thinking and in my work, that work which fights the darkness of disease and soothes the fear of the sick with the light shed by knowledge, it was possible nevertheless, and at times it seemed to me as if I had taken in little Rosa only so as to enter into new bonds in my solitude.

But at bottom this is immaterial and to reflect upon it to me seems almost improper. I feel this way not because possibly I might deny the difference between dream and reality and because in that case I would deem it of little import whether someone passes through this world dreaming or awake, but rather because our essential knowledge has nothing to do with all of that and is totally independent of this or that condition into which we may transpose ourselves or into which we may let ourselves be induced by others: for our life is dreaming and wakefulness at the same time and when the cool breath of the dream at times intrudes into the world we call reality—and this happens more frequently than we commonly assume—then that world sometimes can become wondrously illuminated, illuminated as a landscape after a cooling rain or as a tale which suddenly is no longer made up of mere words and no longer describes events that have occurred in a formless somewhere but which, endowed with the apprehension of a higher reality, all at once is capable of re-creating things as they truly are in all their liveliness and warmth. Yet these two spheres could never intermingle and impregnate each other so intimately were they not constantly receiving their guiding light from that realm which constitutes our prescient knowledge, sunk in the unfathomable depth of our heart and soul.

I still heard the voice of the liquor salesman as I reached the street. "Do you want 'Theodore Sabest' written out in full or only 'Th. Sabest'?"

"In full," the innkeeper replied.

It was a warm and clear September afternoon, interpolated between the coolness of the morning and that of the evening, for the rain with which August had ended soon had eased off again, leaving only a light gray haze which rose during the warm hours of the day and covered the greenness of the mountains, leaving visible only the sunny peaks, a haze reaching all the way to the high drifting clouds: it hung around the whole basin of the valley like a circular curtain and closed it off from the rest of the world, so that one well could have believed that this world no longer or even never had existed. That was fall, both its coolness and its warmth, it was an autumnal dryness, the autumn's mellowness and its light.

The plow was already furrowing the fields.

If there is anywhere an objective criterion for trance-like or dream-like conditions it may well be found in the swiftness with which those things one subconsciously seeks cross one's path all by themselves: ever since my conversation with Irmgard I had wanted to have a talk with her father, and now I saw Miland at the blacksmith's shop as he was loading a plow on his wagon.

Both he and the smith saw me coming. The wagon rumbled as they heaved the plow onto its bed, and now they waited for me with welcoming expressions.

I had no clear idea really in what form I would tell Miland of Irmgard's fears and of the danger to which she was exposed, and I could not broach this subject in front of the smith. Nevertheless, I found myself immediately touching the topic close to my heart. "You're plowing already," I said, "while they're still threshing in the Upper Village."

"Yes," said Miland, "they're always later up there."

"And Marius is still working up there."

"He'll be down for the plowing."

"Lucky there are no machines as yet to do the plowing."

The smith laughed, but Miland remained serious and said, "He's not so wrong about that."

"He's not wrong about what?" I asked, although I already knew what was implied.

"About the machine work."

There could be no doubt that he had been thoroughly infected by Marius's ideas. I looked at him with concern. "Come now, Miland, then you would also have to turn off the water faucet in the stables and once more carry the water in pails."

"Maybe," he said.

But after a pause he gave his justification. "Too many people already have lost their jobs because of the machines."

I knew this to be one of Marius's itinerant preacher arguments, one of his cheapest and probably one in which not even he himself believed, knowing full well that man cannot run counter to the products of his own inventive powers. How then could someone as reasonable as Miland repeat such drivel? To what power was he subject in so doing, what commanded his tongue?

"But, Miland," I said, "you've always taken efficiency into account."

He smiled. "Sometimes one must leave the figures out of one's thinking, Doctor."

The smith said, "No . . . one has to resign oneself to accepting factory-made products . . . Nor will it be long before the blacksmith, too, becomes obsolete."

But the economics preached by Marius could still be invoked against this view and Miland said, "What good is it that production throughout the world is getting cheaper all the time if the purchasing power sinks along with it? . . . That has to be changed, one has to change one's ways . . ."

"Meaning that machines are to be done away with just here in Kuppron of all places?"

"No," he replied quite reasonably, "it will have to be done in many places at once, maybe even throughout the world. A single place is too weak to have any effect but . . ."

"But?"

"But truth can originate only in a single place, for it is always only a single mouth that proclaims it. If there is a single point in the world where right thinking prevails . . ."

"One just man in Sodom," I interpolated.

"And then it's still not necessarily the truth," commented the smith.

"No," Miland conceded readily, "that is only the result of the truth. The spiritual attitude is what matters, then what is right happens by itself."

I dimly felt that the truth he had in mind related to Irmgard and to all the talk about sacrifice, but I merely said, "Well, all that searching for gold is hardly the right thing either."

Again Miland showed his trance-like smile. "The truth is in the soul, not in the mountain."

"Oh yes," I said almost in a rage, "but meanwhile the whole Lower Village is already gearing up to look for it in the mountain . . . I don't think you are aware of the two-faced game Marius is playing with all of you . . . He's got two kinds of truth, one for Lax and another one for you . . ."

The smith laughed. "Let the lads look for their gold."

"Oh," I said, "have you, too, switched to the Lax faction, smith?"

He put his heavy hand on my shoulder. "The gold is the fire, Doctor, and whether folks are talking about gold or about truth, they mean the fire that's in the mountain . . They've got to learn that once more . . . and Marius, too, has to learn that . . ."

"Yes," said Miland, "you may well call it the fire, smith, and indeed it is in the earth, though a bit deeper than the gold . . ."

"It's in the deepest depth," said the smith, "and the gold they want to dig out and which they are quarreling over, that gold is nothing but fire . . . Each grain of gold is a spark of the great fire . . ."

"You've already got your fire, smith," I said, and pointed into the darkness of his shop, where the fire was glowing on the hearth.

"True, I have that," he said, "but people always seek to return to the great fire and that's why they search for the gold . . ."

Miland said thoughtfully, "The smith, too, wants to see the world redeemed . . ."

"Oh . . . ?" said the smith.

"Or don't you, too, wish for the truth to enter the world?" Miland asked in his gentle way.

"The truth," the smith said, and laughed his good solid laugh like polished wood, "yes, the truth . . ."

The sun had sunk close to the mountains, and in the changed slant of the light the rocky walls of the Kuppron, which up to then had been clear and distinct, became flat backdrops, resembling large gray paper cutouts lightly glued to the clouds, mat silver foil shimmering in the haze.

Then the smith said, "The truth is that all of this"—and with his hammer, which he had laid on Miland's wagon, he pointed across to the mountains—"that all this is smoke from the great fire below . . . solidified soot, while the sparks are still caught inside and it is they that are the gold . . ."

"Smith," I said, "not much can be made of that kind of truth . . . It may somehow apply, but what good is it to mankind?"

"Mankind should respect it, is all," he said. And then he laughed. "As Miland said, what matters is the spirit."

As he stood there with his hammer and looked across to the Kuppron, one could have thought he intended to hammer the rocks made of petrified smoke even flatter than they already appeared.

Miland had taken the halter of his team and had turned the wagon to point down the village street. And now he said, tapping his chest, "That's where the real truth is, smith."

"But also the fire," replied the smith. "So long, you two." And he returned to his hearth.

"So long, smith," we responded.

I joined Miland. He had tied the reins to the wagon's frame and walked next to me. At the entrance to Church Street the horses hesitated and were about to turn in, but then continued on when Miland called out to them. It was only half past four and the work in the fields could easily go on until seven; there would still be light then.

"Well now," I said, "what does this truth really come down to, this truth of which there's been so much talk lately?"

He thought it over and it took some time before he replied, "It isn't the fire that burns below that matters . . . That's the smith's own truth but nothing more."

"Quite so, Miland, but you constantly speak of the truth . . . Which one do you refer to, then?"

Lost in his thoughts, he again let me wait for an answer.

But then he said, "You have no wife, Doctor . . . You sit up there all alone by yourself . . ."

"Thank God," I said.

He looked at me sideways and smiled. "Yes, I know, you like to make fun of it . . . and yet you've taken in that ugly little girl of Wetchy's."

"Why, yes, that's true . . . but I don't see what this has to do with your truth."

"You've got to be patient with me, Doctor, I'm only a simple farmer and farmers are slow in thought . . . Nor can one simply say that this or that is the truth that matters . . . The smith has his truth and the eyes have their own truth and so have the fingers of the hand; for the smith it means the fire in the earth and for the eyes it is the green of the trees and for the fingers it means hot or cold . . . All one can say is that this is true or that is not true, this is just or that is unjust, but the one truth or the one justice, they don't exist."

"Yes, all right," I said, and I waited for him to continue.

The wagon next to us creaked, the plow on its bed rumbled, and at times there was a metallic clanking while the large horses, live, breathing tractors, continued steadily on their way. We had reached the end of the village.

And then Miland said, "The man who is alone loses the truth."

"Which one?" I asked. "The truth of the eyes? The truth of the fingers?"

"Those, too, maybe," replied Miland, "but most of all he loses the truth of the heart."

I felt a bit stricken, naturally, and not only because he had touched on my own loneliness. I said, "Are you referring to me, Miland?"

"No, to myself . . . but if you wish, I refer to all of us, for all of us who pursue our business here quite likely are in loneliness and have lost the truth of the heart."

"But, Miland, you have your family, your children."

He stopped, took out the large wrinkled tobacco pouch he carries stuck under his belt, a yellow pouch made of a hare's bladder that long usage had turned black in patches, offered it to me, and filled his pipe. "Ho," he called out to the horses, which had continued in their even gait and now stopped obediently at his command.

We lit our pipes, covering them with our cupped hands as is the custom of all smokers even when there is not a breath of air. The small life of the burning match glowed in our hollowed hands, and I said, "Life is in the fire, Miland. The smith is right, it is the only truth."

In front of us stretched the gentle hills of the eastern slopes slowly rising to the woods, they, too, veiled by the thin haze of autumn. All was still, the stillness of fall, a tart mildness awaiting the moisture yet to come, and even the haze around the higher slopes seemed as if dry, a dry smoke, immobilized in expectancy. Small gray smoke columns rose from our pipes and joined in the stillness all around.

If Miland had not continued to speak, I would not have asked any more questions. All was peaceful and there was no need for the redemption of the world. Though one be lonely in this world, one was surrounded by peace and quiet. And as Miland now spoke, cautiously drawing on his pipe, it also sounded peaceful. "If you give one hand to your parents and the other to your children, one may well assume that there is no loneliness."

"Yes," I said, "no man is quite alone, for he must have had parents, even if he should never have known them."

"But," he continued, "all this is mere outward semblance."

"Oh?" I said, but inwardly I agreed with him.

We had reached the waiting team, and as we approached, the horses continued on their way without even waiting for Miland's command. The road turns here in a wide bend toward the north and leads down toward the end of the valley, cut through by a brook running between steep embankments. "Hee!" called Miland, and the horses turned right into the lane that leads up to his field on the slope.

"Nevertheless," I said, "one hand for the parents, one for the children, and a third hand for the wife with whom one has made those children, that counts for something and could well stand for the truth of the heart."

We walked into the meadow at the edge of the lane. The first crocuses stood in the short grass; it had only taken the second mowing for them to bloom and now they waited for the mists in which to dissolve and were themselves already mist-colored. They suffered silently in the clear afternoon sun which shed its thin watery light over them before drifting up the slope to the sparse birch grove that stood there, a grassy bosk no longer meadow and not yet woods, its light green cloud seemingly levitated by the luminous lightness, a floating sound dying away in infinite space.

Miland said calmly, "There is neither beginning nor end, beginning and end are in us only as long as we live . . . Abraham was ready to sacrifice Isaac and he would have loved the dead child even more than the living; it is only when we speak with our dead that we are able to surmount beginning and end, for the living leave us in loneliness . . ."

Now he, too, had mentioned the concept of sacrifice.

He nodded to me. "It is only to our dead that we reach out truly with our hands."

"So are you perhaps going to kill all your children because of that? What becomes of your truth of the heart in all of that, Miland?"

He remained silent at first, as if my objection had affected his thoughts, but then he shook his head. "You misunderstand me, Doctor . . . It is only that we cannot hope for anything from the living, they leave us in our loneliness . . ."

"Marius, too, is among the living," I said quite bluntly, "and yet you offer him your hand. You're on the wrong track, Miland."

"No," he said, as calmly and self-assured as before, "he is less alive than all of us, even less alive than I . . . He comes from loneliness and goes into loneliness, and even if he remains, he is a wanderer . . ." Then he added, "And because he is more lonely than all the others, because he is not bound by anything living like all the others, because of that he is able to lead others out of their loneliness and into the truth of the heart . . . and that is what the others understand and why they follow him . . ."

"So we're talking about redeeming the world after all . . ."

"Yes," he said, "for it is not enough that men agree with each other in the truth of their eyes and the truth of their fingers, that they understand each other when one says green and another means hot or that two times two makes four, that's not enough, for as long as they don't concur once more in the truth of the heart they will lose the other truths . . . and then not even the truth of the eyes will be the same as that of another . . ."

"You're making things too easy for yourself, Miland," I said.

Again he thought awhile and then he said, "I've always been searching, Doctor, even when I was still very young. And then I fetched Ernestine Gisson from up there"—and he said this with some pride in his voice—"yes, and I may have done it because she resembled her mother so much, and that may well have been a mistake . . . It may be that she would have remained more like her mother if I had taken her only for her own sake and had thought less of the resemblance . . ."

I understood what he meant and asked, "So what was it you hoped for, Miland?"

"Communality," he said, "and not just love."

And then he continued: "It did not come about . . . It's no secret, you've seen for yourself that it did not come to pass . . . It may be also because we down here think differently from those in the Upper Village but that's not all . . . We do our tasks, I do mine and she does hers . . . and you know, Doctor, if I didn't have the hang of my work, the hang of what I've had to do from way back, all the way back to my own father, I would not have the strength in the morning to go out to the fields or to the stables . . . That's how lonely we've become, we no longer know what to do with our hands . . ."

"Yes," I said.

"And then he came . . . one not different from myself, one who could be my own brother, one who set his feet to walking because he no longer saw any sense in using those feet to walk to some workplace . . . and so he wandered . . . but he has put this into words while I, I was not even able to think it . . ."

And then he concluded. "Wherever I look, it is the same . . . The folks do their work, yes, they do, but they do it merely out of their loneliness and they hate each other because of their loneliness . . . They no longer are able to want to be together, they even lack the wish to hate . . ."

"Miland," I said, "you would like to be pious . . . That's what it is."

He looked at me. "Yes . . . if you want to put it that way, Doctor, that's what it is."

"And what you have been saying smacks very much of Christian love-thy-neighbor teachings."

"It is more than love, it is communality."

"Yet you go to church every Sunday . . ."

"Yes, I attend church and so does my wife . . . We all do . . . but that's of no use to us anymore. Even if we tried to understand it, we could not comprehend the ways of God because God should not have allowed our loneliness and our hatred to happen . . . and when the priest preaches and remonstrates with us for our lapse in faith, then why did God allow such falling away? We did nothing to bring about such loss, we were faithful to our duties and we wish to be pious . . . Is it that God does not countenance it? If there is a God, then He plays with us and plays with our suffering . . . but since He cannot possibly do that, He cannot exist . . ."

"And in the face of that, Marius is supposed to bring salvation to the world? . . . Just consider for one moment, Miland, on the one side the church in all its magnitude and on the other side little Marius . . ."

"Marius is a man like us, Doctor, just as lonely and filled with the same kind of hatred, he is exactly like us but he is able to express what is in our thoughts and we understand him . . . We no longer understand Christian love and charity, much as we would want to, but we do know that the Upper and the Lower Village must pull together instead of pulling at cross-purposes, and we understand that the machines are bad and that the earth is good . . ."

I walked next to him, I, too, enclosed in my loneliness, enmeshed in the loneliness of my dream, I, too, lost and astray on a path of which we only know that it leads from the darkness of the maternal womb back into the darkness of the earth, I, too, in the loneliness of the free will that has been granted me and which may be the only hallmark of our course through this world. Or did we, in that earlier darkness, enjoy a greater freedom? Shall we enter a greater freedom in an unknowable beyond? But even in the loneliness of my freedom, in this dream-like freedom, good and evil became intertwined and I no longer could tell whether Marius was leading to one or to the other.

But Miland said, "When man has gone astray, then he needs the leading hand, leading him from stone to stone, he needs his earthly brother . . ."

And to that I could finally reply, "All too earthly, perhaps."

He stopped for a moment. "Why?"

"Miland," I said, "you thought nothing much could be made out of the truth of the smith . . . and you were right because it is only an earthly truth like so many others . . . Marius claims too much for his own truth, which also is but an earthly truth . . . He seeks to make something godlike out of the earthly, he seeks to make a god out of the earth . . ."

We were close to Miland's fields and almost reluctantly he stopped his team once more. I could sense how important it was for him to settle the matter before getting there.

"Doctor," he said, "a whole life long we have been taught to love God and we strove to do so, yet we failed because He made it too difficult for us . . . Should we then not love the earth instead? . . . We are being given the miracles of the saints for our veneration . . . Should we not rather venerate the miracle of the yearly harvest? . . . What does it mean to us if we are told that it is God who accomplishes the miracle of the harvest? It is only when we ourselves truly grasp and venerate this miracle that we may then perhaps be able once more to understand that which has been called God . . ." He smiled a little and then added, "One thing after the other."

"And is this what Marius says?"

"No, he says nothing at all, he acts."

His conviction was almost infectious.

Nevertheless, I said, "Miland, something's wrong there . . . You have no use for God, yet you see in Marius God's messenger."

He put his hand on my shoulder, a slim and yet rough peasant's hand. "Whether God has sent him I cannot tell any more than whether God is responsible for the harvest . . . Maybe it is the earth that sent him, just as it is the earth that produces the harvest . . . But one thing is certain, he didn't come without a reason . . . God is but a name in all of that . . ."

"Fate, then?"

"Maybe fate . . . If everything were merely due to chance one would have to despair."

"Fate, too, is but a name, Miland . . . especially when fate is to have the name of Marius."

He shook his head. "Chance or fate, Doctor . . . When chance comes our way in human form, it is no longer chance . . . Whether a man is called this or that, that may well be chance, but that he should be here, that he came at a given hour, that is beyond name and chance . . . that indeed is fate."

Irmgard was afraid for her father. He was enmeshed in all these things in a peculiarly loose and yet inextricable way, even though he seemed to see them in a most reasonable light. Was she aware of this entanglement? Yet she herself was much more deeply entangled in them! Did she wish to extricate her father by that sacrifice of which lately there was so much talk? The whole world appeared to me like an immense shared dream of all the living, yet all of them asleep, like an infinitely ramified dream, enveloping all sleepers who believe themselves alive and in whom also all the dreams of the departed, the dreams of all the dead since all beginning are embedded. One throws the thread of his dream to the other, so that in his turn he may take it up and weave it into the cloth that is life. Is it God's dream in which all of us sleep?

"If nothing were preordained, my children, too, would have been due merely to chance."

Having hardly anything more to say, I suddenly asked, almost against my own will, "And Irmgard?"

He looked at me in surprise and then he said slowly, "Irmgard is my child."

"Yes, Miland, and if she continues to follow Marius she may be in great danger . . . You say that he has been sent by fate, but there are also madmen sent by fate . . ."

He shrugged. "He may be a madman and it may all be madness . . . but once all believe in a madness, madness becomes reason . . . the old reason no longer serves . . . and something in us must be able to say yes, then it becomes reasonable by itself."

There was something highly dangerous in all that, even though it also contained a kernel of truth in that it expressed the trust in an instinct of humanity which, led astray by its own reason and in direst anguish, would then haltingly grope for a new reason. Were these not the same impulses that had driven me from my scientific work and into my own solitude, now waiting and listening for an uncertain knowledge to come?

"Whether in danger or not," he said, "and if chance is not everything, if it was fated and if she is my child, then her path is the same as mine, then we shall meet each other and"—he hesitated—"and what I once hoped for may still come to pass . . ."

Now I understood. "The daughter is to become what her mother failed to fulfill? So that by way of Marius your path may still lead you back to Mother Gisson?"

He sucked on his pipe. "That's too complicated for me, what you've been saying, Doctor, my head's not made for that . . . But you also said that I want to be pious, and that's true, that's what I'm working on, and if Irmgard, too, achieves piety, then she and I will share true communality . . ."

"Assuming that we share our communality not merely with our dead, as you declared earlier . . ."

"That's how it is now; but after the rebirth communality once more will be shared by the living."

"The rebirth," I said, deeply moved by that most magical of all words that mankind has invented for itself.

He was still busy with his pipe as if he had spoken merely of the winter crop, but his eyes shone with a dark flame.

With some trepidation I asked, "And I suppose the rebirth means the sacrifice?"

"Yes," he said calmly, still looking at me with his flaming gaze, "for it cannot be expected that we shall be granted the rebirth without having to do something for it."

An unexpected urge rose in me that I might also share in this rebirth, even though I did not believe in it and although it seemed to me both dangerous and nonsensical; it was as if the stillness all around us had been transformed suddenly into a sun storm filled with silent thunder, and I said, "The rebirth is death."

"Yes," he said, "but then death is a rebirth; whether seed or harvest, both are death and both are life."

There were many things I could have said in reply, such as that metaphors as such are not yet true perceptions, that our death is stronger than any metaphor, and that our knowledge needs to transcend and penetrate below the metaphor, so that our death may become the reality it truly is and so that our dying may be transfigured into that which we yearn and hope for; all this I could have said and more, but stronger than my thinking was the pull I felt toward the dark gate of the rebirth, toward the earthly death and earthly rebirth, and had the womb of the earth at that moment opened at my feet, for me to descend into its darkness in which lies the fire or the gold, so that I might walk through the darkness toward death or toward a resurrection in the light reborn, I would have done so. And as I realized this, somewhat shaken and disconcerted, I was struck unexpectedly by Miland's question: "Do you believe in God, Doctor?"

"I don't know . . ." I said. "I cannot tell at this moment."

"Oh yes," he said. "You know."

"I only know that I believe in the miracle of my solitude, in that miracle that has been sunk deeply in me and that bids me to see and perceive . . . but who it was that sank it in me, that I am unable to apprehend, I only know that it is in me and that it is my being, whether it be called soul or whatever, and I know that its miraculous power of perception is greater than all that can be perceived, greater than the miracle of earthly ripening and harvesting, and that, sunk into me at the moment of my birth, it can rise again to whence it has come . . . but where that is I don't know . . ."

"Yes," he said, satisfied, "it is the seed corn sunk in the earth, rising again in the rebirth of its ripening . . . it is the same . . ." And content, he called to his team of horses, "Yup," the wagon creaked and rattled, we walked in silence behind it, and in a few minutes we had arrived at his field.

I could have turned back right away, but having gone that far, I felt I had to greet his wife. She probably had waited for his return to break for the afternoon snack, for they stopped work as we arrived—a mound of oats was still waiting to be loaded—and sat down on the low grassy embankment that, bordered with dense bushes, edged one side of the field. There was his wife, the hired hand Andreas, and the elder son along with Cecily.

While I greeted the woman and sat down next to her, the farmer and Andreas unloaded the plow, unhooked the cross-shafts from the wagon, led the horses, with their traces still on, in front of the plow, and fastened the shafts to its hitch bar. After this had been done, both joined us for the vesper snack.

The Miland woman sat there like a man, her legs stretched out and spread, so that her blue calico smock sagged between them and the rough black shoes showed their nail-studded soles. She held herself ramrod stiff, her back sharply angular, and her bony awkwardness was unmitigated, even though she had opened a few buttons of her blouse because of the work. One always had the impression that this woman was doing all in her power to make herself as unfeminine as possible, so as to spite her husband. When in her strong, handsome set of teeth, strikingly similar to Mother Gisson's, one tooth became infected, I was barely able to persuade her to have it repaired with a gold crown; she first had insisted on having it pulled—one gap more or less in her teeth didn't matter to her.

Miland, as was his wont, had drawn Cecily close to him and was sharing his snack with her. Andreas was squatting next to us and cut his bread between his knees.

And then he said, "Wetchy, your neighbor up there, Doctor, is to be given notice on his house."

I had already heard a vague rumor to that effect some time before, but I said, "I haven't heard. What new kind of chicanery is this?" I looked at Miland questioningly. "Only the municipality can give notice, and as far as I know, no such proposal has been submitted to the council."

Miland was visibly embarrassed. "Well, yes, Krimuss is supposed to offer such a proposal in the near future . . . That's on Wenzel's instigation. I don't think it's serious."

I flared up: "And behind all of this is Marius."

Miland shook his head. "He knows very well that you and I and the whole Upper Village will vote against it, so there is only Lax, Krimuss, and Selbander in favor, and even if the mayor were to vote for it, it wouldn't pass."

Of course I would vote against it and so would Miland. But suddenly I had to ask myself whether I really would oppose it. An absurd question, to be sure, and so as not to think about it, I said, "Is this the truth of the heart in which the Upper and the Lower Village are to meet again?"

But Miland, who either had guessed my thought or simply had had the same one, shrugged. "If you come right down to it, a tradesman like that has no business in a farming village."

Every peasant despises the unproductive tradesman. But that this could now be expressed so unequivocally was the work of Marius. My first supposition that he could be a communist propagator, fanning the hatred of the despised unproductive work, gained once more in likelihood, but the surprising thing was that I began to share that scorn. However, I did not wish to admit this and so I said, "One thing is sure, he's being used left and right throughout the village."

"Does he do it for free?" asked the Miland woman with her rough bluntness.

I was annoyed. "Is he meant to work for nothing, by any chance? When he installed your radio, everybody was very happy, including yourself."

"Cost a pretty penny, too."

But Miland, who was cuddling his child and may well have been remembering that I had taken in little Rosa, said soothingly, "At heart he is quite a decent man."

"Well then, in God's name, why does your Marius permit Wenzel to stir up the whole village in an uproar against that poor little wretch up there? . . . Do something about it!"

"Where there hasn't been any uproar in the first place, none can be stirred up," said Miland with great conviction. And then he came close to me and said, "Doctor, in all candor . . . do you like Wetchy?"

"That's not the question . . . What matters is that his wife loves him and that he loves her and his children . . . and that one isn't permitted to make anyone's life more difficult than it already is . . . Or do you intend to make all those you don't like suffer for the fact that you don't like them?"

He put his hand on my arm. "You've taken in Wetchy's little girl although you don't like him, Doctor, and if it came to that I might have done the same . . . but if his little boy had died, you could not have saved him. One can help one's fellow being but one can't shoulder his fate . . ."

"Has Wenzel now also become fate for you, Miland? Even though I may not like Wetchy, even less do I like Wenzel . . ." I had to laugh.

"No," asserted Miland in his greater knowledge to which I had to bow, "if the truth be told, you like Wenzel better."

And then Andreas could be heard to say, "When you come right down to it, he does no real work; an agent like him goes around and talks people into buying this or that, that's all."

No, there was nothing that could be done anymore. Things had already gone too far. Even old Andreas knew the rules of the game, and the young lads were under the leadership of Wenzel. And I myself? Had I not also become enmeshed in their dream? To be sure, it was just another sleeping position into which this small world had rolled. But don't most revolutions boil down to nothing more than a tumbling over of sleeping mankind from the right to the left side or vice versa, emitting two or three sighs or groans in the process, after which it continues its dream of wakefulness? And even the knowledge of that dream is itself dream, sleep and dream, at the beginning and end of which lies the knowledge, even though the dream is without beginning or end.

With his snickering and malicious old man's laugh Andreas said, "Only serves him right if they give him notice now."

The Miland woman laughed. At such moments she could laugh, and even though it gave me some satisfaction that in the process my own work, the gold crown, became visible in her mouth, these were unwholesome occasions: that people strive so vainly to achieve an understanding, that they become trapped in a thought which will not let them go and on which they then pull until, out of clumsiness and in desperation, they hurt each other in sleepwalking numbness, so that even old, good-natured Andreas became the enemy of the agent Wetchy, a being who had never done him any harm, this provoked the laughter of this woman. For she was a clever woman who saw to the core of many things but who had become hardened and was now rooted in that hardness, so that like any hard being, she enjoyed seeing the awkward helplessness of others as a justification of her own hardness.

"Well, I have somewhat different views of what justice is supposed to be," I said, and rose. The vesper break had come to its end anyway.

"Can we ever become just without human kinship?" said Miland, who still stood in front of me with the child.

"Can we ever become pious without justice?" I retorted.

He smiled. "Faith requires justice, but faith itself must be unjust at times."

Was this true? Was this false? I no longer knew.

Nevertheless, I said, "Look here, Miland, these are strange subtleties you are using to justify the nasty tricks being played on poor Wetchy."

He gave me his hand. "No, Doctor . . . you know well enough how I mean it." And then he went back to his plow.

When I had left the group, I heard Cecily's voice, clear and pure, as she sang in the stillness of the late sun:

> . . . Agents and tradesmen we despise
> Our earth they bastardize
> We hold the future in our hands . . .

Behind me the child's song fell silent. I could hear Miland as he called to his team of horses and then some wooden sounds, but then all at once there came to my ears in the surrounding stillness and with utter clarity the word "God." It may have been only a sigh, an "Oh my God," a wafted breath solidified into the audible, the audible inner voice calling for reassurance in the face of the turmoil of loneliness, and it may have been the thought of rebirth which had released that word in me. Had not my whole flight from the city been an attempt at such rebirth? Was my yearning for a knowledge of the wholeness of life, my yearning for an encompassing of its outermost limits, was that not also such an attempt? Mother Gisson's knowledge of temporal times and of earthly depth was great, and inscrutably deep is the innermost chasm of the human soul, but the power of time and of things resides in infinity, infinite the chasm of the soul, and an infinity which is merely a continuous remove, non-encompassable and inconceivable, would remain unfathomable and without a conceivable wholeness for the human mind were it not that a supra-infinity, a supra-inconceivable entity had been placed over it, encompassing it and recomposing it into a whole: God. No individual's thinking can or ever could grasp that supra-infinity since that thinking barely can reach to infinity; man's apprehension had to grow over millions of years and through generations after generations to allow for that remotest image to emerge from the most earthly gropings and searchings, amended time and again and ceaselessly perfected, yet already present in that first moment in which man felt himself as a human being and in which his human countenance had been bestowed upon him, his yearning and his memory, the memory of millions of years and millions of generations, still inconceivable and perhaps merely a faint apprehension of the heart, growing from a continuous rebirth that strives toward him, strives to strengthen the ephemerally remembered image of his dream, holding on to it through rites and deeds so as to be permitted to utter that which is unthinkable and unutterable: God. And yet how deeply tempting it is to draw Him back into the temporal and the tangible, to call Him back into the forms of the earth, to elevate earth itself into His being, and to conceive of the truth perceived by the eyes and the fingers as His reality! And I who dare not pronounce the name of God because for such presumption my knowledge has become too small, my memory too weak, and my yearning altogether too human, I, who became aware of the relapse in faith all around me, in my fear of that potential lapse that resides in every being, I had no way out left to me but that one sigh which in the solitude and stillness all around me had sounded as the voice of the heart.

It may have been a mere coincidence that the route I took back led through Church Street.

The small garden in front of the presbytery was now full of dahlias, they stood in all the colors of the rainbow along the fence, but in the circular center bed the priest had planted his roses, so that he might have them before his eyes and could enjoy them fully when sitting on the bench along the wall of the house. He was busy watering them just as I came by and, stopping at the fence gate, I greeted him.

He nodded at me, for he was reluctant to put down the heavy watering can and then have to pick it up again. Soft and peaceful, the water sprayed from the sprinkler nozzle and a gentle breath of moist smells rose from the darkening earth around the plants and mixed with the quiet dryness of the evening, the light of which, turned golden, sounded in mellow harmony with the yellow and red of the roses.

The priest quickly tipped the remaining water from the can, the fine parabolas joined into a thick feeble dribbling, forming a small puddle between the clumps of earth before seeping away, and after shaking out the last drops, he put down the can and came over to me.

"The roses are beautiful, Father."

A smile crossed his lopsided face. "But the dahlias, too, Doctor." He was fair.

One always looked for the thick scarf over which his face peered out in winter, for it was difficult to imagine him in any other way even when, as now, he was in shirt sleeves, his shabby black taffeta bib hanging out over the open waistcoat.

I told him that I envied him his roses and he invited me in to smell his flowers, as they smelled strongest in the evening. So I entered the garden and found the familiar small fragrant cloud around each plant, a sweet and small sacred life, and once again I found myself thinking that in all probability the faith of that little man did not exceed the fragrant confines of his plants.

He rubbed his thin arms that protruded from the much too short sleeves of his patched shirt; the watering cans had been heavy.

"Yes, the flowers," he said, and a weak inner light illuminated his face.

But then he told me that he had not yet finished watering and asked me to excuse him while he filled the cans once more. I offered to help, and so each of us took a can, from the rough interior of which a coolish dank breath rose, and carried the cans to the pump in the yard. I grasped the wooden pump handle rubbed smooth by innumerable hands, the priest held the cans under the spigot, and after a few strokes the stream of water rumbled into the tin. Then I insisted on carrying both cans because of the better balance and was allowed to help water the flowers under the watchful eye of the priest, to make sure I did it right.

When we had finished, he sighed.

"What is it, Father? Again some church repairs?"

He nodded, pleased because I had understood him.

"Couldn't you raise the matter in the municipal council, Doctor? I can't get anywhere by myself . . . and Lax in particular, I simply can't cope with him . . ."

"Well, Father, if we had the folks from the Upper Village on our side, we might get somewhere . . . but as you know, in such cases they vote with Lax because it isn't their church and because they have a long way to go . . ."

"Always that discord. Maybe that'll change now, God willing."

What was to change? What did he hope for?

He looked at the church in sorrow. As a result of the humidity rising from the ground, the plaster had fallen off the wall all the way up to a man's height, but to my surprise I noticed that the stretch extending between the tower and the church door had been repaired.

He noticed my surprise. "Oh that? . . . Johanni repaired that for me as a favor."

"You see, Father, there are also some white sheep among your flock."

He giggled his arch, insect-like laugh. "But only in return for another favor."

"And what was that?"

"I had to bless his brass moons . . . for the cattle."

Ah yes, the brass moons, which hereabouts are often hung on cows next to the bells like dog tags and which also decorate the harnesses of horses.

"And that was only enough to reach to the church door?"

"Unfortunately."

It was as if any problem that had no connection with his rose plants amounted to nothing more than a petty material worry; his world had a puny core of animation with nothing around it but a bit of tangle, dry and inconspicuous, and yet an entire human soul had to be accommodated within, with all its tensions reaching from the pagan to the devout and the divine, and it seemed to me as if the priest Rumbold were obliged to manage an interior household that was both meager and highly complicated. Though this may well be the case with all of us.

"Yes, Father, if there were always some moons to be blessed it would be simpler . . . but for the Sunday sermon the peasants are less inclined to pay. That's a business that to them doesn't tally as clearly . . ."

"Maybe it'll get better now."

Again this strange hope.

"Oh?"

"Well, yes, there's a man now in the village, his name is Marius . . . and now there may be more of the brass moons around."

He saw my astonishment. "One may well accept a little super-

stition for the sake of the welfare of the church; it's a pious superstition, after all."

I had to laugh. "Well, to me this superstition doesn't look quite
so pious."

He became apprehensive. "Is it really bad, Doctor? . . . I didn't
want to believe it . . ."

"That depends, Father . . . I don't know what you've been
told . . ."

"That, may God forgive me the sin, that they've now taken to
venerating the devil in the earth."

"Well, maybe not exactly the devil but perhaps the earth itself
or something of that sort . . ."

"Dear God, but that's sheer folly . . . that runs counter to all
reason . . . The man must be deranged."

Strangely enough, I felt prompted to defend Marius. "If a single
man believes it, Father, then it's madness, but if all believe it, it
becomes reason and vice versa . . . That's how it is."

"No, no," he protested, "don't succumb to blasphemy, Doctor.
Even if everybody were to stand against the eternal verities, they
would still remain sacred and eternal."

"Yes, Father, that's all well and good . . . but the world has
always gone through periods of madness so as to advance a bit on
the road to reason . . . Where was reason when the war broke out?
And yet, at the time, it seemed reasonable to us to go and fight
. . . The world once more is falling back into the irrational because
it has grown weary of its reason . . ."

He looked at me aghast. "But, Doctor, that only happened because mankind failed to recognize the eternal verities . . . The divine
commandment to love one's neighbor would have prevented all
those calamities . . ."

I really did not wish to tease him, but I was thoroughly fed up
with the invocation of this so-called reason. And although I knew
that the Arabs had burned down the Alexandrian library and yet
had reverted to Hellenism, that the Occidental knighthood had put
the Moorish universities to the torch without being able to prevent
their fecundating all of Europe, and although I knew that there is

an incontrovertible truth which is as indubitable as two times two makes four, I said, "There are patients who instinctively do the right thing, who feel what it is they need, and there are others who do exactly the opposite, even though there isn't one among them who isn't convinced that what he does is right for him, even though it may kill him . . . And the same applies to mankind, which from time to time needs to fall back into irrationality, and sometimes this may even be the right thing to do. At least, mankind has not yet killed itself up to now . . ."

"But it is close to doing so," declared the little gardener courageously. "Yes, indeed, it is close to it if mankind continues to spurn the blessing of divine revelation. Mankind's physician is risen for it in Jesus Christ the Savior and if it accepts His hand it need no longer lapse into insensateness."

"Father," I said, serious once more, "it may be that this teaching is still too great for man in all his imperfections. His reason still has too many cracks and holes from the time of its origin, and even though they are plastered over time and again, there are still too many that burst open anew and reveal underneath the naked madness of its beginnings . . . It will be quite some time before all the irruptions of irrationality have vanished for good . . . Always remember that man is lonely and that the lonely are prone to insanity."

He had bowed his lopsided head and was thinking it over. And then he said, "No, man need not be lonely if he accepts the teachings of the Church, nor are its teachings too great for him, for even the fishermen of Galilee understood them . . . but they are too gentle for him, for man still has not been able to tame his own wild nature."

"Yes, Father," I said, laughing. "There you are quite right for once. One should first teach men to love and tend the flowers."

"Yes, isn't that right?" he replied, beaming. "And may God grant us that the matter stemming from this individual, this Marius, also will turn out to be nothing more than one of those roundabout ways which you mentioned."

"What roundabout ways, Father?"

"Well, that ultimately lead toward salvation."

"Yes, may God grant that, indeed, Father," I said, and shook his hand in parting.

"May God be with you," he said.

I slowly climbed the hill. The sun was about to disappear behind the flat backdrop of the mountains. The whole valley became light gray as if the smoke which had hung all day in front of the rocky walls were now flowing down so as to flatten also the rest of the landscape and leach out all its colors: hills and meadows slid together, the waves in the ground evened out, and the border between woods and rocks could no longer be discerned. Only directly in front of me were the trees and the grass still green, a green island with blurred edges through which I walked and which kept pace with me. When the sun had disappeared completely and only a soft saffron stripe in the sky gave proof of its departure, the new shadows of dusk appeared all around and reshaped all the forms of nature: the clefts and crevices in the rocks had returned and had become twice as deep, the gorges and abysses opened once more in the mountains, on the slopes the meadows cut into the woods became visible again, and the mighty cover of the forest was patterned in all its expanse by the cones of the spruces, each crown clearly defined in its blackish green and becoming progressively darker and blacker.

The woods which I entered now were heavier and wilder than the airy garden of the priest, wilder than the cheerful smell of the roses were the odors of resin and of mosses and of mold, and walking through the darkening shadows I feared for Irmgard. Ineluctable is the lonely dream in which we are enmeshed, inextricable as the well-nigh infinite ramification of the canopy above me through which the clear evening sky still shone on the darkness of my path. A grouse rose with heavy wings in front of me, and when I took a shortcut through a clearing, a roebuck and two fawns jumped soundlessly across my field of vision. And then it became increasingly still throughout the woods. I tried to say "God" and I said it quite loudly but the woods would not answer.

12   If the strange tension weighing over the village had been released during the village fair, I would not have been surprised. And it may well be that a full-blown kermess brawl would have cleared the air. But scheduled revolutions never take place, least of all in bad weather. In the morning I even thought that the whole fair would be rained out altogether, that is how much the water had taken hold of the September world. The woods around my house had dissolved into a rainy veil. Drenched in water flowing down the trunks of the trees, their wood appeared as if tired and ready to rot away, the white moss on the branches had combined with the fog, and the fog that sank down ever more thickly was like white moss, like snow that isn't quite snow and melts away as it is about to solidify. On the electric wires that lead to the house, drop after drop hung in long rows which from time to time were set in motion by their own weight and slid along the slanted wires down to the next mast. And when later I left and had come out of the woods, I could not even see the first houses of the Upper Village. Everything was shrouded in gray, only a strip of the grassy meadow around me was visible and, at its outer limit, a light green birch standing in the thick mist.

Trapp disappears into the fog and then reemerges; at the edge of the fog his legs can no longer be seen and he becomes a gliding float, a strangely animated barge, and the fog seems filled with sorrow.

But the rain hesitated and stopped, the clouds lifted a bit as if to give some room to the people readying for the fair, and when I arrived in the village, mass was already over and the festivities were in full swing. Between the end of Church Street and the pub, canvas-roofed stands stood on both sides of the main street and offered their cheap merchandise, cheap and yet overpriced, for the peasants have no way of comparing prices. The Upper Village was well represented. Sack was here with his boys, and for a moment I saw Irmgard, who, wide-eyed, admired the gingerbread hearts on sale at one of the stands. But Marius was not to be seen anywhere. Children's trumpets could be heard and the shuffling of the crowd as it slowly moved forward and back, their shoes mud-encrusted and pants and socks splashed with dirt, hardly aware of the puddles and full of a ponderous determination to make merry.

Wenzel also stood there, surrounded by the usual band of young lads, and upon catching sight of me he laughed, gave me a military salute, and called out, "Guard! 'Ten-shun!"

A few of the lads clicked their heels so hard that the puddles at their feet splashed all over. The others laughed.

Wenzel snapped at them in his loud, well-modulated voice: "Nothing to laugh at . . . I said, 'Ten-shun!"

They smirked, but most of them obeyed and stood rigidly at attention.

And then something rather strange happened. I, an old soldier, responded with the military salute.

"Like it, Doctor?" Wenzel asked guilelessly. He seemed to have forgotten the incident at the Pit of the Dwarfs and I, too, hardly remembered it.

I look him over; he barely reaches to the chest of his grenadiers and yet, despite his clownish appearance in his overlarge plus fours, this hop-o'-my-thumb has a weirdly intimidating presence. Nevertheless, I kept myself under control. "Have you gone crazy?" I ask him. "Or are you turning the fair into a parade ground?"

His reply is surprising. "Doctor, some of the lads should be trained as medical corpsmen."

Krimuss came over from a group of older farmers. "Today the beer is on me . . ."

"Long live the boss!" commanded the general.

"Hurrah!" responded his men.

"Three cheers!" shouted Wenzel.

"Hurrah! Hurrah! Hurrah!" echoed the troop.

Krimuss tries to make a flattered face but it turns out sweet-sour, for, in truth, the barrel of beer pains his stinginess. I knew it and yet I somehow applauded his gesture, if only as proof that he had overcome his avarice at least to that extent.

Not far from us was a stand selling textiles, and there I saw Agatha having some linen measured out for herself. I noticed that she didn't even glance at Peter, who was playing soldier under Wenzel's orders. Where was the closeness that had once joined these two human beings together? Was it still floating in the air somewhere between them or had it flown away altogether? Had the longing, coming from and directed toward infinity, that longing that takes hold of human beings so that they may live again, escaped into infinity?

Next to me Krimuss said, "Fine lads."

I got my bearings back. "It must be your birthday, Krimuss, for which you have my best wishes . . ."

Together with me he strolled through the circle of his admirers. "The lads deserve a little something . . . now that they're going to work for free in the mine . . ."

On his watch chain dangled a silver half-moon of old peasant workmanship. From the shooting range outside the village the first shots could be heard.

"Yes," I said rather unthinkingly, "the Pit of the Dwarfs."

He looked at me with some resentment. "Yes, I know, Doctor . . . Without your intervention things might have gone differently and we would have it already . . ."

"Have what?"

"The gold . . . Why are you siding with the Upper Village?"

I did not reply; my thoughts were with Mother Gisson and that would not have been an answer.

He continued: "We're no fools down here . . . It is rather they who are the fools with their stories about the mountain . . . The municipality has the mining rights and must exploit them . . ."

"Even Marius," I said, and was embarrassed by finding myself invoking that crackpot as my authority, "even Marius is against the search for gold . . ."

Lax had joined us, tall and stout, and he laughed through his strong teeth. "Marius? . . . We'll get him yet, don't worry . . ."

"The little one is a lot better than Marius," says Krimuss heat-edly, and he flexes his arm and makes a fist to indicate Wenzel's muscular strength. "Marius, he fits in with Miland . . ."

"Yes," said Lax, "yes, Miland . . . If it weren't for him we would be the majority in the council . . . but because he married someone from the Upper Village and doesn't dare have a mind of his own, the municipality is to let the mining rights expire . . ."

I had to defend my friend. "Miland has a mind of his own all right . . ."

"He wants to become the mayor," commented Lax, "that's all; and if he were on our side he could . . . why not, for all I care . . . but as things stand, he must be replaced in the council, I can't help that . . ."

Krimuss nervously plays with his watch chain. "If we don't get it, someone else will . . . and that one will have the last laugh once we're gone . . ."

Lax clapped his huge hand on Krimuss's shoulder. "If Krimuss gets his gold, he'll never die . . . That's how he is!"

Krimuss smiled almost gratefully and then said with enormous conviction, "Yes."

Of course, someone who already possesses the beyond in the hereunder never need die.

"When you come right down to it," ponders Lax, "every single one of us has something that will keep him from dying . . . Krimuss needs the gold, but as for me, Doctor, put a girl in my bed when my time comes . . . and then you'll see for yourself how I'll manage to elude death . . . Better than all your medicines, Doctor."

So even this brute of a man was concerned with death. But then he said, "Are you coming with me to the shooting contest? I'm just about to go . . ."

We had arrived at the pub.

"No," I said. "I can't compete with you at shooting, Lax, but please see to it that we don't have any deaths today . . . With all your talk about the gold you could start the most god-awful brawl."

"You can rest assured," he replied, "the lads will keep discipline."

But Krimuss said, "They're getting their beer today because

they've got to enter the mountain . . . That's where death sits and for that you need courage . . ."

"Oh?" I said. "Did you ever see death sitting in there?"

"Yes," he replied. "When I was a small boy I was inside and I saw him myself."

How deeply must one sink into another's life to grasp it truly? On what deepest level of oblivion rests such a life and how far back need memory be sent? And yet life is a single whole and birth and death are so close together that the dying man encompasses all of life in a single breath! Krimuss was indeed almost ready to encompass himself, everything in him strove to join the beginning to the end, and I was not surprised when he said, "That's where I'll be sitting."

"You go and sit in the pub," said Lax, pushing him in the door.

But I went up to my clinic.

The festival is an occasion on which the folks from the more remote homesteads come to the village not only to make their purchases but also to take care of their medical needs. So my business took longer than usual and it was quite late before I finished my consultations. As I stepped out into the open corridor, the command "Close ranks!" rang through the whole building and was audible all the way to the public room.

I looked down into the yard. Under the chestnut tree, the leaves of which already hung down in autumnal lassitude, Wenzel stood on a chair and commanded his troop. The lads assembled, some staggering out from the pub or from the toilet located at the back of the yard where they had satisfied a call of nature, they came haltingly and in a haze of beer, some attempted to play football with the chestnuts fallen from the tree, but finally they all stood lined up more or less properly.

"Hurry! Hurry!" the general goaded the last stragglers.

And when at last order was restored, he commanded, " 'Ten-shun! . . . Close ranks! . . . Right dress!"

There weren't fourteen now as on that evening at the Pit of the Dwarfs; their number had grown to some thirty and to my surprise I also recognized among them some lads from the Upper Village.

At the door to the glassed-in porch that adjoins the yard there were the spectators, including their patron Krimuss. Lax was missing, since he had gone to the shooting range, but Sabest and his wife were there; he had his arm around her shoulder and was visibly gratified to see that Peter played such a prominent role in Wenzel's troop.

The general on the chair had arranged the sly wrinkles in his face in a mien of commanding severity and inspected his faithful followers. But suddenly he jumps down, runs to one of the soldiers, and slaps him—he has to reach up quite a bit to do so—with all his might across the face. "Button your pants before you come on duty!" he hollers at him.

The spectators laughed. I had expected that the big fellow would react angrily and knock the midget down. But not at all. He buttoned his fly and Wenzel calmly climbed back on his chair.

"All right now . . ." he declaimed. "You all know that we shall now march to the shooting range, where you are expected to do honor to yourself in the presence of the entire population . . . 'Ten-shun! . . . In rows of four! . . . March!"

So it was done. They even had a drummer, who had taken his proper place according to regulations on the right flank of the third rank. I suddenly felt a strange and childish urge to be allowed to march among them, for is it not as if the uniform cadence of man's steps could save him at least temporarily from the helplessness of his dream?

Then Wenzel left his command post on the chair for good to take the lead of his company, and they all marched out of the yard intoning their anthem: "We are men and no mere boys . . ."

I entered the public room as the spectators returned from the porch. There were not many people left, since most of them had gone to the shooting range. But the tobacco clouds hung densely in the air, together with the sour odor of sweat and the beery fumes. Pluto, the St. Bernard, rose in a soft and deliberate motion so as to rub his flanks against my legs and place his giant head under my ruffling hand.

Sabest, his perennial cigarette in his mouth, said, "We're having a good autumn for once, Doctor."

"I can't really see that," I answered, glancing out the window.

As usual, he tested the edge of his long knife against the ball of his thumb. "No, I don't mean the weather but what's about to happen . . ."

"Greetings, Doctor," sounded suddenly out of the tobacco haze from one of the tables; it was the slow-paced voice of Mathias of the Mount.

"What? Mathias of the Mount here? How come you're not at the shooting contest?"

He laughed. "Not this year . . . One of my shots might go off in the wrong direction . . . the one you didn't let me fire, Doctor . . . I'm going home."

"That shot wouldn't have been worth the trouble."

"And how it would have been worth the trouble! . . . We would have peace now."

"All right, if you think so . . . but if you're going home, we can walk together."

Outside, the fair was at its most animated. We pondered what to bring back for Mother Gisson. And since, despite her age, she was a woman and a woman doing herself proud, I bought her a pretty silver pendant, while Mathias was content to buy her a coffee mug bearing the touching inscription: "Hotter and sweeter than coffee dew / is my eternal love for you."

We climbed the road in silence, with the even, steady gait of seasoned mountaineers. The rain had started again. The woods smoked and white wisps of fog drifted along the slopes. But the rain had thinned, the cloud cover had lifted, the birches and pines glistened luminously in the moistness, and from time to time there even was a break in the clouds, so that a band of rain appeared as a singing golden veil in the rays of the sun, though only for a brief instant, for a quick hand up there immediately pushed a few more clouds into the momentary crack so that it would not open again before evening set in. And the mountains remained invisible.

Mathias said, "Now he'll even get into the municipal council . . ."

I stopped. "Who? Not Marius? How would he go about doing that?"

"He probably doesn't even want it himself . . . It's Lax who wants it . . . One of the other councillors is to withdraw, so that Marius can be voted in . . ."

"What nonsense."

"Why? It's perfectly in order."

"Mathias, I think you've had too much to drink."

"Maybe, but now that he's getting a following in the Upper Village as well, it's only right that he should also have a seat in the council . . . Lax is sure to bribe someone to withdraw . . . What he'd like best, of course, is for it to be Miland . . ."

It had been a long time since Mathias of the Mount had said that much at one time; it could well be that he was a bit tipsy, but what he had said was all entirely within the realm of possibility.

I asked, "And the mountain?"

"If men don't protect it, it'll know how to protect itself, that's for sure," he declared with great conviction.

We said nothing further. The skies again became denser, and though it wasn't yet dusk, dusk was already there, not quite noticeable yet present like a guest who has come too early and now waits in a corner: the clouds crumble, as if aimlessly picked to pieces by some unseen hand, they fly around randomly searching, broken free from the sheltering herd, while the gravel on the road is the color of wet evenings, the oceans take a deep breath that reaches all the way to the remotest peaks even though these be still hidden, and what has not yet happened is already a presence.

We arrived at Mother Gisson's with our gifts, and she now read with great admiration the inscription on the mug that Mathias had brought her. Dutifully, though with somewhat less animation, she admired my pendant. Before giving it to her, I had first had to draw a drop of blood from my finger with the sharp point of the clasp so that it might not destroy our friendship.

"Why didn't you come down for the fair, Mother Gisson?" I asked. "Had you come, I would have stayed down there for the dance."

"No one needed me down there."

"Not true, I did . . . You've been promising me a dance for a long time now."

Musing, she stared into space. "I reckon I'll come for the mountain kermess," she finally said. "There may well be a need for me there."

"Sure?"

"Of course, since Irmgard is the Mountain Bride."

The mountain kermess is a kind of appendix to the regular one, or more correctly its precursor, for there can be no doubt that, of the two, it is much the older celebration. This is corroborated by the fact that, like the Blessing of the Stones, it is held on a day of the new moon and that, in addition, it is in intimate correlation with the latter since the Mountain Bride consecrated during the Blessing of the Stones also plays the main role during the mountain kermess. But this ceremony takes place not at the Mountain Chapel but at the Cold Stone and usually it is even more meager than the Blessing: a few stands decorated with twigs, where beer and knick-knacks are sold, and a dance in the open air, that is all that has remained of what in olden times was indubitably a great and significant ritual; a bit of masquerading, and even that only if the weather is propitious.

"Well, so we'll dance together then . . ."

"Why, yes," she said, still somewhat lost in her thoughts. "That we'll do."

On the following Friday—I had long forgotten that there was a new moon and a mountain kermess—I was lured to the window by the sounds of music. It was about four o'clock, the sky, as far as I could see it from the house, was without a cloud, and the firs sang their dark, sharp-pointed chant into the blueness above. But it was not that which I had heard, even though it was quite audible, but the chords of an accordion which had stopped in front of my garden. It was the procession of the Mountain Bride moving toward the Cold Stone and the mountain kermess, and as they now all stood along the fence, with Christian the music maker playing his accordion, it was almost as if they were serenading me. There was quite a big crowd of young lads and girls surrounding Irmgard, the Mountain Bride, and I even made out Wenzel, never one to miss any merrymaking. And then I saw Mother Gisson in her best holiday attire and I understood what they wanted of me.

"I'll be right there," I called down.

"All right," replied Mother Gisson, bidding the others to continue without her and stepping into my garden.

I readied myself in haste and went down. Little Rosa was playing in the sand and Mother Gisson was watching her.

"Are you keeping her for good?"

"Well, certainly for as long as the sordid hate campaign against Wetchy continues . . . That gang needs to see that someone is on his side."

She nodded approvingly, but the glance with which she observed the child held little warmth. When we turned away she said, "I couldn't say she's a pretty child."

I was somewhat taken aback by her obvious dislike but at the same time felt ready to hold Wetchy responsible for bringing such ugly children into the world. And because man is prone to produce cheap wisdom when confronted with aversion, I countered, "Dear God, Mother, your village children are not all of them pretty as angels either . . ."

"No," she said, "that they are not . . . but this child you have here, that one is poorer than the others and that hurts."

"That's why I want to help it."

"That you can't."

In front of Wetchy's house stood his little wife, who greeted us obsequiously. Mother Gisson nodded back.

And then she said, "You're here to give help . . . that's fine and good . . . but don't make your helping too small, for all men are waiting to be helped . . ."

"They'd rather be helped by Marius."

"That's one more reason why you'll have to stand your ground."

We had arrived at the clearing where the cableway had its origin. The sky seemed as if made of silken steel over which the ball of the sun rolled, but over in the southwest soft white clouds began to cling to it, filled with a tepid limpness, layer upon layer, and already they had reached the peak of the Raw Venten.

"We'll get some weather today," I said. "I'm afraid our dancing may be in a bad way."

"There'll be time for dancing before it comes," she answered.

September filled the valleys, dark the Plombent Valley, in which the afternoon shadows were already settling, still sunny the Kuppron Valley, but both valleys were raised somewhat above themselves, as if they were floating above their own floors. The fields lay harvested, plowed earth showed in many places among the pastures, and only the maize still stood yellow, though no longer rooted in the earth but as if carried aloft·by the brightness of fall. In the lane of the cableway, some two hundred yards below the clearing, the fallen mine cage rested in a tangle of wires, already overgrown by rapidly sprouting grasses and weeds.

Though not yet in the fiery final clothing of the year, swiftly consumed in its own conflagration, the world had already begun to show its motley colors, and Mother Gisson said, "The world is dancing."

As we entered the path through the woods, leaving the cableway lane to our right, the air we breathed seemed saturated by springs. The blueness of the sky followed us, but the heavy fragrance of the moist forest floor met us even more swiftly, the cool dankness trickling over boulders and teeming with ferns. It was then that I said, "How can I help, Mother, when I myself seek help and do not find any?"

She replied, "Do not let yourself fall under a spell. Then you'll be able to help."

But I said, "How can we know when we fall under a spell? How can we ward it off?"

"You may well have to pass through it," she replied.

And then she said, "When the trees are dancing, you, too, are allowed to dance."

The path through the woods was almost level, at times interrupted by small clearings, enclaves of moisture in which the grass was saturated with the soil's nourishment and in which the coolness sang as within a shell. But the sea was stretched above us and shone on our way. And she said, "Nothing is ever lost and that's why one must love the children, for they retrieve that which for us is falling away into oblivion."

"Yes," I said, and thought of the fact that I had no children but only little Rosa, who was so ugly.

The old woman next to me walked as lightly as a young girl, as if her being also were raised above itself, as if she were somehow floating in her soul, gliding serenely over the mirror of her own self. Around us breathed all the large, age-old plants that we call trees, breathed all the vegetation, grasses and mosses, the rotted and the rotting, the growing and the yet burgeoning, and the wholeness of all that growing breathed the serenity of its freshness and of its everlasting renewal.

Nothing is ever lost, and the soul, sinking into the cool shaft of its own being, into the cool wellspring of its dream at the bottom of which rests curled the snake and in which the moon mirrors itself, in its shell it sings forevermore from the first child to the last children's children.

We now approached the festive detonations of blank mortar rounds. Broad and shattering, they ring through the foliage set atremble by their reverberations, in which always wingbeats of startled birds can be heard.

For a short distance the trail led down through sparse woods becoming sparser still; here meadowland already trespasses on stands of trees, the heather is displaced by mosses which themselves give way to soft short grass, the path runs through bright meadows, the view becomes ever more open and airy, the larches stand light green and well spaced, their branches touching each other merely with their fingertips, there are ever more birches among them, and after a few more steps, bordered by the brook that wells up next to the Cold Stone and here hurries between rust-brown grassy embankments before curving away to the cableway lane, a clearing gently edged by birches spreads before our eyes, a slightly hollowed-out terrace in the slope of the mountain, crowned by darker woods at its upper edge, where the Cold Stone itself stands, a garden over which tower the crepuscularly blue-gray majestic walls of the Kuppron, as yet only barely caressed by their shadows on their uppermost slopes: the last rays of the afternoon sun still illumined the fairgrounds, the glasses of the beer stand glittered in its gold, the canvas of the gingerbread stand hung like a slack sail on the sea, and the smoke of the sausage barbecue curled up into the transparent light. The glimmering sheen of gold and of human voices hanging over the grounds is at its thickest and has its center over the square of the dance floor which has been erected in the middle of the clearing; it is a humming kind of sheen, mixed up with the dragging and stomping of boots, intermingled with the smiling flowering of the air and with the sounds from the accordion of Christian the music maker, shadow and gold sheen singing toward heaven. The dancing had been well underway ever since the arrival of the Mountain Bride, while up at the edge of the woods and next to the old Celtic sacrificial table the last mortar shells were being detonated, and no one paid any attention at all to the Cold Stone itself: it stands there, shadowed and neglected on its half-buried pedestal, and the role it once played in this ceremony is long forgotten.

Mother Gisson and I had crossed the plank over the little brook and were now in the midst of the turmoil; some greeted us, but most paid us no heed, so deeply were they caught in the joy and animation which they sought to feel and share.

"Yes," said Mother Gisson, "and now you may lead me to our dance."

Christian struck up a new tune.

It was an honor dance to which I led her. But proper as our own dance was, all around us the stomping was wild and bodies and heads, as if lashed by invisible yet stormy waves, bobbed furiously; the dance floor was a steaming cauldron, bubbling with bodies, and the golden sheen, trembling and floating above, was full of hot vapors and quivering into infinity. So we danced, I, an aging man, the old woman in my arms for the dance of honor, and we smiled at each other in the knowledge of it though we were hardly dancing together, each of us dancing the unfathomable mystery of our own life, dancing the heartbeat of our own being, of our still present, not yet extinguished, still pulsing original source, inspired by and part of and feeling the great heartbeat all around us. Does one select the partner with whom to dance when one is under the command of one's own hammering blood? Can there be affection in such random selection? Does friendship still obtain? Or even love? Another dancer plucked Mother Gisson from my arms and I, too, changed partners, changed time and again, hardly knowing with whom I was dancing and knowing even less what was happening around me. I danced a few turns with Irmgard and she was grave and beautiful in her bridal finery; but soon she was torn from me and later I saw her with Lax, whose face bore the smile of one transfigured in carnal pleasure. Absorbed in its own rhythm the brown-bearded face of the blacksmith bobbed up and down, and for a moment I had a glimpse of Wenzel's sly mousy smirk almost smothered in the ample bosom of a big peasant girl, but all that surging mass became increasingly blurred before my eyes, as more and more my own consciousness became blurred and I noticed neither that Mother Gisson had left the dance floor long ago nor my own exhaustion, and though I heard myself being called, it was quite some time before I understood the meaning of the summons: "Doctor, it's high time you got out of there!"

It was Mother Gisson. She stood amidst the spectators outside the ropes enclosing the dance floor and her voice sounded more like a warning than a jolly remonstration. Yet I still could not break away, and when I finally did so, I stood for quite a while among the spectators and watched the turbulent mingling of bodies. They were moving without a pause and apparently without tiring, they struggled for their rapture with the grim determination of people possessed, with a grim passion that no longer had anything in common with the usual carnival merriment, driven by a magic tide which irresistibly rose and tore with it everything in its path, a tide generated in the twilight of mankind and ascending to the twilight of the stars, all to the accompaniment of the accordion. Oh yes, they had to hurry if they meant to reach the stars on this day, and I almost felt that I had to urge them on myself with my cheers and my applause, so that they would persist in their frantic efforts, and indeed they did: they hardly interrupted their strivings even while drinking beer and shouted to Sabest to bring them their mugs, and Sabest, as if he understood their urgency and the imperatives behind it, shuttled back and forth between them and his kegs.

I might have thrown myself once more into the teeming throng had Agatha not approached me and asked for Mother Gisson. I recognized her but was incapable of an answer: under the spell of the dance, under the spell of my own blood in which I felt birth and death so close together that they seemed to have become one and the same, I saw Agatha on a path toward an identical twilit zone and my mind barely sufficed to raise in me the fanciful notion that she might dance her child straight out of her belly. "Don't dance too much, Agatha," I said.

"No, no." She laughed. "I know well enough."

And then she repeated her question as to the whereabouts of Mother Gisson.

I looked up for the first time and saw that it was evening, though I saw it like someone who looks at a landscape out of the window of an overheated room without being able to go out. The shadow of the Kuppron had now covered the entire clearing, and the cool peacefulness between day and night was holding its murmuring dialogue in the air above the treetops.

"We shall look for her," I said.

Behind the spectators, Cecily, alone on the lawn, danced with her eyes closed to the tunes of the accordion and accompanied them with the texts of her own small life. Washed by the gray coolness, she glided hither and thither, at times stopping like a trout that stands still against the current and letting the coolness and the music ebb away from her, only to resume her chant once more and leap up again toward the evening and its singing intercourse.

And that's when we found Mother Gisson. She had bought a gingerbread half-moon for Cecily and called to the child. But to me she said, "So you finally stopped dancing? Good. Keep your senses."

"Yes, Mother," I said. But the dusk itself was drunk with the dancing and it bent under the strokes of the rhythms that continued to rise up into it.

Cecily had come, still half dancing, and let Agatha read for her the inscription on the gingerbread: "Moon and stars in heaven mild, the mother dreams about her child."

"That's true," said Agatha, "and very beautiful."

"No," said Cecily. "It should say: 'The father dreams about his child.' "

"Run along and dance," said her grandmother. "Children may still dance."

"Only the children?" I asked.

"Yes," replied Mother Gisson. "You go and see to Miland." And she took Agatha by the arm and left with her.

Miland sat in front of Sabest's beer stand and I sat down next to him. Our beer mugs between us on the rough white wood of the newly carpentered bench—for there were no tables—our fingers around their handles, without drinking, we both looked out into the evening, which in the deepening dusk had become light blue and pink, as light blue and pink as the frosting on the rows of gingerbread becoming increasingly indistinct on the stand across the way, imbued with a frosty dullness and yet strangely vehement and heated up by the raging din of the dance floor. Were Miland's thoughts also over there? Did he disapprove? Or did he think of leading his own bridally attired daughter to the dance? We remained silent while all around were only roars of laughter, particularly when splinters from the coarse bench seats pricked through trousers and skirts each time anybody sat down on them or moved. Behind his counter, Sabest was in his element. With his shirt sleeves rolled up over his lean muscular butcher's arms, he poured glasses, washed them out, banged an empty mug on the counter in time with the music, almost splintering the wood, and each time he emerged from his shack he grabbed the nearest girl within reach and dragged the shrieking victim back with him into his shelter.

Someone called to him, "If your wife were to see you . . ."

"She'd only be proud . . ." he shouted back.

Lured by the clouds of vapor hanging over the grounds, all the

gnats and mosquitoes in the surroundings had found their way here
and their thin, razor-sharp choir accompanied the music like a
malevolent falsetto descant sawed on some weird fiddle, its single
string tightened to the breaking point. The stomping of boots on
the wooden floor continued uninterrupted, even faster than before,
and in an increasing and peculiarly robot-like muteness; there was
still an occasional shout, a solitary yodeling that rose only to die
away abruptly as if ashamed of itself.

"It isn't right," said Miland finally, "it is not done in freedom."

Did I understand him correctly? Did he mean that this dancing
was removed from the will of the individual? Or was stronger than
the will of a single being?

I asked him, but even as I was doing so, I became aware of a
figure in the dusky haze up there near the Cold Stone. It moved
there, inspired and solemn, and then sat down on the stone altar.

"Isn't that Marius?"

Miland peered up with his sharp hunter's gaze. "Yes, that's him
all right."

"What the devil is he doing there?"

"Hm." Miland had no explanation either. But neither of us was
surprised by his appearance and it may even be that we had missed
his presence.

"Well, he's not going to sit there forever," I remarked. "He's
bound to come down sooner or later."

But for the time being he did not move; instead other figures
appeared at the edge of the woods, to disappear again soon after in
the darkness. Only the outline of Marius sitting on the stone remained immobile. I looked up there with concentration and for a
long time, for so long, as a matter of fact, that I almost was under
the impression that the Kuppron itself, grown ever larger and blacker
in the mantle of the night and growing larger still, that the Kuppron
itself was about to come down to join the raging dance, join in it
more deliberately than the seething human mass, yet it, too, driven
by the pulsing rhythm of its blood, the slow pulse of the earth, the
ebb and tide of eternal fire. I did not believe it, but my eyes wanted
to and they blurred in fear at the menacing approach of this mon-

strously dimensionless dancer, so that I had to turn away and back
to the humanly measurable.

Then the blacksmith came by laughing. "Now the fires are ablaze,
Doctor, and not even you can contain them any longer."

I pointed to the edge of the woods. "What's happening up there,
smith?"

As if holding his hammer, he made a circular movement with
his arm. "Now it's starting all over."

Yes, something was about to happen, something was going on,
something dangerous and alluring, and while it amused the smith,
I was apprehensive. I had to see what it was and got up without
further ado to climb to the Cold Stone, but after a few steps a
strange dread held me back and I looked for Wenzel instead, so
that he might enlighten me; but the midget had disappeared.

Thus I wandered undecided around the dance floor, on which
the music and the stomping had not abated for a single moment.
It had become quite dark and storm lamps were being lit, simple
acetylene lanterns that looked like tin cans, some near the stalls and
four of them on long poles at each corner of the dance floor. The
white beam of their flames whistled in the air with a venomous
sharp hiss and cut through the buzzing of the gnats, and everything
outside their circle of light became even more difficult to discern.

Finally I discovered Mother Gisson, and I was surprised that it
had taken me so long, for she still stood quietly with Cecily in the
same spot.

I approached her. "Mother," I asked her almost fearfully, "what's
happening now?"

"Don't ask," she replied. "When it calls, you must follow or it
will sweep over you."

"Who's calling?"

"Everything!"

"Up there, too? What's going on there?"

She peered into the darkness and then she said, "The spirits are
coming."

"Who? Why, that's something new!"

"It's nothing new . . . it's just that they haven't been here for a
long time."

And, indeed, I now saw a long row of formless unwholesome creatures moving down from the woods toward the dance floor. They came so stealthily that they were able to enter the circle of light unnoticed and with complete surprise, and even when they were there the crowd, intent on its dancing, was not yet aware of them. It was only after some shrill screams by some of the girls that the music fell silent and the crowd froze in fright, face to face with the equally immobile group of spirits.

And the spirits were frightening enough to behold. Their faces hidden by masks, rags, and beards, clad in straw coverings which gave them the aspect of animated tepees, armed with pitchforks like devils, their heads crowned with goat and cow horns between which some had stuck a moon or a sun made of gold foil, they planted themselves in front of us and threateningly and slowly waved their weapons to and fro.

This lasted for a few seconds and then the masked figures started a terrifying din. They rattled their chains and sounded cowbells, they clanked their weapons and tools together and, with foolish and yet intimidating hops and jumps, encircled the whole dance floor, on which the mass of people still stood motionless and silent in frightened expectancy.

And then one of the chief spirits shouted, "Music! Christian! Go on playing!"

Whereupon the accordion again took up its folk-dance tune, but this time, strangely enough, accompanied by two fiddles, discordant and scratchy yet plaintive-sounding fiddles which must have come in with the spirits. The doggedly dull stomping began anew, while the spirits, holding each other by the hand, encircled the dance floor in a loose, awkward roundelay. One of the lads, wearing a witch's mask and a woman's skirts, rode on a broom, while another one, with a white beard and a bishop's miter, obviously represented something like a high priest, and although I knew that someone was hidden under the mask, it seemed to me undignified that a make-believe old man would hop around so childishly.

The smallest of the devils left the circle, limped toward me, and shouted, "Anyone who doesn't dance goes to hell and will be impaled!"

"Well, Wenzel," I said, for that is who the figure unmistakably was, "at last you show yourself in your true colors."

"You'll be the first one I'll come and get," answered the devil; then he waved his pitchfork in my face and rejoined the circle.

The dance continued, and if one stood aloof from the roundelay of the spirits, which, in truth, was performed merely by some peasant lads, one could see it as nothing more than an ordinary kermess dance, even though it had continued now for over two hours with undiminished and untiring intensity. This I repeated to myself, repeated it time and again—and yet despite all the absurdity in Wenzel's summons, hardly calculated to incite someone to join in the fun, I had to restrain myself from jumping once more into the stomping, seething fray.

I looked at Mother Gisson. She stood tall, fair and calm, and I was glad that she showed no inclination either to join again in the dance.

"Don't you want to call Irmgard, Mother?" asked Miland.

"Let her be," replied her grandmother.

The night thickened and the wind of fear blew down from the Kuppron, it played with the flaming beams of the acetylene lanterns and cooled the moist brows of the dancers, who felt not its freshness but merely the breath of fear. Had they found in that very fear the pleasure that they sought? Did they still seek it? Almost free of perspiration, their faces seemed frozen, marked so deeply in the violent carbide light by jet-black shadows and so fractured into ridges and indents as to have assumed a kind of midnightly appearance no longer resembling human countenances, and they were hardly different any longer from the masks worn by the figures in the outer circle. The cutting gassy smell of the lanterns commingled with the fumes, and the wild seething rising from the arch-beginnings of life petrified into a kind of supra-animation which was like the howling of invisible stars. Thus dance the mountains in the light of the comets when no human eye can perceive them. The accordion sang the night itself, the violins fiddled white light, and it was as if they were no longer played by human hands. Sabest, standing in his stall, flanked by the storm lanterns, had turned into a machine and continued to drum the rhythm of the night on the counter with an empty beer mug. In front of us, Lax appeared, his mustache black between the wrinkles of his midnightly pallid flesh, and he bared his white teeth as he howled "Boo!" at us, so that Cecily started to cry; "Boo!" and then he was swallowed up once more in the tumult.

How long could this mad pandemonium go on? Notwithstanding all the perseverance that peasants seem to bring to such merrymaking—but could this still pass as such?—there had to be an end to it, there had to be a resolution, and this assuredly was felt not only by myself but also by all those standing here, waiting for some form of consummation, including even the dancers themselves. Was Marius still sitting up there on the stone? Should he not have been here long ago, so that redemption might come about, the redemption from a state of being that had overintensified itself and had become transfixed into an unbearable state of supra-being?! Cecily had quieted down, with one hand she held on to the skirt of her grandmother while with the other she groped for the arm of her father so that he would, as usual, pick her up, but Miland paid no attention to her, he held his hands in front of him as if ready to accept a gift proffered to him, his glance was on the dancers and yet was directed far beyond them, and there was an anxious expectancy in his expression. Was he looking for Irmgard? She remained invisible; only her bridal crown could be seen, immobile in the center of the dance floor, encircled by all the bodies and masked figures.

But suddenly one of the acetylene lanterns had joined the dancing circle. Its pole, which someone must have torn from its mooring, swayed at a slant over the heads of the devils and spirits and its white flame hissed here and there like a venom-spurting reptile.

"Stop it!" I shouted, and was about to intervene, for how easily could the flame take hold of one of the straw mantles, but at the same moment I found myself surrounded by the masks, my hands and arms had been grabbed, and I was dragged along as the other lanterns also began to move and joined the whirling turmoil.

Had a collective madness taken hold of everyone? Had I, too, fallen in its grip? To be sure, I was helpless, I was being dragged along, I had no choice but to follow, but I did more, I not only let myself be pulled, my legs voluntarily jumped with all the others, I was unrestrainedly dancing with all the others, and the curses I meant to utter froze in my mouth, my tongue and my face were as if numbed, and even when I was punched in the back with one mean blow after another—I guessed it was Wenzel who was doing this—I was unable to utter a single sound. I noticed that the ropes enclosing the dance floor had fallen, and then I became aware of the fact that our circling motion had changed into a straight-line progression: like a multi-legged animal, so close were we pressed together, the dancing herd was pushing ahead to the sounds of the accordion and the fiddles, harshly illuminated by the swaying lanterns. My devils were still glued to me, but even if they had released me, I would no longer have been capable of breaking free but would have continued to hop along with the rest.

Then the music broke off and abruptly we all stood still. My hands were freed, the compact mass around me loosened up, the spirits had suddenly disappeared. And it became apparent that we had stopped in the immediate neighborhood of the Cold Stone and that, indeed, from the beginning this had been the objective to which the spirits had driven us. Although the stone table was now bare and Marius no longer sat on it, the lantern poles were rammed into the ground around its circumference, so that only the stone was lit up, while the human herd, now occupying the slope with faces expectantly turned upward, was illumined by its reflection.

Harsh was the green of the bushes and trees behind the stone in the stark whiteness of the carbide, their leaves trembled gently, the woods farther behind lay in darkness, and nothing could be heard but the hissing of the lanterns and the breathlessness of the waiting.

If there was a master of ceremonies of this event—it may have been Marius or it may have been Wenzel—he really knew his business, for the dramatic pause was held to the limits of the bearable, for so long, indeed, that I thought exhaustion would overcome us all and that all that had occurred would fall back into everyday triteness, yes, indeed, this was about to happen when at that very instant a crackling was heard in the thickets, so that everyone's attention was riveted on that point, and then, after a wait of some additional interminable seconds, all the masks reappeared in a long row amid the bushes and stepped out into the circle of light around the Cold Stone.

Nevertheless, nothing out of the ordinary happened; although the reversion into everyday usualness had been averted, what then occurred was barely beyond the expected, for the unwholesome figures merely began to chant quatrains, the kind that are usual in every kermess, though this time their texts may have been slightly different from those customarily sung on such occasions.

> The priest wants the dragon
> who much frightened shouts: Look,
> if you want a dragon
> just get your own cook.

Applause.

> The dragon has the maiden
> but she has him, too.
> When she tickles his tail
> he goes soft as goo.

Applause.
Some people start to laugh. Immediately the masks stop their own clapping and remain immobile until total silence is restored once more.

> And the earth has the heaven
> and the heaven the earth
> but if they are parted
> there's war and much worse.

Applause, and the masks share in it.

> And the heaven is the father,
> with his bride he has lain.
> Should he lose his wife,
> he can't make any rain.

Of course, some laugh once more and immediately the singing stops. As soon as the laughing has died down, the singing resumes.

> If the father can't rain,
> the whole world is vexed,
> there's hate and no harvest
> and the cattle are hexed.

> The dragons, the giants,
> the creatures of night,
> in the mountain they buried
> his wife out of sight.

No one laughs this time, and after the expected applause, the spirits continue their chant:

> The mothers of evil,
> the witches of hell,
> to the dragons, the monsters,
> the maiden they sell.

And now the witch steps forward and sits down on the Cold Stone, holding her broom in her right hand like a scepter and in her left hand an apple, an imperial orb, the orb of the world, or perhaps the apple of Eve.

> If the mother of evil
> the world wants to boss,
> then the men must expel her
> with one mighty toss.

At that the laughing crowd could no longer be silenced, for now all the good spirits attacked the witch to drag her from her throne while the devils protectively surrounded their sovereign, who swung her broom wildly against the attackers. And in the general tumult and shouting, which was not too different from the customary kermess brawl, the evil forces might even have won out, had the majority of the spectators, following their good instincts, not also fallen on the devils, so that now, bereft of their weapons and helpless, they could only watch as the witch, held down by the most powerful of the spirits, stood without her broom and her apple before her erstwhile throne, in front of which the spirit with the bishop's miter and crozier had now planted himself, white-bearded and imposing.

The bishop nodded solemnly and then said, "So you are the witch."

"It's Alois," shouted a jokester.

"No!" others shouted. "It's the witch, that slut!"

"Are you Alois or are you the witch?"

"The witch," she replied, crestfallen.

"You have committed many crimes," announced the bishop.

"She's sold the Mountain Bride to the dragon," could be heard from the crowd.

"The bitch!"

Whereupon the bishop asked, "Where have you left the Mountain Bride?"

To which the witch replied in a piteous tone, "Abducted by the dragon, devoured by the snake, buried in the mountain."

I wondered who was hidden behind the bishop's mask, for his voice was distorted so unctuously that it was difficult to recognize, but suddenly it came to me: it was the prayer leader Gronne and therefore someone from the Upper Village, a perfect choice for the role.

"Thus you plead guilty, witch?"

"Yes," she whimpered.

"Do you know what you stand accused of?"

"The maiden . . ."

The bishop beckoned, and a large roll of paper was handed to him, from which he read the accusation in a thunderously hollow voice: "Indictment. Indictment of the Kuppron witch."

He paused and then began: "Witch, you have governed the world poorly . . ."

"Boo!" shouted the crowd.

"Ooh, ooh, ooh," moaned the witch, "don't beat me . . ."

"Be silent, witch . . . and kneel while I address you . . ."

The witch did so, and the indictment continued.

"You have governed the world poorly. You held sway over vale and mountain and over all men, and the men bowed before you, powerless were they at your feet . . ."

"Down with the witch!" shouted the crowd.

"Silence!" ordered the smallest of the devils in Wenzel's voice.

"You've made the vales poor and the mountains barren and you have entered into an unholy union with the giants and the dragons and with the devils of the night."

"Ooh, ooh, ooh . . ." All the devils began to howl and the witch joined in the woeful chorus.

"You delivered the maid as tribute to the dragon and you allowed the giants to lift the heavens away, so the earth withered. False rain you called down, the rain of dragons, from which only poisonous weeds may grow; even higher the heavens rose from our reach and ever lower the earth has sunk, so that we can barely discern the heavens anymore. Woe unto you!"

"Woe, woe!" chanted the crowd.

"Man is no more than an island in darkness, the light that once you had brought him you have now snatched back, the creation sinks back into formlessness, the plants grow back into the coldness of the oceans, and woe! the animals themselves waste away into the slime of the past and the sea has become a stronghold of darkness."

"Oh, oh . . ."

Who moaned? Was it the masks? The spirits? The devils? Or was it the woods that moaned? Or the mountains?

"Mother Gisson," I whispered, "Mother . . ." But she did not hear me, she was no longer at my side and I could not see her.

"We who stand at the edge, our ears attuned to the nothingness that gapes at our feet, hearkening to the terrifying voice of this abyss in which lies the great snake, we, the forsaken, oh, we are twice and thrice forsaken, for we trusted the mother and the mother has forsaken us. Never again may she lead us."

"Mother!" many now moaned. "Oh, Mother!"

"Kill the witch! Kill her!" shouted others for whom the play was progressing too tamely.

"Oh, witch! Daughter of the Great Mother, risen out of her and risen with her to establish her empire, hear the distressed grumbling of the forsaken! But we are powerless against you, we may not

touch you, for no one is allowed to lay hands on the mother. You
have forsaken us, leaving us at the mercy of the unformed, of the
demons of pre-creation. Move on, then, witch, mother, daughter
of the Great Mother, we have served you but we shall serve you
no longer."

A great silence set in. Up in the Kuppron walls a loosened stone
tumbled free and struck several times in its fall.

The witch slowly rose from her kneeling position, took her broom,
drew her scarf over her face like a beggar woman, and slunk away.
The group of devils followed her, their pitchforks lowered, a horde
of expelled and miserable wretches.

Was this the end of the play? I hoped so and feared it even more.
Where was the resolution? Where the redemption?

And the crowd was similarly disappointed. "The witch must get
her just deserts!" they shouted, and were ready to follow the fleeing
devils into the woods. "Kill the slut!"

And then I heard Lax call out, "Go ahead, lads, kill her!"

"The atonement! The atonement . . ."

At that moment, as if it were still part of the play, the Mountain
Bride suddenly appeared next to the Cold Stone in all her mag-
nificence, and all eyes fixed on her. But almost simultaneously—
not more than a few seconds could have passed—she was joined
from somewhere by Marius who had jumped on top of the stone,
from which, almost rudely, he nudged the figure of the old priest.
There he now stood with legs spread, and in the white calcium
light one could see that he was unshaven as usual. He looked down
on Irmgard, who, in his gaze, smiled back at him sweetly. Everything was as it had been on that evening in the threshing barn.

All this was so astonishing that the noise and turmoil were wiped
away as with a sponge. Everything had become absolutely still, but
it was not the frozen immobility that had preceded it, it was the
stillness that follows a summer rain.

"The atonement?" asks Marius, and though his voice is not very
loud it carries over the entire clearing. "The atonement? The atonement can never come from the sacrifice of a guilty victim. The
victim must be innocent."

The two, Irmgard and Marius, had locked eyes, and there was another silent pause. But then a young tenor's voice rose from the circle of the spirits, and it wasn't a folksy quatrain like those that had been sung earlier but rather an old miners' chantey that rose into the night, one I had never heard before, with strange elongations of the stressed vowels, archaic and arcane and yet like a primitive dirge of incantation, the first two lines ending with a kind of plangent yodel:

> The sun into the mountain fell *lio*
>   oh, maiden fair
> 'twas the silver dwarf who wove the spell *lio*
> he waits in the golden night of the snakes
> the silver king with glee he shakes.

Whereupon the whole chorus of spirits joined in the syncopated rhythm of the refrain:

> Don't send into the mountain the hero, the son
>   oh, maiden fair
> Silver dwarf will kill him, oh, woebegone!

Thus it is at sea when at night the sailors sing on deck before the rain trickles down from the yardarms and ropes, and sails hang heavy in a slack wind dreaming of what is still to come.

> The hero into the mountain descends *lio*
>   oh, maiden fair
> to do the great deed with his own hands *lio*
> he raises his spear, of stone it was made,
> to force the king to return the maid.
>
> Don't send into the mountain the hero, the son
>   oh, maiden fair
> Silver dwarf will kill him, oh, woebegone!

A single violin had accompanied the chant, plucked like a guitar, but now it was joined by a second, the tempo accelerated to become a serenade of the stars, so that the masts might once more be laden with leaves shadowing the sea.

> The maiden from the mountain returned *lio*
>   oh, maiden fair

but by the whole earth she was spurned *lio*
the lakes and running waters dried
and many fruits and cattle died.

Don't send into the mountain the hero, the son
   oh, maiden fair
Silver dwarf will kill him, oh, woebegone!

The dwarf then carried all the ore *lio*
   oh, maiden fair
from the golden mountain's innermost core *lio*
and walled up the gate with a golden stack
so that the hero can never get back.

Don't send into the mountain the hero, the son,
   oh, maiden fair
Silver dwarf will kill him, oh, woebegone!

The maiden accepted the king's golden crown *lio*
   oh, maiden fair
and wrapped herself in a starry blue gown *lio*
but she shivered and froze in her royal throw
for her empire was cold and deep in snow.

Don't send into the mountain the hero, the son,
   oh, maiden fair
Silver dwarf will kill him, oh, woebegone!

Into the huts came the sickly bear *lio*
   oh, maiden fair
as well as the hungry wolf from his lair *lio*
and so that they may remain on earth
they had to be fed and granted berth.

Don't send into the mountain the hero, the son,
   oh, maiden fair
Silver dwarf will kill him, oh, woebegone!

The chant had become more gentle, it had slowed and become more plaintive, and the nocturnal bark also had slowed its advance; one of the storm lanterns near the Cold Stone had gone out, the wind was in mourning, and the sails had become ribands of wreaths.

The queen of the world arose and spoke *lio*
   oh, maiden fair

> so kill me then at a single stroke   *lio*
> thereby redeeming the hero-son
> with me enthroned forever on.
>
> Don't send into the mountain the hero, the son,
>   oh, maiden fair
> Silver dwarf will kill him, oh, woebegone!
>
> The spear of stone struck through her heart   *lio*
>   oh, maiden fair
> and brought to the dwarf a death most hard   *lio*
> the hero climbed back up the golden way
> with a fiery wheel for the sun to play.

All the spirits had joined the singing in low voices during these last verses, a second lantern had gone out, the faces of the waiting crowd had become darker, shadows fluttered through the air along with the smell of the woods, and Marius and Irmgard still faced each other in frozen rigidity.

"Are you ready for the sacrifice?" he now asked her.

"Yes, I am," she responded.

"Your bridal bed is the stone," he said, "and with your blood the father's rain will flow down once more, redeeming the world and making it fertile anew."

Irmgard merely nodded, and Marius, climbing down from the stone, beckoned to the high priest, who had remained close at hand, so that the play could resume.

The high priest of the spirits advanced and now asked in his turn, "Are you ready for the sacrifice, Mountain Bride?"

"Yes," said the Mountain Bride.

At that, the woolly-bearded figure raised his hands in blessing and declaimed in the hollow voice of the prayer leader:

> Speak now aloud the searing sun's blessing:
> Nevermore shall reign the unholy master
> Of the night's gruesome monsters.
> Henceforth the father's fertile fire commands,
> Grown from the warmth of the wave,
> Blinding the light of the wheel rolling above,
> The lion of life

> Prevailing over the will of women subservient,
> Iron the will of the Lord.

Then he turned toward the Kuppron and bowed deeply three times, so that his beard touched the ground, upon which he straightened up and, throwing both arms upward, called out, "Hear me, O Father!"

The spirits crowded closer to the sacrificial table and they, too, bowed many times toward the Kuppron, the enormous mass of which, without being seen, pervaded the night together with the invisible fires within. One was aware of it without seeing it, and the masks bowed to its presence.

Marius, now strangely included in the play, then said, "Harvest-bearing the mother, she has sent now the daughter that she may reign and sacrificially offer herself, while the rain-making father shall send his own son the sacrifice to accomplish, empowering him as the father once more. Bridal daughter, now call aloud for thy father."

The Mountain Bride replied, "You are the father."

"Not yet."

"When shall you be him?"

"When your blood has flowed back to the earth, when through your sacrifice the mother once again will mate with the father, the earth with the heaven, the siblings of every day."

"And you are the heaven."

Marius, touching the stone with one hand and the other hand raised as if for an oath, said:

> Lion of all of the earth,
> Lightning of heaven above,
> Killing thee as the father,
> I return to thee as the heaven,
> Thou who hast become earth,
> Now thy husband once more.

"Yes," breathed the girl, and it was as if the night itself bloomed in the darkness.

And then she said, "Do it."

"Call for the father."

And Irmgard called, "Father . . . Father . . . Father!" And at the third call Miland stood next to her.

He was pale and his eyes were closed.

And then the high priest advanced and asked, "Art thou the heaven?"

With eyes closed Miland replied, "I do not know."

"Dost thou wish to be the heaven?"

"Yes."

"Then do what is required."

And he lifted his crozier and prayed:

> Joyfully now, O Father, accomplish the sacrifice,
> Wed now the maiden, O lion of light,
> That her blood now may flow, to her mother returning.

But Marius called, "Bride, are you ready?"

"Yes," Irmgard said, still smiling, and knelt down to lay her head and her widespread arms on the sacrificial stone.

"The sacrifice, the sacrifice!" shouted the crowd. And it may be that I, too, joined in the shouting.

Now all the spirits began again to dance around like mad, they gesticulated wildly and made full use of their various noisemakers, all the assembled people joined them, and I may well have been one of them, too, I no longer can tell. But suddenly all is quiet and a reverent murmuring runs through the crowd: "The knife . . ."

Marius is holding up a strange instrument in his hands for all to see, it is a short cleft piece of wood in the fork of which a thing of stone is fastened, and I recognize it as the flint dagger which—so long ago, it seems—Marius had brought to Mother Gisson. Was it with this unwieldy utensil that a heart was supposed to be pierced? Or a throat cut? A crazy disappointment filled me at the sight of this twig holding a meager little stone which was meant to be the goal and the climax of this entire happening, and I understood well why someone suddenly shouted, "That thing won't work . . . Here, this is better!"

It was Sabest, who, with his elbows, was pushing and forcing his way through the tightly packed crowd to get to the sacrificial table. On his way there he had drawn his long butcher's knife from his belt and on arrival he proffered it to Marius, shouting once more, "Here, this is better . . . Take it!"

"No," says Marius.

"Take it," Sabest insists, and tests the blade against the ball of his thumb like someone about to shave. "Look how sharp!"

"It is not sacred," says Marius in rejection.

"What? Not sacred?" Sabest threateningly shakes the fist holding the knife. "My knife is as sacred as yours, you clod . . . Whatever has been dipped in hot blood is sacred . . . What else, for Christ's sake!"

Marius merely made a gesture of dignified repudiation and pressed the flint dagger into the hand of Miland, who still stood immobile, while Sabest, who continued to stab the air with his steel like someone groping for something in a dream without being able to reach it, was restrained by the spirits.

"Do it! Do it!" shouts the crowd, which had become restive.

Irmgard, spread over the stone with her arms stretched out, gazed with transported eyes to the skies, invisible in the white carbide light.

"Do it! Do it!"

From afar, down on the road, the tooting of an automobile horn was heard and something in me called "Do it!"—in me who stood there in my suit sewn by machines out of cloth woven on mechanical looms, minted coins and a knife marked "Solingen" in my trouser pocket—yes, nevertheless, something in my soul shouted "Do it!" while trains and automobiles travel throughout the world and while the ether is filled with radio waves and my head with a hodgepodge of the accumulated medical knowledge of many centuries, it shouted in me "Do it!" but then it dawned on me that now the ram was bound to appear in the bushes, so as to take the place of the intended victim. Had not the ram appeared to Abraham while from afar was heard the clanking of the chain of a draw well and the bellow of a laden camel on the trading road? He, the arch-father, father of all fathers, did he not then perceive the father's ultimate command, dispensing with the bloody and blood-laden mediation, relieved from pagan custom as the humane took on life in and around him?

"Do it!" roared the life, roared all that was pagan.

But it was not the ram that I had almost expected that emerged from the bushes, but the voice of Mother Gisson, which now could be heard: "Beware! Beware, Marius!"

Was she also part of the play? Had her unrestrained dancing also been the prelude to her joining in the drama?

Wenzel, who had remained at some distance from the action, hopped over to her, and bleated, "Don't disturb the sacred proceedings." He was sent on his way with a slap across the face which he would remember for the rest of his earthly days. But the people did not laugh.

And Mother Gisson repeated: "Beware, all of you, beware, Marius! The presence of the Mother is still in all things and each night she conceives of the heaven and its knowledge. The earth still hearkens and it spurns the blood with which you mean to drench it."

The silence had become so great that one could hear the bubbling of the spring up in the woods.

Finally Marius spoke. "You no longer are the earth, Mother, though you once were."

And someone called, "You let the dragons and the snakes enter you."

Thereupon the Mother: "Because you thought of rising above yourself, your fear has turned into the snake."

And then she turned to Miland. "Whom do you obey when you seek to kill your own child? Do you obey your own fear?"

"Yes," replied Miland, "for our fear has become overpowering and the world calls for its redeemer."

But Marius, without glancing at her, turned to the crowd, turned toward the valley and the harvest-bearing earth, and said, "Earth, you let it come to pass that machines crawl over your soil, that your fruit is traded by vile agents, and that the threshing floors have fallen silent. Altogether too much that is alien you have fed and protected. Only the blood of your child, O earth, can cleanse you anew."

And the Earth herself replied, "No blood can redeem me. It is the rain of the father that comes down upon me, time and time again, cooling and cleansing, and it impregnates my mountains. Hearken to me, the father does not spill blood, his knowledge is not in the blood, his knowledge is in the rain cloud of his breath. It is your fear that speaks in the blood."

A child began to cry in the midst of the crowd, over whose heads the dark haze of fear hung suspended.

Lax shouted, "Shut up, you old crone! We're not afraid!"

And Marius laughed and said, "What is the rain cloud without the lightning? I am the lightning bolt sent to kill and to dissolve the rain cloud into rain."

And indeed, he was answered by heat lightning in the sky, and Sabest, who was still being restrained by the spirits, shouted, "Let me go . . . I know my business, I know how to . . . I'll do it!"

"Go ahead, Sabest!" came further encouragement from Lax.

But the crowd was silent, only the child cried, and when more lightning flashed across the skies it called out in its thin voice that broke the silence of the whole assemblage like a trembling luminous beam more visible than the flash of lightning, and it called out, "Mother . . ."

"Do not be afraid," replied Mother Gisson.

"Yes, be afraid, tremble and fear!" screamed Marius.

But then Irmgard, kneeling in front of the stone, spoke, and it was as if she were begging forgiveness. "My fear is sweet, Mother, sweet as the solitude of my dream drifting up from the abyss, sweet as the mirror of the abyss that lies in me and shows me the image of my beloved as I gaze down into it and am reflected by it. Oh, it is sweet to float in the mirroring abyss, floating up toward myself and yet toward the meeting with the father."

Miland had stood silent until then, lost in the dream, and his fingers played with the point of the stone dagger as if he, too, wanted to test its sharpness. But now he said, "What flowed from us, let it now flow back into us, child and children's children, narrow brook of life between the shores of death, forebear after forebear, grandchild after grandchild, for only when the mouth of the river once more becomes its source will fear subside."

"Mother!" wailed some men in the crowd. "Mother!"

Only a single lantern still burned near the sacrificial stone.

Sabest, still struggling with the spirits from whose grasp he sought to escape, panted: "Mouth and source . . . yes, indeed, mouth and source of the blood is the earth . . . Come and watch me, all of you come and watch when I slaughter, see the earth drinking the blood, see my hands dripping with blood . . ."

"Oh Mother, Mother," came the laments from the crowd, interrupting Sabest.

And Sabest's panting died down. There were sighs from the crowd. The crying child no longer was heard. Instead a woman sobbed, a cracked meager sobbing full of tremulous impatience and trembling waiting. I felt gravel under the soles of my shoes which I could press easily and deeply into the soft earth. Ordinary meadow loam in no way thirsting for blood. And yet all my senses had been concentrating on Marius to such an extent that I had not even noticed that it had started to rain some time before. The drizzle came down, dark and mild out of the mild, dark night; I touched my shoulders and found they were drenched through.

And then I heard again Mother Gisson's voice, and it was almost jubilant. "Do you hear the rain? Do you feel the good rain?"

The heat lightning had stopped. On the straw mantles of the masks up near the stone, raindrops glittered in the light.

"Listen to the rain," continued Mother Gisson, "breathe in the knowledge that rises from the rain-sated earth, the star-pregnant knowledge, and open your face and your heart to it."

"Mother, don't leave us!" That had been Agatha in supplication; I had recognized her voice.

"Mother, don't leave us!" was repeated here and there.

A hardly noticeable and yet inexorable motion had taken hold of the human mass, it forced its way toward Mother Gisson, as if it wanted to crowd around her in its anxiety and as if only some last shyness had to be overcome before finding a haven close to her. There was great helplessness in all of that but also some rebellion, rebellion against Marius, for now some calls could be heard: "Send him away, Mother . . . send him away."

"No," came from Lax, "he stays."

"Music! Music! Play on!" The commanding voice of Wenzel drowned all other sounds.

Whereupon the accordion actually began to play a wretched little dance tune. The music maker sat on a low branch behind the Cold Stone, his arms bent into triangles pumping back and forth, the keys of the instrument shone white in the light of the last of the lanterns, and hopping next to it, Wenzel beat time for the maskers, who, on his order, had begun to dance again and now were shuffling rather forlornly over the wet grass. But the shadowy rhythm had also accelerated the motion of the crowd, it advanced by fits and starts, perhaps toward Mother Gisson to seek her protection, perhaps toward Marius to oust him, and I, almost against my own volition and yet following it and helping along with my elbows, I was carried along to the dancing chain of the spirits, who could not withstand the press of the crowd but dissolved and dispersed among it the way a shuffling, scuffling cloud disperses in a larger heap of clouds. All this happened within a few minutes and then the last lantern went out.

"Tremble in fear!" screamed Marius into the darkness, and it may be that he himself had extinguished the lantern.

He was answered by the laughter of Lax. "Time for the womenfolk to be afraid."

With the advent of darkness the human mass automatically had come to a halt and the spirits also had stopped their dancing. But the accordion continued to play and one could hear Wenzel hopping and beating time to the thin music.

Had I thought of my flashlight, had I switched it on, things might have taken another turn, but at that moment I knew nothing of a flashlight, could not and probably would not wish to know of it, as I was all ears, listening for the scream that as yet had not been heard and yet already trembled in the air like an echo preceding the sound. I did not breathe, indeed probably few of us who stood there took a breath at that moment; one heard only the panting of Sabest, who apparently had managed to escape from the restraining arms of the spirits and had pushed his way close to the Cold Stone, for it was from there that his voice now came in hoarse harshness: "Now . . . now I'll do it!" followed immediately by an almost blissful "Ah!" from Irmgard's mouth, then only silence and a swift crackling in the underbrush as of an animal bolting through the woods at a gallop.

The music continued to play and Wenzel continued to beat time.

Whether seconds or minutes elapsed in darkness and without any reaction, I would not have been able to say then and I still cannot say today, for my thoughts only slowly returned, merely knowing that the frozen stillness was first broken by Mother Gisson, whose voice, veiled in deepest grief, sounded out of the night, more nocturnal than night itself, sounding into the darkness, darker than darkness itself: "Now it has happened after all."

Only then did I shout, "Stop! . . . Lights!"

There was one more long-drawn-out, breathy chord from the accordion, and when it ended I was still searching for my flashlight, though it was already in my hand; astonished at finding it there, my fingers had already automatically switched it on, so that its beam strayed over the faces of the immobile bodies, over faces which, blinded, closed their eyes and yet hardly were aware of the light. Awkwardly they made way for me, awkwardly I bumped into them as I advanced, groping and confused, toward the sacrificial table, which itself was still obstructed from my view, while above Marius was now visible in the full beam from my flashlight, standing tall and nonchalant and higher than the other figures, unshaven and with a fixed smile playing on his lips. I called out "Marius!" but he did not move. But when the beam fell on Miland, who stood equally immobile, the flint dagger still in his hand and his gaze riveted on Marius, then and only then did I know that a corpse lay between them.

Yes, she lay there in the sharply delineated circle of light, withdrawn and bud-like, closed in on herself and yet etiolated, the arms widely spread and the head resting on the stone. The colors of the silks of her attire shone richly, the hair at the nape of the neck under the bridal crown was blond, and for one heartbeat I was not yet the physician I was called upon to be, attending first to the business of life and not to that of death: for that one heartbeat I was with Irmgard in a beyond in which her sacrifice seemed to make sense, a harvest sacrifice and a crown in honor of which people danced, and sharing for that heartbeat in a beyond in which Irmgard now resided and which belonged to her, I was without hatred for Marius, partaking for that one heartbeat in a crazy redemption which now was supposed to have entered the world. For one heartbeat. But then Mother Gisson stepped up to the stone, knelt, and grasped one of the lifeless hands of her grandchild, and in the surge of grief I said to Marius, "Give us some light."

Miland let the stone dagger fall.

In shy immobility, as if forbidden to transcend the intangible circle, people and spirits stood still and dared not come closer.

"Light!" I shouted. "For Christ's sake, give us some light!"

"But she is dead," said Marius obligingly as he stepped forward lightly and gracefully, placing one hand on the lifeless body with an almost elegant gesture.

"Yes, she is dead," said Mother Gisson next to me. "Do not touch her, Marius, you are not permitted."

I had rested the flashlight on the stone and tore open Irmgard's silk dress; the shift I pulled back was bloodstained and the blood seeped from a wound below the left shoulder blade. Sabest could not have aimed any better. The blood ran over my hands and dripped on the earth in a steady uncheckable flow. Medically there was nothing left to do.

"The earth drinks the blood," said Marius above me.

Suddenly Wenzel appeared, in each hand a beer mug full of water. "You'll need some water, Doctor . . . Good thing we have a spring close at hand . . ."

Marius continued his crazed declamation. "The earth drinks the blood and once more the springs run pure . . . Strength and justice spring once more from the earth . . ."

I took the water and washed the wound but the blood continued to flow.

"It sure doesn't take long for a human being to die," said Wenzel conversationally as he watched me and played with the tassel of the cow's tail which he had tied to his behind in his role as devil. "I'll bring you some more light, Doctor." He took one of the lantern poles and I heard him rattle the carbide in the tin can.

But then Miland said slowly and as in a dream, "Marius, did I kill her?"

"No," I said. "Sabest did it."

But Marius said, "You have accomplished the sacrifice and the faith will arise from purity reborn."

The light of my flashlight lying on the stone yellowed; the battery was dying and it got darker around us.

"Marius," asked Miland, "are the people around us?"

"Yes," said Marius.

"Are they now sharing in our togetherness?"

"Yes," said Marius. "They have entered a new realm, for now they have knowledge of death."

Was it not as if Mother Gisson was smiling in the darkness? Words such as faith, purity, and justice could have little meaning for her to whom faith always had resided in the concrete, the powerful life in all its immensity, life without beginning and end, life that is cruel but never cruel for the sake of empty words; for Mother Gisson wisdom was in her knowledge of the visible, tangible life and not in some vague generalities with which this non-man preaches and promises the advent of his male creed. Did she not smile in all her grief? And she said, "She is gone from us, beyond her blood, she strides through the rocks, and the trees of the wood are her fluttering hair."

But Marius repeated with the persistence of the demented: "The highest knowledge is the knowledge of death. All strength derives from it."

The light from my flashlight became dimmer still. Soon it would only be a yellow pinpoint, but I no longer required any light, my business here had ended. The harvest had fallen to the fool, a fool we all had followed in our dance, around whom we had danced, driven by the deepest darkness in our lives, we, the many-headed motherless beast of which I was part, men and women, leader or led, wise ones and fools, all part of the nocturnal beast.

Wenzel arrived with fresh carbide, merrily rattling it in the can to announce his arrival. And when he added the water and the first lantern hissingly lit up, the paralysis that had taken hold of the throng around us finally dissolved. The people began to talk, they crowded and furtively crept around the corpse and pointlessly moved hither and thither. Some of the spirits took off their masks, others forgot that they were still in disguise and confused questions were voiced through tousled, half-glued-on beards. Lax was among the first to reach the sacrificial table. He examined the lifeless body for some time while I busied myself rearranging its clothing, and once more the gloominess of the flesh showed in his face as he stood there melancholy, aged and heavy-legged; but since he was attentive to manners, he first proffered his black-haired paw to Mother Gisson, accompanied by a "My sympathy," though without getting any acknowledgment from her, and then he repeated this gesture with Miland, who limply relinquished his hand for him to shake.

And then he turned to me. "Well, Doctor, when you come right down to it, this is a murder . . . no?" He peered once more at the corpse.

"Insanity at the time of the deed is ground for exoneration," commented Wenzel as he planted a second lantern next to the stone.

Yes, I had forgotten Sabest, the murderer, since for me Marius was the real culprit, not the one who had fled to the mountain, and I said, "Sabest? . . . Yes."

Senselessly I snapped at Marius: "Marius, where is Sabest?"

He closed his eyes, his head sunk on his chest, and after a short pause he said, "Dead."

"Nonsense," said Lax dismissively, for he did not wish to hear this. "Let some of the boys search for him."

"It's of no use," said Marius.

Lax thought the matter over. "We have to notify the authorities . . . Such a devil, that Sabest!"

"I'll gladly take care of that," Wenzel volunteered eagerly, and he tore the cow's tail from his behind and disappeared in a trice.

He probably also decamped so quickly for another reason: Mother Gisson had risen and had stepped forward, and her grief was terrible to behold. The people stared at her and retreated slowly before her gaze, and even Marius could not withstand its weight. He busied himself with the two lanterns and then he retreated to the edge of the woods as if he had to attend to something over there and sat down on the branch on which the accordion player had perched; he crossed his legs, rested his head in one hand, and remained in this attitude of reflection.

"Cover her up and leave her alone," Mother Gisson ordered the crowd.

One of the maskers—it was Ludwig, the blacksmith's apprentice—stepped forward, took off his straw mantle, and draped it over the lifeless form, whereupon he disappeared once more in the receding human sea.

Was it out of respect for death that they retreated? Out of respect for her grief? Her mourning? Or did they simply fear the transcendence, the sense of her no longer belonging to their world that emanated from the old woman? It was almost a stubborn rebellion that exuded from this human mass, and I could almost comprehend it. Had they not danced, had we not all danced frenetically to conjure up this sacrifice, so that the heavens might descend to earth and the earth rise toward heaven? Was Irmgard not called upon now to enter the reopened mountain, welcomed by the wide-gaping gates of the hall of gold? Had not all of this been brought to naught as Mother Gisson, with calm hand, took possession of the blessed departed, the radiant sacrificial child, and led her back into the shelter of a land that allowed access to no one? Were they not, all of them who had been waiting here, now cast back into the everyday life from which Marius had promised to free them? Their fear had been great, it had been magnified to an almost unbearable extent, and now that deliverance from this fear was near at hand, they were being cheated out of it, they were being driven back into what had been before and whence the fear arose anew, the fear of the mute night! They did not grumble but withdrew in silence, only a child's whimpering could be heard and it came from Cecily, who haplessly wandered among the crowd.

Mother Gisson looked at me and said in a low voice, "Bring her to him."

Indeed, it was the best one could do for both of them, and so I fetched the child and brought her to her father. At the sight of the girl a part of his dream fell away from him, he knelt down to pick her up, and he even smiled a little as she ran toward him and he bedded her down in the grass next to him. I, too, sat down close to them and watched Cecily playing with the stone dagger that she had found on the ground.

Thus we waited. Mathias of the Mount arrived and, without taking notice of anyone, joined his mother, who now sat on the sacrificial stone at the head of the lifeless body, her hand on Irmgard's blond hair, from which I had removed the bridal crown. Red-bearded, silent and somber, Mathias stood next to her.

We waited. Some lads had gone to look for Sabest. At times a call resonated from the rock face: "Sabest!" and the nocturnal echo replied from ever farther distances. One who already was among the dead was being called, one who no longer hears his name, one in whom perhaps only the "Ah!" of his victim still throbs, echoing in the murderer's hopelessness, echoing in all the deaths, the reverberating realization of a life that has become hopeless. They called him as if they could call him back from the hopelessness of his dying, oh, no one is able to grasp the meaning of hopelessness, no one is able to conceive what goes on in the man who no longer sees anything but his own death. They called him and their calls remained unheard.

Thus we waited. But the festive enclave again filled with the random hum indicative of the presence of a crowd, lanterns had been lit next to the stands, the people wandered about or rested on the lawn, and there was even a real thronging of people around the beer stand, for the innkeeper had disappeared and the beer was free. One might have thought that the dancing had simply been interrupted by a momentary pause in the music.

Thus we waited, and it was about another hour before some lights and torches showed up at the lower edge of the meadow, floating among the thin leafage of the birch copse; led by Wenzel, there appeared the mayor, the village policeman, and an area constable, as well as several others from the Lower Village whom shock and curiosity had impelled to come and see for themselves, all of whom now climbed the meadow with wet shoes and were forthwith surrounded by the waiting crowd.

The usual formalities followed; those present were interrogated and Lax did most of the talking. Everything was quite simple and proceeded without a hitch until the questioning of Miland, who talked confusedly and accused himself of having killed his child, at which Lax only laughed and asked, "And what are you supposed to have done it with?" It was a few moments before Miland finally pointed with a vague gesture to the flint dagger Cecily was still playing with, whereupon the laughter became general, everyone forgot about the dead girl still lying in their midst, and Lax commented, "I see . . . Well, a trouser button would have served better . . ." And since in my own report as physician of the municipality I was able to put on record that the lethal wound incontestably had been inflicted with a butcher's knife, no notice was taken anymore of Miland's muddled talk and the authorities turned away in abrupt disdain from Irmgard's body, an object that had lost all interest, to focus on the fate of Sabest, who, after all and according to law, had to be prosecuted. Irmgard's corpse was released, released to be grieved over and to be carried down into the valley.

This was done on a stretcher improvised from the canvas roofing of the gingerbread stand. The lanterns around the meadow were extinguished and the night sighed inaudibly. When the group started to move, I noticed that Mother Gisson had joined it, too. Quickly I went to her. "Mother, you really shouldn't take that long walk down; I'd rather bring you home."

"No," she said simply.

"Well, then I'll go, too, Mother."

"No, you stay here," she decided. "You'll still be needed up here."

"Sabest?"

She shook her head. "No . . . but you'll be needed . . ."

Flanked by torches, the column disappeared. I noticed that it was followed by Marius. The place became empty of people, and in the stillness the stars appeared between the clouds, one group of stars after another became visible among the cloud mountains that slowly drifted away and the trunks of the birches began to shimmer whitely.

I slowly crossed the clearing; some drunks still staggered around, others snored next to the beer stand, and twice I encountered the usual closely entwined couples hurrying toward the soft moss under the birches. For those, heaven and earth would still be joined together tonight, but for that Irmgard's sacrifice hardly would have been necessary.

Since I no longer had a functioning flashlight, I did not take the path through the woods but walked along the main trail that leads down to the cableway lane, which I then followed slowly upward to reach my own house above the clearing. A strange empty absentmindedness had taken hold of me, the warm southerly September wind played with the cables above me, from time to time I heard voices from up above still calling for Sabest, but I could not focus my thoughts either on him or on Mother Gisson, who was now accompanying the stretcher down to the valley, I only heeded the path and its gravel and roots, merely paying attention to the next step, and I even forgot that I was heading toward home. Like a faraway call, the thought came to me of Peter Sabest, for whom the authorities had looked in vain on the fairgrounds and who undoubtedly was now searching with the others for his father among the rock walls, but when I arrived at the smashed mine cage, the fall of which was supposed to have signaled the beginning of the new era, I suddenly lost all strength: without having noticed it before, I was overpowered by exhaustion and disappointment, maybe simply because I was overtired or hungry, but even more because of my powerlessness and my inability to comprehend the meaning of that madness in which I, wrapped up in a spectral dream-like hope, had myself participated. I was incapable of doing anything at all, incapable of continuing the climb, incapable of even wanting anything. I leaned against the concrete pedestal of the cable mast, already overgrown with weeds, in front of me the torn wires and cables intertwined with the rod skeleton of the mine cage, a jutting man-made tangle weirdly returned to its primordial natural condition, barbarian and pagan by virtue of its utter uselessness, as if to demonstrate that man's ultimate rational creations are as far removed from his humanity as the primordial roots of his blood and of his corporeal being, both prohibited realms, both of them dizzying and leading to fakery, touching each other in that which is most unholy, murderous out of the idolatry of blood, murderous out of the idolatry of technology, both one and the same, for the pagan requires the murderous for its own existence: only in the center of our being is there holiness, the holiness of our life, that life that is ever so short and becoming shorter with every night, a holiness that is not an intoxication and not a machine but rather a continuous blooming, a flower opening and growing out of darkness and into darkness, from unborn to unborn, a rebirth of its own self: it is in the center of our being that the trees stand under the caress of heaven and where time blows, a gentle windblown messenger between infinities from whence it comes and whereto it flows, a short stretch through which it carries us like an autumnal leaf, so that we may apprehend whence we awoke and whereto we pass on, messengers of ourselves: only in the center of our being is knowledge, the knowledge of that which man requires to achieve humaneness, the knowledge of his humanity and of his culture, the devout knowledge that is the perception of the highest culture and is also that of Mother Gisson, not the knowledge of the blood or that of technology but man's knowledge of his own selfhood: in the center of our being and only in its center, neither in the intoxication of man's arch-beginnings nor in the intoxication of his technology, but only within the being of man's own self resides that which in us is truly godlike. The trunks of the pines moved gently in the earthly night breeze, at times a leaf fell from one of the deciduous trees, spiderwebs hanging between the wires like artful miniaturizations of their steely tangle had clung to my face, and my hands were still sticky with traces of the blood that had flowed over them, the skies sank lower in the subdued humming of their swarming stars, the nocturnally singing forest rose higher toward their promised meeting, and the earth floated: I was alive still, still was it granted to me to stand in the center of things, here where the infinities join. Thus I resumed my climb, strolling along, hardly noticing that I had done so and that I had reached the clearing from which I encompassed the stars of the valleys and the valleys of the heavens, both filled with the transparent September mists in which the heights and depths touch each other, powerful in their powerlessness. All this I saw and once more was sheltered by the woods.

Was it a happy state of mind? Surely not. But it was one of certitude. And yet it was to be subjected to yet another test.

For not far from Wetchy's house I was thrown back and stopped in shock. I heard music and yelling, the rough music accompanying the singing of quatrains and the clapping of hands, clear the sounds of the accordion and of the two fiddles, fiddling in a night heavy with heartbreak. Overcoming my own fright and forgetting my exhaustion, I started to run, faster still after a few minutes when I saw the light of torches between the trees, and moments later the whole scene was right before my eyes. The band of spirits and devils, though no longer spirits and devils but simply sweating masked hoodlums, this whole gang, insanely drunk with the free beer from the stand at the kermess, was assembled around a tree to which they had tied a man—even without seeing him, I knew it could only be Wetchy—in front of whom a figure in a straw mantle danced around in time with the music; the others clapped their hands or slapped their thighs, from time to time one or the other stepped forward and slapped the face of the martyred man, all the while singing with the persistence of the heavily drunk a primitive quatrain:

> You wretched stupid agent,
> whence you came go back!
> You stole our money,
> Now we'll break your neck!

Wenzel was among them. They were all in the merriest of moods; there wasn't an unbroken windowpane in the house, and to enliven the merriment further, an additional stone was thrown into the house at intervals. In short, the whole scene was repulsive.

I was fairly certain that despite their drunken frenzy they would not dare raise a hand against me; after all, some kind of trusting relationship linked me even with Wenzel. But nevertheless and to be on the safe side, I whistled to Trapp, who was sure to hear me over in my garden.

The sharp whistling drew their attention; the festivities faltered. Wenzel staggered toward me. "Doctor, a little wholesome fun."

"You turd," I said. I had a good mind to sick Trapp on him.

"Doctor, sir," he said, becoming strangely sober and serious, "it was necessary."

It was necessary? I had no time for discussions, even though his seriousness impressed me somewhat and slightly reanimated my old dislike of this poor devil Wetchy, who now was supposed to have made even this necessary, and so I went to him without another word, took my pocketknife, and cut him free. He collapsed in my arms.

"Courage, Wetchy," I said, "courage, you'll be all right . . . we'll manage to cope with a bit of nosebleed . . ."

"Don't tell my wife, Doctor, it might frighten her," the little hero murmured, and then fell unconscious.

The whole band stood around me, some merely gaped dumbly, some drunkenly smiled. I looked them over and to my surprise found even that sterling fellow Ludwig among them. None of them was really bad after all, they were merely stinking drunk.

"Ludwig," I said, "help me."

He came after some hesitation, then another joined him, and together we lifted up Wetchy. But the house was locked. I called for Mrs. Wetchy. No response. Maybe she, too, was lying unconscious inside.

But I had to get in. Some of them suggested that we break down the door, but I didn't like that idea. So I had myself lifted up to the smashed kitchen window, reached in, opened the latch, and entered. In the kitchen I stumbled over the boards that Wetchy had solicitously placed over the stone floor. I put on the light and walked from room to room, always calling "It's me, Mrs. Wetchy, the doctor!" but all to no avail. Could she have fled? I gave up the search, for I could not let the injured man wait any longer, ran down the flight of stairs, and opened the door to the house, after which we carried Wetchy, still unconscious, to the bedroom. Trapp followed. I then sent the lads on their way, filled a basin with water, and began to take care of the man.

As I was in the middle of it, the dog next to me growled. I listened. A hesitant, barely audible shuffling could be heard, then it faltered. "Come in," I called, but there was no response. "Come in!" I called again. "It's me, the doctor!" No reply. I opened the door. Nothing. But after I crossed the small anteroom I found the woman on the stairs; she sat on the topmost step and her teeth were chattering.

Dear heavens, let her not go into labor now in her panic! I was again filled with anger toward these innocent people. "But where have you been, Mrs. Wetchy?"

Her teeth were beating a drumroll; she could not reply. In any case, it was better that she not see her unconscious husband and so I left her where she was.

I examined Wetchy. At first, I found only a broken tooth. What else was wrong with him I could ascertain only after he had regained consciousness. Arms and legs were intact. But then I also examined his crotch. Of course, someone had kicked him there; peasants are loath to forgo this highly popular maneuver, and that had probably been the direct cause of his unconsciousness. I washed away the worst, applied a cold compress, and then I ran home, past the woman, to get a morphine ampoule so as to protect him from the first attack of pain.

After I had given him his injection, I went to look after his wife, who still sat where I had left her. I had to tear her out of her panicky terror, which still chattered and trembled within her. "Mrs. Wetchy, where is the boy?"

That had the desired effect and she pulled herself together. "In the cellar," she managed to utter.

"Go get him."

I helped her up on her shaky legs. After this, the ice was broken. "Are they gone?"

She had her hands folded over her belly as usual but did not complain of any labor pains; I felt this as a downright blessing.

298 · THE SPELL

"Yes, Mrs. Wetchy, they're gone and not too much harm was done . . . I'll go with you to fetch the child." I was afraid that she would drop him.

After that we sat at the bed of the injured man. He lay in his morphine-induced sleep and looked peaceful. I, too, dozed off in my chair, restless and often interrupted to look after my patient, but finally so profoundly that I overslept his own waking. As I opened my eyes, the woman sat on the bed next to her husband, they held each other's hands, and out of fear of disturbing me they had not dared speak but only gazed into each other's tired eyes.

"Pain, Wetchy?"

He shook his head and smiled.

"Nevertheless, we shall claim compensation for injuries, damages, and loss of earnings . . . I'm not about to let that gang off so easily . . ."

He shook his head again. "Oh no, Doctor, that wouldn't make much sense . . ."

"Well, we'll talk about that later . . ."

"No, Doctor, we'll just leave as soon as possible, that's all . . ."

"And what then?"

He smiled confidently. "I'll always manage to take care of my family . . ."

"Yes," said the woman, "he can do anything he wants."

And the puny little Hercules in his bed said, "To leave bad people is easy, it's only difficult to take leave of good ones . . . and you have been very good to us, Doctor."

Both had tears in their eyes and perhaps I did, too. But they did not complain. And when I examined him once more so as to forestall any further emotional outbursts, I found that he also had a broken rib.

It must have been about five o'clock when I finally went home. The trees stood black against the already lighter sky, in which not a cloud was to be seen anymore. Already the stars had detached themselves matutinally from their cupola, they had become small fixed glittering points floating in an ether that took on a greenish hue and were about to dissolve in it altogether. The world lay below, meaningless and yet rich with meaning in its cruelty and goodness, and in places it had begun to take on color.

13 As urban wastes discharge into a river and, cleansed once more in its flow, are carried off into the sea, all misery and woe, having become once again transparent and pure, turn back into life and revert to what they have been and what they are and always will remain: life, part of the whole, no longer identifiable in the totality, absorbed by it, unrecognizable and submerged in the immutable. Indeed, even shame, this sacred property of man which reaches deeper into him than he usually cares to admit, shame which tends to last longer than grief, it, too, once more becomes transparent and part of the indefinable life, becomes a band in the glow of the sunset, a speck of dust on a butterfly's wing, a passing thought in the sea of thoughts. The grief of that night of terror still lingered in heavy waves and yet already had begun to fade. Irmgard had been buried. Sabest had been found among the rocks, his head smashed in a fall. Wetchy lay in bed woefully beaten up. And yet all had begun to sink back into everyday order, becoming transparent and invisible, a small eddy in the sea of memory and oblivion: not only was Lax bringing his wood up to the Pit of the Dwarfs and not only did Wenzel march and parade his lads through the village as if those lurid events had never happened, these had begun to slide back into everyday triteness even for those directly affected, even though the pub had been closed for two days and although Peter was now to be sent to the city for schooling or apprenticeship, and even though Wetchy spoke of his plans for leaving the village, the dark reasons, increasingly concealed behind all of that, hardly were mentioned anymore, they were already being assimilated in people's souls and a balance struck between their lighter and darker aspects. And Miland, with the help of Andreas and Marius, harvested his corn. The fields lay unchanged in the valley and the plow was pulled over them, square after square of earth turned blackish and brown-red, on the heights the last oats, no longer able to ripen, were being cut and loaded, and soon the potatoes would be dug up. Likewise unaltered seemed the life of Mother Gisson, it appeared to go on unchanged as she silently went about her chores in the house, and she had even set out her annual schnapps to ripen; once I met Agatha at her house and once I came across her and Agatha on my way home as they emerged from the woods. There they stood, on the embankment of the sloping meadow, the two women, one old, the other pregnant, and looked down into the autumnally sunny valley.

That the wife of the murderer, Sabest, had not sold the pub forthwith but continued to run it, at least for the time being, was due partly to the long talks I had had with her about her own future and that of her son. In the course of these conversations and perhaps because she was beginning to feel her age or perhaps simply because of womanly bonds, the idea of Agatha as a prospective daughter-in-law had arisen in her. It had always weighed on her mind that Peter could have behaved dishonorably and left the girl in the lurch; now, after all the horror, surely he would become serious and responsible and would be eager to make amends. She had followed my advice to go and talk directly to Agatha, though without achieving much, for Agatha had said neither yes nor no and had refused to see Peter again before his departure.

I spoke of the matter to Mother Gisson.

"The girl is right," she said. "Peter will never be the right man for her."

"It's too early to tell, Mother, the two are mere children, after all . . . and the right thing can always grow out of love."

I sat with her in her kitchen. On the windowsill one of the new bottles of schnapps stood in the sun, its neck muffled and tied up.

"Agatha stands in the right place," she replied, "but he, he has the greed of his parents in his blood."

"Anyone can change, anyone can be changed . . . and Peter, after all, has had quite a shock."

"No, he's still too young to draw much from that . . . He will still have to pass through a lot of dark greed before emerging from the darkness . . . if he ever does."

"An illegitimate child always remains just that," I remarked, "and it still is unfortunate that this should have happened to the girl."

"For Agatha it wasn't unfortunate, for her it was right and it was beautiful . . . That's how Irmgard should have turned out . . . I only wish I could stay a while longer with Agatha"—and her face again had that far-off look that I knew so well in her, but then she smiled—"but Irmgard may need me more urgently than Agatha . . ."

She smiled but I felt her seriousness and I dared not utter any of my usual remonstrations.

"Yes," she continued, "and why don't you have a talk with Agatha yourself . . . You should be looking after her anyway . . . later . . ."

The sun shone outside, windblown clouds were drifting in broad bands across the sky, Mother Gisson sat in front of me, hale and strong though perhaps a bit tired, next year's schnapps had been put up, and it may have been merely the aftereffects of that terrible night that made her talk like that. Nevertheless, Mother Gisson was not someone given to moods.

On one of the following mornings I visited Agatha.

The weather had suddenly broken. It must have snowed up in the mountains, for through the heavy rain one could taste the snow hiding behind the fog, wrapped around the mountains like stiff old linen, behind which the winter's workshop was already in full swing. Trapp, running in front of me, envied me my loden cape, the hood of which I had raised. But down in the Lower Village the weather was noticeably milder.

Strum was splitting wood under the overhang of his barn; a large pile of winter wood was already stacked neatly against the barnwall, showing the light yellow of its cut faces.

"Always hard at work, Strum. So much wood!"

He beamed. "What can one do, Doctor? A child needs a warm room. It's already October. Winter may be here tomorrow."

Agatha came out from the stable door with a wooden pail in her hand. Her pregnancy was now quite noticeable; her small round belly protruded and her face was stretched by the first signs of burgeoning maturity. But, childlike, it became transfigured by joy: "Another visit . . . the doctor."

"Yes, the doctor, but he's not going to stay out here in the wet for you." And I entered the house, took off my loden cape, and sat down by the kitchen stove.

She had followed me and pointed to the parlor.

"No, no. I'm staying here where it's warmer . . . Or is there someone in there? You spoke of a visit . . ."

"No"—she smiled happily—"but Mother Gisson was already here to see me."

"Really?" I was indeed surprised that Mother Gisson had come down to the Lower Village in this beastly weather.

"Mr. Sack drove her down," she announced proudly.

"Aha." It would have to be an important matter for Mother Gisson to order a carriage to drive her down.

"And now she is at Miland's next door and then she's going to see Mrs. Sabest."

It all began to make sense to me. "Oh, Mrs. Sabest? . . . I guess because of you and Peter?"

She obviously knew that I was in on things and simply confirmed it. "Yes . . . and so that Mrs. Sabest shouldn't think that I said no because Mr. Sabest had murd . . . because Mr. Sabest had done what he did and so that she wouldn't be upset, Mother Gisson is going to see her today."

"Nor, in truth, would there be any reason for that. What Sabest has done has been paid for and people will soon forget it . . . but the illegitimate child of Peter Sabest they won't forget that readily, that stays . . ."

Agatha's face shone happily. "Yes, that stays . . . and they can do me no harm, not to me and not to the child . . ."

"Agatha," I said, "the child isn't here yet, but once it's here . . ."

"Soon."

"Yes, soon, in some six weeks . . . and when it's here you may well want the one you once loved and a father for the child."

At that, a change came over her features, all childlikeness disappeared from them at one stroke, they became ripe and womanly, and she said slowly, "I'm in bliss."

Outside the rain had become heavier and more steady, a joyless downpour, but here inside a human being was joyful because she carried within her another living creature, struck by the rain of the stars, which is rich in joy. And I said, "Yes, Agatha, you are in bliss."

And after a short pause she added, "What has been between us, between me and Peter, that was a beautiful darkness, but there is no joy in darkness . . . But for me, the brightness had to come and the joy . . . and the darkness must never again overwhelm me, for then I'd be shamed in the eyes of the child . . ."

Mother Gisson was right; it would have been futile to try to change Agatha's mind. Nevertheless, I said, "Sometimes there burns in the darkness an inconspicuous light and one need only fan it for it to flame into love . . ."

She smiled. "Peter wouldn't be the one to fan it . . ."

"You probably would have to teach him how."

But she answered firmly, "I don't want to teach him, nor would he want to learn it from me, for all he wants is the darkness and that's why he had to follow Wenzel . . ."

"Agatha," I said, "that may be merely because you don't know how to forgive."

She thought it over and looked down at her hands, folded over her belly as is the wont of all pregnant women. "No," she said, "that's not it . . . for the joy is so great that I need not even think about forgiving . . . The joy is so great that it will still be here after I myself have died and it will still be my own joy . . . I believe it was there ever since the world began, long before I myself was born, and it has received me as if I myself were the child . . . Couldn't that be so, Doctor?"

"Yes, Agatha," I said, "it may well be as you say."

Strum entered. He had folded his hands over his belly and his rolled-up apron as if he, too, were pregnant.

"Strum," I asked, "is it to be a boy or a girl?"

"Twins," called Agatha.

"Yes, but girls," said Strum. "Boys all get crazy."

"That happens at times," I said.

"And how they are crazy!" said Strum. "Today, in this weather, they went to open up the mine."

"Oh?" The thought flashed through my mind that Mathias of the Mount and Sack might take advantage of this opportunity to start a horrific shooting party up there. Fortunately Sack was down here in the Lower Village. But I would not put it past Mathias to go ahead alone, especially now that he might be thinking of taking blood revenge for Irmgard.

"I believe Marius went up with them," reported Strum.

It was obvious to me that Mother Gisson knew something of this undertaking and that her visit to the Lower Village may well have had some connection with it. I had to talk to her.

"I'd like to go over to Miland's as long as Mother Gisson is over there," I said, and stood up.

"Doctor," said Agatha shyly, "I'd still like to ask you something . . ."

"Yes, child . . . Does anything hurt you?"

"No . . . but, Doctor, I'm worried . . . Is Mother Gisson sick?"

"That's something one should never ask a doctor, first of all because he doesn't know the answer and secondly because he's not allowed to tell . . . But Mother Gisson is not my patient and so I can tell you that I believe her to be as healthy as the three of us put together . . ."

"Yes, but she speaks a lot about dying . . ."

"She's an old woman, Agatha . . . Old people sometimes talk about dying."

She was visibly relieved. "She also promised to take me herb gathering."

"So there, you see."

I slipped on my wet cape and went over to Miland's. The rain had become even denser and sky and earth formed a single broth brewed out of October, cold and hopelessness.

Mother Gisson was still there all right; she sat with her daughter at the large kitchen table, and Miland's wife had a slip of paper in front of her, on which she wrote down figures with a pencil stub.

"So there you are, after all," Mother Gisson greeted me. "We wanted to pick you up, Sack and I, but you were already gone."

For the Miland woman I was an unwelcome intrusion; she was busy with her computations. "Twenty-six full days and one half day," she tallied.

"What's all this about?"

"Ah, she wants to settle the account for Irmgard's keep," replied Mother Gisson.

This struck me as somewhat ghoulish, since the last day of that accounting had, after all, ended with a murder.

"Never mind," said Mother Gisson, "she worked it off anyway."

"She didn't work off anything," replied the Miland woman in her harsh stubbornness. "Irmgard is not to owe anyone for any gifts." And she went to the kitchen cabinet, from which she took a china pot in which she kept her money.

"I haven't come to see you about money."

"I want everything settled in good order."

Despite the day of the murder standing at the conclusion of this accounting, there was an amused and ironical undercurrent to Mother Gisson's reply: "What kind of order are you looking for? Do you think all one has to do is pay to get everything in order?"

From the cabinet came the answer: "Irmgard is to rest without debts."

It seemed to me as if the Miland woman meant to invest Irmgard's passing with the greatest possible finality; not even a debt to her grandmother was to be left outstanding. And so I said, "Miland woman, Irmgard rests in peace in any case."

Mother Gisson smiled and then said, "So give me the money; I'll keep it for her."

Her daughter came to the table with her piggy bank and turned the pot upside down. "The dead don't come back," she said while counting out the money.

"Some have to be called and some have to be sent back . . . yes . . ." Mother Gisson's voice trailed into a somewhat mocking remoteness. "Yes, and some are still among us without our knowing it . . "

Did she mean herself? Or did she mean Irmgard?

"Mother," said her daughter, who had sat down again and was staring with deep weariness at the tabletop, "Mother, you shouldn't say such things."

The hoarse and livid broth that filled the world outside was present in here as well, commingling with the shadows of the kitchen, the ever-present odors of human shelter, and the low hissing of the pots on the kitchen stove. And I said, "Leave Irmgard alone, Mother. Souls don't mind waiting."

But I was put in my place. "It's something you don't understand, Doctor."

Then she put the money in her large black purse, and I couldn't help noticing that she counted it perfunctorily while doing so. "Yes," she said, "when traveling one needs some money . . . not much, but some . . . and especially when one has company."

The farmer's wife did not raise her gaze from the chinked wood of the tabletop: "Do you want to take her from me even in death, Mother?"

Mother Gisson shook her head: "Take her away? No . . . but when a child has lost its way in the woods someone must go looking for it."

But the daughter did not listen to her: "Always I paid and paid and nevertheless everything was taken from me and I'm left with nothing. I'm like the water running down from the mountain, I am as the water which owns nothing and which is not allowed to keep anything, not even its banks. I am naked and bare of shame as the water, I hold nothing in my hands and I feel myself running away into nothingness."

Was this the same woman who had stood at Irmgard's funeral, mute, almost indifferent, and without tears?

With a wild, almost mannish movement she now turned on me: "Look at me, Doctor . . . Yes, go on, look at me. I've become bare of shame, shameless as if I were no woman, shameless in my utter loneliness. I've become a man who bears children, less than a man, and Miland, too, has turned into a nothingness, neither man nor woman, and this is how we conceived our children, like the mere menials we were."

Mother Gisson did not relieve me from replying. And I, although knowing that human beings in their loneliness, bereft of love and fallen prey to hatred, become bare of shame and that only the saint is able to gain a solitude in which he is still capable of preserving love and a devout sense of shame, I could only say in a conciliatory manner: "Don't be unfair, woman, you have loved and you've been loved."

She, who had not expected any contradiction from me, least of all any of this nature, came close to pounding the table with her fist as she glanced at me angrily and said, "She who has no father is no woman and he who gets no woman as wife loses the man in himself . . . We no longer had any ground under our feet and we had to take in the stranger because we ourselves had nothing left of our own, yes, Doctor . . . and Irmgard, she, she broke apart over it."

Finally Mother Gisson spoke up. "Daughter," she said, "are you lamenting for Irmgard? Are you lamenting your dead father? Or are you lamenting yourself? I ask you: Whom do you accuse?!"

It was a long time before the toneless reply came: "It is you whom I accuse, Mother . . . Father was shot and it may be that he did it himself."

"No," said the mother, "and you're slandering his memory."

"And even if the poacher did it," continued the daughter in a hoarse and venomous voice, "It was Father who wanted it so, he wanted it because you were always stronger than he . . . you've taken away everybody's strength, you've taken it from anyone close to you, you took Father's strength . . . and mine, too."

"Daughter," said Mother Gisson gently, "your father gave me his strength and I gave it back to him with all the power of my heart . . . That's how we have kept it always and to this day and that's how we shall keep it into all eternity."

The Miland woman had once more sunk into herself; she stared at the cracked tabletop and drew a fingernail along one of its chinks. Finally she said, "I don't believe it . . . A stranger, a stranger from far away had to come, and only over him did you have no power; he proved stronger than you . . ."

"Yes," said the mother, "my time is over but it is without end . . . The stranger, though, he will wander on and disappear . . . and then you, too, will no longer put your faith in hatred . . ."

"I don't believe you, Mother, I cannot believe in you, Mother," lamented the daughter once more, "and even if it was as you say it was, you kept the father for yourself, you didn't let me share him with you, he lay shot to death in the woods, while me, you expelled me into loneliness, into hatred, bereft of a father and bereft of the child, cast out, disinherited, a fatherless menial . . . that's what I am."

A strange stillness set in; it is possible that the rain outside was flowing down more gently now or was about to stop altogether, but it is also possible that this stillness emanated from Mother Gisson, for it seemed as if it were not she but the stillness itself that spoke: "What do all of you know about loneliness, of which the lot of you are forever gabbing? . . . Yes, then, as I lay in the woods on the earth where his blood was ebbing away, there I was truly alone and, daughter, I, too, was full of lament and accusation . . . With my hands, with these, my own hands, I dug into the earth, willing it to give me an answer as to why I, a young woman, was struck by loneliness, and I screamed it high into the heavens . . . Yes, I did so without shame, daughter, I, too, without shame, my screaming was shameless, shameless my accusations, shameless my loneliness . . ."

Her voice became even more quiet. "The heavens did not reply, nor did the earth . . . until I learned that it had been the false loneliness, terrible as it had been, yet it was false, for I had been but as a child left alone in the dark who screams, a child shameless in its fear and in its accusations . . . Only then did the true loneliness take hold of me, not the one that is walled in, the false one for which the darkness is in the walls and the even blacker darkness outside the walls, for what then came was the great loneliness, which is bright as a garden without a fence . . . and I learned that no answer can come from beyond the wall, nothing can penetrate it, and I learned that the answer comes only when heaven and earth and death are within our own center, in the center of our bright garden in which we sit and which we tend . . . our heart and its sense of shame."

The stillness sang its mute song. Were the thoughts of the two women with the man from whom all light had flowed for the one and all darkness for the other? Mother Gisson's kind wrinkled face, even though at the moment it had a somewhat remote aspect, was peaceful and yet had not lost its ever-present hint of a small amused smile, and the Miland woman continued to stare in motionless brooding at the crack in the table along which her finger moved mechanically, but the song of stillness, filling the room now and resonating with the gentle bell sound of holiness, that song now widened, taking the whole room with it so as to become both song and space, becoming landscape and garden, becoming a bright dell of birches, and at its uttermost limits, where the song ends and passes over into the grove of death, there sits a man with a bullet-torn chest, his hunter's jacket comfortably unbuttoned, quietly smoking his evening pipe. Yes, thus and in no other way the song of stillness must have sounded, thus it had become word, for through its inaudible and remote bell strokes Mother Gisson could now be heard, she herself remote and infinitely gentle: "Daughter, all that is part of dying is beautiful."

The daughter did not look up, her expression did not change, and yet, although indiscernible, an intimation of childlike softness had spread over her features and even the finger on the tabletop had become that of a child playing. But then the softness changed to childish obstinacy when, through the slowly opening door leading to the parlor, Cecily now pushed herself into the kitchen, and Miland's wife said, "No child belongs to me."

Cecily, having stopped undecided at the door because she had not expected to find her grandmother and me in here, now clattered to the table in her small wooden clogs and hesitantly looked at her grandmother, trustingly yet ready to slip away at any moment. But the grandmother pushed her toward her mother: "Here, take your child."

A moment of helpless tension developed between the mother and the child. And the hand which had been about to draw the child near fell discouraged once more to the table as from the lips of the little girl, somewhat twisted in disappointment, came the question: "Is Father not here yet?"

For Cecily surely had come only because she had felt the imminent nearness of her father and, indeed, after a few seconds Miland himself appeared, drenched through and through, a shadowy weary automaton in his wet clothes whose feet seemed to have found the customary way home merely by chance. And automatically he took off his wet coat and, now in shirt sleeves, leaned close to the warm kitchen stove.

"Irmgard is dead and I am here," came from the child, as if she knew that this alone could grip her father's attention and direct it toward herself.

"Nothing is dead," corrected the grandmother, "nothing at all, nor is Irmgard dead . . . Children must not talk nonsense."

Miland looked at her in puzzlement. "But, Mother . . . Irmgard is dead . . . I myself . . ." His voice broke.

"Yes," said Mother Gisson. "I know, you yourself . . . but Cecily is to know that Irmgard merely lost her way in the woods, up among the birches and the larches, near the spring and the mossy rocks, and that her grandmother will go and look for her there."

The man at the stove did not move; he stood there, enveloped by the vapors of labor, leather and sweat and tobacco, earth and weariness, he stood there as one who himself has lost his way in a pathless wilderness and finally he said, "Yes, lost."

"Where is Marius?" asked his wife without looking up from the table.

He made a vague gesture. "In the fields, with Andreas."

Did she still want him here, him, the agent of her hatred, the stranger who was supposed to be stronger than her mother? Did she wish for him to confront the mother once more? And almost against my own will I said, "Send him away, farmer."

"That's not possible . . . I can't do that." He said it with quasi-automatic swiftness, but after a short pause he added in a strained, though more natural voice, "I need a hand for the winter sowing."

Yes, he needed a hand, and not the hand of hatred, even though his loneliness was no less than the woman's, he needed the hand of a brother, whom he still expected to reveal the truth of the heart and of his own being, sowing the earth with the power of the seed-casting blessing. And although I knew that this was the way the farmer's mind worked and that this was why he still clung to Marius, I had to reiterate my own conviction. "Miland, you must get rid of him."

And then it was as if his wife suddenly were given to understand the man with whom she otherwise had so seldom been of one mind and as if she were beginning to share my own comprehension of him, nay, even more, as if she were begging me and her mother to spare him and not to rob him of his last support, and as if in an abruptly arising compassion for him and not merely so as to contradict me, she reaffirmed his own refusal: "No, Doctor, that's not possible."

Mother Gisson saw the questioning and imploring glance that her daughter directed at her, but her own expression became as distant as of one who is occupied with more important matters and who cannot be bothered by trifles. "Miland," she said, "you don't have to dismiss him; the stranger will drift away as he came."

From the darkly shadowed corner near the stove where Miland was leaning came his voice as if in deepest alarm: "Mother . . . Mother, don't say that . . . that must not be."

"It is so."

"Mother, then all will have been for naught . . . even Irmgard . . ."

"Irmgard is dead," twittered Cecily, who, cruel and power-hungry, had been waiting for just such a cue.

But Miland, enveloped in shadows, gave voice to his growing terror: "If he were no longer to sow the fields, if the seeds are not to ripen, then the earth and I myself are left with nothing but loneliness and then there cannot be any common bond with the child . . ."

"He will no longer do the sowing for you."

"Mother, then even the sacrifice was nothing but a chance happening . . . It will have been futile, Mother."

"Certainly," said Mother Gisson, "it was futile."

The man fell silent and the shadows that shrouded him thickened in contriteness and shame.

But Mother Gisson took no notice of it as she asked, "What fields is the stranger to sow for you, Miland?"

"I no longer know, Mother, I no longer know my own fields . . . Only after he has sown them will I know them again."

"You come from the fields, Miland, and yet you see only darkness."

"There's nothing around me but darkness, Mother, and I walk toward darkness."

"Yes," said Mother Gisson, "This is how men are. They come from darkness and walk toward darkness, dark the blood out of which they were born, dark the death that awaits them, and they are walled in between. Isn't it so, Doctor?" That submerged amusement of hers blinked again in her eyes and she did not wait for my confirmation to continue. "And because that's how it is with men and because man is filled with the fear of the darkness of death, such a man then thinks that all he has to do is to stretch the dark beginning all the way to his death, so that death may become part of the beginning, so that death may turn into birth in the darkness of the blood. Such a man doesn't have even the desire to rid himself of his darkness but instead wants to drown all the brightness of life, so that the beginning may merge with the end. Yes, Doctor, that's how it is, in case you didn't know."

"I guess that's how it is, Mother," I said.

She became grave once more. "The darkness of his beginning and of his end, he draws to his center, and that's the drunkenness of the blood which he gulps down, that's the dance in which he hops, the scream which he screams, and those are the sacrificial victims which he slaughters, that's the common bond which he seeks in the false loneliness of his darkness, the union of the beginning and of his dark blood which he wants to preserve to his ultimate end, for its sake he spills the blood of his victims, so as to drown in it his own center. But the last jump that he hops and the last scream he screams, he feels it no longer, he no longer hears it, for then there is nothing around him but darkness, senseless the spilled blood of his victims."

There was silence. And for the first time I saw that the Miland woman was able to cry; two tears fell on the tabletop and formed two wet splotches in its cracks. "Irmgard," she said softly, and blew her nose.

But again Mother Gisson spoke, and even though she spoke quite calmly and naturally, surrounded by an ordinary farmer's kitchen in which a shiny radio stood on a shelf and a pot of soup steamed and bubbled on the stove, and although this happened on a perfectly ordinary October noon, it was nevertheless as if Mother Gisson, the old woman in her, the age-old and timeless, timelessly young soul in her, had sunk down to the shadows of an even older memory when she spoke: "Yes, I have seen the great herds, the rams and the lambs and many cattle, they came to the borders of all lands and of all mountains, there were many and ever more, they came without bleating and without lowing, for they had left their bleating and lowing behind them because their throats had been slit. That's how they came in their mute stampede, herd upon herd, and behind them came the men, the humans, screaming and with horsewhips and bloody knives, the men full of dark fear and dark anger, drunk with blood, and they drove the herds in front of them so that they might breach the border and open the way for them. There was no fence at the border, the beasts all crossed it and dispersed on the meadows and in the garden-like woods on the other side; it was good there and they browsed and lay down on the grass to chew their cud. But the humans who ran after them, men and women, they could not cross the invisible wall of the border, and those who rode on the cattle or had grasped their horns to be dragged along across the border, they were all shaken off, and even the sheep proved stronger than they, for all of them were rebuffed by the invisible barrier, and what happened beyond, the meadows and the gardens and the browsing beasts, they were not able to see, for they were blinded, and to them it was as nothingness as they stared into black darkness, and only the smell of the herds, of their blood and of their dung, still lingered in the air. Thus I have seen it. And those were the beasts of sacrifice."

It may be that it had been a dream emerging from her memory, but the shadow of reality hung over her tale. Was it not like a voice from remotest forests, a voice from the border of all lands and all mountains that had recounted the dream? For shadow upon shadow lies in front of the eyes of man, but shadow upon shadow likewise lies behind those eyes, wall upon wall, and the voice that springs forth from the innermost walls of man's soul is invisible and what it conveys is nothing but the truth.

We who heard this voice did not dare interrupt the silence that followed. But as if what had been told were of more urgent import to me than to the others, Mother Gisson singled me out when she said, "Yes, Doctor, that happened long ago, much longer than you can ever imagine, much longer . . . and I saw the shame of man, I saw how shamed he was when he was rejected at the border and no longer could see anything but his own blindness and nothingness and futility . . ."

"Yes," echoed Miland from the darkness near the stove.

And while her voice emerged from the darkening grove of death, in the here and now it gently addressed the daughter: "Those women who follow the men on their way into darkness and who, together with them, seek to draw death into life, become shameless, they become as shameless as the man himself who is overcome with shame when he finally opens his eyes, and they both find themselves in the false loneliness, and false is their feeling of communality, for the man is no longer a man and the woman no longer a woman. It is then that they call for the redeemer who is to put their darkness into words and is to sanctify it, they call for the one who is to be stronger than the center of life and stronger than the center of the heart, they call for the stranger who comes from darkness, so that he may lead them in the dance toward their death."

At that her daughter wailed like a little girl unable to speak through her sobbing: "Oh, Mother, did I dance? Did I ever? While the others were on the dance square, my thoughts were with the father I never knew . . ."

Mother Gisson did not reply immediately, but when she did a smile floated in the darkness and in her remote voice: "You expected the stranger to bring back the father to you because the stranger came from darkness. That was your own dancing ground."

And then she said: "I have learned that we need not die into our death but may live into it and that such a death is neither in vain nor senseless, and that then the bitter death itself becomes alive, and what is alive is never futile. And I have learned that I must not look at the end if I wish to see it but must instead look at the center, the center which is where the heart is . . . yes, the center is so strong that it reaches past the beginning and the end, so strong that it reaches into what is dark and that which is feared by men because they see nothing there but sheer nothingness and darkness . . . But when the center has been allowed to grow freely, then it casts its brightness beyond all borders and to the utmost limits, then there is no difference any longer between what is past and what is to come and we are permitted to look to the other side and to those who have died, we are permitted to speak with them and they live together with us."

Did she address the Milands? Was she addressing me? Did she speak to the congregation of the dead, listening silently in the woods, their transparent backs leaning against the trunks of birches, their mouths agape in amazement at receiving this message of a death reaching into life? She spoke for both the living and the dead, for to her they were as one. The Miland woman had bowed her head again, her face extinguished and no longer seeming to see or hear, but Miland himself had now come forward; he leaned one hand on the table while the other automatically had taken hold of Cecily, and he listened in great concentration as one who steers a boat in heavy fog.

And once more could be heard the voice coming from the grove of the dead: "That is what I learned, then, when the being I loved was shot dead in the woods, and ever since I have lived in death and yet in the center of life, and my loneliness is no longer a loneliness . . . What is dead are merely the empty words and these indeed lead to a death which is a nothingness and a darkness, but that which truly happens hereunder reaches beyond death and invests death with life everlasting, as does each child that is conceived and born in love, each field that is being cultivated, and each flower that is being tended, for the child is knowledge and so are the field and the flower, a knowledge that cannot be lost, that is larger and stronger than time, and it is a joy requiring for its rebirth neither sacrifice nor dancing ground at the edge of death, for it is here and with us always and forever, from eternity to eternity . . ."

Mother Gisson paused and then she laughed gently and continued in her good, warm everyday voice: "But for the one who has not experienced it, these, too, are empty words, and that's why I shouldn't even talk of it . . . For as long as you're looking merely on the outside, for the father whom you didn't know, you won't find him any more than you'll find death and its living rebirth or the truth of the heart . . . First both of you must experience yourselves in your own lives, in the truth of the center, first you must sow your field and tend your garden . . . Are you not a couple? So much a couple that you have children together, the two of you?"

But Miland, still tensed and rigid, stiffly shook his head: "How can we be a couple when I have sacrificed the child? What can be born again when rebirth has turned into darkness and shame? How can there still be a common bond and truth since I was not even allowed to find the truth with the child? I no longer can see the truth of the heart, I can see only the shame . . ." And almost impetuously he demanded my own confirmation: "Didn't I sacrifice Irmgard, Doctor? I, I myself?!"

Mother Gisson had stood up and she now took Miland's hand in her own. "Miland," she said, "do you believe it serves you in your loneliness that you don't let go of the little one here? Didn't you also cling to Irmgard in the same way? You are in the false loneliness, in the darkness standing at the beginning, the one which generates the drunkenness, and that's why you can't let go of your flesh and your blood, what you seek is that intoxication and not the truth and not community, and where it carries you there is indeed nothingness. And, Miland! That is why Irmgard had to end there, too."

It was as if Miland were slowly losing his rigidity at the touch of her hand; the arm with which he had grasped the child became loose and dropped and his voice became uncertain, soft and questioning: "Mother, is there still a path left for one who is filled with shame?"

At that his wife raised her still tear-dimmed eyes, she raised her face bearing the traits of both her mother and Irmgard, and in the old woman's stead she herself replied, "Give me the child, husband . . . and come close."

The man remained immobile; he looked uncomprehendingly into the eyes of the woman, a man who remembers and yet still searches in his memory, a man who suddenly sees before him the sea of remembrance, the gentle waves of the morning murmuring all that is past and all that is to come. And he remained motionless as one who does not believe it.

Whereupon Mother Gisson simply took Cecily and sat her on the lap of the woman.

"Is that right now?" she asked.

And Miland said, "Yes."

The radio stood on the shelf, the pot on the stove hummed softly, the china on the wall shone whitely in the shadows, and for an instant I felt slightly disappointed that the dead had had to be troubled merely so as to restore some homely harmony to the hearts of this couple. But no sooner had I had this thought—triggered perhaps by the sight of the radio—than I felt ashamed of it. For the dialogue of the living is no less miraculous than that of the dead, and the center of our life and of our knowledge is the humble soberness in which there breathes our heart and its truth, the infinite implied in a single breath of the finite. And I, too, felt this breath, heralding the lifting of a spell.

Mother Gisson had remained standing and put on her black woolen cardigan. "I'm going," she said, as if to speed up matters. And when she had it on, she repeated: "I'm leaving, Miland, Sack is waiting for me at the pub with the carriage."

Miland merely smiled musingly and said without altering his stance, "I shall sow myself . . ."

"Daddy," whined Cecily, who disliked sitting on her mother's lap and wanted to return to her father.

But Miland said, "Stay with your mother," and approaching them both, he gave his hand to his wife.

Mother Gisson took her umbrella. "Everything's fine," she said, and was about to slip away unnoticed.

"Wait!" I called. "Wait, Mother, I'm coming with you."

"Then make it fast." There was something in her sudden haste which made me suspect that it was not easy for her to leave.

The Miland woman paid no attention to us; she clasped her husband's hand, and as she wiped the last tears from her eyes, she asked, "Aren't you hungry yet? Call the boys to the meal."

But Mother Gisson was already out the door and I didn't even have time to put on my cape before rushing after her.

She stood in the street and was busy with her large cotton umbrella; only now was I struck by the fact that under her woolen cardigan she was wearing her Sunday best and it crossed my mind that this was as if she were dressed for her formal farewell visits.

"So, Doctor, there you are . . . It was time to leave." She looked at me and then said with some gravity, "It wasn't quite in vain, I believe . . . Don't you agree?"

"Yes, but that was entirely due to you . . . and not to our Mr. Marius."

"And yet his coming served in that, too."

By now it was raining only lightly, but Mother Gisson protectively held her umbrella over me as well, even though I, in my loden cape, hardly needed it. Trapp, his tail between his legs, sniffed into each of the farm gates in the hope of discovering some life, but the yards were deserted and wet, a brown broth ran from the compost heaps, and even the chickens had sought shelter.

"Mother Gisson," I said, "you managed to restore some order in there and it would seem to be up to you now to see to it that this whole Marius business is finally brought to an end as well . . .

I heard that that nonsense of the opening of the mine is to begin today."

"Without Marius, that's for sure. He looks out for himself; it's in the hands of Wenzel and his lads."

"Well, that may lead to a real nice brawl with the Upper Villagers . . . High time, in fact, that I went up there . . ."

"There'll be no brawl . . . Sack I took down with me, and Mathias will keep the others in check . . ."

"That's certainly good to hear, but it would be even better if you were to put an end to that man's game once and for all . . . When all is said and done, it's actually your duty, Mother Gisson."

"Duty? Quite the contrary. I leave him a clear field, in the mine and everywhere else . . . At Miland's, it was different, but otherwise these are no longer my concerns . . ."

"The people need you more urgently than they do Marius, much more urgently!"

"No, they don't need me . . . What Marius is offering them I can't offer . . . My time is over, even though you still see me walking around hereabouts, Doctor . . . That's only the outward semblance . . ." And Mother Gisson laughed somewhat remotely and enigmatically.

We had arrived at the corner of Church Street. A slight easterly breeze blew through the village street, all the way to the wall of fog behind which stood the Kuppron and the Raw Venten, it nibbled at the fog and ate up the white rags drifting down from the peaks. And Mother Gisson, slanting her umbrella, said, "The rain will soon stop, but we may get some snow before we get back up . . . Are you coming with us, Doctor?"

"Why, yes, if you're willing to wait until I'm finished with my clinic . . . But, Mother, you shouldn't always be talking about your time being over. Even though you may already be somewhere else than all the rest of us, that's only one more reason why you are needed here, and for many more years to come . . . There's no one who could take your place."

"Maybe Agatha will be able to do so one day, in about thirty years . . . but you can't understand that," she said, dismissing me.

"Oh, Agatha . . . So that's why you're going to see the widow Sabest."

She nodded. "Yes, for that, too . . . One has to make it easier for both of them."

We had arrived at the pub. "So nothing is going to happen up there, Mother Gisson?"

"You can rest assured, nothing at all."

"And what about the gold?"

"I guess the mountain isn't ready to yield any."

"Well, then this is definitely going to be the end of Marius."

"Because of that? Why, Doctor! How can you believe such a thing? . . . What's important is promising something to the people, not actually keeping those promises . . . The people have always lived on hope alone."

And with that we entered the pub.

Sack sat there drinking a hot grog. Upon seeing us, he set down his glass unhurriedly.

"Are we going already, Mother Gisson? I stabled the horse."

"No, no, no hurry; first I have to speak to Minna Sabest and perhaps the doctor will be going back with us."

"I've plenty of time," said Sack contentedly.

Mother Gisson went to join Minna Sabest in the kitchen, and after making sure that no patients had arrived as yet, I sat down with Sack.

"Don't you also want a glass of grog, Doctor? Warms you up nicely."

Not a bad idea, and I ordered one, too.

Sack radiated contentment. The holes in his cheeks, dug by the grief over the death of his wife, had filled up.

"Well, Sack, they finally got their way, they're working the mine . . ."

Sack pointed to the kitchen. "If she hadn't interceded, they wouldn't have reached even the entrance to the shaft, of that you may be sure, Doctor . . . But when Mother Gisson commands, nothing is to be done . . . one has to obey . . ."

"Hm, yes."

"Back then, in August, you should have let us shoot, Doctor . . . but now it's too late."

"Only because Mother Gisson has so ordered?"

"Not only . . . but she always knows what she's doing . . . You can't rely on the Upper Villagers anymore, the young ones have all shifted their allegiance to Wenzel . . . and since the happenings at the Cold Stone, they've all gone crazy; they loved it, in spite of everything."

"Just you wait, Sack, in the end they may even dig out their gold and we'll be the dumb ones in the eyes of all."

Sack smirked cunningly. "Don't worry, the mountain knows how to defend itself."

"Why, is there going to be another earthquake perhaps?" This mysticism about the mountain was still somewhat beyond me.

"Why not, could well be . . . but the mountain has other means."

Yes, indeed, it had other means, as was to become only too clearly apparent on this very same day.

I had had my grog, Sack had allowed himself a second glass or perhaps a third, and I had gone up to my clinic, where some patients had arrived for dental treatment. No sooner had I finished than I was called downstairs to answer the telephone in the kitchen. I rushed down, somewhat perturbed, for Caroline hardly ever used the telephone without serious cause; each and every time, this contraption impressed her anew as weirdly mysterious.

It was indeed Caroline. "The doctor is to come to the telephone . . ."

"Yes, it's me . . . What's the matter, Caroline?"

"Hello."

She had learned to say hello.

"Yes, what is it?"

"Doctor? . . . Doctor, Ludwig is here . . ."

"What Ludwig?"

"Ludwig is here."

"Ludwig from the blacksmith's?"

"Yes, that Ludwig . . ."

"Damn it, speak up, Caroline . . . What does he want?"

Silence; I hear her whispering with Ludwig. Then: "He says he wrenched his arm . . ."

"What the devil! . . . Call him to the phone, I want to speak to him personally."

Again some whispered negotiations, followed by Caroline's pleased laughter. "He's never telephoned, he says he doesn't dare . . . You are to go to the mine, there was a mishap . . ."

"Hell's bells! . . . What's happened? Ask him, damn it!"

A pencil stub dangled on a string next to the telephone; I managed to tear it off. Finally, still intermingled with Caroline's giggling over Ludwig's fear of the telephone, came the answer: "Something has collapsed . . . There may be some dead."

"Ludwig is to wait for me . . . I'm on my way."

"Hello."

"Yes, hello and goodbye. I'm coming home first and he is to wait for me."

I hastened to the pub room. "Sack! It's happened, a mess at the mine . . ."

He nodded calmly. "Aha . . . in the mountain . . ."

"Of course, where else? . . . Harness the horse while I run over to the smith . . . What a mess!"

"Very well, Doctor." He rose placidly and with obvious satisfaction.

"I just hope the smith is in."

Behind me I could still hear Sack: "Of course he's in, where else would he be?" But I was already out the door to alarm the smith and his fire brigade.

The blacksmith was there and in the process of fashioning long carpenter hooks.

"Smith, something has happened at the mine already . . . Sound the alarm and get your men together!"

"The devil . . ."

"Yes, and your apprentice was caught in it, too, but there may also be some dead . . . That's what comes from all that recklessness . . ."

He stroked his beard. "I guess you're right . . . the young ones are rash and stupid . . . and yet, I can understand them . . . What will we need up there?"

"A few ladders at most, the axes . . . most of all, the first-aid equipment . . ."

"Yes, yes . . ."

We were both already in the street, he to look for his bugler, I on my way back to the pub.

In the yard Sack was getting the harnessed horse between the shafts. The wind blew under the canopy of the carriage, so that the whole light surrey trembled; the first fallen and autumnally yellowed chestnut leaves stuck to the moist ground.

"Did you notify Mother Gisson?"

"Not yet."

"I guess I have to do everything myself."

Running up the steps and entering the Sabest apartment, I found the two women in the cozily coffee-impregnated parlor and they were so deep in conversation that Minna Sabest at first could not grasp the import of the news with which I had startled them. But then, alternately raising her hands to her temples and folding them together, she said, "The dear God in heaven be praised and thanked that Peter was no longer with them."

Mother Gisson remained strangely detached. "Well, that was fast," she merely said, and continued to sip her coffee. "As soon as Sack is ready, we'll go."

"He's ready."

"Good." She quickly finished her coffee, put down the cup, and rose. But while putting on her cardigan she turned to the widow once more. "And don't say that your life is over, Minna; rather, it would have come to an end if everything had remained as it was."

Mrs. Sabest sighed. "But it's hard nevertheless."

"Yes, that it is," Mother Gisson agreed, and opened the door.

But on the steps she took up the thought once more; she stopped and turned to the widow, who had followed us out. "Yes, it's hard and it will also be hard for you in times to come, Minna, but life is never at an end, it always starts anew . . ."

And then she continued on her way.

We stood in the yard.

"All right, Sack," said Mother Gisson, "help me up . . . and many thanks for the fine coffee, Minna, and now we're off."

"And I thank you very much for your kind sympathy and for taking the time to call on me," said the widow formally, as she stood there, blond in her black mourning attire.

The first bugle calls for the assembling of the fire brigade were heard from the street.

"Nothing to thank me for, Minna," replied Mother Gisson from the carriage. "You're most welcome."

I climbed up and Sack pulled on the reins. Pluto the St. Bernard came by, bereft of his master, his expression even more sorrowful than usual, and he looked after us sadly, envying Trapp, who was allowed to sit on the box next to Sack.

People were already gathering in the street; the smith stood in front of his shop, his fire chief's helmet on his head and girded with his ax. The bugler was now in Church Street.

The smith beckoned to us and we stopped for a moment. "Aren't you coming with us, Doctor?"

"No, I've got to get home first and bandage Ludwig . . . He's waiting there . . . After that I'll follow."

We drove on.

It was the high-wheeled surrey with the linen pillows, the one that usually was used to transport the priest, and I sat behind with Mother Gisson under the canopy, the dirty-yellow inside of which showed both old and fresh bands of rain splotches. But the rain had stopped, and after we had left the village, the woods and slopes became visible.

"Hurry up, Sack," I admonished.

But Sack, sitting in front of us on the low box that allowed us to look over his head, would not let himself be hurried. "I can't whip the horse to death." Nevertheless he goaded it on with some "tsks" and "hees," though they didn't do much to speed up its staid trot.

Softer now, the bugle call could still be heard, agitated and alarming. "God knows how many may already be dead up there, Sack!"

"Too few," he replied.

"Sack," I said, "the tunnel may very well have collapsed . . . To be buried alive and suffocate is a terrible thing."

"Oh yes," he assented, "the whole ground is softened up by the rain . . . That can press pretty hard on a man, there's quite some weight there . . . Wet earth can easily start to slide . . . Yes, yes, that's how it is when one tackles a job that one knows nothing about."

"Nevertheless, things up there couldn't have been quite above-board if something like that happened so quickly," said Mother Gisson, and it seemed to me as if all kinds of suspicions could be heard in her voice.

"It's all aboveboard all right," said Sack, looking well pleased with everything.

The wind blew from behind, the canopy thudded damply like a slack drumskin, the thin-spoked wheels creaked and crunched, and to the left and right of us the cold stroked the fields and slopes with a flat and rigid and somewhat moist hand, while up above the mountains rapidly discarded their foggy garments and the first wintry snow patches could be seen on the tops of the firs. We fell silent and did not even speak of the weather.

It was about two o'clock when we arrived at the spur leading to my house and I got off.

"You still have some hard work ahead of you today," Mother Gisson said, and pressed my hand.

"Yes, Mother, that's quite likely."

"I'll come down to the mine later on, too," Sack called after me, and prodded the horse once more.

I arrived at the house quite out of breath, for one must not let a man with a dislocated arm wait and Ludwig had been waiting long enough. His arm was indeed in bad shape, not merely luxated but also fractured, and that made it damnably difficult, for I could hardly take a good hold of the arm because of the fracture, let alone exert a lever traction on it. At first, I thought I would have to send him to the hospital. But finally I succeeded after first putting the fracture in a splint. We both sweated profusely, the patient because of his pain and effort and I because I had to exert my last ounce of strength. But then we were both mighty proud of ourselves, he on account of his courage and I on account of this proof of my physical strength, and we praised each other lavishly when I was done and while I was still putting the arm in a cast. It was only afterward, when we were both drinking a well-deserved brandy, that I realized that in all the work I had forgotten the real catastrophe that had caused it.

"All right now, tell me about the mess you got yourselves in . . . I should be there already."

"I'll go with you, Doctor."

"Are you crazy? It's a miracle you ever got down here in your condition and now you're thinking of going back up!"

He laughed. "But, Doctor, I should be able to stand that, it's nothing at all."

Nor could I restrain him. As fast as I could, I gathered all the dressings and whatever else I might need and stowed them away in my rucksack. And then we started on our way, he at my side, telling me what had happened.

Well, yes, but there was hardly anything to tell. They had worked at clearing the tunnel since yesterday evening. The first hundred yards were nothing, only rubbish had to be carted out, and they had accompanied their work with songs, and even though they may also have thought of the gold that they hoped to find, it had not been truly in their thoughts, for the wish to penetrate ever deeper into the mountain, to sing in it in ever greater depths, had become stronger as time went on, so strong that finally they probably thought of nothing else.

"You know, Doctor," he said, "when one sings in the tunnel there's no echo, but if one could get to the center of the mountain, the center where the pure ore lies, that's where the source must be of all the echoes one hears on the outside aboveground . . . and that's what we wanted to reach."

"Hm, and Wenzel, too, is now looking for the echo instead of the gold? I can't quite believe that . . . It sure wasn't the echo that broke your arm."

"Wenzel? He sang along with us . . . and all he wanted was to get ever deeper into the mountain, and he kept driving us on in our work . . . but after some hundred and fifty or two hundred yards we got into the water, water that shimmered with drops like the eyes of snakes . . . it seeped out of the rock and lay on the rotten wood of the old shorings, and a bit further on the water stopped and instead there was earth, earth like in a swamp which comes at you from all sides, Doctor, an earth full of soft bubbles . . ."

"And it's there that it happened?"

Yes, that's where it happened. Wenzel, who is also an expert carpenter, ordered that the tunnel be bulkheaded. So they brought in the wood supplied by Mr. Lax, they propped up the face, braced the struts, and secured the planks, there had been five men working at that task and they had sung with each stroke of the hammer while Wenzel instructed them how to do it . . . and suddenly there had been an echo in the earth, something like an echo but more like a gurgling, though their singing down there also may have sounded more like a gurgle, and at that the new struts had given way: he had meant to prop up a ceiling strut but it had simply twisted his arm off, three of them had been able to reach safety but Leonhard and Wenzel had been caught inside.

"And that's all, Doctor."

"So that's all . . . And what happened to Wenzel and Leonhard?"

"I don't know, I'm afraid . . . nor can I say how I got out myself . . . I only know that the earth collapsed around me and the other two and that it must have caught those others . . . but it may be that they still can be dug out alive . . . I ran down here, for someone had to do it, and I couldn't have helped with the work anyway, and I also thought it would be best if this shitty arm could be straightened out right away . . ."

"Does it hurt now, your shitty arm?"

"Well, a bit . . . Another schnapps would be fine."

Instead of the road leading to the village we had taken the shorter path which leads along the slope and now met the miners' path. The trees dripped, the patches of snow on the ground became ever more numerous, growing together into ever larger snow islands, though these were still pierced by grass and green heather bushes, at times a clump of snow fell heavy and wet from a branch which then slowly rocked up and down in the aftermath, and the air in the woods was of a dark transparency that high up above the tree-tops thickened to a solid whitish gray, from time to time peering down through the pines. Since we moved quite fast despite Ludwig's injury, we caught up with a number of people who had heard of the catastrophe and had armed themselves with pickaxes and shovels and were now rushing like us to help at the site. Among these, we saw Sack, striding unhurriedly, and when we emerged from the woods on the meadow in front of the Mountain Chapel we had already turned into a rather imposing troop, working its way up through what had become a dense, wetly grained field of new snow.

White were the blackberry bushes still carrying their leaves, brown were the bent and withered fern fronds on the wintry ground; the Mountain Chapel stood in front of us, quiet, unnoticed and unused, sheltering the blessed stones, melted snow dripped from one side of its roof, mighty and cold and surprisingly close rose the walls of the Kuppron behind it, and the head of the snake above the entrance of the mine also wore a small cap of snow.

All around us in the great clarity of the darkly transparent air, the mountains rose starkly against the snow-colored sky, in hard contrast their peaks and rocks, covered in white deep down below the tree line, reaching down into the greenery even lower on the north slopes, and in all that brightness the rocky masses which everywhere had grown out of the snow or had shaken it off took on the color of a yellowish-black darkness: a great and secure coolness, almost cheerful in its self-assurance, spanned the entire space before us, the garland of winter crowning the green and brown valley below in which autumn still nestled softly.

From the Pit of the Dwarfs we could at times hear a shout or the stroke of an ax and the sound was carried forth by the porcelain-like softness of the echo in the reflection and counter-reflection of which winter and autumn, autumn and winter sang to each other, reply and response in ever reiterated colloquy.

Lofty ground in which the echo sounds and reverberates, mirroring garden enclosing the center of being! Did I not myself seek the source of my own echo as I searched for the glance emerging from my being, embracing all that is and carrying me toward it? Had I not, too, been in danger of being buried under the downward-plunging dream, in danger of suffocating in the swamp? Oh, hallowed brightness of the world, bright sanctity of the center, fair bashfulness of autumn, both bared and shrouded by the coming snow! Nevermore can we reach farther than to that loftily floating center in which the perceived joins with that which perceives, source of echo and counter-echo, our cognizance, divine and earthly at the same time, revealing the otherworldly in the here and now: this is the abode of the saints who live in the secular and yet have opened themselves to the divine—wherever their glance rests in this world, in their eyes it becomes lofty and sublime, to whatever they hearken, it reaches their ears as the mirroring song of the echo, for much as they apprehend the remote in that which is close, their whole life has become a loving recognition and thus is invested with sanctity, humbly and bashfully baring and shrouding the immortal in the inadequacy of the hereunder, and the deeper they submerge themselves in the loneliness of their selves, the higher they ascend to the heights of the unnamable—though who then may say what is below and above?—the more the worldly center becomes their high and bright, their sublimely radiant abode, secure in the embrace of all the horizons.

Through such noble abodes of nature we, too, ascended, though in truth without noticing or even wishing to notice much of it. The men stuck their shovels in the snow and used them as climbing sticks to speed up their ascent, the tools penetrated the soft snowy mass with sharp slapping sounds, and thus we noisily reached the chapel. No wonder that most of them cursed with renewed energy the whole gold-seeking adventure and that but few still defended it; but even though they cursed and even though some of them declared that the mountain had now taken its revenge, they felt as little shame on account of this new disaster as they had felt over the murder of Irmgard, and the shudder of horror they nevertheless now felt surely was not that of shame but rather one of anticipation; they were quite ready to dig out hecatombs of dead bodies.

The short stretch from the chapel to the adit was almost Christmasy in its whiteness, but the path had been cleared by the steps of many, as well as by Lax's bringing in the wood, so that we quickly reached our goal, the clearing in front of the Pit of the Dwarfs. Here, surrounded by Christmas trees standing in quiet stateliness, a scene of excited and noisily undignified comings and goings was under way, ant-like in its bustling in front of the yawning blackness of the entrance to the tunnel; the snowy ground had become a blackish expanse with here and there some tired clumps of grass, in its middle the loosely stacked pile of construction wood, while to our right a primitive toolshed had been erected on the slope at the edge of the woods, more accurately a mere lean-to protected on three sides by walls partly secured to the trunks of nearby trees, with next to it an open fire, obviously for cooking purposes, from which the sharp-mellow woodsmoke drifted into the coolness all around and over to us; that is where Lax stood, and his voice could be heard throughout the clearing as he tried to give some sense and direction to all the hustle and bustle. Of course, this was quite futile, for there were patently far too many people present; only a very small number could work in the narrow confines of the tunnel.

He desisted as soon as he saw us and came over, followed by some of the others. I also noticed some firemen, who had tarried long enough to don their full uniforms.

"A fine mess, Doctor," said Lax in greeting, apparently totally oblivious of the fact that he was the main culprit.

"Yes, indeed . . . What is there for me to do?"

He looked somewhat abashed nevertheless. "Wenzel we managed to get out . . . he seems to have gotten off lightly . . . but Leonhard . . . well"—he turned away—"not much hope."

"Where is Wenzel?"

He pointed to the toolshed.

Wenzel lay stretched out on the ground under the roof of the lean-to, covered with two overcoats, a rolled-up jacket under his head, his much-wrinkled wily face snow white and his eyes closed.

I knelt down next to him. "Wenzel?"

He slowly opened one eye and blinked at me sideways. "The doctor."

"Yes, Wenzel."

"Can't talk," he pressed out with difficulty.

On no account had he come off lightly, that I could see already. "Well, maybe you can try . . . Where does it hurt?"

A shimmer of his old mockery flitted over his face. "Better ask where it doesn't hurt."

"Hm."

"Cold, Doctor," he said softly.

"Yes, we have to try to get you out from here . . . Can you move?"

His attempt at joking turned into a wizened grimace. "Better not, Doctor."

And after a while: "Can't move, Doctor."

One could see that the effort had caused him incredible pain; after it had subsided he said, "Doctor . . . I've had it . . . Better let me croak right here . . . Shitty luck . . . Slight professional mishap . . ."

"There's plenty of time before thinking of dying, Wenzel."

He merely groaned.

I began to suspect a fractured vertebra; everything pointed to a spinal injury. I could not even begin to determine what else had been fractured and crushed in the man since I could not risk changing his position. There was no question of any serious examination. What's more, transporting him on the fire brigade's inadequate stretcher posed a well-nigh insoluble problem.

I squatted next to him in utter desperation. People stood in front of the shed and watched me tensely; from time to time wisps of smoke drifted in from the fire.

Finally and so that something might be done at least, I barked at the men standing around outside the lean-to: "Bring the stretcher!"

Wenzel opened his eyes. "Doctor, don't torture me pointlessly."

The smith came. "How is he?"

"He's got his share . . . but it could be worse."

It was almost as if Wenzel tried to laugh; it came out as a wheezing whistle. But then he said, "Smith, someone sawed into the wood uprights."

"What?"

With great effort he repeated: "The shoring struts had been sawed into . . . and that's how it happened . . . I know my business . . ."

"You'd better know how to get well," said the smith, "instead of thinking of such things . . ."

The face of the little rogue filled with hatred. "Those bastards . . . and I'm croaking here . . ."

I looked at the smith; he nodded at me as if to indicate that Wenzel's claim might not be without grounds. Sawn into? Sack? Mathias?

In an even weaker voice Wenzel continued: "And Marius . . ."

"Yes? Shall I give him a message?"

"He has nothing to do with this whole matter . . . It was my business . . . mine alone . . . Doctor . . . only I . . ." He wheezed in exhaustion.

"Yes, Wenzel, don't worry."

He did not indicate whether he had heard me; he had fallen back into a stupor.

No matter what, I had to try to get him to the hospital, hopeless as it seemed, and so I asked the smith, "Does one of your men know how to use the telephone?"

He thought it over. "Yes, young Lax should be able to."

"Then send him down to call the hospital . . . It is now past four, by nine o'clock at the latest the ambulance should be at my house . . ."

But what of the present? It would be best to bring him down immediately while there was still daylight. They might have to work for hours in the tunnel before they were able to dig out Leonhard and I could be back up here long before that.

I asked for a few more overcoats and wrapped them around Wenzel. "Come, smith," I said, "let's go see what's happening in the mine."

"Right; I've got to go in anyway . . . Change of shift is about due."

"How often do you change shifts?"

"Every hour. Six men for the digging and the shoring up and four men for the earth removal."

The unhealthy tension of waiting hung over the clearing, a tension which after some time could only be released in jokes or quarrels. The people had come to help, they wanted to lend a hand, but instead they had to idle away hours before being assigned to a shift. They wandered about with nothing to do and already there was considerable shouting among some of the groups.

In front of the adit Lax was about to designate the next shift.

The smith interrupted him belligerently. "I can't use everyone . . ."

"Oh, the chief of the brigade himself."

"Yes. I am in command and I bear the responsibility."

Mathias of the Mount emerged from the tunnel, his clothing and his red beard encrusted with earth, an ax in his hand, and he laughed. "No Lower One can be in command here, for none of you understand whatsoever about the mountain."

I inquired about the progress of the work.

"Slow, slow . . . new shoring to be put in every two feet."

There was already a large mound of excavated earth next to the entrance, a pure earth of a strong brown color, rich in flint, which hardly looked capable of murder. A wheelbarrow full of that earth was trundled out from the tunnel at intervals and the man wheeling it then returned below on the double after having emptied it.

We, too, now entered the mine. From far away we were met by the sounds of hammering and of dull clanking shovel strokes, carried by a warm draft of decay; along the still largely brick-clad walls torches and pine kindlings burned in holders many of which obviously dated from olden times, and the path led gently upward. Had they let Wenzel rest down here instead of outside in the wintry cold, it would have been better.

But then the path turned and led quite steeply downward into the wet zone of which Ludwig had spoken; the old casement became increasingly rotten and crumbling, interrupted ever more frequently by the white wood of today's replacements. Water dripped and trickled and the tepid cellar breath was impregnated with the sharp smell of freshly dug earth. The men we met on our way in were hard put to push the wheelbarrows up the incline in this section, the noises from the digging drew nearer, and after another slight bend the tunnel widened and we seemed to be entering a roomy chamber, the frontal face of which was still closed by earth while its three other sides were all shored and boarded up with fresh wood: it was this warm enclosure, brightly lit by some storm lamps, that was the site of the disaster.

The carpenters hammered the casement planks onto the walls and four men dug into the face of earth and filled the wheelbarrows.

Ludwig stood next to me. "It can't be far now . . . It caught me right there"—and he pointed backward—"and Leonhard wasn't far away; we were talking to each other."

I had lost all sense of distance; surely we had walked only a few minutes, but I could not tell whether we had penetrated into the tunnel for a stretch of three hundred or six hundred yards. I would have believed anything. "I wonder how deep the tunnel reaches down . . ." I mused.

"Deep, very deep," replied Mathias, "but it's likely that all that has been flooded." He wiped a few drops from the ceiling as if to show them to me. "The same water as that in the Green Lake."

The image of a subterranean lake from the midst of which the spring of all echoes rises, an image itself arising in sweet longing from the sea of all thoughts, of all memories and of all things conceivable, was wedded eerily to the image of the heights through which the echo reverberates, the image of another ethereal lake which, between its snowy shores, shelters autumn on its bottom, and the image arose in me like an ultimate enticement.

Behind me the lads were driving a shoring pile into the earth as they sang, in the face of death, the age-old, obscene pile drivers' song:

> Fair little Mary
> Now we ram it in
> And once up (Pom)
> And twice deep (Pom)
> And thrice up (Pom)
> And four times deep (Pom)
> Fair little Mary
> Now we ram it in (Pom)
> Fair little Mary
> Now you've got it in.

"My God, he may still be alive!"

"If he is, then he'll be glad to hear us," said one of the pile drivers.

"He's dead," said Mathias of the Mount.

> Fair little Mary
> Now we ram it in . . .

Was that the dirge they sang for the dead man? The man who had been rammed into the womb of the earth, a small, truly inconspicuous dirge, as small as the immeasureable is small in the womb of the earth, and nevertheless immeasurable, without distance in time or space, yet containing immeasureably all that is as in a single seed corn. And I suddenly became aware of the strange fact that I could think of Leonhard, though I had known him in life in all his great length and girth, that I could imagine him only in the dwarfish size of Wenzel, nay, even smaller than Wenzel, and it occurred to me that one merely had to step over this dead and buried gnome to reach all the way to the silvery lake lying down there.

> . . . And six times deep (Pom)
> Fair little Mary . . .

"Here he is!" shouted one of the diggers.

At that, the singing stopped at last.

A shoe protruded from the earth wall at about half a man's height and pointed its hobnailed sole to the ceiling.

Everyone fell silent. Mathias took off his jacket and then also his shirt and started to dig with the others. It was not easy, for the gradually liberated body had to be supported time and again by the insertion of planks against the mass of earth constantly pushing from above. He lay slanted downward, his head pressed against the floor of the tunnel. Finally he could be dug out.

I was filled with impatience, for I was worried about Wenzel up there, not knowing whether he might not have awakened again from his stupor, and so it was almost with relief that I found that nothing could be done anymore for Leonhard: he had not even suffocated but had simply been crushed to death.

The men surrounded him in silence. In the excavation from which the body had been extracted, crumbling earth dribbled down and water dripped and the shoring boards bent and creaked. I noticed that all of us looked again and again at that hole in the earth as if we expected something to emerge out of its depth, an animal, a snake, a black cat, or something equally unlikely. And without anyone having ordered it and though it made no sense and served no purpose at all, two men began to board up what so recently had been a grave.

"I'm going," I said. "You'll carry him out."

Mathias undertook to take care of the corpse and I left. Returning, I realized how short the stretch had been, certainly less than three hundred yards. The steep incline was behind me almost immdiately, the half-moon of the entrance appeared up ahead and rapidly grew in size. That's where I met the smith with the new work shift. I told them that they could go back: the work was done.

"So," said the smith, "crushed to death . . . At least he had a fine death."

"Smith," I said, "that's not my idea of a fine death."

"You're wrong," he said. "The good death is wild like the fire." And he continued on his way to look after Leonhard and his fine death.

Some of the men in his shift turned and went with me toward the exit. The waiting crowd meanwhile had grown further. When I announced to them what had occurred, one after another of the men took off his hat or cap, but at the same instant a piercing scream filled the clearing, rising to the tops of the Christmasy trees and reverberating again and again in the walls of the Kuppron. It was the mother of Leonhard, the old Nistler woman, who had been waiting with a group of women standing on one side, and she had understood the meaning of the gesture of respect.

But I had no time to look after her; I had to get back to Wenzel. But another surprise awaited me there, a rather awkward one.

Marius had planted himself in front of Wenzel, who still lay there with closed eyes, next to Marius stood Krimuss and Lax, and Marius, who obviously had already gotten himself all worked up, was in the middle of one of his usual tirades.

"Wenzel," he was saying just as I arrived, "Wenzel, you're claiming that the wood had been sawn into . . . Do you realize that you're voicing a grave accusation? The mayor himself will be here shortly and you will have to substantiate your charge . . . Did I not always warn you that everything you do, you do on your own responsibility? Did I not order you to wait until the time was ripe and until the mountain itself would call us? And it would have called us, in greatness and purity its call would have come, for his first bidding had already been heard! But you were impatient and you laughed at me and now you seek to shift the responsibility to others and you raise groundless suspicions . . ."

"Leave him alone now!" I shouted at the madman.

He stopped short and stared with angrily knitted brows at the maimed dwarf, who, contrary to my assumption, seemed to have heard him, for he had now opened his eyes, eyes in which there was nothing of their former roguish merriment or of their perennial readiness for hatred, but eyes which now were large and grave as they rested heavily on Marius.

Lax was quick to use the pause to interject, "The wood I supplied was clean and impeccable . . . If the catastrophe really was due to the wood, then some scoundrel indeed must have sawn into it."

But Marius would not allow his flow of words to be interrupted, either by me or by Lax, and he now adopted the singsong voice I knew so well. "Only the one who hears the voice and hearkens to it is permitted to act, only I am permitted to do so, I alone, for to me have been granted the voices of the mountain and I alone comprehend them. But the mountain has remained mute and has not yet bid my coming . . ."

At that, Krimuss could no longer contain himself. "Is the mountain to remain mute? Will it remain sealed? Will it refuse to yield the gold?"

But the madman replied in the manner of all charlatans by turning once more to Wenzel. "You committed the crime, you disobeyed me and have offended the mountain, and if it should now remain mute and seal itself off, you alone bear the guilt."

And at that, it was as if hatred, perhaps even a roguish hatred, had returned once more to Wenzel's eyes, strong enough for him to utter audibly what all that time had been simmering in him under the surface, a single word only and that was: "Bastard!"

But then, overwhelmed by the effort and once more succumbing to pain, he groaned and closed his eyes.

Marius crouched like an animal about to pounce on its prey—though, knowing him, I was convinced that he would never do so—but Lax guffawed loudly and, grabbing his arm, he shouted in glee, "Say it again, Wenzel!"

Marius tore himself free of Lax and turned away. "He's paralyzed for good, in any case; the mountain has punished him." He said it and spat.

I had had enough; bluish dusk was settling over the clearing, it was high time to transport the injured man, and in a blazing rage I shouted, "Don't you have enough with one dead man lying down there?!"

Lax became serious. "Leonhard . . ."

"Yes," I said, still raging, "Leonhard, crushed, buried and dead."

Krimuss's yellow face awoke from the consternation into which it had sunk, it cleared up and he shouted, "The gold! Now, now the mountain has been appeased . . ."

And Marius, despite all his craziness still quite conscious of his own advantage and undoubtedly intent on securing Krimuss's support, not only took up the latter's superstitious nonsense but transformed it forthwith into true madness and fanatical zeal as he adopted once more his role as prophet and declaimed with those inward-directed eyes: "Dead man in the mountain, crushed by the mountain drinking his blood, so that once more the dwarf may grow into the giant, the non-man turn into man, and the voice arise out of muteness . . . Now that the mountain has accepted the expiatory sacrifice, it will forgive the crime and loudly raise its voice to call me forth . . ."

"Let it, for all I care," I said, "but I have serious business to attend to here . . . Lax, be so good as to finally remove these two . . ."

"I'm leaving, Doctor," Marius said politely, and departed, followed by Krimuss.

"What a crackpot, that crazy scoundrel!" exclaimed Lax, "but mark my words, Doctor, he'll somehow still manage to get the gold."

"Lax," I said, "I don't give a damn about the gold, least of all now . . . I've got to get this man down to my house."

Much as I hated to do it and dangerous as it was under the circumstances, I gave Wenzel a heavy dose of morphine, ready to counteract its effects with a caffeine injection if he should show any signs of heart failure. I then cut out a broad strip from the canvas covering of the stretcher, so as to shield the patient's back as much as possible from any pressure, and after having made sure of the onset of his by then deep unconsciousness, we lifted him carefully onto the stretcher frame and I strapped him down. I selected some reliable strong men who would take turns carrying the patient, and we took some torches along and set out on our way down.

The clearing we crossed had become quite still. For Leonhard's dead body, which meanwhile had been brought up from below, was now laid out in the middle of the Christmasy grounds on two white pine boards, their edges blackened by the hands that had handled them; he was covered by a piece of canvas, his mother knelt next to him, and all around stood the silent crowd, black in the gentle peace of the vesperal snow.

But Marius had let himself down on one knee next to Leonhard's mother with the artful grace of a dancer, one elbow leaning on the knee of his supporting leg, and when we came by and stopped for a moment out of respect for the dead man, I heard that crackpot say to the mother, "Do not grieve, Mother, for your son fell for a great cause and not only we who are here mourning with you but also our children and children's children will revere his hero's death in everlasting remembrance."

And the mother did not curse and send the shameless humbug away—nor did anyone else in the crowd—but instead, in her greed for consolation, she said, "Oh yes, Mr. Ratti."

And he continued undaunted: "And once mining is again in full swing, you, now grieving for your courageous son, shall not be forgotten . . . Everyone here knows what is your due . . ." And he turned to those standing around. "Is it not so? Do we not stand all for one, one for all?"

No one dared contradict him, perhaps because the silence of death and grief is stronger than any human reason but perhaps also because all of them actually believed that they shared the feeling invoked by Marius.

And Marius, having made death his ally, went on, for his speeches always were endless: "In each piece of gold his name will shine . . ."

But then a voice called out, and I recognized it as that of Sack. "For God's sake, don't fall for all this damn idiotic bullshit!"

An indignant murmur arose and there were even viciously angry shouts of "Shut up, Sack!"

And Krimuss shouted hoarsely, "The gold, now we'll be getting it for sure . . ."

"You'll get shit, that's what you'll get," Sack replied, and was heard departing through the woods.

I would have liked to press the hand of the poor Nistler woman, but as things stood I said to my carriers, "Let's go." I had more urgent things to do, after all, than to get involved in all that craziness, and we could not linger any longer if we were to take advantage of the remaining daylight to negotiate the steep incline below the chapel, a stretch that worried me greatly. The first section through the woods after the meadow was bad enough.

But everything went well beyond all expectations, even the steep part. The dwarf was easy to carry. We formed a double chain and passed the stretcher from hand to hand so as to keep it always horizontal. Some more people joined us, they helped us along, and that's how we managed even the precipitous slope on which the snow had now become quite firm in the evening shadows. Below us the autumnal valley lay in mildness, and a break in the clouds must have formed behind the Kuppron, for the whiteness on the opposite peaks had become a pink haze, a rose-colored silver sheen which was like the ultimate, the very last breath of an echo, the fading echo of an immense red-flaming shame.

We passed through the slowly darkening woods without further incident, returning to the mild shadows of the autumnal regions, and for the last stretch leading to my house we had to light the torches. The ambulance arrived punctually not long after eight to collect Wenzel, but the once roguish dwarf merely blinked an eye and let himself be handled in complete apathy.

14   In those first November days the year roused itself once more and gathered its whole strength in trembling splendor and golden resonance: a late autumn, a second summer of rarest ripeness once more melted the October snow from the heights, a fathomless clear sky once more had soaked up all the cold in the world and had hidden it behind its transparent blueness, a blue that was not that of forget-me-nots or that of gentians but like the shadow within a fully opened white rose, and it gazed down in great rigid mildness through the tracing of the boughs of the trees, a tracing that had become both sharper and more delicate; once more infinity flowed through nature in its fairest embodiment, readily at hand for the perception of man before sealing itself off and withdrawing to the wintry remoteness of the stars. This season is called the Old Wives' Summer, perhaps because more than any other season it intimates the wholeness of the world, its hardness as well as its mildness, its beginning and its end joined in the fullness of the center, feminine the infinite when it rounds itself into plenitude and calm, at last released from its urgency to fulfill itself; thus the earth and the world granted themselves to man once more in their ultimate wholeness.

It was in those first November days that Wetchy moved away to the city to establish a new life. He had given notice that he was vacating his house, and it was good that he did so, for the municipal council, of which Marius was now a member, would not have let him retain it in any case. Immediately after the disaster in the mine, Miland had resigned all his official functions and without much fuss or effort Lax had succeeded in replacing him with Marius. I had absented myself from the meeting of the council at which Marius was officially introduced, and I would have liked nothing better than to withdraw as well, but I was prevented from so doing because of my function as municipal physician.

It was the fourth day of November when Rosa woke me up. As usual, she must have knocked timidly at first, and when I did not hear her, she beat on the door with her little fists as mightily as she could until I finally responded.

"Yes," I called, "come in." It was still dark; I switched on the light. Six o'clock.

She stood in front of the bed. "I'm going to the city," she said gravely. Trapp, who had come in with her, placed his head on the edge of the bed.

"And because of that you're waking me up at this ungodly hour, you little wretch? . . . Why, you're even all dressed and ready to go!"

"Caroline's making coffee."

While I dressed it grew light outside; the mist stood in front of the windows like vapory wax, saturated with brightness like a sponge, and already one could feel the cloudless sky above.

When I came down, the two of them were having coffee.

"So, are you happy to leave, Rosa?" I asked.

Caroline audibly blew her nose, got up, and busied herself at the stove.

Rosa wiped her mouth with the back of her hand. "In the city I'll go to school . . . just like Albert Sack."

"You could have done that here, too," said Caroline from the stove.

"No," said the child.

"Really? And why not?" I asked her. "Is it because you only want to learn with the city children?"

"Papa said that I should go to the city school."

Caroline turned around impetuously. "Your papa should leave you here with us."

"Caroline, don't put such ideas into the child's head; you know quite well that a child belongs with its parents."

Offended, Caroline fell silent. But after a while she said, "And just now when things are getting real good around here."

"What's that?"

"Yes, now everything is going to get better, and the school, too . . . Now the girls won't have to become servants anymore."

"That's all news to me, Caroline."

"Because you don't like Mr. Ratti, Doctor, sir . . . but now he, too, sits in the council . . ."

Fortunately Sack entered at that moment, together with his three boys.

"We've come to say goodbye to Rosa."

He beamed with goodwill. The smallest of the boys, little Franz, held a wooden doll in his hand, artfully whittled and freshly painted.

Rosa slid down from the chair.

"Give it to Rosa . . . Franz brought this specially for you."

"Did you make that, Sack?"

"Of course."

The two larger boys had their school satchels with them. It was high time for them to be on their way to school. Rosa and little Franz went with them as far as the garden.

"Yes," said Sack, "and now I'll help Wetchy load up his belongings."

"Very kind of you, Sack."

But he brushed it aside. "Not at all, I do it to spite Marius."

Caroline joined us. "Yes, you're one of those others."

"Of course I'm one of the others . . . Don't you want me to help him?" He stood there, the carpenter's ax over his shoulder, the pipe in the corner of his mouth, and merrily twinkled at her from between his ruddy round cheeks.

She giggled. "No, and I say good riddance, too."

"But, Caroline," I said, "you wanted to keep the child here."

"Yes, that one I want to keep. She's too good for her parents."

"Don't talk such nonsense, Caroline," I said.

Sack laughed good-humoredly, and I had to think of the shoring uprights that had been sawn into. Was it possible that this kind and good-hearted man could have done such a thing?

"You're an old nag," he said, laughing.

"Old nag! I'll give you one . . . Old nag, indeed! . . . For you I'm still young enough by a long shot!"

"Aha, so that's what you're after."

"Don't you dare laugh, Sack . . . I'm going to get the back payments for child support . . . I'll get it for all the years . . . and then I'll be rich."

"Why, for sure . . . And then you want to marry me?"

"You?" snarled Caroline angrily. "You'll go to prison. Just you wait, Marius is going to have you arrested."

I looked at Sack. For a moment he looked worried, but then he gave Caroline a fillip on the nose and turned to the door. "I'm going," he said. "You can come and help, too, Caroline." And he was gone.

"And who's going to pay you child support, Caroline?"

"The municipality," she said dryly, and began to clear the breakfast dishes.

Around nine o'clock I heard the horn of a motorcar and then its heavy muffled approach over the soft road through the woods. It was the truck that Wetchy had ordered for the transport of his belongings to the city.

A little later I, too, walked over to his house.

The truck rested meekly on its four wheels and one of its side panels was folded down; it was already half loaded and the sun glittered in the mirrored wardrobe from Wetchy's bedroom, which, protected against bumps by two gray-and-red-striped mattresses, had been pushed close to the driver's cabin. The driver stood straddle-legged on the bed of the truck while his helper and Sack, with carrying straps slanting over their opposite shoulders, lifted up Wetchy's belongings—crates, the dismembered parts of the beds, Rosa's little desk—into his waiting hands. The driver seemed to be making quite an art out of their stowing away and their protection. The rest of the furnishings still stood on the lawn under the pines, Rosa and little Franz were climbing all over them, and Wetchy, shuttling back and forth, brought the last pieces from the house.

I had brought a basket of food for Mrs. Wetchy to take along. "Where is the wife, Wetchy?"

"In the kitchen . . . no, upstairs."

The empty house was like a discarded garment which still shows the bodily shape of its erstwhile wearer and has not as yet reverted to the condition of a mere object. The breath of the lodgers who had resided here still clung to the walls, and it was as if the greenish-brown paint, peeling off those walls in many places and forming small dusty heaps along the baseboards, had given up for good and was ready to die, now that it was no longer exposed to any animate life. For of the many layers with which human beings are wont to surround themselves and which they seek to fill out, shell upon shell, so as to fill their world's entity with their possessions and the happenstance of their own presence, clothing and lodging are the most basic and the closest to them, and since these partake most immediately of their essential reality, they represent for most of them both the totality of their world and the total world reality. Wetchy had resided here close to ten years, it is here that his fate had cast him, a favorable or an ill wind, just as now he was cast out by that same fate, he himself hardly conscious of these circumstances and of his reality even though he perceived it as tangibly real; for close to ten years these walls had represented shelter and reality, he had filled them with his life and with those furnishings that now found space on the bed of a single truck, hardly objects any longer in their amorphous compaction, those furnishings that again were to become his reality once they were spread out one more time among new walls, shell of his being, shell of his sleep, erected around this sleep and mirroring it, world totality surrounding his resting, place of his rest where he sleeps with his wife, at times hand in hand, united with that other animate creature, body with body and yet also soul with soul, begetting other bodies, begetting souls, as a family evolving into a single body and a single soul, oneness of life which also filled this dwelling the way running water fills a still pond. On the wall of the bedroom the headboards of the two matrimonial beds had rubbed a sharp cross-line into the paint and still hanging over it was a homely blessing: "Where love abides, God's blessing dwells." Slantingly nestled into each other, the two chamber pots stood in a corner and patiently awaited their removal.

Mrs. Wetchy was in the adjoining room, her eyes red with crying, busy taking down the curtains. Little Maxi crawled around on the floor and dragged part of a curtain behind him.

"Courage, little woman," I said. "As long as one keeps a stiff upper lip, anything can be borne."

"Oh, courage we have, Doctor . . . Where would we be if my poor husband weren't blessed with such courage? . . . And the main thing is to love one another, then indeed all can be borne."

"Yes, then all can be borne," I confirmed, although I well knew that even such a blessing is far from being capable of surmounting all vicissitudes. But since I heard Wetchy approaching—his tread sounded eerily hollow in the empty house—I quickly got rid of my basket and escaped any effusions of gratitude by taking flight.

Wetchy was just entering from the stairs.

"All ready downstairs?"

"Yes, I'm just collecting the last things."

Then I heard Wetchy's imperious squeak from inside. "And why is the house blessing still hanging here on the wall?"

Under the pines outside I sat down with the children on the sofa, which was to be loaded last because of its upholstery.

"Thoroughly cleaned out the house," said Sack, who was in the process of shouldering a dresser. "I even took down the light switches."

"Really," I said, only half listening, for my attention had been distracted by a new arrival. Two figures had appeared over by my own fence and soon enough I recognized them as Marius and the village policeman.

"Sack, look who's coming . . ."

Sack put down the dresser and looked. Then he leaned his elbows on the top of the dresser in the manner of a salesman behind his counter. "We could have done without him . . ."

Wetchy appeared, a washbasin in one hand, in the other the two chamber pots, the house blessing clamped under one arm and the curtains draped over his head and shoulders.

"You're going to be real pleased now," Sack told him.

The myopic Wetchy asked what there was to be seen.

"Well, Marius in person is coming to say goodbye to you," said Sack behind his countertop, and he pointed with his beard toward the garden.

"I'm going," Wetchy said, but remained stock-still as if paralyzed.

"Then go," said Sack unfeelingly.

"Girlie, come with me," gasped Wetchy in his fright, as if wanting also to protect the child.

"But, Wetchy," I said, "no one is going to harm you, you've nothing to fear."

He tried to wipe the sweat from his upper lip and brow with the back of his china-laden hands and said timidly, "Yes, Doctor."

Proud, nonchalant, and unshaven, Marius entered the garden. He shook hands with me and Sack but was relieved from so doing with Wetchy, who still had his hands full. He nodded toward the latter a distinctly formal "And a good morning to you," which Wetchy acknowledged with a bow of his curtain-loaded head. But Sack said, "There's still someone else," and he shoved Rosa before Marius, so that he could not help but also take the hand that the child had stretched out toward him.

"And now make a nice curtsy," ordered Sack with obvious amusement, for which he was rewarded by Marius with a contemptuous stare.

But Sack was in an aggressive mood and would not let matters rest there. "Don't you want to give the uncle a nice kiss?" he asks hypocritically, and lifts up the snot-nosed girl and thrusts her right into Marius's face. The child butts her face against the chest of the unwelcome uncle, Sack laughs, Wetchy murmurs "No, please, no," the china in his hands raised in helpless imploration, and it is actually the first time that I observe Marius in real confusion and not master of the situation as he looks in embarrassment from one to the other and even attempts a winning smile, which, however, soon fades when the struggling girl pokes her fingers in his eyes. At that he retreats a step, regaining his dignity, and says severely, "Don't you see that the child doesn't want to?"

"Yes, indeed," says Sack, well pleased, and lets the girl down. "I wouldn't want to either."

In spite of his polite bearing, Marius has to make a sour face. Such jokes are not to his liking.

I ask, "And what brings you here, Mr. Ratti?"

Once more he has regained his usual somewhat overbearing manner. "I'm here to take over the house for the municipality."

"Savoring his triumph," Sack corrects the statement.

Marius gestures as if to imply that the remark does not deserve to be answered, but then he says, "The municipality has agreed to the premature cancellation of the contract . . . That's hardly a triumph."

"Don't be such a coward," says Sack, who is again busy with the dresser. "Admit that it was you who got rid of Wetchy and that you rejoice in it, you coward."

The charge of cowardice hits the mark; the reply is a bit too convoluted. "The municipality has found that it is for the best."

That's a little too much even for me. "What the hell, Marius, don't try to fool both us and yourself with all that rubbish . . . What you convinced yourself of and tried to convince others of is beyond belief, but that doesn't mean that everybody agreed with it."

"The devil take it all," Sack says, and marches off toward the truck with the dresser on his back.

Marius gets a hold on himself, for he doesn't want to lose my goodwill altogether. With a small elegant gesture he points contemptuously to the lawn. "Is this supposed to be a garden, Doctor?"

"Whatever . . . What of it?"

"Not one bed of flowers, no vegetables . . . nothing."

"Mr. Ratti," can be heard from Wetchy, still rooted to the same spot.

But Marius, once started, cannot be stopped so easily. "He who lacks love for the earth is no man, he rapes the earth with each step he treads on it, such a man must be banished, for he rapes whatever he touches . . ."

I try to slow down his rhetoric. "Ho, ho, not so fast . . . there you go exaggerating again."

It helps slightly, for he moderates himself. "Doctor, that's how it is, all evil comes from those men who have become alienated from the earth, it comes from the city . . . I've wandered far and wide, Doctor, I've seen a lot, and I found time and time again that

the peasant is right in his instinctive dislike for the city dweller
. . . The peasants throughout the world love each other, if there
were nothing but peasants, there would be no wars . . . Man grows
from the earth, his fellowship grows from the earth, there would
be a worldwide human fellowship if there were nothing but peasants
. . . But the cities are outside all fellowship because they are paved
over, because they have lost the earth . . . that's where the hatred
grows . . . and the peasant feels that and that's why he dislikes the
city dweller, and anyone who tries to push his way into the fellowship of the peasants he expels, he takes up arms against the
interloper, but his hatred is directed against one and all who are of
the city . . . Peasants do not engage in wars against peasants, they
don't hate each other, they are the victims of the hatred born in
the cities."

That sounded quite reasonable, for a change, though it was not
exactly courteous toward me, a former city dweller. In any case,
it struck me as strange that someone coming from the lower middle
class—for that is where Marius quite obviously had his origin—
should feel himself so vehemently a peasant and should make himself the spokesman for the peasant class.

I made the mistake of nodding in assent, for this was enough to
get him going with renewed zest.

"It crawls from the cities, baleful and full of hatred, it brings
with it the machines and the radios and the mortgages, and in
exchange it wants to be fed with our bread . . . They insinuate
themselves and tempt us with their wheeling and dealing like women,
yes, like women, for they only pose as men, and though they still
may manage to grow beards, those beards cannot hide the womanly
greed staring from their flaccid faces . . ."

I'm reminded of what Mother Gisson has said about his mas-
culinity, but he now closes his eyes, opens his mouth a bit, and
with thumb and forefinger pushes back his Italianate mustache, as
if first breathing some secret into his hand before he portentously
continues: "They beget children, but they are no longer men, and
their children and children's children are even less so . . . The older
the cities are, the more they become womanized . . . Those men

sport the beards of women, they have the hands of women, and their fellowship is one of trafficking, nor can it be otherwise, since they get their livelihood not from the earth but out of each other's pockets . . . They are swollen with poison in the manner of women who act like men, their hatred is that of women, soft, insinuating, and bustling, and like women they do not even know that they hate and are compelled to hate but believe an injustice is inflicted on them if finally they are expelled from where they never did belong in the first place . . ."

His voice became increasingly shrill and hysterical.

"Addicted to hatred and greedy for power they are, they and all their brood, a womanly hatred and a womanly power lust, with no love for and no interest in the earth except to own it, to possess it and plant their mortgages on it. And thanks to womanly cleverness and cunning they almost did succeed in attaining dominion over the entire world . . . world dominion, dominion by the women, a dominion of hatred . . . The cities are the evil in the world."

"Why is he shouting so much?" asks Sack as he returns.

Wetchy, ruler of the world, stood there, the chamber pots in his hand, and it was obvious that he would have liked to interject something, silently he moves his lips, his spare blond eyebrows are knotted with effort, the skin over his bald pate twitches, but all this is to no avail against such an avalanche.

Marius now points to him over his shoulder. "Has any one of them reverted to the earth? Has any one of them ever learned once more how to draw a plow? No, not one of them has ever found the way back from the city, for that way can lead only to the city but never back to the earth . . . He who has been lost among the womenfolk can never disentangle himself, he can only draw others into their ranks . . . But now the end has come for the dominion of the women, the dominion of the cities is over, back to their burrows the whole brood will scuttle, to where they belong, a new era has dawned, the fellowship of men is reasserting itself, it shall rule the land because it is the fellowship of the earth, and the cities shall wither away in envious greed, reconciled once more the earth from which we drove the contemptible brood, reconciled the heavens which once more shall bow down to the regained purity of the earth when the alien and the godless have vanished from its soil . . ."

But at that point he is interrupted by a clattering clash. Wetchy had simply let the china fall from his hands and, stepping over the shards, he plants himself in front of Marius, who, in utter surprise, has fallen silent.

"Mr. Ratti," says the little agent, the curtains over his shoulders, gasping for breath, "Mr. Ratti, that's enough now . . . You've insulted me, you've insulted my family, and I've taken it all without objecting, and for all I care you may call me avaricious, too, although I have never encountered as much avarice as in these villages . . ."

Haughtily Marius tries to silence him. "Any man clings to his possessions but your kind clings only to money . . ."

"Fine," says Wetchy, "although I fail to see the difference, but I'm from the city, and there, too, you may be right for all I care . . . I accept all of it except one thing, I won't let you call me godless . . ."

"God comes from here," says Marius as he bends down and scoops up a handful of earth and shows it to Wetchy.

"There are also some shards in there," says Sack. "Better watch out, Marius, you might cut yourself."

Wetchy blinks myopically at the little brown heap in Marius's hand. And then, strangely calm, he says, "I wouldn't know, Mr. Ratti, I'm only a very poor man, I've got to worry a lot about where I shall get the bread for the next day, so that my family may eat. Bread doesn't grow for me, I have to look for it. And that's how it is for most of us in the cities. But in so doing I've learned something, and some others in the city surely must have learned it, too, for why should only I have learned it, seeing that I'm only a poor simple man like all the others—I've learned that one mustn't consider merely what one can touch and take into one's hand but that greater weight is to be given to what occurs, to what cannot be taken into one's hand such as this earth, and that nevertheless is there and is visible . . . and this may be so because most of the things in the city are man-made, and that's why one rather serves the invisible that is not contained in things, that which is invisible and yet visible . . . Yes, and that is what one serves . . ."

"Serve, yes indeed," interrupted Marius, "the city folks are to serve, they are to serve like womenfolk instead of aspiring to rule . . ."

"You'd better listen for a change, Marius," said Sack. "Today you might learn something from Wetchy."

"No," said the little agent, "Mr. Ratti can't learn anything from me, he belongs to another world . . . and when I speak of serving I mean that I have to take care of my wife and my children, in honor and decency, so that life may go on. That, too, Mr. Ratti can't understand, for he has neither wife nor child, and he may well feel that this has nothing to do with serving and with the invisible . . . yes, that's what he may well believe . . . but I know that the opposite is true, exactly the opposite . . ."

He paused, his head sank to his chest, and he seemed to ponder what he had said.

"Go on, Wetchy," I encouraged him, so that Marius would not overwhelm him again.

"Well, yes . . . I'm not a very educated man . . . I'm not good at expressing myself, but you see, Doctor, when one can feed a child and make it happy, then . . . yes, then one feels the invisible granted us by God just as much as He has granted us this earth and even more so, it is invisible and yet so great, greater than the child one has fed and greater than this short life and even greater than death, it is the consolation, yes, the great consolation in life . . . and for that one need not be very pious and yet one clasps one's hands to thank our Lord that He has ordered it so, and one knows that He is there . . . invisible yet there . . ."

"Bravo, Wetchy," Sack says, and takes hold of the sofa. "You're a good man."

Marius, with a supercilious expression on his face, has listened with only half an ear.

"That's the womenfolk's religion," he now says, "and it only reaches far enough to fill the bellies of their brood, city religion it is, and for that they steal the peasant's bread."

That went a little too far for my taste and I put my foot down. "Now listen here, Marius, your impertinence is getting a little steep, for, after all, I, too, come from the city . . . Are there to be no other professions outside of farming in your fanciful world? I'd like to see the reaction of the peasants if they didn't have a doctor here and a hospital in the city. If that were the case, your Wenzel would have been a goner then and there, I'll have you know."

He shrugged but was quick to make amends by saying, "I certainly wouldn't presume to disparage the medical profession, Doctor."

"But that nursing is a womanly vocation would fit in quite nicely with your crackbrained theories."

He thinks it over, then comes to a decision and declares candidly, "Well, Doctor, yes . . . for that, too, is part of the city's ways of thinking and part of a religion of cowardice . . . Man must be ready to die and shouldn't expect to be nursed back to health, that's the law of nature and the command of the earth, and if you had let Wenzel lie where he fell it would have been better for him . . . What has broken shall perish and what the earth wishes to heal heals by itself . . ." Once more he had talked himself into a dither. "Everything else is womanly cowardice, city cowardice, the funk of little agents . . ."

Although fully aware that I was dealing with a madman, I started to get truly angry. "I'd like to see you really sick sometime and would be curious whether you would then still spout such utter nonsense . . ."

"What matters is the courage, Doctor, the courage to die . . ."

But that is as far as he gets. Wetchy had followed our argument by evincing all the symptoms of growing impatience, he had raised a finger and it was not clear whether the finger was meant to point to Marius or was that of a pupil in school requesting leave to speak, though it was probably both, the finger trembles and all of Wetchy shakes with nervous boldness as he now cuts Marius short: "No, no, no," and although it is said in a low and restrained voice it sounds like a shout, "no, no, Doctor, let him be . . . That, too, Mr. Ratti can't understand . . . He speaks of courage but in truth he's full of fear, yes, fear, he's afraid, he fears the invisible because the invisible would forbid him to do wrong, and he seeks death rather than the Lord . . ."

Marius looks at him as if thunderstruck, he is about to interrupt but is not allowed to.

"Yes, Mr. Ratti, you talk of death . . . I'll tell you something . . . For our Lord we indeed may have to die, one may well have to do that and if it comes to that one must be ready to do so, but otherwise we can serve Him only in life, for that is why He has granted us this life . . . You deride us as being cowardly, Mr. Ratti, because we are attached to this small life, this small hard life of which we know so little and which is so much harder than that of the peasants . . . but precisely because this life is so puny and shoddy, the life of nothing more than a shabby little agent, we people from the city know that we are not allowed to waste this life, that we have to tend it carefully . . . we are not ready to die for the earth . . ."

"That's what I've been saying all along," exclaims Marius.

A smile appeared on Wetchy's face and it was almost his obsequious agent's smile. "For us little people life has a high price, a very high price, Mr. Ratti . . . yes, and . . . and that price is invisible . . ." He faltered and then said, "Doctor, I can't express it well . . . for that price is within life and yet transcends it into death, that's how high that price is . . . I don't know how to put it into words . . ."

"Because you really have nothing to say. He who has something to say can also express it," lectures Marius.

"A whole life is contained in that price and also all of death, that's what I mean. And that is also where our Lord resides."

I understand him, "You mean the infinite, Wetchy."

"Yes . . ." He didn't grasp it right away, "The infinite . . . to feed the children, beyond one's death . . . yes, I guess that is the infinite . . ."

But then he said, "The eternal in the soul."

Marius straightened up majestically and pointed to the heights of the Kuppron with a grandiose gesture. "There . . . there is the infinite, there where the sea reaches up to the sky, where the ore radiates from the heart of the mountain, where the elements are joined, and where no living creature and no plant subsists, that is where the infinite resides . . ."

"What's going on up there?" asks Sack. "Why are all of you looking up at the summer pastures?" But he, too, raised his eyes over the pine tops to the stillness of that azurine eternity which bathed the immobility of the sunlit meadows and the crags of those faraway heights.

"Yes," shouts Marius, "that's where the mountain has its throne, risen from the earth after having accepted the blood of the victim, and it spreads its arms in a rainbow reaching from the skies to the sea, the sea floats up to its peaks and once again glides down to earth, that is how the mountain breathes the blood it has drunk, placated now and utterly pure and cool . . . that is the infinite"— and he spreads his arms as if he himself were the rainbow—"yes, that is where it is . . ."

"There, too, yes, maybe . . ." the little agent says, and nods. "But without a soul there's nothing up there either."

Marius turns around abruptly and drops his arms. "You can't ever see anything at all up there; the city dwellers skulk in their spunkless burrows, they are blind to the sun that strives toward the earth, blind to the earth rising toward the sun . . . they cannot give utterance to the infinite and they can seek it merely in the brood they breed."

But Wetchy said, "No, Mr. Ratti, we seek it in the invisible soul . . . and . . . yes, that is what you fear."

Marius glances at me as if expecting my corroboration and some help in the face of so much dullness and stupidity. But I place my hand approvingly on the shoulder of the little agent, and Marius turns away to look solemnly once more at the far-off mountain.

An impatient tooting is heard from the truck driver and I say, "I guess everything is loaded up."

Wetchy is exhausted; he again assumes his helpless downtrodden expression and his eyes hunt roundabout. "Yes," he finally says, "everything's loaded, but in the house . . ."

Sack breaks into Marius's solemn silence. "If you now seal up the house, is that also going to placate the mountain?"

"That can be done just as well by the municipal clerk," Marius replies haughtily, and he goes to join the policeman, who is leaning on the garden gate, conversing with the driver. And then he leaves without another word and stalks away with his lofty, yet shuffling gait.

"Well, in spite of everything, all that high-flown talk about the mountain was quite beautiful," comments Sack, "but it's hard to take for any length of time . . . Hurry up, Wetchy, see what's left inside." And with that he drives Wetchy into the house.

Mrs. Wetchy appears with a large basket full of household knick-knacks, and after everything is stowed away amid much running to and fro and in an ever-growing hubbub, and after the ropes are thrown over the whole load and fastened to the rings on the sides of the truck panels, there draws near that always slightly embarrassing moment, the moment of leave-taking, a moment already pointing faintly to eternity and in which all participants apprehend a part of their own dying, so that I quickly lift up Mrs. Wetchy and the two children to the seat next to the driver, while Wetchy, his eyes moist and stammering much unintelligible gibberish, is being pulled up by the driver's helper to the sofa topping the load, with Sack hoisting him from below and cutting off any possible retreat, and before Wetchy, much flustered, is even able to find his bearings on his lofty perch, the truck has started up joltingly, so that Wetchy, wanting to lift his hand to wave goodbye, has to hang on to the ropes instead. And then they are gone. Sack and I look at each other and our eyes, too, are a bit moist.

The fine weather held.

Two days after Wetchy's departure—I had intended to be down in the Lower Village for my clinic punctually at noon and was about to sit down to a quick snack with Caroline at a table on which we both missed Rosa's plate—Agatha came rushing in breathlessly.

"Doctor, come . . . come quick!"

I'm used to being called in a hurry and was not overly alarmed. "All right, Agatha, but first catch your breath . . . In your condition you shouldn't run so hard . . . What's happened?"

She shook her head. "No, no, Doctor, come right away . . ."

And she drew me outside by the sleeve of my jacket.

"It's all right, Agatha, but I've got to get my instruments first . . . Who's taken sick?"

"Mother Gisson . . ."

That frightened me. "Oh God . . . did she send you?"

"No . . . Come, let's go, Doctor."

"Has she fainted? Is she conscious?"

I thought of heart failure, a stroke, and tearing myself away from Agatha, I ran upstairs to get my satchel with the essentials. "I'm at Mother Gisson's," I shouted into the kitchen when I was down again. "Let's go, Agatha."

But when we reached the garden gate and as I was about to turn left toward the village, she stopped me. "No, she isn't home . . ."

"Where is she?"

To my amazement she ponders this for a moment before she says, "At the Cold Stone."

"Yes? . . . Did you leave her lying there?"

"No . . ."

The whole thing became utterly puzzling. "Did someone tell you that she was lying at the Cold Stone?"

There is anguished panic in her eyes. "No . . ."

Pregnant women sometimes show evidence of a slight mental derangement. "Tell me, Agatha, where did you come from now?"

She points to the village. "She isn't home . . . A candle in a tin holder is burning in her window . . ."

"And?"

"And the house is locked."

"Agatha, I think you should rest a bit now . . . while I go look in at Mother Gisson's just in case . . . and then I'll take you home— I've got to get down to my clinic anyway . . ."

She had grabbed my sleeve again, but now she let go of it and said with strangely mature firmness, "If you're not coming, I'll go alone."

"But, child, you don't even know that she is at the Cold Stone if no one has told you . . . and why should she sit home in this fine weather; she'll be home in her own good time."

"No, no, Doctor . . . I just know . . . I felt it and rushed up to her house . . . and the candle is burning in the window . . ."

I had taken her hand. "Agatha, when one is carrying a child one sometimes has such forebodings . . . It's like a bad dream . . ."

Her schoolgirl's face becomes somewhat pensive, but then she says with surprising conviction, "No, this can be no dream . . ."

"Well, shouldn't I first make sure by looking in at Mother Gisson's nevertheless . . . ?"

At that she becomes strangely sensible and grown-up. "If I only dreamt it, then she is sitting at home hale and healthy and the walk would be for naught . . . but if I didn't dream it . . . you'd better come, Doctor . . ."

She is very much in earnest; and I, too, am suddenly gripped by fear but don't want her to notice. "All right," I say, "at worst we'll have had a nice walk together, you and I, Agatha."

Whereupon she nervously grabs my hand again. "Doctor, now . . . now . . . I feel it again now . . ."

And she won't let go of my hand, either out of fear or because she thinks she has to lead me. Hand in hand we rush on, almost jogging, past Wetchy's house, now closed and mute; we run through the pine woods, hand in hand like two children, the gray-bearded doctor and the pregnant girl, the forest is summery and yet hibernally bare of all fragrance, the sky looking down through the trees is paler, harder the gridwork of branches under which we run, a midnight sky at noon, and the woods, mute and closed upon themselves, no longer grow toward the sky, nothing grows any longer, and not a single root is heard snapping. We run through all that stillness and arrive at the clearing above the two valleys, which now are like two lakes in which, for one last time, summer is reflected. That's where we stop, for her hand gives a sharp little jolt like the twitching of a divining rod.

Then she draws me on.

"But that's not the way to the Cold Stone, Agatha."

"No, now she's up there."

It is one of those narrow paths that grazing cattle have trodden and that were then cleared and used by lumberjacks, and Agatha, half turned toward me, draws me behind her like a small boy. The path leads along the steep wooded slope, the trees are sparser with much underbrush among them to obstruct the way, from time to time it passes along a barren escarpment, protruding like a small promontory into the airy space above the valleys, and from one of those one has a view of the meadow below the Cold Stone with its pale larches and yellowed birches, their softly clear angelic tune singing above the heavier chords rung by the backdrop of dark firs and the downflow of the mountain's waves. Like a single cymbal stroke, a solitary point in the ether, a falcon hangs motionless over it all and then vanishes.

"Are we going to the Pit of the Heathen?"

She drags me on. "Yes . . . perhaps . . ."

We come out of the woods at the Lower Heathen. It is a small swampy clearing under the opening of a broad cut in the rocks; the cattle have trampled the soil and broken it into deep clumps and hollows, tufts of grass, dull and autumnally tired, grow on the mounds and water shimmers on the bottom of the deep imprints of the cattle tracks; a few logs have been placed across the broken ground to make it passable and from time to time a drop is heard falling in the moist stillness. The little brook which feeds all this wetness comes from the cut in the rocks, it runs over the path leading from the Cold Stone to the Upper Heathen, and in front of us, on the other side of the brook, the adit of the Lower Heathen lies hidden and buried behind dense bushes.

We have crossed the swamp and, having reached the path, Agatha turns upstream with the brook.

"So it's the Upper Heathen after all?"

She doesn't answer me but, breathless, merely accelerates her pace; her hand in mine is moist, I feel her hammering pulse but I also sense her fear, coming from her hand it penetrates me as if we were joined in a single current of fear, running from one to the other and back again, as if prohibiting us from letting go of each other's hands. And as if it had been her thought and not mine, I am struck as by lightning with the realization that the hunter Gisson had been found shot dead at the Upper Heathen.

We have reached the cut in the rocks. To our left, the little brook runs counter to our path, its water unearthly pure as if coming straight out of infinity; the stony slopes on both sides carry some firs and a little higher, among the rubble screes which frequently reach down all the way to the path, dwarf pines already can be seen growing in the rock walls which draw increasingly closer together, so close that finally the narrow gorge, grown rigid and wintry, is filled with mossy shadows, cool and blackish the firs, and the golden brightness above floats as a liquid glow on the darkness below.

To the Pit of the Upper Heathen.

And then the gorge opens onto an immense curved basin, a bowl thunderous with sunny stillness, filled to its rim, nay, overflowing with golden splendor, encircled by a crown of trees, and across, on the sunny side, even a few larches are interspersed in the stand of pines, their gray trunks gleaming with a mat sheen like tin candlesticks.

Agatha presses my hand. "Quiet," she says, and stops to listen.

The Upper Heathen.

Its adit is on the other side within the grove of pines, a natural cave, and one does not even know for sure whether it ever really had a mine-worked continuation or whether it merely had been adorned with such use by popular imagination because it seemed fitting that from that wildest and most grandiose natural setting the heathens had attempted to tear the ore out of the Kuppron. Whatever the truth, it is an eerie place, shunned in fear, even though the pine grove rises ever so gently along the slope and the spring of the brook emerges ever so pure from the entrance to the cave. And that Gisson the hunter had fallen precisely in that spot made the place even scarier.

We stop and listen.

In the center of the bowl the brook forms a small pool; stony and lidless, it stares in soulless smoothness toward the jagged peaks and the blueness above and drinks it all in.

It is so quiet that one would be able to perceive any sound, even the slightest sigh, but I hear nothing, only the sloshing murmuring of water running over stones at the outlet of the pool.

As if entering a hallowed room we walk slowly and almost on tiptoe through the hollow, still holding hands, the young pregnant girl and I, an old man, and when we reach its center and the pool, I fancy that we should submerge ourselves in the mirror of the sky to rinse the summer away and the heat of our bodies before being allowed to proceed any farther. And as the sun plays on the stones, an infinite playing on the earthly lyre, it is as if we heard a singing, a singing ordering our fear to join in it, because that fear, emanating from Agatha's hand, had become a strangely lively, an almost cheerful fear in the face of the invisible toward which we advance, cautiously still, yet knowing full well that we may not conceal ourselves.

And yet in truth it is a singing.

For it is Mother Gisson.

She stands under the pines or, more accurately, she floats there, pacing and yet resting among the tree trunks, and it is solemn and mild at the same time, a flowing immobility sheltered by the broad transparent crowns of the pines, welcomed by the light shimmering branches of the larches, and the light, trickling down through the sparse boughs and filling the luminous grove, is both mild and rigid. Rigid and mild and solemn is Mother Gisson's speech and it is as a singing. We dare not draw closer, we stand hand in hand, but she herself comes to meet us, smiling at us and yet hardly aware of our presence but speaking with someone else, an other far removed:

—"Yes, Irmgard, yes, your crown is light, so light you need not ever take it off, and white and green it sings and lighter than a kiss . . ."

She pauses then as if listening.

—"Do not lament, dear heart, do not lament, lament not for that which has stayed unfulfilled, be not ashamed and do not hide, for always you remained yourself and what you were, nothing has been destroyed, no spell is binding you, you too are now fulfilled . . .

—"Irmgard,

—"Irmgard, do you now hear the birds as they converse with you? Hither they flutter and beyond, their boundary made of light.

Now can you hear the flowers? As they grow hither and beyond, they know no boundary . . .

—"Irmgard, my soul, do you remember it still? As you sat on my lap and could not understand as yet the language of the humans but heard and understood the language of the cat, that of the doe that came to us, and even earlier when you spoke the languages of plants and grasses, of all waves? Those tongues, are they now yours again?

—"Together we shall be, Irmgard, both you and I, both without names and shall not notice it, both nameless we shall know of our togetherness.

—"Irmgard, Irmgard . . ."

She now stands at the last trees at the edge of the grove, close to the slope at the foot of which we had been waiting, and I see that she is barefoot.

And then she raises her arm, her flat hand turned palm upward, as if supporting with it the air and the sky and the entire sun-drenched day, and says:

—"The light comes from beyond and from beneath, soon it will merge no more . . . and shadowless the blossoming rays will be that shall be carrying you, Irmgard, my child and soul . . .

—"Lament not, my dear heart, do not lament, for your lament is hurting me, my search for you in vain . . . and cease your wandering, your shivering with cold . . . we are a couple soon, together evermore . . ."

Again she listens. Then smiles. —"Yes, child."

She falls silent.

I would not have dared to speak, but Agatha says quite naturally, "Mother."

She nods to us and I feel almost as if I, too, could be counted among the blessed spirits with whom she appears to hold such easy colloquy, as she now says, "So you, too, are here, and that's how it should be . . . yes, come with me."

We follow her up to the spring at the Pit of the Heathen. And as she walks in front of us from pine to pine, soundless on bare feet, and rests and leans against each of the trunks, I notice that she is very weak even though her progression appears more like a weightless floating.

But she pays no heed to her lassitude. In front of the entrance to the grotto where the pine grove begins to steepen its ascent and where the stony rubble crops out from the ground as in a small quarry, she stops and leans against the trunk that grows in a long-drawn S next to the spring and dips its roots into the stone-green water, awaiting our arrival. From the spring upward the ground is more densely overgrown with shrubs, masterwort and nightshade are among them, and a branch of a rowan tree, bare of leaves but still carrying its red berries, hangs over the edge of the scree. Beyond life and beyond death is the late fall, a cloud of crystal, weatherworn where it touches the earth. And Mother Gisson smiles at us:

"I guess you want to remind me of my promise, Agatha, and came to look for herbs?"

Agatha has no answer. She has arrived and she is tired; she stands there, big with child, and she places her hands over her high belly. Finally she says quietly, "Mother, we ran to join you up here . . . the Doctor and I . . ."

At that she scolds us, "Look at you, the condition you're in . . . What is your child to think of you, Agatha?"

That is true. I, too, am exhausted. Like two schoolchildren who took fright in a storm and came running home, we stand in front of her beneath her indulgently reproachful gaze.

"Nevertheless, you shall have your herbs . . . there are still some left . . . as a gift for the child . . . Did you bring some grains?"

A child's sly smile flits over Agatha's face as she rummages in her pocket and holds out a handful of grains to Mother Gisson.

"Fine," she says, "but not in that condition, that would be a disgrace . . . First dip your hands and your face, too, into the water's flow."

Agatha kneels down to the spring, dips her hands into it, and washes her face, but as if this were not enough, Mother Gisson bends down and, scooping up water with her hand, lets it drip over Agatha's hair and neck.

"And you?" she prompts me.

But because I am an old doctor, habit is stronger than my will, and I say, "Mother, isn't all that bending too much of a strain for you?"

She laughs. "You can't help it, can you? Not even today? . . . Better come here and dip into it, too . . ."

She straightens up and becomes serious once more. "Irmgard," she calls in a low voice, "Irmgard, dear child, are you here, too? And have you drunk of the water . . .?"

I wait with her. But I am told off forthwith: "Don't you bother about Irmgard . . ."

Obediently I go to the spring and do as I am bid. The water is ice-cold, and as I cool my pulse at length in its transfiguring flowing constancy and moisten my temples and gaze into the ever-recurrent birth of the spring, it seems to me as if there were also an ever-recurrent flow and counter-flow between the hither and the beyond, so incessant that no boundary remains between the two, and that this flow need only touch my head as well in order to open me up altogether, flowing into my heart, encircling my heart like a silvery band, penetrating to my deepest and most unattainable core, that core that had been patiently waiting since all beginnings to transcend all boundaries. At the bottom of the spring, the pine root can be seen, a strong coil, gnarled and much contorted, the rim of the spring is lidded by tear-moist grasses and mosses, and I hear Mother Gisson's command: "Drink," whereupon I bow down to the liquid mirror and obey.

This done, she says to me, "See . . . this is where he lay, here on this spot . . . He managed to drag himself up here to drink . . . It is as if it were today and yet had never been, an ever-present now . . ."

And after a very long pause, in so low a voice that I can barely make it out, and as if it were a legacy to me alone, she adds, "Old Mittis did it . . ."

Her bare feet on the forest soil, she leans against the pine trunk; she has wound an arm around it, and when she sees my confusion, a smile appears among her wrinkles, her usual slightly amused smile, so that one can readily imagine that she would merely have to go home to her kitchen for everything to remain as it had always been and that tomorrow she would again send some sugar and herb tea to the Mittis couple. And she smiles as she says, "Keep it to yourself."

"But, Mother, you have . . ."

At that, she gently strokes my bearded cheek, still moist with spring water, and says, "Whoever doesn't see to it that life goes on is himself not alive, nor does he know what death is really like . . . That is the reason life has been granted us, you are aware of that as well as I myself . . ."

In my mind's eye I can see old Mittis, whom she has granted his life and who now counts on Marius to raise the shooting of all hunters to a sacred duty, but the stillness nestling in Mother Gisson's hands is like a homecoming, larger than old Mittis, larger than any life, a stillness that, rising, fills the baskets of the tree crowns, filling all of life.

"But now off with you, Doctor . . . Agatha is getting impatient . . . and Irmgard, too . . . No male has any business near us when we look for herbs."

"Yes, Irmgard"—she nods to herself—"from now on Agatha will gather herbs in our stead, and as she thinks of us, she'll have no trouble finding them."

At that, it is as if a sigh wafted through the surrounding stillness.

Agatha dries her hands on her apron and says, "Yes, Mother." She, too, is now barefoot.

As for me, I leave. Slowly I walk down to the pond as the most dignified place to wait. I cross the bosk of dwarf pines which girts its edges, and then I stand at its stony shore.

Not a sound can be heard, no fragrance can be smelled; I taste the air and it is as if it had been distilled. Only the visible is extant, filled by the stillness, incorporeal as if it itself were the universe. The rocks all around the vast bowl loom above me like the inner walls of some gigantic hollow tree, a tree that no longer has any outer side, the pond resting in its midst like the sap of its roots, the shaft of its roots penetrating deeper still into still deeper stillness, reaching deeper still and all the way to the center of the world. Thus rests the pond in the midst of all. The echo of the walls sings silence and the echo's spring silently sings from the depths. Thus death itself dreams, and the noonday stars, glittering above the rim of the well, are reflected in the still mirror—nocturnal noon at the bottom of which mortal man circles the crystal. Dream resides in dream, the infinite in the infinite, the invisible in the invisible, but the eye of the pond and the eye of heaven reflect each other. All this I perceive, perceive it without fear as I pace slowly along the shore of the pond, and yet my fear is still present, that almost cheerful fear which inhabits even the most luminous dream because it has its roots in inaccessible infinity, it is the fear of the unawakened and of the unawakability within time, and it shines next to me in the mirror of the water carrying the blossoming light of the blueness above in its silvery blackness and drawing the image of the towering bark rocks down to ever greater depths, supporting the weight of the air in which I walk, that mirror which draws me as well, draws me in so that I may step through it and sink into its dying and into the mirroring transfiguration of my life. Where is the image, where the arch-image, image of image? Border mirroring itself, thus are the stones on the shore immersed in reiterant repetition and ever again emerge from the liquid element, and like glimmering swarms of stars, the fish stand in its luminous radiance, drifting at rest and barely moving along the circles of the Milky Way, their path circling over the crystalline snake in the invisible blackness of the deep. Do I circle my dream? Oh, forever are we mortals circling the shaft of our dreams, forever encircling the abyss in their center, that abyss rushing upward and down at the same time but welcoming us only in death, the soul plunging and rising into its mirrored image, echo of the soul and yet its essence when all images are transformed into truth eternal. Slowly the tree's hollow shell of bark swings around me: behold, the heavens are its crown and its boughs strive upward in crystalline invisibility, they bend and intertwine, gridwork of knowledge, the silent knowledge of all existence, so immense that the future, too, becomes memory, knowledge limitless as the infinities join together like day and night, giving birth to each other, echoing each other, mute knowledge filled with blossom eyes, and these are the stars. Floating upward, gliding downward, thus I stroll along the edges of the pond, along the shores of the heavens, still pacing though hardly moving, hardly feeling my body anymore, my whole being no more than an eye, an eye alive and perceiving, thus I am being propelled gently forward into the image which slowly circles and rigidly glides toward me, nor do I flee in my fear but rather it is that fear which securely holds me and carries me fairly through the circling of that inconceivably great shell in which alone the pond rests in its center, invisible the fear in its depth, all of time circling toward me: this is how I return homeward to the pines and the spring, thus pines and spring return to me, homestead that I recover and which recovers my own self, and as the landscape all around slowly ceases its motion and my feet once more are able to notice the mossy gravelly forest soil beneath, I come in sight of the Mother, resting next to the spring, she sees me and nods for me to approach. Agatha sits at her feet, the herbs in her lap.

And Mother Gisson says, "Come and rest next to us and do not dream of fear."

She has leaned her head against the tree trunk, her face is much wrinkled, wrinkled is the bark of the tree and they are almost the same color. I am not dreaming. The same life is in the tree and in the face, deathless and boundless. Time once again has slowly taken up its course, ever so slowly as if it were a constant and ethereally light breath wafting out of the Pit of the Heathen, on which the torn shadows of the pine boughs airily play, shadowless shadows.

I sit next to her on a fallen boulder in the crevices of which the green moss grows both tender and brittle. The stillness deepens further.

Agatha says, "Now I am home."

Tree crown intertwines with tree crown all along the upward slope of the grove and entwined in them is the sun and the stillness.

Agatha sorts the herbs in her lap.

And once more I hear the sighing of the stillness.

Mother Gisson's hands rest on the earth on which brown pine

needles lie spread like aged and brittle sun rays; she says, "It's only tea, Agatha, and schnapps and sometimes some medicine, and yet it's more and you must keep it safe."

"Oh, Mother, I shall find them and keep them safe and always think of you."

At that, the silence becomes a plaint and I hear it: "Mother, oh, Mother."

"Yes, Irmgard," replies Mother Gisson.

"Oh, Mother, she has her child and for the child she will gather the herbs."

"Do not lament, Irmgard, dear soul. Was it not also larger than yourself?"

The light falls like a veil through the pastoral crowns of the trees and now it speaks: "I no longer know."

"Irmgard," says Mother Gisson, "you are here."

Woven into the stillness hanging in the boughs and reaching up into the azure heights is the compassion, and then the silence says, "Yes, Mother." And it is Irmgard's voice.

She smiles. "Now all of you are here, only Mathias is missing, but he, too, is on his way . . . We'll wait for him."

She closes her eyes. "The day is like a rose, a rose that opens more and more and turns into the sky itself."

"Mother," says Agatha, "the child in me is like a singing heaven and his sleep is full of bluest stars."

And the silence speaks: "All being has become a swift recovery recovering from itself. Though still with you and here, I find myself removed, scattered in farthest reaches, a nowhere out of mind, forever I and yet I nevermore."

"Yes," says Mother Gisson, "that's how it may well be, that's what it will become . . ."

The crowns in the grove are breathing shadow over shadow, breathing them ever fainter on themselves and on the trunks and earth, but the shadow of the tree of life is light itself.

And once more she says, "Yes, Irmgard . . ."

She is silent as if pondering, and then she says, "In each man's depth reigns night and it is warm as earth; that's where he's mother of himself, and then, returning home, into his deepest womb, he's like the child of his own life and being."

She falls silent and my own life seems as a dark stillness embedded between the brightness below and the brightness above, a shadow shadowing itself.

And yet I, wondering, doubt: Can man in his dream's deepest shaft ever become the mother of himself and also his own child? Is not the deepest ground for him that knowledge in himself from which he rises through infinities, to which he wanders through infinities, as if there had been day before his night-dark path, a day awaiting him anew after eternities?

No answer came to me. The rocky entrance, busy with itself, glows silently toward the sun and drinks the silence burning from above as if the rocks had never known a night. But suddenly the silence speaks and it is Irmgard's voice: "Not night, not day, not knowledge and not non-knowledge, neither oblivion nor memory. But both."

Mother Gisson now gives me a look that seems almost amused: "You see infinity only in time, and every man's like that, he gets afraid when learning from his dream that time also can rest within itself. Is it not so, dear Doctor? Deny it if you can . . ."

"Yes, Mother, that is so," and then I realize that on this earth there is no path that can be followed to its end and that only in infinite eternities may the unattainable greet us like a cherished smile.

As gardens sing in springtime nights the silence now its sweet assent is singing: "Indeed, the infinite is always virginal."

But she now says, "The fear of man in his own darkness lies, he dreads the snake that on its bottom rests, and all his longing strives toward this far-off light, invisible and only faintly sensed, merely in image after mirror image communicating a dim semblance of its glow, a light so powerful that no human eye may ever apprehend it, no future generation . . ."

Is it still she who speaks? Is it a tree, a rock? Her head is lowered and her voice is but a murmuring of light as that of branches rimed by frost in the first dawn, as that of rocks by the sun's rays caressed, it is as if the gaping cave itself were speaking in a human voice.

And she continues: "Your world would hold no images if it were not at rest. And all your striving would be but empty rushing to and fro from what cannot be grasped to what is inconceivable were it not at the same time at rest. The time that you perceive, its source is lost in time and timeless it returns to that same source, celestial abyss in the deepest depth of which—your own source and your issue, too—your soul dwells in its solitude, and as a mother shows her child a picture book, the images displayed in it, thus points the soul for your faint apprehension the light infinitely remote, your knowledge rising, image after image, out of your darkest self. For only in the image of your earthly happening can you perceive that light whence homeward always you do strive, nor could there be, without your steady pace on earth, the heaven above in which you float at rest. But in its center lies your goal most infinite, remote."

She now falls silent. Rock and cave and tree and grove, the yellow of the larches and the green of pines, they all once more turn into silent light. As into timelessness I gaze, I hear Agatha speaking to the sky: "All of the flowers are awake in me as blossoms of the stars awakening in the dusk. For, Mother, I'm in deepest bliss."

Twined are the branches of the pines together with the sky, its crystal boughs, knowledge and thought are intertwined together with the crags and rocks, the limpid spring, and shining rays twine with Agatha's eyes. But in the center rests the pond. A breathless eye.

The Mother looks at us in her serenity. And once again it seems as if all time had stopped, the sunny stillness echoing her speech addressing me: "Do not lament the past, those years were fair to you. And fair and strong time rests in its center now, her borders limitless at rest; immense the circle's round but larger still the center innermost in which all fear forever dies away."

Agatha calls in faraway gentleness: "Time's fairest measure is nine moons."

The silence sings, a plaint is its reply: "And no infinity can ever be that fair."

Mother Gisson assents and turns in kindly understanding to the pregnant girl. "It's beautiful and yet it's not immune from fear . . ."

With her flat hand she gently strokes the ground. "This is where I was filled with fear . . ."

And then she says, "This then was where he drank his last, this was where his death came and it was here that with my hands I dug into the earth, and I was filled with fear . . ."

She now becomes quite still and stillness fills the woods, the silence is so great that one can hear the passing of the years as they assemble here, each after each they come and silently they stand and form a second forest made of glass.

But then she speaks: "Yes, I was robbed of him and I was filled with fear.

"In breathing in another being's breath our happiness is indeed great, for then we feel as if we well could be forebear and child of our self at the same time, as if we were not born as yet and yet as if we were in death, as if the kiss in which we live in sleep the center were of all existence and eternity. Of that I had been robbed and I was filled with fear. No pacing and no search can ever be the equal of that happiness, nor can its equal be the striving for infinity, already in itself it is infinity, a being without end transcends ecstatically all boundaries, it is the wholeness of this world, boundless its overflow over its rim in silvery sheets, dark spring-born kiss bestowed, the font's dark-shrouded gift. Of that I had been robbed and heavy was my fear, not fear of night, oh no, but fear of the clear days to come when pitiless and hard the rocks stood bright, my screaming went unheard and nothing moved except the snake that slunk over the stones, my hands were raw with blood as hearts torn open, then I felt fear, fear for my mercy and my womanhood: for she who can no longer feel the wholeness of the world, no longer either can a woman be."

The silence weeps, it weeps the silent light and rays of sun like tears, each drop of tears an arrow made of gold.

And Agatha is heard to say, "The wholeness is my child and I only a part thereof."

The years stand motionless, transparent, a wood surrounding us, invisible, the sun stands still and burning mute as if to permeate this summer day through all eternity.

Thus grows the waiting. Dared I to speak, my voice would fade away, from my lips blown and by the light absorbed.

Her hand placed on Agatha's brow, Mother Gisson now says, "That's how the light is and the fear, the woman's fear, Agatha, and if it should befall you, Agatha, my child, then take it both in joy and grief."

She then continues:

—That's how I searched for him who had been torn from me and with my hands I dug the blood drunk by the earth; no longer could I see the wholeness of the world, nor did I see its edges. I saw nothing more.

—Nothing but me I saw and yet I did not see myself, for stony was the hurt surrounding me, it was a grayness hard as stone.

—A woman I no longer was.

—I did my day's work like a man but when the evening came I ran up here, here to the spring and to the blind remove.

—My children I took care of and clothed and washed and fed them every day, did it not knowing what I did and hardly seeing them.

—And yet they were his children, too. But I no longer was the woman who once had conceived them all.

—Death within me, it grew, it grew around me and in me until its rocks fairly had buried me.

—So in my dire straits I took the children up, here to the spring, so that they, too, might for their father call. They failed to call but played instead with stones.

—But I, I lay right here, my hands deep in the earth, and all the light was stone and every cloud was hollow, bursting between clamps. That's how I lay, entombed between these walls that grew to ever greater heights, a deadly shaft, and all my longing was directed at sinking into it, to sink into its bottom to ever deeper depths. And buried in the night, I was as if released. For then I felt my fingers being loosened up, one after one, until dug out. It was my boy and he had crawled to me, and he it was who, as if playing with marbles, had dug my fingers from the earth. And he went on to play with them, all the while crawling over me as if I were the earth.

—Upon which I went home and never did return.

—I did my daily work, I lived my life and it was good. I gazed at the remote remove where he now dwelt and slowly it became infinity, in it I realized the goal that lay beyond all death, the goal to which he strove and which he now, like a belated child, had placed below my heart that it might grow in me. I tended plot by plot and, planting shoot by shoot, I myself grew. I grew in closeness to the one who's waiting over there, awaiting me, who knows about my coming as if it never could have been otherwise.

—There was a gentle murmuring first, below the earth, of subterranean springs, but very slowly it became a light, and suddenly I knew: I am a woman once again whose knowledge may renew this world for now and evermore. What once was sweet and dark, now it was bright, the world had grown, becoming whole once more, in growth it overflowed the rim of every font, a mirrored garden, spell-bound pond, the source myself though hardly more than wondering gaze, alive in him, I living him, an overflow of trust, a birth of knowledge ever new. Thus grew the world with every day to greater day, with every night to brighter night, the earth became the firmament, a growing into death, constant and luminous.

She's silent now, all those transparent years surrounding her, a ghostly woods, they take a breath and then declare: "Because you saw the light remote despite your earthly strife, transmuted shall you be, Oh woman, in the hereafter's life."

"Oh, no," says Mother Gisson then, "we know it better, Agatha and I, first you must love your child."

But once more Irmgard's voice is heard in grieving song, a silent plaint arising from the pond: "I never became earth, no child was granted me."

Then came reply from Mother Gisson's lips. "You, Irmgard, had a lighter task though heavier your fate: for you dwelt in a higher

peace, your life an easy dying since its start, your death a light-
born life; while on this earth you lived a gentle death and dying
you were born."

Her eyes are closed, once more it is as if the rocks were speaking,
the heaven's shadows and the grotto's depth.

"He stayed with me since then but since he was as yet not quite
fulfilled in death, I walked the rounds for him, he granted me
infinity, the wholeness we both shared: I lived for him his life and
he lived mine. And only in this wholeness shared did he then find
his goal infinitely removed, infinitely returning as between world
and worlds all boundaries fell away and although he is far, so far
away among the silver clouds, he stayed with me, in me who followed
him in waiting, and as he grew in age his face in beauty gained."

And the assembled years could then be heard to add: "The earth
was your appointed circumstance, as spirit thus, O man, you keep
your human countenance."

She winks at me as if this had concerned us both and says, "Yes,
Doctor, that is true, so you attend to it."

She is quite still. But then she says, "I turn toward the center's
light and as a drop of my own self I overflow my rim."

The light turns white. And though she sees it not, she is aware
of it.

And then she asks, "Irmgard, are you still shivering in cold?"

To which the silence answers: "Oh, Mother, it's neither cold nor
warm. It's only beautiful."

Mother Gisson replies, "Indeed, it's beautiful. And he is where
no knowledge or oblivion still pertains; but, Irmgard, can you hear
him now?"

The light, about to vanish, yet replies, "No, Mother, I can hear
him not, and your voice, too, I hear but very faintly now."

Hardly perceptibly she shakes her head and smiles. "Irmgard,
my soul, I cannot raise my voice, for soon our speech will be no
more than light."

The heavens have slid down and wrapped Agatha in an azure
cloth, but we float, all of us, above the waters still, with us there
float the mountains, trees and grass, the stillness floats in fair rig-

idity, floating the stars and all the brightness floats, the years, they carry us on crystal wings like those of angels high into invisible realms, and floating still they carry us into the center of all worlds.

And resting on the ground though floating still, she now remembers: "When evenings we were bedded down by Mother and the candle doused, it became bright and then we flew away."

The world is lost, lost in the dream.

"Then it was, too, as if one were not born as yet."

The earth itself now holds its breath and silent falls the spring. Are we, as we have opened ourselves to the dream's spell, already far beyond the threshold that cannot be seen? Is this not as a shadow's flight in shadowless realms?

At that, she says, and almost cheerful is her voice, "You have escorted me but now you can go home."

Agatha weeps but it cannot be heard.

Her face is closed, her head against the pine's trunk rests as if it meant to grow into the tree. And now she calls, "Mathias!"

"Yes, Mother, I am here," and he steps to her side.

I had not seen him come.

"You go now find a good wife for yourself. The time is ripe."

Once more a shimmer of her usual merriment flitters around her mouth. "And when a little one comes, it has already now all of my love . . . that you can tell it later on from me."

"Yes, Mother."

She gazes at Mathias, at me and Agatha, and shuts her eyes for good. And thus she waits with us.

Then reaching down toward the spring, she scoops some water in her cupped hand and drinks.

And speaks no more.

The forest of the trees invisible has disappeared, no longer courses time, it has been overcome. But through the pines a silence walks, the silence of a mighty man, a loving silence, and it now calls, "Come."

At that, once more she breathes and she smiles.

And then Mathias puts his hand over her eyes.

A soft wind breathes through the valley's length, a rustling runs throughout the woods, a shivering of the branches in the sun.

And that is how it happened.

As I hurried down to inform the people in the village and arrange for Mother Gisson to be brought down, the gorge at its lower end was already shrouded in crepuscular shadows and the smells of autumn, cool and moist, mossy and moldy, flowed with the wind all around me and down to the valley.

When I arrived in the village, the people had already assembled in front of Mother Gisson's house and some were about to climb up to the Pit of the Heathen. Sack was among them and I didn't ask how they'd come to know already. The candle in her window still burned and flickered in the evening sun; it had burned down to a small stump and the wax had run down and caked on the tin candlestick.

She was brought down as dusk settled in and the Milands and the priest came to administer the last rites. Mother Gisson had been laid out on her bed, and it occurred to me that I who had known more or less every villager in his or her bed, had never seen her in hers. The room was full of people, the womenfolk knelt around the bed, and the little priest, almost extinguished himself and his face as lopsided as ever, recited with them the Lord's Prayer.

The summer weather still held until the funeral of Mother Gisson. Straight from the sun she went into the earth. But that same evening winter set in with a blizzard like a bolt out of the blue. Within a quarter hour the temperature fell by forty degrees.

EPILOGUE

WHEN I STARTED THESE NOTES it was winter, and now another summer is close again: summery is the wind drifting outside the opened windows, summery the drifting sky pregnant with clouds, the woods are filled with summery warm rustlings and the dahlias below my window are already in full bloom. But they are far from being as perfect as those of the little priest. The clover in the fields of the Lower Village is fragrant and stands high and green, and when one walks through the meadows one's steps form a small alley which only slowly closes after one is past; soon the mowing will begin. Agatha's boy shortly will be six months old, and that, to me, may well be the most summery fact in all the growth hereabout, a source of wonder to me, even though so many children have been brought into the world by my hands, and when I stroll through the village I see them thrive, growing no differently from Agatha's child.

But if other children simply came into this world by passing that boundary which at its entrance we call birth and at its exit we call death, it seems to me as if this boundary had shifted slightly in the case of Agatha's child and Mother Gisson's death and as if that child had started its life a bit earlier and Mother Gisson's life had ended somewhat later than actually would have been determined by that boundary, and the longer I ponder this strange phenomenon, the more I am convinced that these two happenings are connected by an even deeper and more intimate link than the one that quite naturally resulted from the given circumstances, a link that interweaves these two happenings more closely and deeply with nature as a whole, nature which only in the case of man draws such a sharp line between life and non-life, between the before and the after, and thus distinguishes man from all other living creatures, though distinguishing him perhaps only by investing him with the longing urge to overcome that boundary and still remain a human being. And this urge appears to me as a kind of piety known only to man.

Mother Gisson has died and Agatha has her child. I am loath to put down my pen, for what is an aging man such as I to do with his evenings if he does not record the events of his life? Though what is there to record if not that Marius still sits in the municipal council? And for whom should I record that fact since I would rather not think about it myself? And even though everything still follows more or less the old beaten track despite all the crazy talk and outlandish antics of Marius, and even though the peasants continue each day to go out to their fields and each day milk their cows, and even though even this year most of the threshing will be done by machine, so that the overall view of the world has hardly changed at all, and neither can it be expected to change, the farms, stables, and huts still lying peacefully all around as heretofore, peacefully sending their smoke heavenward, still I cannot forget the fate of Irmgard or the wrong that has been done to poor Wetchy. And it seems to me as if the latter were of even a graver and more far-reaching nature than the death of Irmgard, which came as an almost natural end to her life: for an injustice does violence to mankind and to what is godlike in men, and that violence is the source and origin of the horror in which Irmgard, too, perished. What an evil spell! And how far astray has it led us all by purporting to bring us back closer to nature! And how much revenge will nature still wreak on us as a result! For it is always nature herself who vengefully punishes the violations visited on the spirit of man, because nature and spirit are but one and because there is but one path for man toward nature and infinity and that path leads by way of his spirit, the blessing granted to man as his divine distinction.

Mother Gisson has died and Agatha has her child. This was and is important because the spirit can be active in both the act of dying and the act of childbearing, indeed therein perhaps more than anywhere else. And therefore next to this the fact dwindles to nothing that the Pit of the Dwarfs has been ordered sealed up by the Bureau of Mines and that Marius has appealed this decision and, in order to do so, has had to call upon many city-based institutions, such as lawyers and engineering experts, the fact fades to nothing that Krimuss is paying for all this and that in the end Lax will probably succeed in grabbing the Krimuss holdings for himself. In comparison, all this fades away into an insignificant mist. Mother Gisson has died and Agatha has her child. And I suspect that the new era will be brought in rather by Agatha's child than by the rantings of Marius, for it seems to me as if it were rather in Agatha's spirit that the new piety is being prepared, the new piety the world needs and seeks, and that one day its realization may be brought about by Agatha's child. And it may be that I was present at the birth of that future.

AUTHOR'S COMMENTARY

THERE IS NO DOUBT that events involving mass-psychological occurrences can be brought to life by means of "objective" descriptions: a procession of medieval flagellants, the spectators' roar at a football game, the enthusiasm of the crowds in front of the Reich Chancellery in Berlin listening to the weird inflections of Hitler haranguing them from the balcony, or the horrors of a pogrom—all these can be depicted in a most convincing and lifelike manner. But all such descriptions—even though based on historical events—in a sense remain empty statements, merely confirming that mass-psychological forces are at work but failing to reveal anything of their true functions and impact. If these are to be elucidated at all, one needs to address the mind of the individual, one must probe why and how such an individual falls prey to these incomprehensible forces and participates in such mass behavior, a probing all the more called for precisely because of the incomprehensible nature of such occurrences. For it would seem that within the realm of mass-psychological impulses the individual suddenly becomes quite ready to accept the crudest lies as gospel truth, otherwise perfectly sober and intelligent men allow themselves to be enlisted in the most outlandish undertakings, and archaic forces believed to be long buried break out together with a mythical set of mind that runs counter to all rational thinking. Why this is so can be explored only by probing the minds of those who themselves have fallen under the spell of such mysterious forces.

Nor is there any sense in trying to discuss such matters in a "sensible" way. No poetic talent is needed to write a scientific essay, and least of all are subjects belonging to the realm of science to be dealt with in the form of a novel meant to entertain, for this would be tantamount to both blasphemy and frivolous dilettantism. The subjects of all true writing must be "eternal"; that is to say, they are to deal with the most basic human experiences, human birth, growth, eating and sleeping, lovemaking and death. Therefore, the protagonist of any true work of art is always "Everyman," so that any true work of art is also bound to create personages who are archtypically human.

In this novel I have attempted to approach the problem of mass-psychological phenomena by respecting these two fundamental considerations. On the one hand, I have set the action in a primitive mountain village which, in its remoteness, allows for the depiction of the most basic human interrelations; and, on the other, I have entrusted the probing of the individual minds to a journal kept by the village doctor. For a journal is the simplest and most honest means of reflecting on psychological phenomena, and since peasants do not keep journals, I had to assign this task to an intellectual, particularly because such a person may be credited with a measure of discernment and self-criticism, the ultimate overpowering of which by mass-psychological forces then appears all the more dramatic and surprising.

The plot is quite simple: A stranger makes his appearance in this remote village. At first, the reaction to him is not one of sympathy; on the contrary, he invites derision and hostility since he soon reveals himself as a crackbrained lunatic who obsessively importunes everybody with his pseudomythic ideas about the sacredness of the earth, the subjugation of the mountain, etc. But gradually he begins to gain followers, first among the youth, then among the adult population, until finally the whole village has fallen under his spell, last but not least because some of the more prosperous farmers believe that it is to their advantage to support his activities. Events then rapidly take an ever more demented turn, though always with apparently rational motivations; even the most aberrant notions find credence, and finally, on the occasion of a village fair that gets out of hand and deteriorates into a kind of pagan sacrificial rite, even the main antagonist of the interloping stranger, a wise old woman who embodies the spirit of humaneness and of kindness, falls victim to the general madness: her succumbing appears symbolic, as if matriarchy once more had to be annihilated. After this climax the village begins to recover, civilization reasserts itself, and even the crackpot stranger, once he has risen to the domination of the village, is absorbed by the inalterable rhythm of everyday life. Nevertheless, a portion of humaneness has been lost forever.

All these events are experienced and told by the doctor, who, without being aware of it himself, and although he had initially been much more critical in his sober appraisal of the stranger than all the others, also falls increasingly under his spell. And without really noticing what has happened, in his journal, too, the doctor reverts to a recording of everyday life, as he feels secure in the belief that nothing in him has changed since he began to write.

It is in the nature of every poetical work that stands midway between two cultural epochs that it is bound to be concerned with the search for a new faith; indeed, that well may be its highest claim to distinction. Wherever poetry draws close to religious aspirations, it seizes on mythological concepts, and it does so not by intention but because this is in the nature of things. This can be illustrated by any number of contemporary examples, such as the biblical mythology of Thomas Mann, the Hellenistic one of Joyce's *Ulysses*, and the pagan one of Giono. Nor is this an accidental coincidence but rather the result of a historical imperative, the same imperative which in the present novel dictated its turn toward the mythological.

In addition, this mythological coloring resulted from the inherent nature of the thematic material: for it is one of the essential elements of the present era that it attempts to compensate for the decline in religious faith by an almost feverish worship of "nature," on the surface motivated by hygienic, sports-related, ecological, or other such rationalizations, though in truth its sources lie much deeper and, indeed, within the metaphysical sphere. I have tried to trace these sources by having the doctor consistently take note in his journal of the concordance between inner and outer landscape, of the interplay which constantly links the landscape of the soul with the scenery of the action. And if one thus takes heed of this interplay which indubitably occurs in every human being to a more or less obvious extent, one quickly discovers how readily these mythic intimations can arise from the depths of the soul. And because this is patently so, one would not be wrong to see in this constant readiness of mythic and nature-oriented tendencies to reassert themselves one of the main reasons why our present epoch is so vulnerable to mass-psychological forces.

Hermann Broch wrote this commentary on the novel in the spring of 1940. Its two-page typescript is deposited with the Hermann Broch Archives in the Yale University Library (Item #12).

BRIEF GENESIS OF THE NOVEL

HERMAN BROCH wrote the first version of what, at the time, he referred to simply and generically as "the mountain novel" in 1935. It is only this first version which constitutes a completed novel, consisting of fourteen chapters plus a foreword and an epilogue.

In February 1936, the author began to rewrite the entire novel, considerably expanding all its parts, particularly the descriptive and philosophically speculative sections, and changing some of the names of the protagonists. This work, however, was broken off in June 1936 and extended only to the first eight chapters and the beginning of the ninth chapter.

In January 1950, while residing in New Haven, the author once more started work on the novel, in preparation for its translation into English and its publication by an American publisher. This third version constitutes a considerable abridgment of the second version and a tightening of its form; the "journal" style of the first and second versions was abandoned and the novel was to be compressed into twelve chapters without a foreword and epilogue. Hermann Broch died on May 30, 1951, while working on the fifth chapter of this third version.

The first version of the novel, and the only complete one, was published by Suhrkamp Verlag, Frankfurt, under the title *Die Verzauberung* in 1976.

❁

The collected works of Hermann Broch were published in seventeen volumes, in German, by the Suhrkamp Verlag in Germany under the editorship of Professor Paul Michael Lützeler of Washington University in St. Louis. They consist of the following volumes:

I. *The Literary Work*: Vol. 1: The Sleepwalkers. A Trilogy (1978). Vol. 2: The Unknown Quantity. A Novel (1977). Vol. 3: The Spell. A Novel (1976). Vol. 4: The Death of Virgil. A Novel (1976). Vol. 5: The Guiltless. A Novel in Eleven Tales (1974). Vol. 6: Novellas. Miscellaneous Prose. Fragments (1980). Vol. 7: The Dramatic Writings (1979). Vol. 8: Poems (1980).

II. *The Essayistic Work*: Vol. 9/1: Writings on Literature/Reviews (1975). Vol. 9/2: Writings on Literature/Theory (1975). Vol. 10/1: Philosophical Writings/Reviews (1977). Vol. 10/2: Philosophical Writings/Theory (1977). Vol. 11: Political Writings (1978). Vol. 12: Theory of Mass Psychology (1981).

III. *Letters*: Vol. 13/1: Letters 1913–1938. Vol. 13/2: Letters 1938–1945. Vol. 13/3: Letters 1945–1951 (1981).

TRANSLATOR'S NOTE

THIS TRANSLATION was based on the first and only fully completed version of the novel, which was published by Suhrkamp Verlag, Frankfurt, in 1976, under the title *Die Verzauberung* and edited by Professor Paul Michael Lützeler of Washington University in St. Louis, Missouri.

The one exception to this statement pertains to the so-called "Barbara Story," the autonomous tale of the doctor's great love affair appearing in Chapter 10, the translation of which was based on the *second* version of the novel, in which this story is greatly expanded (by nine printed pages as compared to the first version); its descriptive sections are stylistically much more polished and rounded, and the insights into the doctor's personality which the story affords are more sharply focused. This would have been reason enough, in the translator's opinion, to prefer the second version in this case, but there operates an additional factor in its favor which has to do with the importance the author himself attributed to the story: namely, the central position that this story occupies in the structure of the novel, a centrality all the more surprising in view of the story's apparently total independence from the rest of the novel—until one becomes aware that the author has placed the story in this strategic location because it is the only key to the character of the doctor and his development in the course of the novel's action. It is then hardly surprising that this story also contains a great many autobiographical elements—possibly more than any other writings of the author—and this alone would have prompted this translator to use for his translation the version that the author himself considered the final one.

The German printed version contains a few textual inconsistencies of a topographical and chronological nature which probably resulted from later insertions by the author in the first draft of the first version, insertions which, in some instances, the author neglected to bring into full concordance with the earlier text simply because he already knew at that time that he would write a second version of the novel. All such inconsistencies, as well as typographical errors or mistakes resulting from oversights or negligence, were eliminated in the translation as a matter of course and have been recorded in a List of Corrections ("Korrekturen zur *Verzaub-*

erung") which the translator has forwarded to Suhrkamp Verlag, Frankfurt, as well as to Professor Paul Michael Lützeler in St. Louis and to the Broch Archive at the Yale University Library in New Haven, Connecticut.

Some of the names of persons in the novel which to English-speaking readers could have seemed visually and verbally rather unpalatable have been changed slightly:

> Thus, Zäzilie, younger daughter of Miland, became Cecily. Strüm, both the father and his daughter Agatha, became Strum. Suck (and his whole family) became Sack because of the connotations of the word in English and also because the frequent use in the novel of the verb "to suck" (as in "the sucking power of the earth," "the sky sucked it up," etc.) would have led to confusion if that word also had been used as a proper name.

All other proper names have been left unchanged, but something should be said with regard to the name Wenzel, the nickname given by Marius to his roguish sidekick. In German, the name Wenzel has a number of connotations, which may be listed here more or less in the order of their evocative strength:

1. As a diminutive of Wenzeslaw (or Wenceslas, first king of Bohemia), Wenzel denotes in German, often in a somewhat derogatory sense, a person of Bohemian or Czechoslovak origin.
2. *Wenzel*, a dialect variation of *Winzel* (from winzig = something tiny); also as in *Winzelmänner = Heinzelmänner* = tiny ones, dwarfs.
3. *Wenzel* is also the jack or knave in card games, more particularly the jack of spades in a game called Black Peter, in which this card is to be avoided at all costs. By extension, a *Wenzel* is a rogue of sinister potential, someone to be feared.
4. And finally *Wenzel* (also *Schwenzel*) in Tyrolean dialect means a penis, an allusion to the novel's Wenzel's much-vaunted and aggressive virility.

All this is completely lost in English, and the translator initially thought of giving Wenzel a name that would preserve at least some of the above connotations in English (Jack was one possibility), but it was found in the end that all such substitutes sounded a false note, one out of place in the locale of the novel. Thus, Wenzel remained Wenzel and, instead, an attempt was made to imply in words some of the German connotations.

As in most translations from German, there arose the vexing problem of the German familiar form of address, the *Du* form: rather than resort to the stiff and awkward "thou" and its even more stilted corresponding verb declinations, the translator decided to ignore it, to stick with "you" and to indicate familiarity of speech by the choice of words and style.

Every effort was made to respect authorial intentions and to preserve in English—though always without doing violence to the language—the pronounced stylistic idiosyncrasies of the author, in particular with regard to Broch's broad syntactic sweep and his "symphonic" sentence structure, his cadences reiterating and reflecting echo-like between opposites and metaphoric images. If nevertheless the translator well may have failed at times to equal in English Broch's lofty lyrical thrust and grand stylistic design, the translator begs the reader's indulgence for such inadequacy.

I wish especially to thank my editor, whose patience is exceeded only by his enlightening knowledge and without whose kind encouragement and help I never could have tackled, let alone accomplished, this daunting task.

H. F. Broch de Rothermann

September 1986

PICADOR *Classics*

Fifteen years after the launch of the PICADOR imprint, Pan have introduced PICADOR CLASSICS. This important new list brings together the works of distinguished authors (in excellent translations where appropriate), carefully chosen from the wealth of the world's great literature.

Landmarks in World Literature

Hermann Hesse
The Glass Bead Game £3.95

Eleven years in the writing and published three years before his Nobel prize award, this is Hesse's great novel, the epitome of his creative credo. Taking the form of a biography of Josef Knecht, it is set centuries into the future in the province of Castilia, a disintegrating society where an intellectual elite play out the game of the title – a quest for perfection that synthesises the *I Ching* and the astrologer's art. When Knecht rejects the esoteric in an attempt to resuscitate his dying homeland, his final suicide is at once a symbol of despair and an exemplary supreme sacrifice.

Translated by Richard and Clara Winston

'A new English version of *Das Glasperlenspiel* which lifts the whole novel onto a higher plane' THE TIMES

John Steinbeck
The Grapes of Wrath £3.95

The novel that won Steinbeck the Pulitzer Prize in 1940 endures as his masterpiece. His torrential narrative follows the destiny of the family Joad, loading their home into a beat-up truck and heading west out of Oklahoma towards the golden dream of California. It is the story of all those disinherited who came out of the dustbowl to find themselves in labour camps filled with hungry men and broken dreams, drawn into the black and bloody conflict of migrant worker against company thug. No novelist has so vividly evoked the America of Woody Guthrie and Joe Hill.

'This is a terrible and indignant book; yet it is not without passages of lyrical beauty, and the ultimate impression is that of the dignity of the human spirit under the stress of the most desperate conditions'
THE GUARDIAN

Erich Maria Remarque
All Quiet on the Western Front £2.95

Of all the literature that came out of The Great War, this novel by a soldier in the Kaiser's army gained the widest public and is still today regarded as one of the great novels of men at war. Its title – *Im Westen nichts Neues* in the original German – is an ironic echo of the headlines that shrugged off a generation living and dying in trenches under fire as not worth reporting as news for the home front. Two and a half million copies were sold within eighteen months of publication, but by 1933 the book was being publicly burned in Berlin, declared 'defeatist' by the Nazis.

Translated by A. W. Wheen

This is the original English translation from the German first published in 1929.

All Pan books are available at your local bookshop or newsagent, or can be ordered direct from the publisher. Indicate the number of copies required and fill in the form below.

Send to: **CS Department, Pan Books Ltd., P.O. Box 40, Basingstoke, Hants. RG21 2YT.**

or phone: 0256 469551 (Ansaphone), quoting title, author and Credit Card number.

Please enclose a remittance* to the value of the cover price plus: 60p for the first book plus 30p per copy for each additional book ordered to a maximum charge of £2.40 to cover postage and packing.

*Payment may be made in sterling by UK personal cheque, postal order, sterling draft or international money order, made payable to Pan Books Ltd.

Alternatively by Barclaycard/Access:

Card No.

Signature:

Applicable only in the UK and Republic of Ireland.

While every effort is made to keep prices low, it is sometimes necessary to increase prices at short notice. Pan Books reserve the right to show on covers and charge new retail prices which may differ from those advertised in the text or elsewhere.

NAME AND ADDRESS IN BLOCK LETTERS PLEASE:

Name————————————————————

Address————————————————————

3/87